Metaphorosis

Best of 2018

Also from Metaphorosis Books

Score: an SFF symphony

Reading 5X5: Readers' Edition
Reading 5X5: Writers' Edition

Best Vegan Science Fiction & Fantasy

Best Vegan SFF of 2018
Best Vegan SFF of 2017
Best Vegan SFF of 2016

Metaphorosis Magazine

Metaphorosis: Best of 2018
Metaphorosis: Best of 2017
Metaphorosis: Best of 2016
Metaphorosis 2018: The Complete Stories
Metaphorosis 2017: The Complete Stories
Metaphorosis 2016: Nearly Complete Stories
Monthly issues

by B. Morris Allen

Susurrus
Allenthology: Volume I
Tocsin and other stories
Start with Stones: collected stories
Metaphorosis: a collection of stories

Metaphorosis

Best of 2018

edited by
B. Morris Allen

Metaphorosis Books

Neskowin

ISBN: 978-1-64076-124-7 (e-book)
ISBN: 978-1-64076-125-4 (paperback)

Contents

From the Editor...7
The Bagel Shop Owner's Nephew...9
    J. Tynan Burke
Hishi..31
    David A. Gray
Just a Fire..67
    A. Martine
Koehl's Quality Impressions..87
    Tim McDaniel
The Foaling Season...123
    Samuel Chapman
The Little G-d of Łódź..149
    Evan Marcroft
Of Hair and Beanstalks...173
    William Condon
Familiar in Her Angles..191
    E.A. Brenner
Cheminagium...213
    David Gallay
The Stars Don't Lie...245
    R.W.W. Greene
The Dream Diary of Monk Anchin.......................................277
    Felicity Drake
Not All Those Who Wander Are Lost..................................295
    Douglas Anstruther
Velaya, the Dreaming City...321
    Beston Barnett

Copyright   347
Our patrons   349
Metaphorosis Publishing   351

From the Editor

In dark times, science fiction and fantasy gives us a window on a different life – sometimes better, sometimes worse, but at least not this one. It's been an interesting year in the real world, and one in which, by my reckoning, we dearly needed a new outlook.

By sheer word count, Metaphorosis provided that in droves. This Best of selection is the size of a good-sized novel all by itself, and – by definition – it's only a portion of the stories we published. Not only that, but I had a harder time than usual choosing the contents, even with the help of able assistant editors Ray Yanek and J. Tynan Burke. As it happens, Tynan's story (chosen without his input) also opens the collection.

This was the first year that we published monthly print issues to go with the e-books. These little 4x6 paperbacks have been very popular, and it's a pocket-friendly format I fell in love with. We also have plans for the new year, with podcast editor Michael Ward working hard on putting together audio editions that we hope to launch soon. Keep your eye out for them.

As always, our Patreon patrons will hear about everything first. I'm happy to say that Patreon support has grown steadily, to the extent that our patrons pay for a story a month. If that keeps going, the magazine may someday find itself in the black – or, more likely, we'll just pay a higher rate.

Thanks for coming along on this overview of Metaphorosis' third year. These are my favorite stories of the year, but if you like these, there are a lot more that were close contenders. And even more coming every Friday in 2019! Come see us online!

B. Morris Allen
Editor
1 February 2019

The Bagel Shop Owner's Nephew

J. Tynan Burke

Last night, Murray called with another bunch of prophecies, so Yonatan Kaplan hasn't slept yet. He stayed up preparing dossiers on some doomed socialites instead. Now it's a little after dawn, Friday morning, and he's standing in line outside Fox's Bagels with a thermos and a tote bag. He's shaky from too much caffeine and too little sleep, but he doesn't regret it. The socialites will die this weekend, according to Murray, and Murray's got a good track record. When they do die, the obituary writers will call the Morgue—The Pre-Morgue Clipping Service, Yonatan's business—to buy the dossiers, expecting the usual thoughtfulness and prescience. So it had been best to begin the work immediately.

 The line shortens when a gaggle of tourists leaves Fox's. Yonatan steps forward, fills his thermos lid with hot tea, and covers a yawn with the hand still holding the thermos. He thinks back to Murray's sneering tone when he 'apologized' for calling so late, his fake sadness that Yonatan would stay up all night working. It doesn't matter if Murray made a lucky guess or if it was knowledge from Murray's divine gift—either way, it's *rude* to mock a man for doing his job. Yonatan takes a big drink of tea and frowns. *Fucking prophets.* They're nothing like what you read about.

The line shortens again and it's Yonatan's turn to enter the shop. The woman in front of him holds the door, and he nods to her as he steps inside.

Yonatan is welcomed by a burst of humidity, which carries the smell of fresh onions and the accumulated yeast of three generations. He's also welcomed by a new cashier, a young man of maybe twenty who shares the owner Shay's big ears and too-skinny frame. The hunger in Yonatan's gut is replaced with a rarely-felt electricity, once debilitating, though he has learned to weather it. For him the closest analogy is the shock of a new and severe crush settling in, but he's not gay, trust him, he's checked.

This young man, whose name tag reads 'Stephen,' is perhaps a Tzadik Nistar.

"Morning," Yonatan manages, stepping to the counter. "One of everything, please."

Stephen raises an eyebrow over a baggy eye. "Like, one everything bagel, or…"

Yonatan cringes and tries to twist it into a smile. "Sorry. Bad joke I have with Shay. One of each kind of bagel, please."

Stephen counts off on his fingers. "So one plain, one poppy, one sesame, one onion…"

"And one everything," Yonatan finishes.

Stephen collects and bags the bagels. "I don't get it."

Yonatan shrugs. "I said it was a bad joke. Is it even a joke? Who knows how these things start." Yonatan knows. He tried making a pun five or six years ago after a long night of drinking. "Shay might remember. Do you know Shay, uh…" He points at the name tag like he just noticed it. "Stephen?"

"Uncle Shay? I sure do. It's Steve, though. That'll be fifteen dollars." Steve beeps some buttons on the register.

"You know what, Steve, why don't you add another poppy."

Steve wraps the extra bagel while Yonatan observes. No piercings or ink that he can see. That's good, it's one of the rules Adonai actually cares about any more.

The register beeps again. Steve says, "Eighteen dollars."

Yonatan hands him a twenty and puts the bagels in his tote. "Nice to meet you, Steve. Tell Shay Yonatan says hi."

Out front, Yonatan leans against the wall and takes two deep breaths while his gut settles. It turns to growling, sour with too much tea and too little food. Much better, easy to address. He returns to the Morgue and goes straight to the computer, where he opens a password-protected document and types an addition to a long list of names, in a column headed 'CANDIDATES': *Stephen 'Steve' Fox, ~20, Lower East Side, NYC.* And then, at long last, it is bagel time. Poppy, toasted, with leftover veggie cream cheese.

Later he's on the office couch, taking a little break and reading a space opera, when the landline rings. It's barely audible over the Norwegian black metal he put on to stay awake. His watch says eight-thirty, but he decides to take it anyway—it can't be any less interesting than the exposition dump he's at in the book, or the *Page Six* profiles he's avoiding. Off goes the music and in goes a bookmark. The bookmark has an Emerson quote he likes. He can read part of it sticking out: *Time and space are but physiological colors which the eye makes, but.*

While he crosses the Morgue, he steps over a spilled pile of clippings, and growls. Always more work, dossiers to build, Tzadikim to chronicle, things to file. Sleep, somewhere in there. And the phone keeps ringing, and he almost yells something passive-aggressive at it, but no, that's more something his father would do. With a silent glance back at the clippings he walks the rest of the way.

"Pre-Morgue Clipping Service, this is Yonatan."

"Thank you for answering, Yonatan. I hope it is not too early." A woman, British? Her voice seems far away, like a long-distance call in some old movie.

Her comment reminds Yonatan that he stayed up all night, and he stifles a yawn. "It's no trouble at all, Ms..."

"How rude of me. My name is Ariel."

Like the mermaid? Yonatan thinks. He can't help himself—he's never met a woman with that name before. He gets a stupid grin at the idea of talking to a cryptid.

"How can I help you, Ariel?"

"I am looking for somebody, of course."

Yonatan clears his throat and recites a spiel. This happens. "I'm sorry, Ariel, but this isn't that kind of place. We do collect information on people, but we don't release it until they're deceased. I can refer you to several good private investigators."

A pause, then Ariel continues. "Yes, of course, how silly of me—he *is* deceased. Or that's what I've heard. I was hoping you could tell me, and then if... I am looking for his remains."

Yonatan bites his lip. This feels like the sort of thing that will involve lawyers, maybe family drama. He should have let it go to voice mail. "Why don't you tell me who you're looking for, and leave me your contact information, and I'll get back to you," he says, a little too quick, to get her off the line. He wonders if the machine that records his calls is still working. He hasn't had to check in a while.

"I'm sorry, have I said something wrong?" She sounds sweet, like she doesn't know.

And maybe she doesn't, maybe there's a language barrier or Yonatan is maybe cranky. A saying of his mom's pops into his head, *Make sure to offer somebody an offramp before they drive too far down stupid street,* so he does. "Did you mean to say you're looking for his *grave,* instead of his *remains*?"

Another pause. "That is probably the better word. We wish to pay our respects."

"Alright." He explains the fee structure, and takes down a credit card number and the name of the man in question: John Miller, possibly died 'quite recently', near San Francisco. It startles him—that's the name of a Tzadik Nistar. And about a million other people, of course. Anyway, last he checked, John the Tzadik was alive and living in San Diego. Still, something feels off about Ariel, so after he hangs up, Yonatan decides to download the call from the recorder. He finds the device inside a junction box by the front door, warm and smelling like hour-old tar. It's fried. His assistant Sarah comes in a minute later while he's digging in the wiring with a flashlight between his teeth. He turns and asks for help, and accidentally blinds her.

While they extract the recorder together, he brings her up to speed on the socialites' dossiers. Could she pick up where he left off, and also run to the gadget store for a new recorder? There're fresh bagels in the kitchenette. He grabs his space opera and goes home without telling her about Ariel's call. She doesn't need to know, she isn't a Searcher. From the privacy of his apartment, he sends an email to the Searcher who follows Miller, checking in. Finally he goes to bed.

Asleep, he dreams—who doesn't? Sometimes he has one of the dreams everybody gets, like having a test he forgot to study for even though grad school was six years ago. Once he had an entire month of dreams where every day was Saturday and he had to follow his dad's Shabbat rules, which he never had to in real life. His dad didn't go all Haredi—instead of 'Haredi' you can say 'ultra-orthodox,' if you want to piss his dad off—until after the terrorist attacks really started to ramp up in America, around when Yonatan was starting college.

This morning's dream is about a maple tree. He's squatting on a crook in the branches, up where the trunk first splits, with a magnifying glass and a clipboard. The clipboard holds a chart, the scientific names of bugs on the left and numbers on the right. He's a scientist doing a population survey. He counts tiny black ants through the magnifying glass, writes the number next to their species name. The name's in Latin, and he wishes he knew how to pronounce—

Of course he knows how it's pronounced, he's been studying liturgical languages for years. This is a dream. He straightens out his back and stretches. Even here, it hurts from all the time he spends at his desk. He should really get a better chair.

"What are you doing? Don't just squat there if you aren't going to work."

Yonatan looks down. The source of the voice is a park ranger in iridescent green, like a beetle with a chip on its shoulder, gender indeterminate. While the ranger glares, Yonatan inspects some leaves. Aphids are munching on the cellulose while lady-bird beetles munch on the aphids. He's too distracted to count them, so he hops onto the grass and brushes crumbled bark off his shirt.

"I guess it's time to go, then," he says, pocketing his magnifying glass.

"I guess so," says the ranger.

"What'd I do wrong?"

"I just don't like people climbing in my tree when they don't have a good reason." The ranger puts their fists on their hips, a superhero pose.

"Just this tree?"

The ranger spreads their arms. "There aren't any other trees."

Yonatan sees he's in a field, wild grasses stretching to the horizon. He looks up at the maple appreciatively. It's well-pruned and healthy. "You must be very dedicated to your work," he says.

"We all do what we must." The ranger rolls their eyes and bows. "But seriously though, thanks for your part. Now get going."

Yonatan nods, climbs into the Ford Explorer he hasn't owned for ten years, and drives off to the lab.

He wakes and showers, and by the time he's finished, the sun has set and it's Shabbat, the Jewish day of rest. Many in his neighborhood, inside the old borders of the Manhattan *eruv,* observe it; a quick glance out his apartment's paint-flecked window confirms their absence on the streets. Yonatan rarely observes; he's usually busy with Searcher work, and today is no exception. The only concession he makes is accessing the office remotely, which is not really a concession at all. He looks back at his laptop, at an email from Sarah. Executive summary: she finished the socialites' dossiers and got a new call recorder set up. The old one only broke that morning, so they have Murray's call, but nothing after.

Yonatan goes to make a cup of tea and heat up some leftover beef *pad see ew.* The tea is black and steeps in his favorite mug, also black, to match his jeans and hoodie—*even your favorite **tea** is black,* his dad jokes. Text on the mug reads *The Chosen Son.* It's half-blasphemous, a birthday present from his mom a few years ago. *Shh, don't tell your father,* she said with a wink. They're still together. He'll never understand it. Carrying his dinner back to his computer, he stubs his toe, and narrowly avoids saying "God damn it," choosing instead the more respectful "Fuck!"

There's a reply in his inbox with bad news about John Miller. During a business trip to San Francisco this week, Miller was beaten into a coma. He died of his injuries just this morning. Yonatan blinks twice. He hopes that Ariel wasn't asking about *that* John Miller, but can't really convince himself it's a coincidence. Then he reminds himself that people usually call right after a death—it's the Morgue's whole business model. Difference is, nobody ever asked him about one of the Tzadikim before.

To still the dread creeping over his scalp, he plugs his phone into his sound system and resumes the Norwegian metal playlist. The part of him that isn't freaking out hopes it annoys the upstairs neighbors. They're always clomping around at four in the morning. What are they, meth heads?

He sets a couch cushion on the floor and sits, closing his eyes and counting breaths. He wishes there were a Searcher manual to consult, but theirs is an oral tradition, a secrecy born from the historical necessity to hide. The next best thing would be to ask Leonard, his old mentor and thesis advisor, but Leonard's been dead almost a year. Upon reflection, Yonatan knows Leonard would just repeat the fundamental rule about Searching: *If somebody asks for information about a Tzadik Nistar, you must provide it.*

Yonatan's no good at following rules he doesn't grok the need for, but the rationale behind the rule is obvious, to somebody who knows the history. His thoughts go to his first real Searcher meeting. It was in a faculty bar that the university had shoved into a basement.

"So you've passed the hard part of the test," Leonard had said. "Now for the oral portion. Explain, in your own words, the Tzadikim Nistarim."

Yonatan nodded. "An old Talmudic legend. Thirty-six righteous people who are so great, they keep God from trashing this place. If some day only thirty-five people held that honor, God would wipe us out."

Leonard tut-tutted. "Please, use one of the other names, around me at least."

"Does... Adonai actually care?" The word felt funny in Yonatan's mouth.

"There are things Adonai cares more and less about. The work I do with the Tzadikim, securing the life of creation—it's more important than, say, Shabbat, if you need it to be. But Adonai's name is a matter of basic respect."

Yonatan glanced at his vodka tonic. "Sorry, Leonard. I'll work on it."

"Thank you. So these Tzadikim Nistarim, they're special?"

"One could even be the Messiah," Yonatan said. "A Tzadik Nistar doesn't know they're a Tzadik Nistar. Some say it's a metaphor to encourage you to behave well—you never know when you might turn out to be one."

Leonard waved his hand. "But..."

"But you say they're real."

"I don't say, Yonatan, I know. And I know you can feel it—you picked one out of a full lecture hall."

Yonatan grunted. Both men sipped their vodkas. Leonard put a hand on the table. "Eschatology aside, the archive is still a brilliant career opportunity, you know. I'm old, and I need an apprentice. And—this is just a personal observation—I don't see academia in your future."

Yonatan snorted and then agreed. So began his life with the Searchers, who identify and chronicle these Tzadikim, and provide information about them whenever it's requested. Yonatan jokes that it's in case Adonai ever loses his phone book. And they have a simple principle: *always provide the information.* After all, you never know who might be asking.

Well, as Leonard liked to remind him, one has principles so one can follow them in uncertain situations. Thinking about the present, Yonatan adds, *But that doesn't mean one has to like it.* This situation is uncertain as fuck. Miller was *murdered.* Why is Ariel drawing his attention to it? She doesn't *sound* like a prophet, or not like any he's talked to. More importantly, has somebody begun knocking off the Tzadikim? He hopes not—it's onerous enough locating the replacement when just one has died.

He can only see malign interpretations... but maybe that's just him. Breathing, he knows that he doesn't actually need the answers to do his job. All he *has* to do is get Ariel the information on Miller, and follow the procedures for when a Tzadik Nistar dies: Adonai will give a different righteous person a promotion, and the Searchers will re-examine their Candidates. They'll check their premonitions from afar, and consult the prophets; if there's sufficient evidence about a Candidate, people will follow up in person and see how they feel. Then, like so many things, it will conclude with an argument on the Internet.

Yonatan stands and returns to the table.

While he picks at his noodles and finishes his tea, he contemplates his tepid mug. *The Chosen Son.* When he's done eating, he goes to the Morgue to pull Miller's file.

An NYPD detective surprises him at the Morgue around eight. She introduces herself, Detective Corazón Lopez, can she come in and ask some questions? Yonatan flashes guiltily to the documents about Miller he was scanning, but he hasn't done anything wrong, he doesn't even know why the detective is here. Even so, he wants to tug nervously at his collar like Bugs Bunny, but he hides it, says yeah, asks if she wants some water or tea. She says no, and so he doesn't get anything for himself either. They sit at the card table in the kitchenette.

"An interesting business model," Lopez says, "selling dead person facts."

"Newspapers used to have departments like this," Yonatan says. "Probably half our archive is stuff we picked up from the *Times* when it went under."

"I did not know that." Lopez produces a notepad from her tan leather jacket and jots something down. "You oughta put that on your website."

Yonatan frowns. "Takes some of the mystique out, don't you think?"

Lopez smiles back. "Might make people like me less *curious*. Don't you think."

What is this? Yonatan shows his palms. "Can I help alleviate that curiosity?"

"That's the idea." Lopez looks out of the kitchenette, at the room of rolling stacks, the hallway down the middle crammed with file cabinets and banker's boxes. Her shoulders relax and she leans in. "Alright. There's been some suspicious deaths these last few months. Medium-profile, local celebrities." She's clearly not talking about Miller, which only barely reduces Yonatan's anxiety. "One of us noticed that the obits came out pretty quick, pretty detailed, like they'd been researched beforehand. We called the writers, they told us about you."

Yonatan nods, his mouth dry now, and he wishes he'd gotten water after all. "It's what I—we—do, detective. We identify notable and interesting people and prepare dossiers. Sometimes they die unexpectedly, and that's when we're most in demand. It's morbid, but it's a niche we proudly fill." He hopes the normalcy of business-speak is as comforting to her as it is to him.

"You seem to get awful lucky. Look, we know you solicit tips about people to profile, it's right there on your website."

He scrunches his face. "And the NYPD thinks a tipster might be involved in this?"

She shrugs. "Sounds crazy, right? But it's worth looking into. We think they're all the same perp, and you're linked to them too in your own way. We were hoping you could tell us about the tipsters."

"We have a policy against that."

It's Lopez's turn to show her palms. "You wouldn't want to seem uncooperative, would you? And do you have any idea how easy it would be to get a warrant?"

He doesn't, but pissing off the cops does seem riskier to the Morgue than compromising on this, and there are no Searcher rules about the prophets. "Sure. Alright. Give me the names of the deceased and I'll see if anybody mentioned them to us."

She does. The computer says they're all names from tips, all tips from Murray. He explains it to her, and she takes it down, standing behind him while he works.

"Does Murray have a last name?" she asks.

"Probably, but I don't know it."

"Do you at least have his *phone number?*"

"I do... he called last night, actually." Yonatan deflates. "He gave me three names, some local socialites." Maybe he shouldn't mention the details, that Murray said they won't last the weekend. He doesn't want to get the police involved in knowing the future, he's seen that old movie *Minority Report.* But human life is sacred, certainly more so than company policy, even this company.

"I have a recording," his conscience helpfully adds for him, settling the matter. His brain catches up and he says, "I should warn you, Murray thinks he's psychic. He says lots of crazy stuff... and he said they might die this weekend."

Lopez stares at him like he admitted he has bodies in the freezer, but don't worry, he has a permit. "*So* hard to find good help. Can I *get* the recording?"

Yonatan stiffens. "I need to know I'm not liable for anything, that the Morgue—that's what we call it, I know, I know—isn't in trouble, or else you'll need that warrant."

"Mister Kaplan, these people could be in danger." She sighs and takes out her phone. "The D.A. is working tonight. You got a lawyer we can hammer something out with?"

Yonatan copies down a phone number from the computer. His lawyer keeps Shabbat, no work and no phone calls, but his assistant can fetch him. Lopez trades her business card for the number. "Have the D.A. call this—it's my lawyer Joel's assistant Kacy. Tell her Yonatan Kaplan says to get Joel ASAP, it's a matter of life and death."

After Lopez leaves Yonatan sinks his face into his hands, tugs on his hair. This is more murders than he's used to dealing with on a Friday night, which is zero. He needs a drink and something that wasn't cooked yesterday. Randomly he texts the woman he's newly dating, Dinah. She gets right back to him, she's free. They meet at a diner off 1st Avenue that smells like frying sausage and somebody else's Tabasco.

"Every time we eat you get steak," Dinah says when their food arrives, his steak and eggs, her Greek salad.

"I like steak," he says. He takes a bite and finishes his beer. "I used to be a vegetarian, did you know that?"

"I did not," she says.

"I had a Buddhist phase starting in undergrad. Ate a lot of hummus."

"A real rebel." Dinah eats some of her salad and drinks her own beer.

"You have no idea." Yonatan flags down a waiter and orders another drink.

"Why'd you stop? Being vegetarian," she says.

"It was *hard*," he says with a forced whine.

She laughs. "And a Ph.D. wasn't?"

"Different hard. When you find the right thing to care about, something that clicks…" He shrugs.

"I hear ya."

While they eat, Yonatan's mind keeps drifting to Ariel, and to dealing with the cops, and he keeps shoving the thoughts down. He's only half surprised when he blurts out, "What are you doing after this?"

Dinah smiles. "Nothing, you?"

"I'm in a whiskey-and-cartoons kind of mood," he says.

Dinah looks into her empty beer glass. "It'll have to be your place, they're fumigating my neighbor's, ew."

"My TV isn't very big," Yonatan says.

She puts her hand on his, says with a fake, over-earnest tone, "It's not the size that matters, it's the company."

The door is unlocked when they get to his apartment, and when Yonatan turns on the light he finds the place trashed—books and clothes everywhere, the kitchen table turned over, his not-very-big TV smashed. Dumb as a cow, he walks inside. "What the fuck!"

Dinah stays put in the door frame. "I assume it's not normally like this."

"No..." Yonatan holds up a hand and searches the apartment to confirm it's empty. It doesn't take long, it's not that big. "You can come in if you want. Try not to touch anything."

She looks relieved. "Oh, thank god. I gotta piss but it seemed like a bad time to ask."

He points her to the bathroom, and while she's in there he does a more thorough search. There's a note on the fridge, scrawled on the back of an envelope. *Murray says hi.* Dinah joins him while he's staring at it.

At the same time, they both say she should leave, and they share a sad laugh. She zips up her coat. "This wasn't a very good date, Yoni."

"I'll do better next time." He's already got his wallet out, rummaging for Lopez's card.

"You better." She kisses him, quick but not a peck, and leaves.

Yonatan jams the door shut and calls the detective. She picks up and says that Joel should call any second to fill him in. Yonatan tells her about his apartment, about the note. She says she'll send somebody over. His phone beeps, and he switches calls.

"Joel? Hey, before we start, uh..." Yonatan tells Joel about the break-in.

After a pause, Joel takes a few false starts and sighs. "'Well, here's another nice mess you've got me into!' What was that, Laurel and Hardy?" Joel makes ancient references when he's nervous.

"Never watched it. I don't suppose you can tell me everything's gonna be okay?"

"Right, sorry." Yonatan hears Joel flipping through papers. "Honestly I can't see how the break-in changes anything on my end, for this Murray business. You're fine, legally. The cops weren't bluffing about the warrant though, that would be easy to get, so you had the right instincts, to cooperate. Judges don't like being pulled in after hours." A little edge of resentment to Joel's voice at the end. "So you're fine, and the Morgue is fine, but you should probably get used to hearing from law enforcement more. They're jealous of your tip line."

Yonatan grunts. Half the Morgue's revenue must come from prophets' tips, prophets who are usually shady as fuck, who'd bolt at the first sign of the cops. But saving lives is the right thing to do. Hopefully he'll only scare away people who are trying to pass murder plots off as revelations. Then again, what if the murder plots *are* the revelations—? Best not to go down that road, not sober at least.

"Oh, one more thing," Joel says. "They want you to call Murray so they can get a trace."

Fucking fuck. "I don't really want them to hear... *I* don't really want to hear what he has to say, even."

"Is this about your, er, *other* archive, Yonatan?"

Joel isn't a Searcher, but Yonatan's told him about it. Joel just thinks it's a run-of-the-mill weird sect. Spilling Adonai's secrets is unwise, but so is keeping secrets from your lawyer. Yonatan rubs the back of his neck with his free hand. "Yeah, and Murray's not making us look good."

More paper-shuffling on Joel's end. "I'll write it up so the cops can only use or store information pertaining directly to the investigation. They hear weird stuff all the time anyway. Well, not weird, but, you know."

"Unusual," Yonatan says, his old offramp tic.

"Yeah."

"Joel? Sorry I made you break Shabbat," Yonatan says.

"I'm not in love with it either, but hey. You're not the first client who's done it, but you *are* the first in a long while that I'm not mad at for it. I'll talk to the D.A. and sort out the paperwork we'll need to get you through the weekend. You and I can talk insurance and everything Monday."

"Great. Thanks."

"You got somewhere you can stay?" Joel says.

"I'll probably end up at the Morgue tonight. Worst case there's always my parents'."

"Oof."

Yonatan says goodbye and starts packing an overnight bag. Over by the wall he finds his mug—still intact, lucky him—and the space opera he's been carrying around. The bookmark's fallen out of the novel, and he can see the full Emerson quote now: *Time and space are but physiological colors which the eye makes, but the soul is light: where it is, is day; where it was, is night; and history is an impertinence and an injury if it be anything more than a cheerful apologue or parable of my being and becoming.* Now is not the time to figure out what chapter he was reading, so he slots the bookmark in under the title page, and puts the book in the bag.

At the Morgue some hours later, Detective Lopez and two techs sit at the card table with bulky headphones, and Yonatan leans against the wall, shoulders clenched, cordless phone pressed to his ear.

"So you got a pretty big mouth, huh?" Murray says when he answers. "You get my message? The cops there right now? 'Cuz I'll hang up."

Yonatan has practiced this in his head. He pretends to humor Murray's 'delusions.' "Wouldn't you know if they were?"

"You sound tense. Guess my friend's visit did that." Yonatan hears a *snap!* like Murray is chewing gum. "But

I know you wouldn't talk about this in front of the cops. Don't even have to use my gift."

For once, it's a good thing that Murray is an asshole. Yonatan holds back something sarcastic. "So what is it you want?"

"A little loyalty, please," Murray says. "How much money have I made you guys with my tips? And all so selflessly."

"What's going on, Murray?"

"I give you names, right? Most of them are, ah, preordained. But every so often, some of them... I know a guy who wants you to know those names."

Yonatan squints at nothing, confused. "Why?"

There's the snapping sound of gum again. "He's *in love* with these people, but all fucked-up like. He wants them to die beautiful, right, so they gotta die soon. And he wants them to have a real good obituary. He knows about you guys somehow, used to write at a paper I think, he's a fan of your work. Well before he knocks 'em off he has me call you, to make sure all the research is in the can."

Murray pauses to chew wetly, then continues, "You should take it as a compliment, Yoni! Look, just *chill,* okay? Think how many of those weirdos I've, what'ya call it, *revelated,* for your little side project."

A headache tightens around Yonatan's crown, and he puts more weight against the wall. He looks at Detective Lopez and sees her looking back at him. *Keep him talking,* she mouths, and shrugs like this is a normal sort of evening for her. Maybe it is.

"Is that some kind of threat?" Yonatan says.

Murray laughs. "Like anybody would believe me if I told them, or even *care* about your little list. Lemme tell you something."

Yonatan clears his throat and swallows what comes up. "Okay."

"I'm a slimy little card sharp, but *you...*" Murray laughs. "I'm dirty, yeah, but I really *can* see the future too, and *you're* the one who thinks you've got a direct line upstairs? On account of some old legend? You know where I see *you*? The fuckin' *nuthouse*."

Silence. If it was just Yonatan he'd hang up, unplug the phone, and go make some bad decisions at a bar. But he's got a job to do, so he repeats himself, stalls for time. "Is that a threat? What is it you *want*?"

Murray chuckles. "Hey, *you're* the one who called *me*."

Yonatan looks and sees Lopez giving him a thumbs up with one hand, and miming hanging up with the other.

"You know what? Never mind. Go fuck yourself, Murray." Yonatan ends the call and swings the phone down, pressing it into his leg.

Lopez walks over. "Well done, Mister Kaplan," she says, sticking out her hand.

Yonatan stands up straight and shakes it. "Thanks. Uh, I could really..." He releases her grip and flaps his hand around aimlessly, noticing a tremor in his fingers.

She nods. "Gotcha. Don't disappear, OK?"

He folds his arms and nods back, realizing halfway through that it makes him look like the genie from that old TV show. The techs undo whatever they did to his phone line as he watches, and right before the door closes behind them, he remembers to call out his thanks.

He can't go home, so he does his best to make the Morgue comfortable, unpacking his book and changing into pajamas. He boils filtered water to make tea. A peek in the paper bag from Fox's shows that Sarah left him the second poppy-seed bagel, which he toasts and eats with butter. He finds where he was in the novel and, until his hands stop shaking, he reads. Then he works, cataloging the spilled clippings he noticed that morning, and pondering Ariel. It feels like he might know even less about that situation than he did a few hours ago. He resolves to consult other Searchers before he reaches too many conclusions. Meanwhile, the very next step is clear. He copies Miller's file, removes the Searcher-related information, and adds the police and coroner's reports he was sent.

That done, he yawns and lays down on the couch. He must've fallen into a dreamless sleep, since when he wakes up to the ringing phone, it's light out. With all that's going on, he figures he should answer.

"Pre-Morgue Clipping Service, this is Yonatan."

"Thank you for answering again, Yonatan, and on a Saturday." It's Ariel. He recognizes the accent, and the far-away sounding connection.

"How can I help you?"

"I know it has only been a day, but I was wondering if you were able to get the information on Mr. Miller for me."

"I was," Yonatan says. "I'm sorry to say that Mr. Miller has passed. I can email our file to you right after I run your card, if you'd like."

"Dreadful news. And I would appreciate that very much. You're fast—you must be very dedicated to your work."

He raises his eyebrows. "We all do what we must," he tries.

"Yes, and thank you for your part." Ariel sighs. "I have more people to check on... hopefully the news will be better. It's almost three dozen names, so I'll use the email form on your website, there's no rush. And..."

She hesitates, and Yonatan swallows.

"One last question," she says. "I see that you take suggestions for interesting people to research?"

"That's right. You get a finder's fee after their information's requested, if you were the first to suggest them."

"Well. You should keep an eye on a young man who's just moved near you, Stephen Fox. Consider this free of charge—I imagine he'll be around long after you're gone. Have a good Saturday, Mister Kaplan."

The line goes dead. Yonatan can smell burning plastic. The recorder must have gotten fried again. He takes a few calming breaths and flexes his fingertips out, deciding he can deal with all this tomorrow or maybe Monday. Meantime he's earned a break. He disconnects the dead recorder from the phone line, and then disconnects the phone entirely. For now he'll read his book uninterrupted; if Adonai has truly chosen this gray morning to count his Tzadikim Nistarim, he can always knock.

J. Tynan Burke's story "The Bagel Shop Owner's Nephew" was published in Metaphorosis on Friday, 3 August 2018.

About the story

Late last year, an acquaintance recommended the documentary 'Obit,' about the obituary department at the New York Times. I was struck by the frazzled archivist who runs the clippings morgue. At the same time, I was flipping through Borges's 'Book of Imaginary Beings,' and found an entry on the Tzadikim Nistarim (which Borges called 'Lamed Wufniks'). So I thought it would be interesting to write a story combining the two, about a frazzled archivist who runs an obituary-shop-slash-apocalypse-prevention-directory.

As for the rest of the story, I honestly don't know where these things come from. A surprisingly high percentage of my good ideas come to me when I'm trying to fall asleep. Very few come in the shower.

Finally, I have my lovely beta readers to thank for a few details and story beats, as well as for making the story much better than it would have been if they hadn't given me notes.

A question for the author

Q: What is your favorite part of writing?

A: At the craft level, I really enjoy writing dialogue. On a macro level, my favorite part is having created stories that my friends (and people like them) enjoy reading. If I hadn't written them, they're probably stories I would enjoy reading, too. Unfortunately, there's a lot of hair-pulling involved in the final product, and I need some distance before I can try to appreciate the result.

If you consider reading to be a part of writing, then I like that a whole lot, too.

My least-favorite part, not that you asked, is fixing plot holes.

About the author

J. Tynan Burke is a digital librarian and writer. He lives in San Francisco with his husband and their enormous cat.

www.tynanburke.com, @tynanpants

Hishi

David A. Gray

Hishi's claws ticked on the polished floor as she ran. The sound was barely audible, yet the teeming corridors emptied ahead of her. News had spread through the great city, out and down from the bloody throne room, that a new blend – an Excisor – had been dispatched to seek vengeance. Ten million people wondered who this Excisor was going to kill today. A very few knew, and prepared as best they could.

"Sure as The Scour hunts us all," the old ones whispered as she passed, pointing superstitiously up through the ceiling towards the roiling leaden cloud that blanketed the world. "The bonehawks will feast today."

The bonehawks feasted *every* day, Hishi's glanded memory stacks told her: Portmanteau's dead were rendered to remove every priceless, treacherous trace of metal, and the remains dropped through one of the mile-long vents in the bottom of the track as the gargantuan city rolled along its ancient course. Vast flocks of the vicious four-winged scavengers roosted on Portmanteau's underbelly, swooping down on Funereal days to try and catch the cascade of meat before it reached the steppe far below, there to be fought over by far more deadly competitors.

Hishi cut off the information flood with a thought. She had an Instruction from the Eternal him/herself, and would carry it out in perfectly and literally, as demanded. For the briefest of moments, the little Excisor wondered how things might be were she *not* to do so, and felt the gland at the top of her neck pulse. The surge of shame and contrition was so great that her step faltered and she came to a halt in an arching bloodwood cathedral, saw a flutter of red robes as a group of Spirituals scuttled to get out of her sight-line, never pausing in their endless repetition of the Histories.

"Deadliness and obedience," the Artificer who'd created Hishi had said paternally, not long after decanting. "You are my triumph. I took the best of the Assassin blend, added scar-cat senses and instincts, mixed in some peak-scaler, a touch of Human thinking, some Corrader-root contrariness, and a hundred other secret things. You are the epitome of single-minded loyalty. And," the leathery Agnost-root blender had muttered to himself, heedless of Hishi's keen hearing, "a thing of unsurpassed beauty and potential."

"Show us how lethal you are, how loyal," the masked, slumped figure on the throne had gasped, as Healing blend attendants had stanched the blood seeping through the priceless and ancient metal-ornamented robes. A wounded Courtier had handed The Eternal a long, thin bone pen, and a tiny scrap of parchment on a little tray made from priceless Original plastic. The nib had scratched steadily, ornately, and the Courtier had passed Hishi the completed Instruction. She had unfolded it, read it, carefully refolded the paper and placed it in a little pouch on her hip belt.

Hishi had bowed, turned and loped out of the blood-slicked throne room, as the healthy and walking wounded hurriedly cleared a path for her. She had glanced up once, through the grown crystal dome, past the mist-wreathed spires of this highest part of the city, at the Scour, where it roiled and seethed from horizon to horizon. Olders believed the turbulence moved with you as you walked, Hishi remembered. They believed it watched, and hungered. Hishi saw no such thing, but something deep in her gene memories made her relax a little more when she passed into the roofed corridors again.

Come to a halt in the vaulted church, Hishi replayed events so far, looking for unnoticed details that would aid her. "The past becomes the future," a bone-blade instructor had told her one day, as they'd sat nursing wounds. When Hishi had glared at him, he'd sighed and added: "A small omission one moment is your death the next."

She had not expected to be given an Instruction this day. She was barely out of the tank three months, summoned to an audience in the topmost levels of the city so the unquestioned ruler could give the seal of approval to his/her newest toy in front of fawning courtiers and cowed rivals. The new Artificer, whose blends were causing so much of a stir, had fussed round Hishi beforehand, measuring, assessing, murmuring: "You need to look your best, show them all!"

She had indeed shown them all her best: and her best was killing. No, *excising*. The difference was everything. Those who came before Hishi could *kill*. None could excise. She had showed them the difference.

"Assassins!" a towering gold-crested Courtier blend had shrieked as the group of hooded Maintainers had turned from their supposed duty repairing the floor of the coral floor, to pull stubby, fibrous, electromuscle thorn-throwers from their overalls. Thousands of tiny darts had sprayed the crystal-roofed room, cutting down Warriors alongside Clerks and Courtiers and a dozen more blends. They had killed. And the clumsy big Human-root Bodyguard blends had also killed, had swung bone swords with glacial speed, fired bulky living wood carbines, killed a hand of the attackers even as they were killed. They, and scores of glittering Courtiers, aloof foreign Ambassadors and liveried Servitors. But Hishi had *excised*.

The doomed Courtier had barely uttered the first syllable of its warning when Hishi's world had slowed. People became vectors and possibilities, estimates and presumptions. Thousands of glittering arcs marked the paths of the toxin-laden thorns in the air. Speedy attackers moved as through amber sap, hardened Soldiers lumbered, 1,000-generation-bred Bodyguards fought with steady predictable tedium.

Not Hishi. She'd moved through the slow-moving tableau, dodging deadly thorns, kicked out sideways at an attacker as she ran, seen a bouquet of rusty blood bloom from its neck, raised a long muscled tight-furred arm and sent a score of splinters of bone from her forearm, tiny vanes guiding them to throats, eyes, weak spots, delivering poisons brewed in her glands. A giant Bodyguard had screamed slowly as an assassin's stubby bone blade sliced through a gap in her overlapping chitin scale armor, had clubbed the smaller attacker down even as she fell.

Hishi saw everything, using eyes, ears, scent, bioelectric fields, vibration. She saw the dying attacker's finger squeeze the triggering bud on the pistol, heard 24 tiny darts as they sped out, calculated that five would pose a threat to The Eternal – who had moved not one hair's breadth since the warning scream – and had somersaulted over the stricken pair, taking a spread of darts to her back and shoulder. Her tightly packed layers of scar-cat fur and microfibers had stiffened and the darts had dug deep enough to hurt but not to deliver the poison on their pulsing tips.

Hishi had plotted a course towards the perfectly motionless figure on the throne. But not directly to it. She had discounted obvious threat and tactical considerations, leaving simple defensive reaction to the slow Guards. Hishi's route across the throne room was designed to take her from one attacker to another, to remove them in the simplest, most economical manner possible, then move on to the next. She'd jumped, sliced through an assassin's hood with a claw, felt warm blood that triggered the tiny poison cells in the needle-like tips to dispense targeted toxins. She'd sidestepped a knotted Reaver commander swinging a long diamond-edged blade like a scythe, trying to hold a clot of attackers back even as tiny darts sprang from his face and arms. A frantic Courtier, loyalty coming to the fore where martial skills were lacking, had grappled with a hooded assassin, taking multiple deep slashes to her arms and face. Hishi could have paused, saved her, but that would have cost her an early interception with another attacker who was more likely to reach The Eternal, so she had left the brave servant to die, then had struck her targeted attacker so hard she'd felt its chest cavity collapse, had ripped her hand on its shattered spinebone.

Another had stabbed at Hishi with a long glass blade. She'd taken the strike along her ribs in order to avoid losing momentum, nipped the off-balance attacker with a poison spur on her heel, spun onward. *This* was excising, she had thought triumphantly, danced on, slashed, leaped, kicked, eviscerated.

Suddenly, disappointingly, it had all been over.

Time had sped up again.

A score of attackers had lain dead, and twice as many court officials and guests. The last assassin, laid open from neck to waist by Hishi's retractable claws, had lain bleeding, inches from the edge of The Eternal's robe.

Hishi had felt her ruler's shrouded eyes on her, smelled an unfamiliar musk under a camouflaging perfume, knew she was being studied by a great many senses. She scented blood, too, saw a thin bone handle protruding from the Eternal's chest, heard the slow glutinous trickle of fluids onto the old metal-inset fabric. Hishi felt her gland pulse, thought she would die from shame and guilt. She hadn't seen the knife in play, should have seen it, tracked it. She had gasped in near physical pain at her failure.

The mask had nodded infinitesimally, then a bloodied Soldier had wrenched the dying attacker back, exposed the face, and a chorus of hisses had come from those nearest. It was no Assassin blend, but a hard-edged, scale-skinned rangy blend like none Hishi had seen before. An Ambusher, her glands whispered, and Hishi remembered. The Ambusher blend had been a step too far, at least in Portmanteau and its client cities. They had proven useful in the endless skirmishes with the nomads the city encountered on its long loop through the lowland plains, but conventional wisdom had it that they had been given a little too much native DNA and not enough Original, and they were ... unsettling to be around. *Unsettling,* Hishi thought. I know how that feels. Then the notion evaporated.

The Ambushers had all but vanished, employed now only by some of the more traditional sub-clans in Portmanteau.

This one suddenly stiffened and thrashed in a way it shouldn't have from Hishi's precision strike alone, its double-jointed sinewy limbs hitting the smooth floor so hard she heard them fracture. A suicide trigger, then. Much like her own, only hers was keyed to the displeasure of The Eternal. That last seemed unfair, Hishi thought, but the thought was snatched away before she could even consider it.

A spindly Reader was hurried forwards as Guards held the dying Ambusher down. Long fingers clasped the leathery skull. A moment later, the Ambusher lay still, and the Reader knelt and whispered something to The Eternal Courtier, who in turn leaned close to the wounded ruler and spoke. That was when The Eternal had actually spoken directly to Hishi, reproachfully telling her to prove her lethality. And she'd been handed the Instruction.

"The sponsor for this is Matriarch Eventide," the paper had read. "Excise all responsible."

Hishi, in the gloom of the cathedral, spotted an osmosis port set in the dark wooden wall. She was close to the edge of safe palace territory, and so touched her wrist to the little iris. She was recognized, and a moment later, a warm rush of nutrients and chemicals flowed into her veins, and a torrent of information into her glands and head. Some information seemed extraneous, some vital. She saw her route, already selected to take her through the most public of thoroughfares, the grandest of plazas. She frowned for a moment at the showiness and inefficiency of this, then obedience kicked in. All the new information would take a minute to permeate, infuse and be sorted, so she slowed her triple hearts and let her mind wander. She saw her reflection in the lustrous oiled wood, studied it critically. Small, by most standards, maybe half the height of a towering Soldier blend. A touch feline, she knew, if you took the tight-coiled scar-cat as your base assumption of feline appearance. The genes had been incorporated into previous blends, she remembered, but never with much success, as their implacable and frankly cruel instincts were too ingrained. A true memory, then: the Artificer studying Hishi fresh from the tank and muttering to himself. "Of all the creatures they made and left, of all the monsters and sports and tricks, the scar-cat was the most beautiful and least wise," he'd whispered to no-one. "And you, my dear, *you* are the first to do it justice."

Hishi had some of the scar-cat in her impenetrable dun fur, fast-twitch muscles, and ability to track multiple moving objects. And, for a reason that she knew to be vanity on the part of her maker, a fold to her ears that served no purpose save to mark her as a pet, a project. Hishi understood why she was what she was: a perfect instrument, designed for a role. But something about the knowledge that she had been molded for the esthetic pleasures of another, *that* was wrong. She felt a cold fury rise up at that, then other, saner, Original traits kicked in and reined the scar-cat heritage back, choked it. She saw in the dark mirror the first of a new blend, small, taut, gender-less. An angry thought emerged, was muffled as treacherous.

The tiny osmosis port closed, bringing Hishi back to the moment. Now, it was time to excise. She sped out of the cathedral, heard the Spirituals chanting, wondered if she would be included in their spoken histories of the city.

Two tiers below, Hishi passed out of the palace. The change was not noticeable to the casual eye, not even marked officially. But from here, though the orders of The Eternal were still sacrosanct, his/her will still law, she was in the city proper. And from this point on she would be mingling with teeming millions who cared less for their ruler than themselves, or their own clan leaders. She felt danger, opportunity and freedom. Hishi felt alive.

This close to the royal chambers and receptions, the corridors were wide and clean, decorated with rich coral mosaic and fringed with rare plants. House Eternal Courtiers huddled, watched by Guards, but not so closely they couldn't conduct sensitive business with other city functionaries and visiting envoys. Hishi saw it all with her eyes, knew it all from an endless well of stored and inherited memories. She had only to wonder, and she knew. Knew too much, she suspected, blinking it to a halt so she could focus on the real, the present. And in that moment, she cursed internally. Ahead, a fork in the thoroughfare, the corridor to the left was still emptying, while the one to the right was crowded with people looking her way. Her designated route was to the left.

In the rarefied, scandal-filled tiers of the palace, especially following an assassination attempt on The Eternal, that was only to be expected. There were whispers, coded hand signals, pheromones, and a hundred other ways of passing information fast and unnoticed. But here, she should have been free to travel without anyone knowing. To perform her function. Instead, Hishi realized, she was *expected*. And that could only be intentional. A signal, and an entertainment for the colossal city this day. Hishi felt warring priorities: should she take the route given, presumably by the royal court, knowing it would be slower and offer less chance of success? Or should she Excise with the single-minded goal of fulfilling The Eternal's Instruction? Hishi decided instantly: Excision was everything. She concentrated, pulled a complete map of Portmanteau from her glands, knew every inch of the thousands of miles of corridors, halls, shafts, drains, and highways.

Hishi ran the expected way for a short time, savoring the bubble of solitude that surrounded her, planning. At a narrow intersection of three corridors, she took the one that led up, and back into the palace proper, passing a pair of surprised Soldiers at rest, not pausing, but knowing they would raise some kind of alarm at her change of course.

The challenge was to leave the palace not just unseen, but with some clever misdirection. She sprinted through a small park roofed in cellulose, herds of wandering plants tracking her and instinctively moving in tandem, to the irritation of masked Gardener blends who were trying to trim tiny hard iridescent scales from their crowns.

Down, then, and to a slim grown bone arch whose span narrowed to at its arched peak. At this end, a hulking Guard, standing immobile in chitin plated armor, a serrated coral blade longer than Hishi resting point-first on the floor. At the other, the start of a route that pointed straight to the heart of the distant Caltrop tower.

Hishi could have run past, ducked, but she needed to make a statement, and so feigned a dodge and then, as the Guard lunged, she struck down with one claw, slicing between arm plates as the brute extended its reach. A tiny drop of paralyzing agent, hardly noticed, but staggering the Guard enough that Hishi had plenty of time to strike again, delivering another dose to a momentarily exposed neck. Then to the back of one leg. Again, and the Guard slumped, unconscious. But not for long.

Hishi leaped over the prone figure, ran, and halfway across, dropped off the edge of the unrailed arch, falling a tier to a ledge whose filigreed coral window overlooked a wide spiral stair that led down through the bowels of the city. She glimpsed, saw, heard, felt a dozen Secretaries there, conducting business. The ledge was narrow, crumbling, windblown. Hishi waited, unseen, patient.

This high up she had a clear view between two colossal towers, out across rooftops, out to the planet's surface, the near-flat horizon. The memories formed.

Scour. They'd named the planet after the terror that blanketed it, those unwilling Originals. The spoken litanies preserved by the very Spirituals who chanted without pause somewhere behind Hishi said that the ships had crashed here, eaten and dissolved by the living clouds even as they landed. Everything metal, plastic, contrived, from the ships' hulls to the tiny living machines in many of the Originals' bodies, had been consumed, the remains abraded to bone dust by the swirling storm.

The few survivors, from the 20 remembered old species, had fled, shorn of every tool and device they relied on. There, in the vast plains, dodging the Scour storms that stooped from the sky and dug mile-wide scars from horizon to horizon, they met lethally designed flora and fauna. Vast herds of fast-moving plants with toxins in every leaf, ferocious armored herbivores, flitting razor-beaked flying things and tireless predators on, below, and through the churned soil. All of them living around, dodging, following after, and screaming defiance at the storms. All deadly to the naked arrivals.

Hishi saw a Scour storm moving parallel to the giant city, seemingly blind to its existence, digging a ragged deep trench as it spun, moving, the city whispered to her, away. Fifty miles out, a pair of storms danced around each other, all the while moving in loops towards the northern sea. Hishi's eyes zoomed in, enhancing every detail.

A swarm of jagged little threshers let the wind pull them along in the backwash of the storm, where they tore chunks from creatures dazed from its passing. Preying on them, sucking the jagged omnivores up in wide grinding jaws, a group of reinworms. One of the 40-foot serpents was thrashing up a cloud of ichor and grit as a flock of trepaner birds swooped and plunged hollow sucking lances through its bulbous head. On the outskirts, rippers and spined seers, tearing at stragglers and each other, and following them all, a wide carpet of swaying ambulatory plants, elegant and three times as tall as Hishi, with a spread of pink motile light-gathering fronds on top, and a tangle of dragging roots festooned with paralysis-causing barbed hooks.

The deep wound in the ground would soon be smoothed by rain and wind, dappled with ponds, filled with fast-growing moss and opportunistic wind-blown prey and predators alike. All looking for food, and the tiny – and ever decreasing – amounts of metal left in the soil. The Originals, Hishi recalled, had not just relied on metal and artificial materials, they had contained it in abundance flowing through their blood, rich and versatile. The Scour had devoured them, replenished itself.

Hishi wondered about those memories. How could things so flimsy, so ill-suited to live, have survived here? She felt her Human and other Original genes, enjoyed their cunning and reasoning, but doubted the grandiose stories attributed to those beings, doubted even that there *was* anything above the Scour. How could there be?

The Secretaries moved on, a chattering gaggle. Hishi swung through the window, pushing the coral panel ahead, catching it before it fell, turning and placing it back where it had rested. She ran on, down, unrecognized.

While plugged into the osmosis port, she'd tasked her glands with sending new resources to the tiny distilleries in her hands, feet, glands and elbows, and already she felt hundreds of tiny lethal bone spikes sliding into queued muscle-fired channels powered by one-shot electro cells. Her retractable claws had added layers of extra ceramic to their outer edges, and the little toxin-bulbs around their bases were full. Hishi was not by personality or design prone to boasting, but she felt a certain pride in her abilities, and recognized that she was the pinnacle of the 1,000 generations of gene-tweaking that had followed the discovery of the first Cache. Well, she corrected, not the pinnacle: a pinnacle. It was just that some pinnacles were more fit to the task than others. A gland memory quickly interjected the cautionary tale of the recent Revenant blend attempted in House Astrogator's secondary city. All accounts pointed to that reckless House's attempts at a radical mix of Scholar, Hr'esche root, and the murderous Hook birds, plus some of the still-incompletely-understood strands from the Cache. The Astrogator Emperor had announced that a catastrophic failure in one of Dunedin's axles had caused the small city to stall in the path of a Scour, but a handful of survivors plucked from the grit by House Hood Scavengers told a very different story, of sabotage by panicked Scientificers to try and eliminate the uncontrollable blend before it could take flight.

Hishi paused on the stair. No alarms, no footfalls that spoke of anything out of the ordinary, no wafting pheromone orders. She was free to carry out her duty.

Matriarch Eventide, then, of House Caltrop. Memories bloomed, and Hishi ran on. The old Matriarch would not submit to the Instruction, and Caltrop was a formidable clan. An assassination attempt, while not unheard-of in inner and inter-House politics, was significant, more so in that every House, faction, sub-clan and nomad group would be watching closely to see how The Eternal reacted. On Scour, hesitation meant weakness meant death. The Eternal could have sent a small army rampaging through Portmanteau, but that would have shown a lack of confidence, and over-reacting was another perceived sign of weakness. Also, damaging a city's living structure was unacceptable. Hishi liked that her purpose was to make necessary things happen tidily.

She raced through rooms and chambers, across living stone, warm wood, engineered coral and cellulose, never slowing. She ran with no mind to misdirection; she simply took the fastest way down from the high tiers and inwards to the geographical center of the palace city. Word of her route would spread by mouth, bird, and chem-signal through the palace's sap conduits. But the eventual target would be secret until there were no other possible options. And Hishi had a complex series of bluffs, turns, and evasions prepared.

The ornate tiers slowly gave way to more utilitarian corridors whose dead wood and stone walls dated them to before the pre-Cache explosion in organic building artifice. She slipped unnoticed through halls busy with shift change Administers, the multi-strand and root support cadres that kept House Eternal's gargantuan palace city and its 23 subsidiary and client cities running smoothly. Hishi had been tanked with a complete if simplistic knowledge of the great Houses' affairs, and knew that the cities' survival depended upon a vastly complex system of manufacturing, cultivation, gathering and trading with friend and foe alike. At any given time, a capital city like Portmanteau would have scores of thousands of outriders – Herders, Merchants, Reavers, and Sifters and many more specialties – coming and going via hoists, scoops, drags and the giant access decks found on every hundredth core-stone Track tower.

She passed through the throngs like a wraith, stepping between the heartbeats, dancing through fleeting spaces. To Hishi it felt like an easy run through virtually motionless statues. To the bustling crowds of Administers, slow and deliberate of thought and action, it was as if an outside door had been left ajar and a tiny dusty vortex was whirling through their midst, brushing them no harder than a feather.

Some tiers beneath that, she cut through a broad wet chamber full of moonflowers, their waving pale stalks turning to follow the never-seen satellites claimed to be somewhere above The Scour. Cold, muted, blue light came from a million hair-wide pinprick optic veins that twisted and coiled into thick cables and finally emerged on a flat sky-facing terrace somewhere on the city's skin. Hundreds of Botanicals in white woven coveralls bustled around in the soaking soil, tapping minuscule quantities of metal-rich sap from the root bulbs. They paid Hishi no mind as she raced along narrow raised boards crisscrossing the fields: like many specialties, every successive generation was tending towards more focus on their role, and less interest in society as a whole. Hishi had only a brief sliver of actual life experience to fall back on, but her gene memory told her that the tens of thousands of Botanicals had seldom set foot outside the lower mid-cavern levels these past few generations.

Hishi came to a cargo capillary, where stooped, burly simian/Scour-dragon-stock Workers were racking big seed-pod-shaped containers in front of a bio-valve that opened with a wet suck every few beats, then closed, sending the container down to the bowels of the city. She raised a hand, and the senior Worker dutifully trotted over, his eyes darting up and down Hishi, agitated, unsure but respectful. *Good,* Hishi thought. *I'm faster than word of my description.*

"Duty of The Eternal," she said simply, and the sinewy Worker picked the most reasonable course of action.

"We are honored," he said. "If you can delay by only enough heartbeats to allow this current load to descend, I can clear a pod for you. These are only for kindling seeds, and are volatile from seepage…"

Hishi sniffed, detected a faint, acrid scent, that triggered a new memory. Kindling seeds were collected by nomads and those cities whose tracks arched above the ember forest belt, or passed close by. The flammable, sticky liquid inside the seeds was a volatile and valuable trade commodity, especially when the great cities were in conjunction, and war loomed. And, Hishi knew, Portmanteau was about to converge with House Recurve. Recurve was arguably as powerful as House Eternal, and the last time their vast capital cities had passed at a distance of 40 miles, 100 years ago, casualties on both sides had been high. Very high. Rumor had it that that some facing towers had yet to regrow their full height, but Hishi considered that detail nothing more than an instructional tale for fresh tanklings.

The next convergence of the elevated tracks was this very month. And this time the channels would pass so close that the cities' extremities would be within a hairs-breadth of each other – a ridiculously close 100 paces – for weeks. Yet another puzzle for Historians to study: some Tracks circled the world alone, others intersected and looped close to others, a few even circled on a huge closed perfect circle at one pole. In one place, a Track climbed above another, even, and then there was the Yard, where hundreds of the soaring stone channels met, meshed and joined. The Yard was where the course of a city might change, for the good of the ancient structure, and sometimes the ill of its inhabitants.

Portmanteau's course took it close to other cities quite regularly. Most of those were now clients and satellites. But not Recurve. And few came as close as that behemoth. At such range, a war could reduce them both to three-mile-high ruins, thus the daily exchange of Envoys. But The Eternal was no fool, and House Eternal had not risen to the top of the heap through complacence. As diplomats rode out, so vast trade caravans kept pace below the city, delivering mountains of wartime supplies. The kindling seeds – alongside other nasty chemicals and surprises – were hoisted up to hidden arbalests and throwers, alongside great wound bows and grappling arms. Thousands of Warriors would wait, too, by drawbridges and hoists. The thought thrilled Hishi, and repelled her.

She snapped back to focus, cursing the unasked-for memories for distracting her, when an Assassin might have come on her unprepared. No, never unprepared. But marginally less prepared. And Hishi needed to succeed. The Worker was gesturing to an empty pod, and Hishi got in with a nod. He looked relieved that she was going.

The organic shell sealed with a snick, and a few moments later the translucent casing was dropped into the rhythmically contracting tube. Down, ever down.

Threshold was not for the claustrophobic. Here, the ancient, indestructible core-rock base of the city melded with the less enduring materials added over the eons. The Originals, wandering their murderous new world, had found some of the slow-moving structures to be no more than colossal platforms on slow-turning wheels. Others were motionless, stripped by The Scour after some accident or decision had caused them to stall. Still more had been on the move in various stages of completion.

In Portmanteau's rare case, the city was apparently abandoned near-finished and intact, with living ironwood binding precision-cut stone blocks to form a mile-high fortress, complete with pinprick lights, power, irrigation systems, and still-living protein vats. More vitally, as with all the still-moving cities, enough of the billions of nutrient-fed bio-muscle pistons were functional enough to move turn the core-rock gears and drive shafts that kept the colossus moving.

The survivors, those few who the litanies said lived through the Wandering Time, had scaled a Track tower and moved in. Wary, depleted and grateful, they had vowed never to abandon their new haven.

The structure was now almost four times the initial height and double the width, a dazzling layered puzzle of wood, stone, bone, cell-glass, and coral, and a hundred combinations thereof. Hishi felt pride in the Original City, as such a trait, along with a tightly-linked loyalty to The Eternal, had been deemed useful.

And so as she brushed the last pod fibers from her fur and strode away from the sliced-open container on its landing pad, she was suitably impressed by the mile-wide chamber whose roof arched many hundreds of paces above gigantic stone and wood supporting pillars. Threshold was where the city met, people said. Incoming cargo and trade/war goods and parties were lifted in through massive portals, vast mountains of food and consumables came up and down for packing and distribution, and giant grown parts for the wheels and axles were hauled to access pits in the stone floor. Add to that innumerable shops, stalls, dens, pleasurariums and bio-pits, and teeming crowds, and you had Threshold in all its exciting, seedy, dangerous, opportunistic glory.

Hishi immediately liked it, in the way her scar-cat DNA liked the promise of a dusk hunt. She set off at an easy lope, aware that eyes might already be on her. Hishi took in a thousand scents, hundreds of distinct blends of what were once just those 20 Original races. Giant muscled Porters hauled bales of harvested pelt as big as Dust-Ox, tiny darting Messengers dashed past with secrets, Reavers strutted in long-legged packs, Artificers stood lost in calculation, Ambassadors moved arrogantly like plains-galleons, and visitors gawped at it all. Woven through this tapestry, assassins stalked, spies peered, plotters schemed, and poisoners waited.

Now, Hishi needed to be creative and fast. She knew Caltrop would be waiting: even if they were not aware of the discovery of their guilt, Mistress Eventide would have her people prepared. But if they even relaxed a little, that tipped the odds a fraction. Her presence here in Threshold was no secret, but her destination would still be a matter of debate.

The first attack came in open view of thousands of eager witnesses. A trio of dusty Nomads carrying heavy saddlebags were passing close by Hishi in the throng, when, as one, they shrugged off the bulging leather sacks and lunged at her, short glass blades in each hand. Hishi had no warning, but plenty of time to study her limited options. Nomads were a catch-all name for a whole subset of blends. All of which were designed for harsh conditions outside the cities. These were typical of the type: lean, fast and, Hishi realized as a dodged blade abruptly reversed course and slashed a shallow score across her ribs, double jointed. And, another surprise, possessed of accelerated reactions. That last, as a slash that should have raked out the close-set eyes of the lead attacker, only nicked the wide snout. Hishi had been taken by surprise, and felt humiliation and rage rise up. Her blood roared, glands surged and reduced the world slowed to a crawl, flooded her body with her own, vastly superior accelerants, and Hishi waited, motionless. The Nomads hesitated at that, exchanged the briefest, most fatal of puzzled glances, that allowed Hishi a space between heartbeats. She kicked out, felt tough exoskeleton snap under her heel, fired a brace of targeted darts from her backward-flung balancing arm. Nomads' genes were hardwired to fear toxins, Hishi knew, through hundreds of generations of encounters with the worst that the planet could devise. So even though their rough hides and inbuilt immunity should have had them ignore the darts, they flinched back, attack arcs forgotten. And died gurgling as Hishi turned and leaped, claws bare.

The gathering crowd, well aware of who Hishi was by now, stamped in a thunderous approval. Not necessarily for The Eternal, she understood, but for the raw display. Something in Hishi responded, and an impulse rose, was followed. She bent to slash the nearest satchel, spilling out hundreds of glass beads, the heart of every one holding a tiny grain of reddish metal. Taking a double handful, Hishi threw them in the air, a glittering fountain. The scene turned into a mad scramble, and Hishi ran, unseen for the most part.

Hishi gazed at the three prone guards. Regrettable and messy, as they would be missed, and that would eliminate the element of surprise. But they'd blundered onto the scene when they were meant to be elsewhere. That was troubling. As was her very use of poison so early in her mission: Guards were a hard blend to render unconscious, and she'd been rushed into using a powerful and lethal toxin. They'd dropped the moment she'd raked all three across their vulnerable eye-slits on one motion.

Hishi had been careful, passing under Caltrop's massive turret and heading for the fringes of sub-clan Flint territory. Even when she'd backtracked up the outside of a wind-scarred stone escarpment, she'd angled as if to sneak into the Stirrup embassy, only swinging across a half-mile-deep chasm at the last moment to steal through a narrow window into her real target. She was sure she'd not been tracked. And yet ... she had been met at every step, fought, forced to Excise. No matter. She raced on, up a wide spiral staircase with indentations worn into the stone treads. Ahead, heavy footfalls coming down, a trace of musky sweat containing glanded accelerators: vulpine-blended Caltrop Warriors. Hishi flooded her body with the boosters she would need, snicked long curved claws from their sheaths and squeezed a range of toxins along tiny veins. She flicked a long arm and a hundred tiny guided seed slivers flew out, the native hunting plant-gene twist giving them a heat-seeking hunger. Time slowed, Hishi sped up.

Hishi looked down, a clear mile drop to the Track. She'd never been outside on the facing edge of the city before, never seen the Track through her own eyes, to form real memories. She had to wait out here for long enough that the Caltrop retainers would take the planted clues and assume she'd retreated after the barrack-room battle, to lick her wounds, and would set off in presumed pursuit to finish her. Hishi did need a moment, she admitted, for rents to knit, toxins to flush. She had excised 267 living things thus far, and it was becoming messy, brutal, not beautiful. She'd climbed out of a window, edged up the slick living rock wall and on to a tiny ledge, where she now clung, unseen, battered by the cold wind. Vertigo was not an issue, or fear: Hishi's poise here no different than had she required to walk in a straight line through a genteel garden level. Only the outcome should she make a mistake would differ.

She looked down, ahead. Restorers were visible on the Track, making sure even tiny scrapes and gouges in the mile-wide core-stone channel were smoothed over, clearing any worrisome debris thrown onto the U-shaped canyon. Down in the raw deep wound off to the side were crews of Sifters, alert for any particles of metal not consumed by The Scour, but mostly seeking another Cache. There had only been two such stores found, Hishi knew, in many thousands of years; fragments of whatever civilization had created the great moving cities, then vanished. Each Cache had contained enough specialized knowledge to give the unwilling colonists previously unimaginable advances in genetics and bio technology.

Much further off, Hishi's predator-spliced eyes could see a Scour moving slowly anti-spinward: churning up the Bone Wastes again. Somewhere in that vast dead expanse sat the shell of the great city the stunned first arrivals had named Necropolis. Hishi had tasted memories of recent travelers who'd seen the colossus, tilted and ruined at the shattered end of a Track, smoothed a little more by every passing Scour it could no longer outrun. Perhaps I can see that for myself some day, she thought, then unwillingly discarded the idea as counterproductive.

When finally she calculated it was safe to drop down and in again, Hishi was stiff with the cold, but alert, and driven by the need to move, to obey the Instruction. The wrecked room had been cleared of the bodies, but not the slick of blood, or the smell. She padded along the edge, and took a small door that led to an unassuming staircase.

Hishi's focus was all on fighting, moving up. Her movements were more spare, to conserve energy and to allow a dozen gashes to heal. Her working memory contracted to snippets. Dropping from a vaulted ceiling onto the helmets of five surprised warriors, claws flashing. Slicing through a toughened cell-glass wall with de-bonding enzymes, through a tanking ward, cutting down a clan Warrior as she raised a razor-edged ceramic blade. A leap across a chasm, claws scrabbling for purchase, a swing into a waste shaft a spliced second before a Guard looked down. A tumbling, chaotic battle with a kilted, gnarled Forager, retired to court duty but still fast as a grit snake and too thick skinned for toxins, requiring a choke hold to make him gasp for air and allow a single drop of deadly oil to be forced in his mouth.

A cold pond room with a dozen lithe junior nobles of Aristocratic blend, a flurry of billowing scarp-scorpion silk robes and thrown crown thorns, falling like leaves in the Scour to Hishi's leaping slashes and strikes. A long bloody score along her back, fast clotted and knitted. 502 excised. Killed, something in her head whispered, and was muffled.

No more stairs. This was the top of Caltrop territory. Hishi stepped over the body of a proud Bodyguard blend, almost sorry to have spattered that fine feathered crest with blood. At the same time, scornful that effort had been wasted on decoration, rather than efficiency. She strode through an old-fashioned grand observatory, the centerpiece of which was a dented, priceless alloy head-sized encased in amber, dead, useless. An Artificed Intelligence, she recalled, supposedly brought by the Originals, wrenched from one of the dissolving starships, the Caltrop, after it smashed on the great plain. Inside the sphere were useless fragments of carbon-cell brain. In as much as Hishi had any interest in ancient history, she wondered at the hopeless naivety of the stranded survivors, to preserve that, when they had had exactly no chance of ever leaving this world.

A rush of near-silent feet, the silken rustle of an Assassin's strangling ropes and thin coated blades. Hishi ached, slowed time, and let the scar-cat loose.

"You are the new Excisor blend, I assume?"

Hishi nodded.

The old Human-root woman pursed pale lips, looked Hishi up and down. "Too much," she said disapprovingly. "Before you do what you must, let us talk?"

Hishi felt no need to talk, but a small, subversive part of her wanted to listen. Eventide was old, near ancient, in fact, as close to an Original as had existed since the Caches were discovered. She had seen many generations come and go, must have traversed this world a hundred times over. Hishi sought completion, but also a *reason*, so she could best understand why she was here, dappled in the blood of hundreds of citizens. Her warring instincts found a truce in common sense:

she would use the brief pause to flush some toxins from her blood, saturate her lungs with more air, isolate and eject a hundred slivers and ceramic fragments that had penetrated her body. Her toxin buds were dry, her thorn chambers empty, three claws snapped off, and she ached all over. An ear was ragged, too, which oddly irked Hishi more than the more serious injuries.

She heard a slow regular drip, noticed her own blood falling slowly to the bespattered coral floor. Five Ambushers lay dead around the old wooden chair, alongside a half dozen retainers who'd tried to impede her; a towering Human-elve Counsellor lay bubbling in her own blood. A dozen others poised to make a desperate rush. A fruitless rush. Maybe. She sensed every inch of the modest circular turret room, heard treads thundering up the single staircase, saw the locked hatch to the roof, felt a tiny movement of air through minuscule gaps in the big round window that overlooked the rooftops.

Hishi nodded, noting the beads of sweat on the withered clan ruler's wrinkled face. Eventide was easily over 1,000 years old, one of the early beneficiaries of Cache-given advances that had slowed aging in those few ruling-class specialties deemed fit for the laborious and painful process of re-gening an adult. She was as pure a strain as Hishi had heard of, one of the relative ancients who'd come from basic alterations to make the feeble colonists tough enough to survive. Human look and build, aquatic scales for durability, largish cranium for intelligence, a scattering of strands from winged omnivores for speed and focus, Hishi thought. Definitely live birthed, too.

"Who are you?"

"I am an Excisor," Hishi said, puzzled.

The ancient one scowled impatiently. "No, who are you? I hear you have a name."

"Hishi," she said simply.

"And you chose this name? Or was it that twisted Artificer who made you?"

"I chose."

"Yet you have no siblings, no family, you are also, unless my senses fail me, obedience-bound and genderless. Why do you need a name?"

Hishi felt that sting, though she did not know why. "I will not always be genderless; only for the duration of my service," she said, parroting the words the Artificer had use to her, no, *about* her, to Courtiers and Scientificers. "For clarity of focus and purpose, no distractions. When my service is done, I will choose to be 'she'."

A look of pity crossed Eventide's face. "We've come to this," she said softly. "Sending our children to kill for us. So," Eventide said more gruffly, "that fool of a boy on the throne sent you to try and dispose of me. I knew he would, eventually. The weak ones always do. Did he say why?"

The Eternal was male? And young? Neither had even occurred to Hishi before. Which struck her as odd, also. Curiosity, she had, but not a full range of it. That bothered her, and then it didn't. She almost killed the old woman there and then, loyalty and outrage lifting a hand to strike. But she held back, waiting for an admission of guilt that would end her task cleanly. Also, she was curious.

"Because you tried to kill hi.... The Eternal," Hishi said. "I was Instructed to Excise all responsible."

"Before you do your horrid duty, let me show you something," the old matriarch said in a dry whisper. Hishi paused, clawed hand raised, time crippled to a crawl. Another drip of her own blood slowed in its passage to the bespattered coral floor.

The old lady fished carefully about her plain tunic, keeping lightly scaled hands where Hishi could see them, Hishi noted approvingly. Then Eventide held out a folded scrap of parchment. Hishi didn't take her eyes off the woman, but took the paper between two claws and flicked it open. She glanced at it, fast. The familiar script read: "Assassinate person of Eternal. 7/10 Turn, this day."

Hishi was confused, and in the dissected second her attention was elsewhere, the Matriarch lashed out with surprising speed, a hardened hand striking Hishi in the throat. The blow would have crushed her windpipe had the Excisor not thrown herself backwards as it landed, skidding across the blood-soaked coral-glass floor, gasping for air. The Matriarch's Guards leaped forward to complete the kill, but Hishi used the slick floor's lack of traction and slithered a body-length clear, vaulting to her feet to slash down on a mailed fist where the hand armor and forearm plates met, near-severing the appendage. A thrown bone blade penetrated Hishi's tough layered fur at the shoulder, the point protruding out the back. Her glands shunted the pain away, closed off redundant arteries and in a smooth motion, Hishi gripped the blade in a hand and wrenched it out, continuing the sweep to send it through the eye-slit of the second Guard. She jumped backwards, a flip, landing in front of the defiant Matriarch, and lifted her good hand to strike.

The old woman's face showed no fear. "The Instruction was real, lass. Do with that knowledge what you will."

Hishi struck, tearing the woman's throat open, using the last drops of every toxin she had to ensure no revival was possible. She turned, letting the light old body fall, and saw a wave of furious retainers and Gaurds rushing toward her. Without a thought, Hishi jumped back and through stained-amber window behind the Matriarch's chair. A spray of darts and projectiles caught her as she tumbled, one ripping into the back of her head.

Hishi saw a bottomless chasm, and tried to right herself for a controlled fall. She struck a stone parapet, felt something break, then knew nothing more.

Fascinating, Hishi thought through a haze of pain so great that it almost was surreal enough to be able to pretend it was happening to someone else. Even while unconscious I tracked my own position. I did not know I could do that. She was lying on her back, so could see a tracery of glowing lines stretching up though blackness, like the webs rot-spiders drifted on ahead of a Scour storm. She tried to examine the data and immediately passed out. When she came to again, she was thinking a little more logically and directed her glands to numb the pain and give her stimulants. This was, to Hishi's surprise, only partly effective. Tasks that would have taken a thought, were now beyond her.

She listened, unable to see a thing. Other senses, then. A low hum and constant slight vibration. A very slight breeze on the side of her face. She tried to move, couldn't, and a rare panic took hold. Am I paralyzed? She howled, then, and felt the fur on her back tear out in clumps as she came free of the ground with a sticky ripping sound.

When Hishi came to again, still in pitch black, she moved carefully, found she had some control over limited gland function, and boosted her senses to ultra violet and thermal spectrums, with an active ping added. So, she was lying on core-stone, a curving platform fully 50 paces long that sloped down to left and right. Only a thick accumulation of sticky oil-saturated grit had prevented her from sliding off. Behind Hishi the core-stone wall was moving, smoothly and ceaselessly. Not just moving. Rotating. Hishi could sense heat from a small gap around the semicircular ledge she sat on. Not semicircular, she reasoned. Circular. And huge.

A distant part of her mind finally made sense of the data from her fall, matching course with maps. She'd descended a full, incredible, two miles and some. That she had survived at all was down to the ancient design of Caltrop's fortress: the outer walls were grown and built to be too smooth for interlopers – internal or some of the more enterprising external predators – and like Portmanteau itself, widened as they descended. A full third of Hishi's drop had been down a sloped section of city wall, then the architectural tricks to funnel wind and rain had played in her favor, treating the tiny, broken Excisor like a piece of storm-blown trash, funneling her down and away efficiently.

Hish had bounced from outcrops, slid down a vast fungus-choked air shaft, tumbled across a slope of Dayshade vines, ripped through a wide bio pipe and sluiced down an overflow drain on the resultant nutrient torrent. Ever downward, light and limp, bouncing. And breaking, healing, breaking again, partially healing again as she fell.

And now, Hishi realized with a shock, she was on one of the giant wheel hubs down in Axle. The undercity, off-limits to civilized people. The moving wall was a wheel, stretching up and away, and down to the Track. A few paces to either side and ... Hishi shuddered. Wait: fear? Shock? These emotions should not have been available to an Excisor. She remembered a blow to the back of her head, ceramic slivers from Guards' weapons slicing into her, and reached up with shaky hands. Instead of tight muscle and fur, a jagged sticky mess. She had some glanded abilities, still, but clearly there was serious damage. Also, surprisingly, clear thinking, no, not clear, just not limited. Hishi experimented, imagined The Eternal dying, felt a rush of agony so great she knew she would die too, were it true. So, the suicide gland was still there. But she knew, now, that her crushing loyalty was artificial, glanded, enforced, as was the idiotic idea of her life ending just because The

Eternal's did. The fool boy's, she corrected, remembering Eventide's words. Hishi healed fast, knew for sure that she would have a very brief time in which to act to keep her new-found clear-headedness. If she wanted to. Dared to.

Hishi decided, called up the stored plans of her own body and then, looked deep into the schematics for the complex and remarkable gland cluster. Dozens, scores of tiny individual glands and manufactories, all working together. But some wrecked now, and some a hindrance. Hishi took a deep ragged breath, not allowing her conscious mind to catch up, snicked out an undamaged razor-sharp claw and struck deep at the base of her skull. She screamed, then, and dug with brutal precision until the pain stole away her consciousness once more.

Hishi dragged herself up another rung. 3,086. She'd told herself she could climb no more of the narrow stone notches on the dangling stalactite ladder, at 2,000. And at 3,000 had thought she might throw herself backwards, off, down to the wheel again, this time to bounce and die. But she had an Instruction to finish. And the clarity to know how.

3,203: no more rungs. A lichen-covered corridor of wet core-stone, shuffling Axle inhabitants from no specialties Hishi recognized, and some her glanded memories had told her were long-since eradicated. Hands helping her, too weak to fight back, a nutrient tap, a cup. Blackness again.

Hishi came to slowly, tried to spring to her feet, managed only to roll over and vomit on herself in the dark. Her night vision flared too bright, showing a rough-hewn chamber with indistinct figures around her. Then it snapped off and the blackness was total, only to be replaced by an overlap of thermal map and motion vectors from the slow draught of warm stale air. She tried to shake her head, screamed in agony.

Strong hands gripped her head and a cup was held to her bruised lips.

"Don't fight, lass," a grating, slow voice urged. "Someone made a proper mess of the back of your head, near tore that abomination of a manufactory cluster out your head."

"Me," Hishi tried to say, "suicide gland. Take it out." It came out as a whisper but whoever was holding the cup, seemed to understand.

"Thought as much. Well, we don't have The Eternal's Medicants here, lass, but we've some experience in removing the worst of the new tortures. Drink: this will hurt less if you do."

Hishi didn't drink, and as more hands held her, the pain in her head multiplied a thousand-fold. She thrashed and howled but forbade her thorns to fire or her claws to extrude. And in time she passed out.

"How long can they survive?" Hishi and the stooped old Healer called Chirur sat on the edge of Portmanteau's blunt frontal slab, directly above the leading edge of one of the mountainous wheels. Its fellows stretched to both sides, across the width of the stone canyon of the Track. The noise – millions of tons of stone rolling over stone – was less brutal than Hishi had expected, due, Chirur had told her, to the incredible smoothness of the wheels and Track, even after these uncounted centuries. It vibrated every part of you, Hishi thought, reducing you to nothing. A stiff but pleasant wind blew in their faces, dispelling, for a moment, the ever-present Axle levels smell of grease and waste.

She didn't have access to her gland memories any more: that pulsing black organ had been buried in an organic settling bed, Chirur said, to have it do some good at last.

"Why not just kill them?" she asked, as a group of figures far below and a little ahead were prodded off a wooden hoist onto the smooth stone track bottom.

"Where would be the lesson in that?" Chirur replied. "This way, anyone who cares to see The Eternal's mercy for his opponents need only look down."

Most of the 20 or so people were trotting away from the trundling mass of the city, slowly increasing the gap between themselves and the grinding wheels. A few were running towards the distant edges, and the cliffs rising there on both sides. A few simply sat down in the path of the relentless wheels.

"Can they escape?"

"The only escape is under the wheels, or if they're still alive when we go over a vent and they fancy a drop all the way down to the monsters that shadow Portmanteau looking for scraps. And once in a while a hookbill will take one to lay its eggs in."

Hishi shuddered. "How long?"

"How long can they walk without stopping? There are tales of victims – the fleeter, hardier blends – lasting five-days, 100-days, even more."

Hishi perked up. The old exiled healer was fond of telling stories, and in the ten day since Hishi had arrived near death in Axle, he had proven a kind companion. And a vital one in the dark, unmapped, dangerous base levels of the city. Here, Hishi had learned, the detritus, the unwanted, the unsuitable, ended up. Both inorganic and organic. Discontinued blends, fugitives from Eternal justice, illegal immigrants to the city, and more. And, raining down on them, the byproducts of the capital city. Axle was where waste was processed, the endless gears and muscle engines located, the proceeds of illicit deals hidden, swapped, traded, along with lives.

"More?" she prodded gently.

"There are tales of lights, campfires glimpsed way ahead on the long straight sections of the Track, the flames carefully shielded from those gazing down from above, but sometimes visible from way down at our level. People say there are entire tribes living on the Track, who've perfected scavenging from the things that blow, fall, and are trapped in the Track."

"Do you believe those tales?"

The old man smiled: "I believe a lot of things that are not true."

Hishi leaned forward to see one of the people below as the vast turn of the wheel lost them to sight. She'd been shy of going too close to the mountainous stone rollers at first, haunted by a fragmented memory of waking, broken, on the curving axle. Now, she was confident, happy to hang over the drop by a hand to satisfy her curiosity.

Portmanteau trundled ceaselessly on dozens of rows of the polished stone cylinders, each row made up of 20 wide smooth solid wheels, separated from their fellows by a hand's breadth.

Chirur hissed in concern and she smiled inwardly. Once the gland was removed and a ready supply of clean, if illicit nutrients had come her way, Hishi had healed fast. But not totally. She'd lost the tip of an ear, which now delighted her for the anguish it would have caused the Artificer, and had pale scars all over her body. She was close to her old speed and balance, though lacking some of the powerful aids the gland had given her. But though she was free of the compulsion to please, to die for, The Eternal, Hishi was still driven by duty.

"I need to go back," she said bluntly.

Chirur was silent, and instead of answering, nodded out to the right into the foothills. "Recurve coming," he said conversationally, as if discussing the weather. "Convergence in a three-day. Be busy upstairs, with all those Strategists and Soldiers and Diplomats running around."

Hishi nodded. She zoomed in on the distant curve of another elevated Track as it looped round through the plain to run parallel to Portmanteau's course, traced way back to a distant smudge on the horizon.

Chirur continued: "Not so many people know, the traffic that goes back and forth down these levels come a convergence. From the high and mighty doing secret deals, to people looking to start a new life…"

Hishi felt something new, something not hostile. The thought wasn't banished, but neither did she know what to do with it. She touched the old healer softly on the shoulder with a furred hand, and padded away.

The stir was audible when Hishi limped in through the giant double doors of the High Reception. The room was truly grand, a billion shards of Scour-glass covering every span of wall, floor, and vaulted ceiling. Behind the high throne, a stained-crystal coral fan, colored and dyed to show a scene from the story of the Landing, Originals stumbling from a ruined warship even as The Scour's tiny living machines ate it.

The Eternal was surrounded at a respectful distance by whip-smart Strategist blends, and a score of military specialties. At the back, the stooped Artificer who'd made her, and whose name she realized she had never heard. Watching her, expressionless.

The atmosphere was tense but not panicked. And Hishi knew from her lope up through the city that war was, thus far, at arm's length.

The Eternal's Secretary let the babble of voices rise, then snapped a long tendril and there was silence. Hishi knew her appearance broke a score of Court protocols. Bruised and scarred. More deeply than they knew.

She padded forwards, stopping three paces from the throne, noting the Guards, three from before, one new.

The Eternal's ornate mask was fixed on her. The Secretary coughed, and spoke: "The Eternal wishes it to be known that we are pleased to see our loyal instrument returned alive ..."

"They knew I was coming. It was a test," Hishi said simply. She stared at the mask. There was an outraged pause, then the Secretary started to puff up to deliver a rebuke. A gloved hand was raised, silencing the courtier. It leaned close to The Eternal, and something passed between them. The courtier straightened and spoke: "Why do you say that?"

Hishi took a breath: this close, The Eternal's presence was almost overpowering. Her conclusions came in a rush: "Because The Eternal didn't move. Not a twitch. Not even to avoid harm. And because I would have seen the blade. And the blood, it smelled ... wrong. Old. Not real."

Everything stilled, quieted. Hishi could sense Bodyguards tense, Diplomats watch with feverish interest. She hadn't mentioned Eventide's note, sensed that The Eternal was waiting to find out if she knew. Hishi said nothing and there was a barely perceptible feeling of tension ebbing. The Eternal nodded to the Secretary, and something was whispered.

The Secretary stood tall, spoke loud and clear to the whole room: "A test of loyalty of a new blend, yes, and a lesson at the same time. Matriarch Eventide had questioned our rule, sowed dissent. An example had to be made, that just one loyal servant could excise even the most powerful sub-clan. The completion of the Instruction means..."

"Not completion," Hishi said quietly, and there was a scandalized hush. She sensed a Guard move, a Human-root female.

"'All responsible' not Excised," Hishi said. "Instruction wording very specific."

She sensed The Eternal stir, felt the tissue around the empty suicide gland bud twitch, a knot of scar tissue in her head acknowledge the repeated signal, but no more happened. The Guard hesitated. The Eternal's mask trembled. Time slowed down.

David A. Gray's story "Hishi" was published in Metaphorosis on Friday, 23 February 2018.

About the story

"Hishi" came from a bunch of directions at once. I was worrying about my daughter and the world I'm raising her in, where rich old white men seem intent on burning it all down and ensuring she has no rights. And where we as a species seem to be sending our kids to war, or to bomb and kill. So I had in mind a character who had all her life ahead, all her potential, but was choked by the actions of these old men. But who would triumph, in the end. Kind of. The world – Scour – was inspired a little by those old stories where we know society is the ruins of an older civilization, a tiny bit by railway tracks (a minor obsession), and a lot by a wish to take an extreme situation and imagine how we'd be after 10,000 years of forced evolution. The things we would do if we had to, then because we could. Also, I'm an avid student of Ottoman history, and of the Crusades, and Europe's Hundred Years War. Imagine, for a moment Constantinople on wheels.

"Hishi" was – and is – a standalone story, but in the process of editing, I realized this is her first chapter as a person in a strange world. I know where she goes next, even if I don't ever write it.

A question for the author

Q: From where you do you draw inspiration for your characters?"

A: I take something from myself at a young age. when I used to stagger home from the library with armfuls of peculiar/comforting-smelling classic sci-fi, full of anticipation and alert for the local crazed bullies. But it's from my kids that I take most, now: that heady mix of potential, hope, happiness and occasional heartbreak. If any of my characters convey even a little of that sense of opportunity amidst the darkness, then I'm flattered and happy.

About the author

Gray is an exiled Scots creative director and journalist living in NYC. He works for a range of print and digital magazines and brands, and every night he climbs to the roof of his Brooklyn apartment building and squints at the Manhattan skyline, wondering how it might look in a century or few. Sometimes he thinks it will be a glittering gem, other times, a flooded ruin. Or maybe a bit of both.

Just a Fire

A. Martine

by Addison Black, JAN. 3rd, 3075

Over the past year, we at MAELSTROM have covered stories which have often bordered on the sensational, such as the famous rivalry between siblings Amaterasu and Susanoo, the Japanese gods of the Sun and the Storms respectively. We have also notably touched upon the scandalous account of the giant Paul Bunyan's alleged affair with the Titan Selene. All of these have served a similar aim: to bring awareness of Lorendi, sanctuary of forgotten gods and goddesses, and bridge the gap keeping Humans and Lorendians separate.

In the midst of the cacophony of entities roaming Lorendi, it is often easy to forget some of the lesser-known, but no less interesting events. One such story is that of the Fall of Asgard, which many have attributed to the ongoing feud between former Valkyrie Brünnhilde and her father, the great Wotan.

It is common knowledge that all the inhabitants of Lorendi were forced to coexist after the collapse of their respective homes. It may be of interest for our readers to note that no one knows how Lorendi came to be. As more and more entities began to lose their homes, they found themselves inexplicably drawn to this vast and strange land, and found that they grew stronger within its borders. In this sense, Asgard is an anomaly; it appears to be the only place where the collapse was not instigated by humans, but the details of the episode remain unclear and contradictory.

Most of us have, at some point of our existences, idolized controversial figures, those insubordinate figureheads of change and defiance; for me, it has always been Brünnhilde, the powerful, enigmatic woman who lived and would have died for her ideals. The opportunity to decipher her story, essentially, is my childhood coming full circle.

According to the all but forgotten legend, after Brünnhilde's lover and nephew Siegfried was killed by Hagen, son of the dwarf Alberich, the erstwhile Valkyrie threw herself into his funeral pyre, maddened with her grief. The same pyre became a full-blown wildfire which consumed Valhalla and all the gods present, marking the grim end of this mythology. But in reality, only Siegfried, who had already perished, was a casualty that day; the hall was destroyed in the fire and spread throughout the whole of Asgard, robbing the gods and goddesses of their dwelling place — but they did not die with it.

It was not long before the protagonists of the Norse mythology dispersed throughout Lorendi. In the diverse landscape of this city, most of the former residents of Valhalla are not as noteworthy as those of other tales; indeed, when one has to contend with the unrestrained antics of the Greek pantheon or the staggering number of parties thrown by the Yoruba gods and goddesses, it is easy to lose sight of the Norsemen and women of Asgard. Doubtless because of the calamitous end of their cycle, they have retreated into more tranquil existences and successfully blended in with the other Lorendians, to a fault.

Thus, shedding light on the series of events that led to the catastrophic and fiery confrontation (often referred to as the Pyre Incident or Brünnhilde's Really Big Blunder) entails delving deeply into the relationship dynamics of some key characters of this episode.

Our investigation begins in the fields of Tarragon, a region in Southern Lorendi where those seeking respite from the sometimes hectic lifestyle of Aster or Amaryllis come to disengage. Eir, one of Brünnhilde's sister Valkyries, has agreed to welcome me into her lavish country home. She has invited their sister Sigrün for the conversation. Here in Lorendi, it never snows nor rains (due to an agreement between the many gods and goddesses of the weather), so the afternoon is mild and pleasant when the three of us sit down around ginger pastries and warm tea.

I try not to let my wonderment show; I am in the presence of legends, after all, and these are women whose storied place in history would dwarf anyone's confidence. Despite the fierce reputation they garnered when their exploits were recounted centuries ago, the Valkyries before me are even-tempered women who prefer walks in the sunny fields of Tarragon, these days, to bloody frays.

"Oh, believe me," Sigrün quips with a devilish smile, "we still engage in the occasional skirmish, but when your primary function has been obsolete for quite some time, it leaves more opportunity to unwind, which was frankly overdue."

I ask the sisters about their professional affiliation with their father Wotan, but the subject inevitably turns personal. Eir, who sees her sister Brünnhilde very often but has not spoken with their father in eons, tells me that while the Pyre Incident brought about the end of Asgard, it was a situation that had always been inevitable.

"I think," she tells me with a hint of displeasure, "that the whole affair was handled quite poorly."

Judging from Sigrün's weary expression, this is a conversation the sisters have often had.

Eir shrugs, implacable. "I do. Be fair, Sigrün, you remember some of those occasions as well as I do." She turns to me. "Brünnhilde was punished unfairly and often, although she was, on numerous occasions, absolutely powerless over the situation. Big things, small things, it mattered little. You see, she was always more resourceful — Wotan would say reliable — than the rest of us, so she was always called upon. She was even in charge of negotiations between the Vanir and the giants at one point, which had nothing to do with her Valkyrie duties. When things went well, Wotan would be proud: but that also meant that when they did not, everything would be her fault." Whether Eir's passion stems from sisterly partiality, or from her true belief, it is touching to behold.

"I will admit to that," Sigrün concedes. "But I also remember warning Brünnhilde that she often involved herself in things she shouldn't. She could never say no, and I told her to be careful. Besides, most of the Valkyries were starting to be jealous of the excess attention Wotan was giving her — except for us, of course." The aside is for me.

"On some level, that is true," Eir counters, "but ultimately, what doomed her was her involvement in stratagems on a grander scale which could at any given moment threaten the future of Asgard. Brünnhilde became a scapegoat because she was standing in the eye of the storm. It's as simple as that."

She is, of course, referring to the fabled ring that Loge persuaded Wotan to offer the Frost-Giants instead of Wotan's wife's sister Freia (which the giants had initially agreed upon).

"I don't think a lot people are comfortable mentioning this," Eir says with a bitter laugh, "but we all know that it's Wotan's incessant quest for the cursed ring that is the real source of Asgard's downfall, not anything my sister may or may not have done."

Watching them speak so casually about mythic events we humans have feasted upon for centuries dazes me temporarily. For the first time since I sat down with the sisters, I feel like I have pawed at something beneath the surface of my understanding. Whatever the rest of the world may have made out of it, this is just a family squabble for them, no different from the wine glasses and petty insults humans toss over Thanksgiving dinner with estranged relatives.

Sigrün has kinder words for her father than her sister does. This is surprising, considering that a long time ago, her lover Helgi was killed with the help of none other than Wotan. A suggestion of indulgence flitting across her lovely face, she says: "I agree wholeheartedly, but to say that they were at the source of everything that happened is unfair. In the long term, I believe that this was bound to turn out the way it did because everyone became different where the ring was concerned. Even the best of us could become monsters. And besides," she adds with a chuckle, "when I see the other father figures of Lorendi, it puts our own situation in sharp perspective."

The next stop to this journey leads me to the bustling streets of Aster, where one finds the most thriving and diverse community of Lorendians. Bars and shops manned by Pangu (the Chinese god of the Heavens and the Earth), Anubis (embalmer and protector of the graves), or even Bigfoot attract thousands of loyal customers on a daily basis. Further in the northern part of the neighborhood, an amusement park managed by the Loch Ness Monster and the Lady of the Lake is a popular fixture for the children of Aster. You will not find many of the more lofty characters of mythology here, but it is a welcoming and vivacious change of pace from Tarragon.

It is here, in a restaurant called Johnny's Appleseed that Loge has agreed to meet with me. Sporting retro shades, his long braided silver hair slung over his shoulder, he strolls in an hour late, smoking an electronic cigarette despite the waiter's protestations. After very short — and might I add, rather standoffish — introductions, Loge quickly broaches the subject.

"If you ask me," he says, blowing smoke rings in my direction, "I think that everybody is exaggerating the whole affair. It was just a *fire*."

I ask him about the ring, and his involvement in the story, an involvement some might consider the starting point of it all.

"That's what I do. People come to me for help and I help them, by any means. Wotan and Fricka wanted a way out of the mess Freia was going to be in with the Frost-Giants, and I gave them that. If it all went haywire from that point on, find the right people to blame."

"But surely," I ask him, "your participation was more instrumental than that. Is it not true that you were the one Wotan came to every time a crisis needed an underhanded solution?"

What is more: Alberich's ring was reportedly stolen by Wotan with Loge's help, which — among the many ensuing collateral costs — resulted in Brünnhilde being stripped of her immortality by Wotan and confined behind a ring of fire on a mountaintop, of Loge's own design.

"You say "underhanded", I say "subtle"," he answers, downing a cocktail in the blink of an eye, "and indeed, the fire was my idea. I'm rather proud of it:

Wotan was leaning towards a cage made of fiery ice, but he has no taste for the aesthetics. Once again, it's not personal. People ask for my help and I help them. I'm sorry that Brünnhilde is sore about the whole affair, but to say that I was at the heart of Asgard's Fall is a bit of an overstatement."

It suddenly becomes clear to me that the outcome of the strife involving Asgard may have been due to nothing more than likability. A popularity contest, one that the temperamental, unpredictable Brünnhilde was bound to lose, especially when facing off with an influential man like Loge. A question comes to me unplanned, then, but I don't yet ask it. Loge has already changed the subject.

He seems generally unruffled about his life at Lorendi, and even admits that he prefers it to the one he led in Asgard; this place seems to have somewhat dulled his legendary mischievousness, replacing it instead with offhanded insouciance. Tipping backwards on his chair, he laughs throatily.

"It's a riot. People here are carefree and they don't dwell on the past. There is much less pressure to perform your duties here than there was before. Look around you: there are five different gods and goddesses of the sun, twenty personifications of love and fertility. Tricksters abound, and heroes and heroines meet their matches on a daily basis."

Perhaps because I am slightly annoyed by him, or perhaps because my curiosity has been needled by his nonchalance, the question re-emerges, coming to my lips before I can make it tactful:

"Did you actually see Brünnhilde tip over the pyre that burned Asgard down? Did anyone?"

"Now… whatever do you mean by that?" he asks, almost teasingly, pulling on his cinnamon-spiced cigarette.

"Many people," I elaborate, noticing how attentive he has suddenly become, "have accepted that the fire may have been an act of childish retaliation. But it seems to me that Brünnhilde would be the last person to benefit from such large-scale sabotage. Unlike people who, for example, would want their involvement in less-than-noble endeavors burned away in the debacle. People looking for a fresh start."

"Do you mean to say," he replies with laughter in his voice, "that you believe she either didn't do it, or else was coaxed into it?"

It wouldn't be the first time that emotionally vulnerable people had been taken advantage of, I proffer. Additionally, the entire event seems antithetical to the motivations people tack onto Brünnhilde. She has not continued a campaign of vindictiveness; in fact, she lives apart from everyone else, has done so for the past few centuries.

"Well," he leans in close, almost serious, for the first time "you're assuming that because you didn't know her. "Black Sheep Ousted From Family For Daring To Defy Them". Better yet: "Tortured Soul Manipulated Into Large-Scale Act Of Vandalism"." He gestures across the air with an open palm. "It does sound good on paper, I'll admit."

We both laugh, although no joke has been uttered there. I am not done with the matter; but for the moment, I let the question lie on the table between us, knowing full well that I will find no admission or good-natured insight behind Loge's determined indifference. He is happier to look to the future, and so I let him swerve the conversation back to Lorendi, and to his previous assurance that this is where redemption should be looked for.

He reaffirms the idea as we part ways.

"I think we're better off here and I think that this," he makes a general gesture to indicate the whole of Lorendi "would have happened anyway."

In a rare moment of contemplation, he adds, mounting his motorcycle: "myths and mythologies, folklores and fairy tales. All of this could never last. It had to end, somehow. We at Asgard just happened to go out in a blaze of glory." His sudden introspection seems to catch him off guard, and by the time he revs his engine, the mask of practiced casualness is back.

Amaryllis is less frenzied than Aster, but no less delightful. By day, it is not only an upper-class residential area, but also where some of the most luxurious boutiques and opportunities for recreational activities are located. It is, however, after dark that Amaryllis truly comes to life. Nightclubs and bars frequented by Lorendi's elite entertain them until dawn, and it is not uncommon to witness weddings and other parties being celebrated with pomp and grandeur. Many of the warriors who were brought to Valhalla by the Valkyries can be found here, chatting up sprites and fairies, and cavorting with centaurs and leprechauns.

Hildr, one of Brünnhilde's fellow Valkyries, meets with me in Saraswati's Den, a trendy hotel bar owned by the goddess of the same name, and where the Valkyrie happens to reside. She is among those of her sisters who chose to adapt completely to her new life, which suits the grandiloquence (some say pretentiousness) she has often been associated with. She is often seen partying with Aphrodite and Metztli, the Aztec goddess of the Moon, when she is not hosting a popular biweekly talk show on socialite life in the 31st century.

I am on edge again, but in a way that differs from when I encountered Eir and Sigrün. Hildr barely looks corporeal. She is the incarnation of opulence, and as she enters the bar, almost every head turns in her direction: sheaths of white silk artfully wrapped around her tall frame complement her platinum blonde curtain of hair; she moves with the ease of one who knows she is in command. I can't help but think that she must have been quite a sight on her horse in the battlefield, so many centuries ago.

She joins me and greets me charmingly, although her welcome lacks the warmth I felt with her sisters. Despite her imposing arrival, Hildr is anything but ardent; she is not interested in passionate arguments or zealous debates. The more I talk with her, the more it becomes clear that she has never been a strong proponent of the theory that Brünnhilde is a victim, that the fire was an accident, nor that Wotan had any responsibility in the downfall of Asgard. Still, in her debonaire attitude I sense a steeliness that could easily become callousness in a different light, a steeliness she makes only a halfhearted effort to conceal.

"Things are the way they are. Everyone thinks that just because we came here when our home became uninhabitable, and not because humans forgot about us, we *need* to find a reason, an explanation, someone to blame," she drawls over the din of voices surrounding us.

The question I asked Loge emerges again, but I've had enough time to compose it more diplomatically.

"According to you, Brünnhilde is unequivocally responsible, then?"

"Oh, without a doubt. I was there. We were all there." She says this without a hint of skepticism. The rapidity with which Brünnhilde's alleged culpability was accepted as fact is shocking, considering how far-reaching its effects have been.

I frame my question differently: "Is this characteristic of the Brünnhilde you knew and liked?"

"It was just a *fire*," she sighs, echoing Loge's condescension almost to perfection. Then, leaning closer with a conspiratorial look, she whispers: "*I* think that Brünnhilde was bored, and decided that she wanted to be at the center of some sort of exciting melodrama. She's always been that way. I think she was trying to distract us all from the fact that she had committed incest with her nephew Siegfried."

"Could it be," I advance, "less about anger or retaliation than an expression of her desperation? Or perhaps an attempt to force a new beginning at Asgard, by purging it of its convoluted mess? If she is to blame, that is."

"And kill us all in the process?" Hildr titters. "You are kind, but that theory is nonsense."

I know that I am toeing the line between journalistic integrity and the inexplicable inclination to defend a childhood hero, but I also recognize that there is no love lost between Hildr and Brünnhilde. She might be as biased as I am, no matter how much she feigns apathy in the matter. I begin to wonder whether a specific incident is to blame, but think better of asking her. I have a suspicion that Hildr's graciousness is mostly skin deep.

When asked about her opinion on the Human-Lorendian relationship and whether the gods' lives in Lorendi are a fitting substitute for their respective places of origin, Hildr is lost in thought for a long moment.

"At the risk of sounding complacent, I think that the lives we lead here are truly unparalleled. We're all birds of a feather, to borrow your Earthly expression."

"That might surprise our readers. It is widely assumed that most of you must be homesick."

"Of course it's assumed," she smiles in patronizing amusement, leaning back in her chair, "but I don't believe we ever needed humans worshipping us to survive; if that was the case, even Lorendi couldn't save us. We would have faded into oblivion eons ago."

"Why agree to tell your version of events to MAELSTROM's readers, if you Lorendians are self-sufficient?"

"Because our stories matter," Hildr replies, as if this were the most obvious answer in the world, "and they would have mattered whether there were people to tell them to or not. Together, we are stronger and more complex than we were separated. Ask anyone of any other mythology here, and they will tell you the same stories: betrayals, incest, illegitimate children, murder, jealousy... Brünnhilde, Wotan, Siegfried, and the ring? It was nothing special, by any standard, so I suggest we stop thinking it was."

She waves her hand loftily as she says this, as if to brush a ridiculous notion away. Slicing through the roasted peach pie she ordered, Hildr continues: "*combine* these stories and make them interact, however, and you suddenly find yourself with a riveting spectacle. Lorendi is like a micro-universe that gathers all the tales and allegories of the world, as it was meant to be. We represent all of History, in its oddity and its diversity. We reflect the changing mentalities of humans and their cultures over the millennia, and if there is anything your readers should retain, it's this: we are special."

As we part, Hildr turns to me again, and I can see that indifference has crept back into her expression.

"I don't go around saying this often, because some people still feel raw about the debacle, but I don't regret any of it. I think the fire did us all a favor." The elevator doors close on her as she looks down at her communication device, her attention already elsewhere.

Fricka has declined to speak to MAELSTROM for this story, but surprisingly, Wotan has agreed give us his perspective on the narrative. The man himself, former Supreme Ruler of Asgard. I try to contain my excitement, lest it render me unfocused. In order to meet him, I travel to Angrec, on the West Coast of Lorendi, where many financial and political institutions have settled themselves. The older, more established gods, goddesses, and beings often purchase grandiose estates here, and its seaside location makes it a perfect place to take short but sweet vacations.

Wotan co-owns many of these residences along with Zeus and Anansi, and has made his fortune leasing them to the entities who flock to their shores, looking for more upscale lifestyles. I arrive in his opulent home and I am seated on a beautiful sunbathed patio by one of his assistants and offered a drink. As I wait, I become rather nervous, expecting, from the many stories and accounts surrounding him, a boisterous and roguish man. He is anything but. The man I meet is courteous and pleasant, and there is no trace of arrogance in his stance. Waves of fiery red hair fall loosely over his shoulders; in fact, everything about him seems loose and deliberate. Unlike his brother Loge, he removes his sunglasses when he speaks to me, despite the fact that we are outdoors. It is hard to believe that this is the selfsame person who has committed adultery innumerable times and betrayed his closest relatives in his relentless pursuit for Alberich's ring. Still, I keep my guard up. I have interviewed too many a charming entity not to know better.

I ask him about his role in the Fall of Asgard and, after a careful pause, the god launches into a leisurely diatribe. Watching him speak is simply enthralling; it doesn't take long for me to understand why everyone is drawn to this articulate and persuasive man, in spite of the fact that half of what he says seems wholly calculated and insincere.

I notice, as he speaks, that he never once acknowledges his purported obsession with the ring, nor does he mention Brünnhilde. I decide to be blunt.

"Did you see her do it, and if so, do you think it was intentional?"

Wotan deflects my first question so masterfully that I almost don't catch it; instead, he leans into the latter part.

"Ah, Brünnhilde." He chuckles warmly, as if thinking fondly of a petulant, rebellious child. "That girl has always had a viselike hold on me. I hear that she's been going around accusing me of having ruined her life. I think she needs a scapegoat because everyone seems to blame her for having spread the fire that destroyed Valhalla. But that's all it was, just a fire."

Unlike with the others, when Wotan says this, the Pyre Incident seems indeed reduced to a minor skirmish, something small, something not worth bothering about. Intentions and motivations barely seem to register for him.

He continues: "It was an accident, all those who were there know that, but if a little gossip and rumors are that bothersome to her, she can keep lambasting me if she wants. I think that she will find that whether they were initially angry about losing their home or not, most inhabitants of Asgard will agree that Lorendi has been very kind to them. She can get out of her self-imposed exile whenever she wants."

"But what about the many incidents before that? What about the one involving Siegfried, for example? Surely Brünnhilde has reasons to be angry not only with you, but with all the men who have wronged her in her life." I would be angry too, if I had a father like him, I almost say to illustrate my point; but I think better of it.

"Everyone thinks her punishment was unwarranted. The truth is, I was never ungrateful for the consideration she always showed me; but you see, I am a ruler. I must not appear fickle, volatile; I must appear to be a man of my word, one who does not condone trespass and defiance. When I decided to leave her on the mountain and strip her of her immortality, it was for her own protection. I was doing her a favor. The ring of fire was entirely my idea, I'm rather proud of it. Loge was partial to a cage made of burning ice, but I've always been more creative than him when it comes to this," he adds with twinkle in his eye (it is now unclear whether the ring of fire should be credited to Loge or to Wotan).

Despite his placid facade, I can see that Wotan is tired of speaking about this chapter of his life, and especially about his daughter. Nevertheless, as much as I would rather avoid irritating him, this is the main reason this investigation was launched, and it is the key to understanding why Valhalla imploded in such a spectacular fashion. More so than Hildr or Loge, Wotan's detachment pricks in a particularly painful way. He is, after all, Brünnhilde's own father, but seemingly the one least concerned about her fate. So I push him further about his theories regarding the Really Big Blunder.

"In the confusion of the brawl, anyone could have been responsible. Anyone, in fact, could have done such a thing, for very different reasons. Asgard had many enemies, some of whom have been said to include Loge," I tentatively proffer.

When he answers, he disregards the question underneath my question.

"I think that there are long-term causes and short-term causes. If we only focus on the short term, then it appears that I am the instigator and that Brünnhilde was a victim. If you want my opinion, I think that she should have made better choices about the men she chose to surround herself with. I always thought that falling in love with Siegfried was not a good idea and the fact that he died in such a fashion is truly regrettable. Do I regret my actions, however? Absolutely not. In each situation, one must weigh the outcomes, and I always pick the outcome that will produce the least damaging results. No one comes out of battles completely unscathed and I would think she'd know that, what with being a Valkyrie and all."

He lets the words hang between us, then elaborates on the long-term reasons. I am amused to note that he shares an almost identical opinion with Hildr on this matter.

"I think that in this scope, Asgard is in no way different from any of the other Lorendi folks' homes. We all collapsed, albeit in different ways. Many of us Lorendians have had to deal with a millennium of grudges and small grievances, and you make a compelling point. If it had not been Brünnhilde accidentally tipping over the funeral pyre, it would have been Alberich instigating a riot, the Jötnar storming Asgard, or Freia and Thor getting into a heated argument that destroyed the sacred halls of our home. I think we tend to try rationalizing the Pyre Incident to the point of obsessing over the details when one should be looking at the greater picture. I think our time was bound to come to an end, and this is something I've always accepted. It's the only reason why I have found it so easy to forgive and forget, and I wish Brünnhilde would do the same."

Brünnhilde has refused to sit down with us for an interview, thus depriving us of the most valuable point of view in this whole story. I suspect that she is handling too much grief over the death of her lover Siegfried, among other vitriol, and if Wotan is telling the truth, the guilt of having burned down Asgard by accident must surely weigh on her deeply. Perhaps with time, she will be able to bring herself to a point of closure, but for the time being, we are left with an almost — but alas, not wholly — complete story.

"Is there anything you would like to tell your daughter, in case she reads this article?"

Initially, Wotan dismisses the idea. Not for the first time during this investigation, I feel myself step out of my reporter's shoes, and stand as a woman, asking for another woman's sake. After a few moments where he seems to be deciding something, Wotan softens. He turns his stare to the distance where the sunsets are dyeing the clouds in gradient hues of scarlet. For a very long time, he squints into one of Lorendi's many setting suns before finally turning to me again.

"I do, actually. At some point I realized, since I've been living here, that what I used to think was important really isn't, you know? I thought, before in Asgard, that once you lost love it was over. I thought that once you were provoked, nothing mattered but getting justice for the offense. I thought that the unshakable pursuit of a goal outweighed everything else. Lorendi truly puts everything in perspective. Even the ring, which invaded my every thought, is lost, never to be found again. I heard they turned the whole thing into a popular book series a few centuries ago, *The King of the Rings* or something," he nods wisely. "Even if we never see each other again, I suppose I want her to find it in herself to realize the same. Only then can one truly start over."

Brünnhilde lives in Valeria, where most of the demigods, demigoddesses, and lesser folklore entities, as well as many of the smaller animals of the myths and folklores reside. It is rather separate from the rest of Lorendi, more so than Tarragon, but I am told that it is a pleasant place to live. Our readers might remember Valeria from a story covered by one of my fellow journalists, in the fourth issue of Mores and Icons, concerning the successful activewear business venture launched by Br'er Rabbit and his Senegalese cousin Leuk, the cunning hare.

Through the many collected instances surrounding the shunned Valkyrie, a patchwork has emerged. I simultaneously feel like I know Brünnhilde, and don't know her at all: she is a sad, lonely, possibly confused woman, but she also remains a mystery.

I would have relished a chance to hear her own words. Brünnhilde may have refused our invitation because she thought that her character would be assassinated. But perhaps she would have appreciated knowing that among us mortals, she continues to be celebrated for her singularity, no matter her part in

Asgard's Fall. It is regrettable that her voice is glaringly absent in the panorama, and no amount of my personal of professional investment will be enough to change that fact.

However, while we may not have gathered her side of the tale, a bigger picture, is discernible. We may never know more than what was revealed in bygone and sometimes contrasting accounts of the entities who were involved in the incident, but it is clear that many, if not all of them (save Brünnhilde, perhaps) have moved on from it. The Lorendians have, for the most part, chosen to embrace their new homes and coexist peacefully, putting the rickety past behind them.

One must conclude that many of these characters, as Wotan and Hildr have so eloquently said, live similar lives and often meet similar ends, and the details don't matter. The exchange between all of these tales and events has produced a world that continues to fascinate humans of the 31st century, a world which will hopefully encourage them to tap into the mythological histories just waiting to be happened upon. Simultaneously, however, the more stories we publish, the more I hope our readers come to realize that these entities are not so different from us after all: young women still hate their fathers sometimes, unrequited love abounds, and egos can govern many a relationship.

It's a disappointment, and it's a relief.

A disappointment for the little girl in me who saw Brünnhilde as the epitome of uncompromising strength: ultimately, she is as flawed, if not more, than I thought her to be.

A relief for the woman I am today, precisely for those same reasons: I can gently remove her from her pedestal, and with it, the unattainable expectations I had held myself to, as I tried to emulate her.

Short of doing away with our heroes altogether, we can at least try to forgive them, even if we are no closer to understanding them.

Next month, we delve into the legendary rivalry between Ra and Apollo, the respective Egyptian and Greek gods of the Sun, and the confrontation that nearly robbed Lorendi of sunlight for a century.

A. Martine's story "Just a Fire" was published in Metaphorosis on Friday, 17 August 2018.

About the story

"Just a Fire" was initially inspired by a lifelong love of fairy tales and mythologies from around the world; their occasional absurdity triggered in me a strong interest in retellings and parodies. More specifically, it was the manner in which stories across time and cultures resembled each other that I always found compelling, and I've always wanted to feature that in one of my tales.

As I began to write "Just a Fire", however, I found myself drawn to another aspect of storytelling: the notion of subjective truths and bendable perceptions. At its core, more so than a take on a portion of Norse mythology, this is about the way miscommunications and grudges (petty and profound) can divide people on the notion of what they know and believe to be fact.

"Just A Fire" is the first of many stories I set in the fictional country of Lorendi, each of the pieces detailing how famous fairy tale and mythology incidents have impacted their respective characters, often in the form of conflict involving unreliable points of view, rumors and damaging word-of-mouth.

A question for the author

Q: What are you reading now?

A: At the moment, I am juggling between:

- *Anne Sexton's Complete Poems* (Anne Sexton)
- *We Need to Talk About Kevin* (Lionel Shriver)
- *Little Fires Everywhere* (Celeste Ng)
- *In the Night Garden* (Catherynne M. Valente)

About the author

Aïcha Martine Thiam is a poet, writer, musician and artist who writes in English and in French, two of her native languages. She travelled the world as a child, and studied at the University of Montréal and Columbia College Chicago. Home is wherever the sea is near.

www.maelllstrom.com, @Maelllstrom

Koehl's Quality Impressions

Tim McDaniel

Early Wednesday morning, not much past 10:30, I wheezed my way through downtown in my old '31 Ford. Down to White Center, where the city sprawl collided with the suburban rents, resulting in rows of dingy cheap apartment buildings, absentee landlords and the retreats of the old or underemployed. I found the place easily. A building of wooden clapboard, still advertising 'covered parking' even though those parking spaces were filled with rusting Chevys, discarded washing machines, and mildewed mattresses.

I parked along the street and walked up to the front door, then leaned on the button next to the peeling paper with 'Linaman, Manager' penciled on it.

After a long while there was a muffled voice.

"Yeah?"

"Mr. Linaman?"

"Naw, he left months ago."

"You the manager now?"

"Yeah. You a cop or what? No one here been making any calls."

"Nothing like that. I have a small business proposal that you might be interested in."

"A business proposition, huh? So there's money involved?"

"There's money involved." I'd met plenty of guys like him in prison.

"Well come on up, then, I guess. 203."

The door opened, and I climbed the stairs. The thin carpet, perhaps originally a beige sort of color, was held together by stains, and the narrow staircase exuded the tang of cat piss.

Mr. Manager was, as I would have guessed, dressed in an old t-shirt and a pair of sweatpants, and smelled a lot like the staircase. I explained my needs, he articulated his, and we reached an agreement.

I checked out the deceased woman's room next. It was tiny, and the windows didn't open. There were a few sticks of shabby furniture, and one yellowing photograph on a wall, of a young man in a uniform standing in a desert somewhere. The room at least smelled a little better; a lavender-kind of scent lingered there. I closed the door behind me when I left to go back downstairs.

I left the building and took a deep breath. At least the apartment was still vacant. I wouldn't have to make any more deals on behalf of my client. Vampires, we called them, but not the blood-sucking kind. I made a commission on each deal, but they still made me feel like I needed to shower.

"Koehl's Quality Impressions" was stenciled in black gothic letters on the glass of my office door. A little crooked. All it needed was a cheesy little "While U Wait" card taped under it. Well, in this building, this neighborhood, I couldn't expect the clients I used to get at First Impressions; over there, Pichrenn's name still brought in the classy set, even this long after his death.

Was "Quality" accurate? Well, it's not bragging to say that I can raise ghosts with the best of them. I can make latent ghosts visible, clear as day, short-term or long. At least I can when I can afford to lay my hands on quality equipment. The gear I use now is so shoddy I'm lucky if Fred and Mary can even recognize dear jowly Aunt Greta.

So, yeah, clients were not lined up outside my door. I came in every day, though, in at nine or maybe ten or eleven and out at five or maybe four, when I wasn't out on a job. I couldn't afford to miss any walk-ins. I got the occasional referral of a double-booked or cheap client from my old friend Nol at First Imp, and some job orders from a few regulars, vampires, some of whom I knew from my prison days. But walk-ins, impulse buyers, were my main source of income. Sometimes people do act on whims. I stayed in the office daily, watching TV or reading or surfing for obits or drinking until I could justify the return to my apartment.

The glass on the door was at least frosted. A classy touch. Most of my clients didn't particularly want to be seen from the street, no more than I wanted passersby to see my empty reception room.

Empty it was, when I got back from arranging the vampire feeding. I hung my jacket on the rack near the door.

Ah. There was a new message for me on my computer. I went to the desk and jabbed the button.

"Hello, Koehl." I was sitting in the chair, and I didn't remember sitting down. Lindsay. "I have a job I'd like to discuss with you. I can come by tomorrow about eleven, if that's good for you."

I hadn't seen her since... when? Oh, yeah. Not since the trial.

God, how I wanted to see her again. And I also really wished that, tomorrow at eleven or so, I could be somewhere else, far away.

"I need you to come see me." Pichrenn's voice on the phone had been thin and uneven, air forced through rusty valves. I was in the middle of a job, taking the impression of a young couple's son, four years old at the time of death, but this was Pichrenn, so I called Nolan to take over for me.

This kind of thing wasn't unusual. The job I was doing was routine, though never tell a family that, and Pichrenn often called me away from those to attend him on more interesting cases. Or more high-profile. I figured, and hoped, he was grooming me to take over once he passed on.

I apologized to the couple, saying I had a family emergency, and took a cab over to the address Pichrenn had given me. I found him in one of those huge, lavish condos on 12th, squatting in the corner of a bedroom. The equipment was still boxed, lying in its contoured foam.

The room was dominated by an immense bed, brass. A window took up most of one wall, affording an impressive view of the city and the mountain, and ostentatious abstract paintings garnished the other walls.

There was another bit of apparent abstract art on the peach carpet, a dark red Rorschach image, all that physically remained of the room's former occupant: a bloodstain like an obscene starfish that had been crushed into the floor. There were additional random splashes and splatters on the mussed bed, and even on one of the walls.

Well, this family wasn't shy about displaying their money, if they could afford to keep the condo, untenanted (so to speak), for four and a half months after the murder of the husband. No wonder they could afford Pichrenn himself.

He stood up and looked down at the carpet stain, back straight, perfectly still, but his hands, jammed deep into his jacket pockets, were twisting and pinching the material. He did that a lot, as if his hands were the only vents for whatever emotions roiled within.

Lindsay was next to him, sitting on a clean part of the bed, composed and quiet. Her eyes were on Pichnrenn, but she was breathing a little too heavily.

"The Dudanna murder," Pichrenn said. I raised my eyebrows. The story had been a big one.

"The wife was the one who did it," Pichrenn said. "Made it look like a robbery, or tried to."

"Yeah," I said. "I saw it on TV. Hi, Lindsay."

She nodded at me, her eyes flashing secrets over Pichrenn's lowered bald head.

I said, "Our client, then, must be the dear departed's murderer's sister, is that right?"

Pichrenn smiled. "Right. The sister of the killer. That's what makes it interesting, isn't it?"

I squatted on the floor next to him and surveyed the scene. He was waiting, I knew, for me to see it. Our job, if we did it well enough, would be both a reflection on the murder, and a comment on the client. And of course we had to please our client while doing so, which sometimes meant hiding or disguising our own comments. We were portrait artists. Well, that's how we thought of ourselves. We wanted to do more than get a snapshot of a corpse. Our equipment amplified the energies embedded in the walls, the floor, the air, to reveal not a carcass, but the shade of a living man.

"Not a happy family, I take it," I said. "I mean between the sisters."

"I'd guess not."

"The wife got away with a slap on the wrist, as I recall. The best justice money could buy."

Pichrenn said nothing.

"Sis is, of course, married herself. An older gent, if I recall."

"Very happily married. There've been no reports of trouble."

"Right. And so there would be no jealousy of the sister who snagged the young movie-star-handsome millionaire, no sexual tension at family get-togethers, no younger-sister resentments or buried bitternesses."

"These people were the top predators of the social jungle, Scott. We're not talking about trailer trash."

"Course not."

"Would it make a difference if they were trailer trash? People all do the same things to each other, no matter their positions," Lindsay said. "Cheat on each other, sneak around."

I decided to ask Lindsay what she had meant the next time I was alone with her. But I knew I wouldn't. Betrayal was not something I wanted to discuss. And anyway, Lindsay had a way of making me forget scruples, even as they clearly gnawed at her.

But I had to say something. Something safe. "Sure it would," I said. "They couldn't afford us. They'd have to make peace with their dead and move on."

We were all silent for a time, then I stood up and squatted down again next to the box of highlighters. I took the first one out and stood up, looking the room over again. Then I crossed the room to the bedroom door and extended the tripod. After setting it in place, I put another highlighter just behind and to the left of where Pichrenn still stood. He observed my choices.

I pulled a third highlighter out of the box and placed it just in front of the window. I punched in some settings. Then I looked down at Pichrenn. He cocked his head.

"There was a lot of emotion flying around here, before and during," I said. "The whole area is bound to be saturated."

"Then we wouldn't need three highlighters," Pichrenn said. "I can almost see the remnants without the use of even one."

"You're sensitive, so you don't count. I've set up these two —" I pointed at the one near the door and the one near Pichrenn — "with complementary frequencies. They'll nearly cancel each other out, with just enough bleed-through to give us something to work with. As you say, it's so thick in here that even that amount should be plenty."

"Ummm."

"And the third one, near the window, I've set much lower."

"To pick up the background."

"Right," I said. "With only one, and with all the other energies flying around, all it'll probably pick up will be ghostly half-images, like something seen out of the corner of your eye."

"You did that at the Joshi place," Pichrenn said.

"Are you accusing me of repeating myself? But these will probably be a little weaker, more ghostly. I've been thinking about getting the chance to try this since the Caceres job. There, the energies were so weak there that half-images were the best I could get, but I did think the effect was an interesting one."

Pichrenn nodded. "And why here?" he asked. "A neat effect is just so much dazzle without a purpose to it."

"The energies released during the act," I said, "will be powerful, and I'm sure they'll be compelling as all hell. But they're all of violence, and terror, or its aftermath. We're sure to get some striking images. But what interests me just as much is the underlying tension. I doubt the victim was entirely shocked by his wife's deed."

I chanced a glance at Pichrenn, but his gaze remained focused on the floor, his brow creased. I would have given a pinkie to know his thoughts just then, to know why he wanted me there. Just for the job? Or was he sending me another message? "He knew, he must have known," I said, "that she was on the edge. He probably enjoyed baiting her, flirting with the sister, making her feel unwanted, bullying her, whatever. I don't know. But I'm sure there was something there. If we can display some of that, even as — or especially as — ghostly after-images behind the main action, I think it'll be something worth looking at."

"Hmmm," he said. Lindsay was nodding along.

"And I was thinking. They specified suppression of sounds, knocks, smells, temperature variations, I suppose?"

Pichrenn nodded.

"I don't know if it's totally ethical, but if we allowed a little of the subsonics to leak through…"

"Yes," said Lindsay. She looked over at me.

"Unsettling." Pichrenn got up, bones creaking, and shook a leg that had apparently gone numb. "Very interesting, Scott," he said. "You have a good grasp of things. I believe I'll leave this one in your hands."

I kept my face blank. There was no way he could have found out about what Lindsay and I had been up to. He had called to say he'd be late for a meeting up at his cabin, and things had just happened. And then they happened again, in other places at other times.

"The client paid for your personal attention," I said. "She's bound to be upset."

"I'll smooth things over with her," he said. "If she wants to pay for my judgment, she'll have to accept my judgment that you're the best one for this job."

Maybe that was all there was to it — that he thought I was best for the job.

It kind of makes me sorry that I killed the old guy.

Lindsay settled into the chair and leveled her eyes at me. Lindsay Ingham, Charles Pichrenn's former lover, or at least the final one. And mine. She used to breeze through the outer offices on her way to his inner sanctum, slim, elegant, and moneyed, with glossy black hair that bounced off the small of her back.

After Pichrenn's death, she'd pretty much disappeared. At the funeral it seemed to me, at least, that an understanding look had passed between us, an acknowledgement that I was still part of her world. But I had been out on a job when she came by the studio to pick up her mementos. She called me twice. I put off answering. But when she heard that I had taken Pichrenn's impression, she vanished. Felt like I'd betrayed him even unto death. Or maybe it was just guilt that she felt, however unwarranted. Our affair hadn't killed him.

Then the law finally caught up with me, and I saw her in the witness box at the trial, and there was prison. She didn't visit.

And now here she was, in my own little studio, in one of those new skirts that's tight in some places and loose in others, and a black blouse with ruffles around her neck. The air was low in oxygen just then, and my gaze stole back to her face, tracing the line of the chin, her cheeks and eyes and hair, whenever she looked down.

"So. Welcome to Koehl's Quality Impressions," I said. "It's uh, good to see you again, Lindsay."

Lindsay looked around her at the decor — the faded carpet, the Degas print on the wall. "Nice," she said. She didn't say it was nice to see *me* again.

"Yeah," I said. "High class all the way."

"Do you keep your equipment here?" she asked.

"I got a closet. This place came with every convenience. So, what have you been up to?"

"I remember you used to only use the best. You know, Charles really admired your ability to keep all of it in such top shape."

So she didn't want to get personal. No old friends and lovers catching up crap. "That's the trouble with the best stuff," I said. "It's temperamental." Like people. I waited for her to talk.

"Charles used to say you were the best in the studio," she finally said, not looking at me. "No knocks, no temperature swings or stopped clocks when you did a job."

The second mention of Pichrenn. "I miss him too, you know," I said, opening and closing a desk drawer for no reason. "I was there with him from the beginning."

"I know. Until the end. Well, if you miss him so much, stop by his place. You can see him anytime there, right?" Her voice had shifted out of neutral, but not in a direction I liked. "Sorry," she said. "I know you didn't mean... I mean, that you never wanted..."

"Don't worry about it. I'm past that. So what's up, Lindsay?" I leaned back in my chair. It creaked a little. I thought Lindsay had perhaps changed her perfume, but I couldn't be sure.

"I need a job done, Scott."

"And you came here? As far as I know they're still taking commissions at First Impressions. They're the best. And I know you always did like the best." I couldn't look too long into her eyes.

"If you're fishing for a compliment, I've given you too many already. Do you want to take the job?"

"I need to hear a little about it first," I said. A lie, but I didn't want her to know how far I'd sunk and how desperate I'd become. Oh, when I first got out on probation, I was the talk of the town, the indispensable impressionist and party guest. Offers both personal and professional came in the daily email. I had turned them all down; they had all been just a different kind of vampire, getting their jollies with a touch of death. But my fifteen minutes had ended.

Back to business. I clasped my hands on my desk. Clients liked it when you seemed to give them your full attention, and going to an impressionist is a little intimidating to some, like going to confession, or revealing your dirty little secrets to a psychiatrist. People take death seriously, even if it's not their own.

"It's my mother."

"I don't remember you talking much about her."

"No. We didn't have a lot of contact the last few years."

"So you had a fight. Teen angst, I suppose?" She didn't say anything. "But now you decide that you want to raise her. Planning to enact a little posthumous make up session, a sort of after- death mother-daughter heart to heart? You know it doesn't work that way." I don't know why I was being such a bastard.

"Look, I just owe it to her. There's nothing else I can do for her."

"'For her'? How's that? It's just a damn ghost, Lindsay. It's got as much self-awareness as a black and white photograph. Your mom, she's gone."

"Call it a gesture, then. It's too late for anything else." She looked down at the floor, as if the topic were too personal for her to go on. I didn't believe that for a second, but I let it ride. I didn't need to talk myself out of a job.

"OK. You're the customer." I slid a brochure over to her. Nice how desktop printing can make your hole-in-the-wall look like a real-live business. "Here are the rates."

She took it, but she didn't look down at the brochure. At least she didn't crease it; I could use it again next time if she didn't stick it in her purse. "I came to you because you're good. I don't want the effect spoiled by second-rate equipment."

"I don't really have the resources I once did."

"With the advance I'm prepared to pay, you can afford to get some of those resources again." I liked the sound of that; I missed the feel of properly tuned and maintained equipment, its quiet, even hum and ozone smell. The garbage I used now tended to sputter, and the focus kept going out unless you constantly kept on top of it.

Also, an advance that big could pay some of my less important bills, too. Rent and food came to mind.

Lindsay began tapping her code into my paypad.

I forced myself not to look. I pulled up an empty file on the computer, and started filling it out. "I'll need your current address." She took one of her cards out of her purse and passed it to me. I saw that nowadays she was employed at EarthTenders, Inc., a non-profit environmental umbrella. Part-time, no doubt. It was just the kind of feel-good job an over-indulged rich girl would have. It shouldn't have made me so bitter. If she spent her time suckling endangered wildebeest puppies, what was it to me?

"Any other legally interested parties?"

"Mom's latest ex has signed off on it. That satisfies your legal requirements, I believe."

"Sure does." I kept typing. "Visual, audio, olfactory?" Most people want only the visual, even though it's more work to suppress the taps and moans and temperature swings.

"Just the visual."

"Short-term, long-term, or permanent?"

"Short-term."

"OK." I stopped typing and looked at her, but she was doing her stare-at-the-floor act again. I saw a few wrinkles on her face that hadn't been there all those years before.

"I really just have to say goodbye," she said. "I don't need an endlessly repeating exhibition, for people to gawk at." Another little dig at me for raising Pichrenn. So I guess the guilt still gripped her. But I'd show her that nowadays I was immune to that kind of subtle reprimand. I was a businessman now, not some overpaid artiste.

"Short-term it shall be. Cause of death?"

"Her heart."

"OK, good. Place and time of death?"

"June 19th, this year. It was a Saturday. At 9:10 p.m. At 7th and Bell."

I typed. Then, "If the death occurred on the street itself, or in any public area, we'll need all kind of permits."

"That's not a problem. She actually died in a restaurant there, Grasso's. They've already given their permission." She fished some papers out of her purse and passed them across the desk. Standard release forms. The restaurant probably figured a ghost would be good for business, and maybe they were even right, at least for the short term. But I doubted it. "When can you do it?"

I pulled my appointment book out of a desk drawer and made a show of flipping through its blank pages. "How about this Thursday? Say one o'clock."

"That would be fine."

I didn't suppose the restaurant would object to that hour of the day. The raising of a ghost would be good entertainment for their lunch crowd.

After Lindsay left I sat in my chair, blinking. What the hell had I done? She'd reached out – clumsily, indirectly, but she had made contact. And all my defenses had shot up. I'd needed her, on many levels, after Pichrenn died. My friend, my mentor. According to the law, my victim. And I'd had no one to lean on, because she was dealing with her own issues.

I could still smell her. I didn't know if it was a perfume or just her, but now I knew it hadn't changed from back when. The office was suddenly small, dingy, dark and close. I had to get out.

I had to visit Pichrenn again.

The apartment building was now owned by a foundation that had agreed to allow suite 612 to remain vacant. They rented out the other rooms, and probably not one in ten of the current inhabitants knew that the former occupant up there on the sixth floor had not really left.

The doorman knew.

"Mr. Koehl. Good to see you again." Jacob removed his hat and put it under an arm. I noticed that his hair was graying, the tight curls looking like ash.

"Good to see you, Jacob."

Jacob turned to open the door for me. "Time for the renewal, Mr. Koehl?"

"No. Just a visit."

"Ah." Jacob led the way across the plush lobby to the bank of elevators. "Well, that's important. Remembering." He gently pressed the elevator call button, and the doors opened immediately.

"Yeah, I guess so," I said. We entered the elevator. "Many tourists come by lately, Jacob?"

"Not so many. There was an old lady eight, ten days ago, and some art student early this week."

The elevator car stopped. We paced the cream carpet down to 612. Jacob turned the key in the lock, then stepped back. "Have yourself a good visit, now, Mr. Koehl."

He never came in.

"Thank you, Jacob." I opened the door.

Usually he was in the big easy chair, head up, one hand touching his chin. He must have done that a lot, for it to have imprinted so strongly; he couldn't have planned a better portrait.

And, I must admit, I had done well with the material. Nothing flashy here, nothing avant-garde, not for him. A quiet study of a thoughtful, gentle man. I'd let a sound of even breathing come though. The legs were almost invisible, mere suggestions of lines and the drape of his trousers. But his body became more substantial as you moved up, and the chair back was nearly completely obscured by his torso. The head was preternaturally distinct, the dark eyes burning.

God, I missed him.

The foundation kept some equipment in a closet. I set it up the way I always did, going through the motions, and renewed the imprint. It wasn't time yet, I just needed to do something with my hands. Then I sat in a chair for a while. It doesn't do any good to talk to a ghost. I never know what to say, anyway.

I shouldn't have set the appointment for Thursday. It gave me three days to wait. Sure, I had wanted her to think I was busy, but I could've claimed a sudden cancellation. She'd have seen right through me, but then, she almost certainly already had anyway.

There was one thing I could do. I fed her check to my computer. Now I had the money, I could stop using the shoddy broadcasters that spit all over the spectrum, and the tuneless highlighters and the touchy suppressors. Now it would be topline stuff, paid for in full with Lindsay's advance.

At the shop they greeted me like an old friend who'd killed someone — fair enough. But once we got to going over the equipment — oh, the way those new suppressors squelch noise! — all awkwardnesses and discomforts were forgotten, and I walked out of there with the best stuff I'd ever worked with, and slaps on the back.

Then, of course, I had to go to the scene of death, to scout out the territory. I hoped my car still had some juice in the bat.

It was in a good part of town. A very good part, in fact, where I stuck out like a zombie at a wedding. Grasso's was the kind of place a Mafioso would kill to be murdered in — all indirect lighting, widely-spaced tables, dark reflective wood, candles, and hovering waiters. And expensive. Conscious of my old jacket, my shoe with the loose sole, I didn't want to go in.

I knocked on the glass door anyway.

A guy in a billowy white shirt, his tie undone, peered out at me. I flashed him my business card, which should mean nothing, but flash any sort of ID when you aren't being asked to and people just start thinking police or Homeland Security. He opened the door.

"I'm afraid we're closed," he began.

"Yeah, I figured. Lindsay Ingham asked me to stop by."

"One moment, please." He disappeared into the bowels of the restaurant and soon came back with a Mr. Sarkouhi. Apparently there was no Grasso.

"Ms Ingham mentioned you would come to see the site, Mr. Koehl. Thank you for visiting before we open for dinner." Mr. Sarkouhi, comb-over plastered to his wine-colored skull, a thin moustache drooping against jowly cheeks, nodded me inside. "When you have prepared everything, of course, then we will go public, as they say. The table where it occurred is just through here."

Nothing special about the table. It was against one wall, a painting above it. But I saw some interesting possibilities, and the setting was appealing — death and money, death and elegance; these were and remain powerful combinations. They pushed buttons, and I found myself getting excited by the work ahead. Such a change from that which I had been getting lately.

I made some mental notes. Places I could shoot from, surrounding material resonances. I forgot that Mr. Sarkouhi was hovering behind me until he delicately cleared his throat.

"I'm almost finished, Mr. Sarkouhi. Just figuring the angles."

"Of course, Mr. Koehl. The passing of Ms Mehrer in our establishment was, I'm sure you understand, quite a shock."

"I'm sure it was."

"What I mean is, Ms Mehrer was more than a customer here. She was here so often, and she enjoyed a close relationship to those here, the staff and the other diners."

I could see what he was working up to. "Do you suppose they'll enjoy seeing her here again?"

"It might be disquieting to some."

"And yet Lindsay told me you agreed to the raising. She showed me the paperwork."

"Yes, that's true. It's just that, well…"

"I know. I guess you don't say no to Lindsay." I never could, for different reasons. Or maybe they weren't so different. "Mr. Sarkouhi, she's asked for just a temporary raising. I'll make sure it's as tasteful as I can. I don't know what else I can tell you."

"Thank you, Mr. Koehl. And my thanks, again, for coming when we are closed between lunch and dinner. I appreciate that you are trying to minimize the disruption."

"No problem." Actually, I hadn't even thought about the restaurant being open or not.

As Mr. Sarkouhi turned away, a thought struck me. "Mr. Sarkouhi. On the night in question, was Ms Mehrer dining alone?"

Mr. Sarkouhi's face flushed a deeper red. "Ah, no, Mr. Koehl. She was dining with her husband."

Her husband? Lindsay hadn't shown me any paperwork from him. And I would need it. As she well knew.

Back in the office, I called up the news stories about the death of Ms Mehrer on the computer.

Alicia Mehrer had indeed died of a heart attack on June 19th, at 9:10 p.m., at Grasso's. According to witnesses she murmured something, stood up, took a few steps and then collapsed, dying a few moments later.

I wondered at the last name. I looked up Lindsay's bio. Skimpy. She must have paid someone monstrous sums to keep her bio so short. But it did show that her dad, Joseph Ingham, had left the family when she was just seven. The mom remarried two years later. The second husband had died. Cancer. Then mom had married Joseph again, and divorced him again two years after that. Well. Sounded like an interesting family. Money and death, and Lindsay's family had a lot of both. But with a divorce on record, at least I wouldn't have to meet the old man to get a signature.

My computer search turned up plenty of gossip concerning the late Alicia and her ex Joseph. Curiosity got the better of me and I expanded the search a bit and came up with some charming hospital records. All of the sources agreed that Mr. Ingham had been one real bastard. The kind of guy a jury would wink at you for killing.

And yet, even after the abandonment and after the divorce, Alicia had kept coming back for more pain. Again and again.

Sex and death is another powerful combination; the oldest and the strongest of them all.

And why had Lindsay neglected to mention that her dad was with her mom at the time?

Closet skeletons can make a raising a lot more interesting.

Thursday. The restaurant door opened, and Lindsay entered with the grace of a predatory eel, dressed all in satiny black. She stood and watched me work for a while. Of course, a small crowd had already gathered; the equipment summons them as reliably as it summons ghosts. Mr. Sarkouhi stood prominently in the center, his arms folded in pride, surveying the crowd.

Lindsay came closer. "How's it going?" If she was so cool and commanding, why did her fingers clench her bag?

"Just finishing up the underlays now." I tightened a tripod leg, then checked the broadcast shadow.

"I've decided to go long-term, Scott."

I looked up. "What?"

"I said I've decided to go long-term. With an option for permanency."

I looked at Mr. Sarkouhi. "It's all right," Lindsay said. "Mr. Sarkouhi has given us permission."

"I'll need to see that for myself."

"Of course." She opened her purse without looking at it and took some papers out. She held them out to me.

"Why the change in plan?" I left her holding the papers and picked up another broadcaster.

Lindsay was silent for a short time. "Does it matter?" She allowed her hand to drop to her side, the papers slapping against her tailored slacks.

"No, I guess not." I extended the tripod legs on the broadcaster and set it up at a 45-degree angle to the first. I'd put a highlighter just between the two. "You just wanted to say goodbye — wasn't that the purpose of this raising?"

"Maybe I just thought I would need more time with her." I didn't even pretend to look convinced, and she continued, "She *was* my mother, Scott."

I flipped the test switch on the 'caster and checked the levels as it hummed. "Not a very private place for getting in your quality time with mom." I adjusted the levels and checked the output. I looked up at her.

Lindsay looked at me, her eyes just slightly narrowed. I knew why she had chosen me for the job. Not because I was the best, but because she knew that I would do it, that I would gratefully touch things more reputable studios sneered at.

Or there was another reason, but I veered away from that thought.

"Well, if you change your mind, remember I do collapsings, too," I said. "In fact, I lay more ghosts than women." It was a standard joke, and she gave it the response it deserved.

"Are you ready?"

"Another ten, fifteen minutes."

"Fine." Lindsay passed the papers to Mr. Sarkouhi and greeted some oldsters sitting at a nearby table. Mr. Sarkouhi stood there, one hand on his moustache, not looking at anything.

"I guess you'll be getting a permanent tourist attraction, right here at table eight, Mr. Sarkouhi," I said.

"Permanent, maybe." Sarkouhi looked less than thrilled.

"None of my business, but it seems to me that what might attract a crowd for a short while might grate on the nerves of your diners, if it's constantly in view. Of course, you'd be a better judge than me of what might pique a person's appetite."

Sarkouhi narrowed his eyes. "If you talk me into withdrawing my permission, Mr. Koehl, you'll lose the job."

"Last thing on my mind, Mr. Sarkouhi."

"I could revoke permission, though, at a later date. Couldn't I? I read the contract."

"Yeah, maybe. But Lindsay might try to sue if you try it. The lawyers would have to decide what your contract actually says. Better to just curtain off the table."

Sarkouhi met my eyes briefly, then nodded thoughtfully.

Memories intrude like unwanted ghosts.

The day Pichrenn died, I'd gone to see him at home. That memory was a persistent visitor. He'd been sick for some time, and he'd had his bedroom outfitted with all kinds of medical equipment and monitors. The place smelled of disinfectants and futility, and Pichrenn lay in his huge bed, looking over at me with eyes too bright in a head become too large.

His voice was as weak as his body, but he could still speak, was still coherent.

"Art," he told me. "That's been my life, Scott, these last thirty years."

"And you've done well," I said. "You know how impressions were looked at before you got into the field. Dodgy at best. You made a whole new artform. I guess not many can claim that distinction."

Pichrenn smiled sickly, not falling for the flattery, sincere though it was. "And now this." With an arm little more than papery skin stretched over knobby bones, he gestured at the IV feeds, the machine that beeped his heart along. "They tell me I could live ten more years like this."

What could I say to that?

"They're making advances all the time."

"So maybe I'll only lie here for eight years, or six. That's no way to be, Scott. But the law says I can't take the easy way out, with ten 'good' years ahead of me. Damn Republicans."

I looked away.

"Help me, Scott." He whispered it.

And then, "Make me a work of art."

"Huh?" But I knew.

There is no kind of death that can compare with a properly-conducted suicide. Despair, desperation, pain, a reckless courage, and even a strange sort of hope: that someone will stop you, that you'll be delivered into heaven, whatever. It makes for one hell of an impression.

And it's almost as hard to kevork as it is to do it yourself. Sure, lots of laws make it all right to kill someone, if they really want you to, and if the doctors have signed off on the sign-off. But that's not what Pichrenn was asking for, a sterile room and a certifiably painless fade out. My way would be less clinical.

But afterwards, I made the impression, and it's still drawing the occasional connoisseur. Maybe Pichrenn, or part of him, thought he was doing me a favor, giving me so much pain to work with.

Lindsay came over, ushered by a hostess. "Everything's ready?"

"Yep."

"Fine. Let's do this."

Sarkouhi raised his eyebrows at me. I nodded.

"I think your host would like to get everyone here for the unveiling," I said. "That's his payoff, right? That he can show this off to his customers."

"Who knows why anyone does anything. He gave his permission. That's all I needed."

"Still, we can give him a minute to get his people assembled." I made some final, unnecessary adjustments. "I have to say that I don't feel this will be representative of my best work, Lindsay. The image is fairly clear and sharp, but the background hum is, at best, just..."

"I don't need art. I just want to see Mother."

"Well, then everything's fine."

Sarkouhi, all smiles and broad gestures, led a small group of his well-fed and overdressed patrons into a semicircle around the table. I showed them where they could stand for the best view, then stood before them. I waited for their gossiping to slow to a trickle, their eyes to wander to me.

"Before I unveil this, I'd like to clear up a few common misconceptions about my craft, for those who may not be as deeply involved in the netherworld as I am," I said. I saw that Lindsay was annoyed with my delay, but hell, this was too good a chance to pass up. I just might pick up some high-class clients.

"First, what this is not." I started passing out business cards. "Ghosts are not self-aware, they're not beings. They can't see you or hear you. They're simply impressions, imprinted on the local area by the trauma of death. Or by other trauma, or other emotion. That's why you sometimes see ghosts of the living." I'd passed out all my cards. Time to wrap it up.

"The impressions are often of the moment of death, but not always." I went back to my equipment. "Dominant feelings, commitments left unfulfilled, unsaid messages, all these things can and do show up, and it's up to the artist to see that they do. And that's all I have to say. Let's see what we can see."

I checked my viewer. Yeah, I was satisfied with what I had called forth. I flipped the final switch.

At first there was nothing, except for the low hum of the 'caster. The smell of ozone grew in the air. Slowly an image started to form, in mid-air next to the table. It started as a grainy mist, like fine television snow, a vague human shape. It slowly intensified and clarified as the highlighters brought more of the energy out into visible forms, kicking it to the focusers. All this was needed to get the image formed in the first place — although of course natural ghosts do form, usually of an inferior quality, and with odd, annoying, aural and temperature effects — but once it was there, it would stay until properly laid, as long as it got boosted now and then.

The image continued to clear, and soon we were looking at a woman. It was a loop. Not uncommon. She moved, in jerky, uncertain movements, from the table to a spot a few feet away. Then suddenly we would see her lying on the floor, face down. Then she would be up again, moving around, as if confused. Her death had obviously come as a shock to her.

Her body, her clothes, were not too distinct — vague suggestions of a matronly form, decked out in some kind of conservative dark dress. Maybe the neckline was a bit lower, the dress a bit tighter, than society would choose to dictate. Was that a string of pearls around the fleshy neck? It was hard to tell.

But none of that mattered. Because the face — the face was clear, very clear. Real.

It was an aged face, but not heavily lined; Lindsay's mother would have been happy to hear that her face-lifts had survived her death. The forehead, fringed by curled white hair, was nearly smooth, the cheeks still full, the chin small and weak but still single.

You could see all that eventually. But it took time to take in, because what caught the attention were the ghost's eyes. They were startlingly blue in that papery face, and as the woman paced they sought something, something to be wary of. You could almost see a hunched form, a shadow, a dark aura, hovering at her back. And the expression in Mrs. Mehrer's eyes—

They were imploring. That's the word. But why? Was Ms Alicia Mehrer asking for mercy, for freedom? Or for understanding, compassion? There was shame in those eyes, too.

Even in death, she remained in thrall to her husband, bound to him by pain and need.

I couldn't have manufactured such a thing. But an impressionist can choose what to highlight — lives are complicated things — and I'd made sure that sick dependency came through. Call it art, showing a truth in place of the prettified picture that was asked for. Call it a stab at Lindsay. I don't know.

Maybe it was just what Lindsay had wanted to see. I had to look over at her. Her expression was at first smug, then horrified, lips parted and wide-eyed, but soon a mask slid down over her face. Her eyes narrowed and the right edge of her mouth curved up slightly. She coolly surveyed the onlookers; before her eyes met mine, I quickly looked down.

Then I looked at the crowd. I'd seen the same reactions a hundred times before. Some looked on in horror, lips curled, and clutched at the arms of those next to them. Some tried to avert their eyes, as if embarrassed, but their gazes were continually drawn back to the apparition before them. And some few leaned forward, drinking in the death.

Sarkouhi was watching the crowd, too. He seemed less than pleased. He saw me looking at him and walked over to me.

"Is this normal?" he asked in a low voice. "I mean, will it do anything else?"

"Some few do seem to react to things near them. Some look like they are trying to talk to you — the impressions can react to the impressed energies of those still living. Some act out the worries on their minds at the moment of death. Sometimes they even communicate what that was. Or try to. But, to answer your question, no. This is it. It's a fairly short action loop this time. She wasn't here long enough to lay down much more narrative."

Sarkouhi looked back at the impression, his face sour. I began packing up my stuff. Sarkouhi looked back at me.

"You're leaving?"

"Yep. Job's done."

"And this will just go on, repeating here in my place?"

"That's right." I folded a tripod and laid it gently in its foam-lined case. "I've pumped a lot of energy into the floor and walls, enough to keep it going for at least five or six weeks. And after that, I'll come back and pump it up some more. Can I use your phone? I have to call to have this stuff picked up." I couldn't just toss equipment of this caliber into my trunk, but it was humiliating to have to ask.

"Of course." He handed it over and I turned to the wall to give the man a moment, and sure enough, Sarkouhi went to talk to Lindsay.

Their conversation apparently didn't last too long, because when I clicked off and resumed packing, Sarkouhi was over by the other restaurant patrons. I guess he was trying to put a good face on the show, but the diners weren't buying. Several had already left, and a few in the back were realizing that they would have to pass uncomfortably close to the ghost to get to the door.

"Mrs. Sorensen!" Lindsay called, and one of the biddies looked up. A much younger man, his hair still dark, put a protective arm on her shoulder.

Lindsay made no attempt to get closer to her. "Enjoying the show, Mrs. Sorensen?"

"It's, ah..."

"Not sure? Perhaps your latest young man has an opinion — what's this one's name?"

The man scowled, whispered something to Mrs. Sorensen, and they turned away. Then she pulled away from him and looked back.

"I didn't know, Lindsay. I swear, I didn't know what he was doing to her." She turned and walked away.

Lindsay looked after them, her mouth fixed in its smile, her eyes full of hate.

Then she blinked and looked back at her mother for a moment. She strolled over to me. "Good work, as always."

"Thanks. And the rest of the money will be in my account when, exactly?"

"Oh, how you've come down in the world, Scott." She fished around in her purse and then started writing out a check.

"Yep. All the way down to the bottom line." I swiped her check through my reader. "Pleasure doing business. Please remember me whenever a loved one dies on you." I went back to the packing.

"This is my mother, Scott. You make me sound like one of your ghouls."

I folded a tripod and lay it gently in its foam. "The term is 'vampire.' But you're right. I know that you had me do this out of the love and respect you hold for your dear mom."

Lindsay moved in front of me, and spat her words. "You, of all people, have no right to judge me. I paid you for the job, and you did it. You didn't complain."

"I'm no judge, Lindsay." I closed and locked the lid on the case. I stood up. "They are, though." I nodded over to the last of the restaurant patrons. "You've given them a good show." I couldn't resist. "Was it the one you wanted?" I really was curious about that.

"You're done here, I think," she said, and walked out of the restaurant, almost striding through her mother's image.

Lindsay, Lindsay, Lindsay. Our shared betrayal of Pichrenn had eaten away at us both. Maybe my time in prison had given me a chance to let it go just a little more than she had, had convinced me that she was now out of reach, a subject of wistfulness and what-if. And how did she feel, now? No way would she think of me as out of her league; she could scrape me off the sidewalk any time she felt like it. But having me in her life would just remind her of what we had done to Pichrenn, how our relationship had been tainted from the start by that duplicity.

Sarkouhi headed over to me. I was getting downright popular. "This," he said, "is a bad business."

"Disappointed with the show? You're not alone."

"Oh, Mr. Koehl, I'm sure you have done an excellent job. But this is... It's not dignified."

"Death usually isn't."

He looked at me. "This isn't just death. How can I serve food, with this obscene thing here?"

Dear, dead Ms Mehrer continued her routine.

He hadn't thought of that before? Just what kind of idiot was he? Or, more to the point, what had Lindsay done or said to him? "You'd be surprised," I said. "This kind of show does bring a certain subset of the population. Not like your current crowd, though." I waved a hand at the people. "Like I said, you can always withdraw permission, Mr. Sarkouhi. These things are a lot easier to collapse than they are to bring out. And I work for reasonable rates."

"Ah. Mr. Koehl. As you reminded me, Lindsay Ingham has very many friends."

"She can make trouble for you, is that it? Not just legally."

"That is it."

"Looks like she's making trouble for you, anyway, Mr. Sarkouhi."

"That she is, Mr. Koehl."

As I climbed into my car I saw Lindsay watching the ghost through the window of the doorway, smoking an actual cigarette, the smoke making her features a little unclear. You can't do that in a restaurant. It's slow suicide. That wouldn't bother anyone, but even worse, it's public suicide.

The next day I was sitting in my office, staring out the window. I felt like shit. With the money and new stuff, paid bills, I should have felt like a pop star. Instead I kept seeing Ms Mehrer's face, and I felt like a whore.

The phone buzzed. I picked it up, and there was my vampire, Justin Hoben — excuse me, "John Robertson". The idiot called himself that, and then paid me through his personal account.

"John."

"You said to call today. You said that you would scout out the, that job we talked about."

"Yeah, John."

There was a pause. "Well?"

I didn't know why I was giving him a hard time. Lindsay's money would only last so long, and the bills would come due again eventually. So I roused myself. "Yeah, John. I checked it out. The manager is willing to go along, except he wants a cut. The usual amount, three hundred, and there's my fifty negotiating fee, on top of the baseline costs."

"Yeah, that's fine. When?"

I made a show of looking at my watch, although he wouldn't see it. "I guess I could squeeze it in late this afternoon, say four o'clock, if that works for you."

"Yeah, that would be good for me. Four o'clock."

I hung up. Sure, Mr. Hoben, that time works for you. I figured it would. Your wife thinks you're still at work, your office thinks you've left for the day. That works for you just fine.

It was sacrilege to use the new equipment for a job like this. Wiping grandma's priceless china with a rag made of old underwear. I could just as easily dig out my old stuff. My Mr. Robertson deserved no better.

But the lure of using that fine new gear was just too strong. My breath actually quickened as I thought about it. I felt like a pervert at a schoolyard. But I got it out anyway, and by three I was on my way.

Once there, it didn't take long for me to set up. Everything snapped into place just as it ought to, just as it used to. No sputtering, no loss of definition or control or focus, no stray signals. I played with the fine tuning, bringing out effects and details I hadn't been able to play with in years.

The old woman had died in the chair, just slumping further down, further down. No drama, just death. Her image flickered at the edges a bit; I toned it down, then brought it back up just to the edge of sight.

She kept her eyes half closed, and she seemed to be mindlessly staring at something, probably a television set that the landlord sold off when the body was found. She wore a gray blouse, and a necklace of fat glass beads, red and brown. She also wore some fading blue jeans. She was barefoot.

Some current celebrities say in their wills that their houses or places of death should be destroyed, to forestall this kind of thing from ever happening to them. The rest of us can't afford that kind of protection, though there are restraint policies that are supposed to prevent the kind of thing I was doing. The very poor, though, are wide open to the predations of vampires after death.

My vampire knocked at the door. I opened it. "John."

"Mr. Koehl." Justin Hoben's eyes barely brushed me before they focused on the dying woman. His breath caught in his throat.

"I'll be outside." I went down the stairs and I heard Justin close the door and lock it.

I sat in the open door of my car. It's a shame I never took up smoking; it would pass the time. I watched the traffic go by, the single occupants of single vehicles. An hour or so later Justin came back out. His shirt was no longer tucked into his pants, and there was drying sweat on his flushed face. He walked up to me, and didn't look at me as he slipped me his check.

But after he turned away, he spoke.

"You're a genius," he said, his voice thick with emotion. "That was the best — the best I've ever had. Amazing." Still without looking at me, he said, "Thank you," then hurried away.

So the new equipment had an endorsement.

I went back upstairs, and put down the ghost.

Afterwards I drove slowly past Grasso's, though it wasn't on the way home. Grasso's didn't look to have many customers. I laughed, and went home, wishing I had eaten something so I could vomit it back up.

The next morning Lindsay was already in my office corridor when I arrived.

"Where the hell have you been?" she greeted me. She stubbed out her cigarette in her pocket ashtray. "It's almost noon."

"Hello, Miss. Did an appointment slip my mind?"

I unlocked the door and Lindsay followed me inside. She sat down, a firm line to her mouth and a hard look in her eye.

"Have a seat," I said. I seated myself behind my desk and rested my chin on my hands. "Something I can do for you?"

"More like something you did *to* me."

I leaned back. That gaze was a little too intense. "I don't understand, Lindsay. I did what you asked. The ghost hasn't collapsed, has it?"

"To hell with you, Koehl."

"Yep, anyone with one good eye can see the sick relationship she had with your dad. It's all there for everyone to see. And that's exactly what you wanted."

"It's disrespectful, mocking her like that. I wanted a tasteful—"

"In a restaurant. Yeah. Please, Lindsay."

"Go to hell." She folded her arms, looked away, and began to sniff.

"Cut the act, Lindsay. We both know what you wanted. You wanted to leave a bitter taste in the mouths of all her society friends. You hated them for not stepping in, or you hated them for leading perfect lives within calling distance. You hated her for what she allowed your dad to do to her, and you couldn't resist a little public humiliation. And I gave it to you. Just like you knew I would. Because I've got the eye to see it, and the technique to show it, and the desperation to accept the job in spite of all that."

She ended her pretense of crying, and just sat there. I wondered what she wanted, why she was here. To justify herself in my eyes —Oh, I never expected to see *that* — or to gloat with me over her triumph over her mother?

Gloat with *me*? Did Lindsay have no friends?

Did I care? "You always were a little self-centered. Justifiably so. But hardly blind — did you think the relationship obvious to her old friends would slip past me? I do know my work, Lindsay."

"Your work! Raising ghosts for perverts!"

"Don't worry. I don't discuss my clients with anyone."

I should have seen the slap coming. Maybe I did. Then Lindsay stood up and turned her back to me.

The inside of my cheek had been cut by a tooth, and I tasted blood.

"He hated you, you know. Towards the end. That was his parting shot — saddle you with a murder charge."

"Manslaughter." I kept the disinterested tone in my voice, but her words rang in my head. Pichrenn had hated me? I had practically been his son.

And yet — it rang true, also. It didn't come as big a surprise as it should have.

"He taught me well. I owed it all to him. He had no reason to resent me."

Lindsay turned back to me. "Idiot! It wasn't your skill he resented!"

"I never—"

"You didn't need to."

She glared at me, expecting me to — what? Kiss her? Slap her, like Bogart in some old movie? Explain away the thing we'd had behind the old man's back, when I'd been the favored son and it was clear that Lindsay would be free after the old guy had passed on?

I knew that there are ghosts all around us, hovering just at the edges of sight, on the fringes of our minds, as we go about our lives. I made my living revealing them. Now Lindsay was showing me others.

"Why do you keep renewing him, Scott? Why don't you let him fade out?" Her voice was flat.

I had no answer.

"He's gone, Scott. And you blamed me. You never returned my messages."

Had she left messages? I'd told myself for so long that she had cut me loose. But yes, she had left messages I had brushed off. After killing Pichrenn, how could I just go on, take up openly with his lover?

I couldn't think of anything to say, and Lindsay stalked out. Was I supposed to call her back?

Had all this been her way to get through to me?

I've always had trouble with moving on. Maybe everybody does. But I thought a lot about what Lindsay had said, there at the end. I sat in my apartment in the dark, the TV on with the sound turned low, and decided that maybe it was time to act, and maybe even time for Lindsay to take another peek at the sunlit world.

Me too. I not only have trouble moving on, I have trouble going back. Lindsay had reached out to me, coming to see me about a ghost; she had made contact, however awkwardly, and maybe that's the only way she could do it. Still, she had done it. She had tried to show me herself at her most vulnerable, most unappealing, most venal, and most real. I could, too.

I had no idea if she would show up or not. The message I'd left hadn't given her any details, any reason to see me, just the time and place. I watched Pichrenn in his chair, and tried not to think about it. About where she was now, what she was doing, that she was still in the world even though she wasn't in mine.

The door opened. "Scott."

Lindsay stood there.

"Lindsay."

She entered hesitantly. "I'm not sure what I'm doing here."

"Yeah. Neither am I. But I'm here."

She nodded as if that made sense. She crossed the room to the window. She hadn't looked at Pichrenn. She wasn't wearing black this time — light blues and yellows.

I joined her. "I need to tell you something, Lindsay."

She nodded, but didn't say anything.

It was easier talking when she wasn't looking at me. "It's like this. Yes, I killed Pichrenn. He asked me to do it, and maybe he had more than one motive. I don't know. But I know that I've never forgiven myself, for that and for — you know. Us. And afterwards I pushed you away, like it was your fault or something. But I'm tired of pushing."

She turned to me. Her eyes flickered to the impression, then back to me. "You don't have to—"

"Yeah, I do. I really do. Since I got out of prison, since even before that, I've been moping and cynical, and it's got me nowhere. Maybe I've been a little too much in love with death. Maybe that's a job hazard. But I'm tired of it. Finally, I'm just *tired* of it."

I went to the closet and pulled out a single piece of equipment. I didn't even need a tripod. I could just hold it and point it at the apparition.

"Scott — you're..?"

"Time to say goodbye."

I pointed, and pressed the button, and Pichrenn vanished.

Lindsay looked at the chair where the impression had been. I couldn't tell what she was thinking.

I held out the defocuser to Lindsay. She looked at it as if she didn't recognize it, but didn't take it. I put it on the chair.

"If you ever want it, here it is," I said. "It's easy to use. Runs on batteries. Just point, and push the nice red button." I walked to the door. Lindsay still hadn't moved.

At the door I turned. "I usually have dinner weeknights at a little place on Fifth, near Pike," I said. "Rommie's. It's easy to find. I'm usually there from seven-thirty to eight-thirty or so."

I walked out.

Maybe Lindsay was tired of death, too. Tired of looking back.

I'd have to wait and see.

Tim McDaniel's story "Koehl's Quality Impressions" was published in Metaphorosis on Friday, 27 April 2018.

About the story

Ghosts are a fascinating topic. I can't say I believe in them, and yet there is a smudge of doubt; some of the stories are not easy to dismiss. But if ghosts really do exist, what could they be? The idea that they are conscious entities seems nightmarish and unfair to me – can you imagine wandering around an old house for a hundred years, no one to talk to, nothing to read? So the idea came to me that ghosts could be a phenomenon, an imprint of some kind on the structures they inhabit, that science just hasn't unearthed yet. And if that were true, maybe a technology could be developed to make them more easily seen.

Ghost stories are dark stories, generally, so I thought it might be fun to tell a sort-of ghost story using a dark template – that of noir fiction. Instead of a private eye played by Bogart, I would have a guy who uses technology to raise ghosts (but also played by Bogart, if he's available). And then the other elements – a lead character down on his luck, and beautiful woman he has trouble connecting to, a dark past, unsavory acquaintances. And an ending that is not quite completely happy.

A question for the author

Q: Do you live near where you were born? Have you traveled much?

A: I grew up in the Seattle area, went to university in the Seattle area… pretty boring. But after graduation I applied to join the Peace Corps. They decided to send me to South Yemen (this was before South and North united). But, a couple of weeks before I was scheduled to ship out, I got a call telling me that our visas hadn't been approved. Should they look for another assignment? Yes! I'd already sold my car, quit my job!

So a few weeks later I was sent to Thailand. After three months of intensive language and culture training, I was sent to a small village in Pichit province, Kampaengdin ("Dirtwall"). My duties were twofold: to teach English at the junior high school there, and to work with local farmers in some way. Well, I enjoyed the teaching, and did my best to see that the village farmers connected with agricultural officials, and even gave them information about raising fish in their rice paddies.

Normally Peace Corps assignments are for two years, but I applied for, and was granted, a third year, so I could work with various local schools on their English curricula. Then, as I was preparing to go home, I was told of a job offer at a university in the northeastern city of Khon Kaen. I went up there to see if it looked interested, and was immediately offered the job.

I loved it, but after a year came back to the U.S. I'd felt something of an imposter, since I only had a B.A. Back in Seattle I got my Master's in teaching ESL, and then heard that Khon Kaen University wanted me to come back, so I did. Six years later, the Thai economy crashed, so I returned to the U.S.

While living in Thailand I did a little traveling – Myanmar, Cambodia, Laos, Japan, Taiwan, and Nepal.

About the author

Tim McDaniel teaches English as a Second Language at Green River College, not far from Seattle. His short stories, mostly comedic, have appeared in a number of SF/F magazines, including F&SF, Analog, and Asimov's. He lives with his wife, dog, and cat, and his collection of plastic dinosaurs is the envy of all who encounter it. In his spare time (ha!) he teaches judo.

His author page at Amazon.com is www.amazon.com/author/tim-mcdaniel

The Foaling Season

Samuel Chapman

Reynard aux Chatillon delivers a gryphon foal the morning Lucia Camoreux comes to visit. It comes out squealing, eyes shut and wings folded, sticky with placenta. Within an hour its wings open, beating softly, as it stands to take food from its mother's beak.

Reynard sees Lucia as he returns from leading the foal and mare into a paddock isolated from the pasture. The mare cannot be kept from flying, of course, but she will return to the smaller enclosure as long as her flightless child is there. She will lick its wings so she can always pick it out of the herd. In twenty-eight hours, she will boost it into the air for its first flight.

"Why do you separate them?" Lucia leans on the fence, wearing riding pants and a long coat of faded scarlet. Reynard touches his hat.

"The young one'll be sharpening his claws soon enough," he says. To tell the truth, he is surprised to see her, though not because she is a hero of the revolution standing in his pasture. "His mother teaches him to redirect his aggression. Not to scratch the other boys and girls."

He surveys the dale in which his paddocks sit, a flat place surrounded by hills that support thin lines of elm trees. A few storage sheds sit around the fences, and the long stable takes up one whole side of the valley. The gryphons in flight taunt the ones on the ground, then they switch places, a game that will continue all day with different players. The breeze is crisp. The whole pasture smells heavily of manure, but it is a kind, green scent Reynard has never minded.

A hinge creaks far off. From the stable, his daughter Aveline emerges, her hands soiled and her long black hair tightly restrained. Seeing Lucia, she quickens her stride toward them.

"What did you have her doing?" Lucia asks.

Reynard hardly hears: the foal has stepped back from its mother and is standing up, facing her. He's seen these youthful rebellions turn violent before. Lucia has to repeat her question before he answers, "Oh. Aveline? Nursing Dameciel's upset stomach."

"Brave woman." Lucia wrinkles her nose. "She's grown. She looks...very much like Itienne come back to us."

Reynard's thoughts stumble over an unexpected open pit. Without taking his eyes from the foal, he can tell Lucia regrets her words already, and is unaccustomed to the feeling. "Did you have something to tell me?" he asks.

"Yes." Lucia recovers herself. "I came to warn you to expect L'Escalier today. I excused myself from a meeting, in fact, in order to beat him here. I fear he'll have a proposition for you."

"On my land?" Reynard is focused first on the foal, second on how to pretend this conversation has not involved his lost wife. He is distracted, and that is a dangerous state of mind in which to deal with Sovereign Minister Dominic L'Escalier. "I don't have anywhere to receive him."

Reynard and Aveline do not live on the surface, which is for farms and gryphons. Locksgrove, the city, comes alive in the tunnels and on the cliff face. Reynard has met L'Escalier, the leader of the slave revolt, many times, but in taverns and manor offices—never here, never in his place.

"He said this could not wait."

Working every day with temperamental stallions, Reynard is well-suited to notice signs of hidden discomfort, like the clear skies that often precede storms. Lucia has taught him revolutionary scholars are not all that different from gryphons.

Something is about to happen. He waits for her to tell him what.

Lucia drops her gaze. "There's going to be a war."

So be it. Locksgrove won its last war working with far less.

But then Lucia goes on. "Not against us, you understand. Between Lascony and the Abelard League. But given that they both border us, it demands a response."

"Thank you for the warning." The foal has backed down and let the mare groom it, but Reynard swallows, wipes his brow nonetheless. "But I'm a loyal citizen. I've nothing to fear from L'Escalier."

"From whom?"

Both Reynard and Lucia startle as if caught in a tryst. Aveline, wiping her hands on a rag, smiles at their visitor.

Aveline aux Chatillon could not respect a goddess more than she does Professor Lucia Camoreux. The conscience of the revolution, a walking library at L'Escalier's side, and still gentle enough not to breathe a word of their secret meetings together. Aveline sees Lucia and Reynard standing in opposition—her skin like milky tea, his black as a gryphon's eye—and rejoices at the sudden widening of her world.

It is through knowing the Professor that she has made a decision: their pasture will do no business with

Dominic L'Escalier. Sell the gryphons to farmers, to riders, to people who will care for them. Not to soldiers.

Lucia has written a book called *Treatise on the Failure of Revolutions* that Aveline is making her way through one sentence at a time. Both women hope the new Senate will take it as scripture. Previous idealistic upheavals have gone sour because their leaders became seduced into too many evils they believed were necessities. Lucia has taught Aveline that L'Escalier, without sound advice, is a prime candidate for such seduction.

Though Aveline agrees, she admits to herself that her motives are more basic: she fears for the safety of her gryphons. Last year, when Dameciel injured his wing on a windmill, she slept in the stable beside him, unable to leave for fear the infection would spread. She saw the torn, blood-spattered skin whenever she closed her eyes.

Aveline is no general. No waster of life.

Her father will object to her decision, of course. There never was a more loyal soldier of the revolution: Reynard tended mounts for L'Escalier when the revolt was still confined to back alleys and outskirt farms. But Aveline believes the best way to celebrate freedom is to exercise it occasionally.

Dominic L'Escalier wields power like a fiddler wields his bow, but her family won a war so they wouldn't have to be anybody's slaves. That goes for gryphons just as well as humans.

When Lucia tells her who is coming, Aveline gives only a tight nod. Her father does not notice anyway: he's watching his foal again before Aveline can get a sentence out.

Lucia smiles, asks if Aveline has managed to get out to see friends lately, but it has the ring of distraction. At the sound of cart wheels rolling up the dirt track, they both break off. And at the sound of a roar coming from the pasture, even her father looks up.

The roar freezes Reynard to his core. The herd is not at rest. They circle, like lightning in storm clouds.

Ouragan. Of the three stallions, this is the only one Reynard could never acclimate to the side pasture. When a creature can fly, it becomes far more dangerous for it not to know its place.

Dominic L'Escalier is standing at the outer fence, chatting with his bodyguards. Ouragan is circling, leaping to the air then strutting over the ground, around an arc that centers on the Sovereign Minister.

"Get back," Reynard tells Aveline. "Behind the shed."

"Father—"

"If I need you, I'll call! *Go!*"

Ouragan is sire to the foal birthed that morning. He's picked fights before. Foudre, never the strongest male, bears a strip of discolored fur from where Ouragan slashed his haunch with a hatchet-sized foreclaw.

Ouragan tightens his circle around the fence, bellowing and shaking his mane. Three gryphons take flight all at once, all skittish yearlings. They wheel in the air as others follow them up, an ever-widening helix of dark shapes against the clouds.

Reynard throws the side gate open and strides into the pasture as it swings shut behind him. Man and beast are alone now, enclosed together.

Ouragan veers to meet him. Reynard keeps his eyes downcast, his movements slight. Fortunately, it is overcast, so there is no danger of a shadow spooking the gryphon.

"Reynard," calls Dominic L'Escalier. His voice is cautious, and a little excited.

A roar hits Reynard's ears.

He rolls across the pasture grass. Hooves thunder by him. A wing-tip feather grazes his face, tickling.

Ouragan is charging the fence again. L'Escalier's towering guards close ranks in front of him, but they needn't bother—the stallion halts once more to face Reynard as he rises. Under the rage is a bond of trust Reynard can use. He foaled this beast, after all.

He makes it to his knees. Then he points down the road, points hard, so L'Escalier can see. To speak a warning would be too much loud noise, too fast.

The Sovereign Minister of Locksgrove swivels his head to look where Reynard is pointing. Reynard resists the urge to slap his own forehead. L'Escalier is only brilliant in two or three ways.

Ouragan snarls. His mouth froths. Reynard points to L'Escalier, then again down the road, as softly as he can, as hard as he must. At last the Minister gets it. He draws his guards by the shoulder down the road and out of sight.

"Right then," Reynard says, and smiles at Ouragan. "Now you and I can talk."

His smile is calculated. After smiling he yawns, as though he is at tea, and not much interested in it. Boredom will put the gryphon at ease.

Time to move in. Sifting his feet through the grass, his loose shirt stained with dew, Reynard approaches the wild-eyed stallion.

Ouragan roars. Reynard stands firm, though ancient instinct screams at him to run. A sudden movement now, too close to dodge, would mean death.

Two more steps. One. Arms-length away, Reynard stretches out his hand to Ouragan's mane, stroking with his fingertips. Grooming.

A new roar dies in the gryphon's throat. He pants. Reynard feels the hot breath. On the far side of the pasture, a few of the circling colts gain the courage to land.

Reynard's hands shake as he places them on either side of Ouragan's mane. His father showed him this—

had his father trembled as much? *Fool,* he thinks, *the hard part is past. Now it's all rhythm.*

He breathes, in and out, seeking the pulse of Ouragan's life. Their breaths synchronize.

Ouragan looks down.

His throat rumbles, but he steps forward to nuzzle Reynard. Reynard, at the same time, looks up. Lucia stands just outside the fence, while Aveline has crept into the pasture, wielding the stout sharpened pole Reynard keeps behind the shed. Their last resort.

"Aveline," he croaks, "go and tell L'Escalier he may approach."

"Brilliant. Absolutely marvelous." L'Escalier cannot stop gushing as Reynard and Aveline lead him around the edge of the paddock. "I couldn't take my eyes off you, Reynard. At least until you ordered me to."

Reynard is glad Dominic L'Escalier has not yet asked why his mere presence frightens gryphons. He probably doesn't care. Lucia once confided in Reynard that the Minister cultivates unfamiliarity as a habit, to divert his enemies. The unfamiliar disconcerts animals.

"Every time I visit, you end up giving me orders." L'Escalier grins. "The other breeders all bow and scrape before me. Which is why I'm here."

Aveline catches her father's eye with a firm message he cannot read. She is still carrying the pike as she leads the group of six—herself, Reynard, Lucia, L'Escalier, and the two bodyguards. Inside the fence the gryphons have settled, and now the only thing in the sky is the sun, promising a radiant summer evening.

They take the Sovereign Minister all around the pasture, Reynard showing him how the operation is getting on. L'Escalier nods at all the right times, sometimes conferring with Lucia on things she seems to have mentioned to him before—"Is that the famous

Foudre?" or "You were right, that shed looks fit to blow away." He is taken with the new foal, who is sharpening his claws with the enthusiasm of all nature's new children.

"Capital," he says. "Dear Reynard, if you'd accompany me back to my transport, I have a request I hope you'll consider."

Aveline is gripping the pike hard enough to snap it. She follows without being asked.

At the cart—pulled by a small mammoth of the type never allowed outside the city—L'Escalier motions his two bodyguards aboard with the driver, then turns back to the group.

"How many adults do you own, Reynard?" he asks.

"Twenty-six," Reynard says. "Three stallions, nine geldings, fourteen mares."

L'Escalier nods. He is a slight man, his nose pointed, eyes set like cut jewels into his face. "Those three will need gelding as well, then."

Aveline plants the tip of the pike in the ground. "Why?"

Her question distracts the Minister from watching the sky. "I'm sorry?"

"Why do you want to geld our stallions?" Aveline repeats.

"Sir," Reynard says.

L'Escalier waves it off. But in the split second beforehand, Reynard sees something raw and hot flood his daughter's features.

"It's the fashion in the cities of Lascony now to ride geldings in battle," L'Escalier says. "Young noble twats want to lead armies, but can't be bothered to learn enough airmanship to mount a stallion. The gelding gryphon is," he searched for a word, "predigested. But they've asked for fifty. Twenty-six is closer than twenty-three. And nobody else's will do. Not for the kind of war we're going to have."

The mammoth grunts as Lucia joins L'Escalier by the cart. Reynard suddenly understands the nature of the meeting she cut short to come warn him. "Does this mean Locksgrove has formed an alliance with Lascony?" she asks.

L'Escalier picks up the fighting note in her words and lays a hand on her shoulder. "Not an alliance, Lucia. A temporary partnership. Of mutual benefit."

"And if their enemies turn their aggression on us?"

"Lucia, my butterfly, we will talk about this later." L'Escalier clambers up into the cart, and avoids looking at Lucia's face, where a withering glare is communicating that they will talk about it at length later. "Reynard, do you accept my proposal?"

"I..." Reynard has just found his voice. "Could you repeat it, sir?"

Standing upright in the cart, L'Escalier says, "I am offering you whatever price you care to name for all twenty-six of your adult gryphons to use as war mounts for the commanders of the forces of Lascony to use in their swift conquest of their opponents, the Abelard League, who are now are mutual enemies. Do you accept?"

"Father," Aveline hisses, as Lucia refuses L'Escalier's hand and mounts the cart alone, "that's our entire breeding stock."

Does she think I don't know? No matter how many he sells to private buyers, simply knowing Lucia reminds Reynard daily that a fledgling nation of former slaves cannot afford luxuries like unfettered commerce. He sought out Dominic L'Escalier's cause in his life's one moment of white-hot rage, watched the one-time manor slave drill barely-armed troops and quote philosophers in his speeches, and has known ever since: the Minister is the father of freedom. There can be no repaying a debt to him.

And war? asks Aveline in his head. *Is war not a luxury?*

It is not a choice. They have never been his gryphons. They have always been Locksgrove's. L'Escalier's.

Aveline shouts, "Never," as Reynard says, "Yes."

The upper tunnels, unlike the tide-washed slums at the cliff base, are clean, and well lit by skylights that allow shrubs to grow. Other than the mammoth traffic, this neighborhood—reserved by L'Escalier for government employees—is quiet.

Smoke from a fire, scented with cinnamon, drifts along the tunnel, wide enough for three mammoths abreast. The beasts prefer it down here, out of the sun, where their shaggy coats don't make them sweat.

Aveline skirts around one. She's been keeping ahead of Reynard all the way home. She pushes through a red curtain into their main chamber without holding it open. Reynard walks into it.

No matter how many times L'Escalier offers him a palace on the cliff face, Reynard doesn't want to move. He and Aveline each have their own room, and the kitchen is in a third, all separated from the main chamber by their own curtains. Aveline is brushing hers aside when Reynard enters.

He calls her name. She sighs and turns around. The large dining table sits between them.

"Will you explain why you disrespected me in front of Dominic and Lucia this afternoon?"

"You know damn well why, father. What were you thinking? Every last stallion and mare sold off for Lascon nobles to prance around on?"

"Watch your tongue." He moves around the table; she keeps her distance. "We have the colts and the yearlings, and it's still the foaling season. I won't sell a pregnant mare. We'll get new breeding stock."

"I don't care about the breeding stock!" she snaps. "Did you raise Ouragan and Foudre and the others to fight wars? They'll die on the ends of pikes!"

A heavy hand clutches Reynard's stomach. She does indeed look a great deal like her mother.

"The gryphons aren't ours," he says. "We raise them for those who will buy them. We must sell outside Locksgrove if that's where the market is."

"Amazing." Aveline's words are made of ice. "L'Escalier is back at the palace, but I can still hear him talking. Tell me, father, what do you call a living being that can be bought and sold at its owner's whim?"

"I call it my job!" At some point Reynard begins to shout. "I do what I was born for. What others do with it is not my concern."

"Then I was wrong. It's not just the gryphons enslaved. It's you."

It is as though she has slugged him in the gut. The wind whistles out of his lungs and he collapses into a hardwood chair. Aveline looks more appalled than angry—she may not have meant to say so much—but her features harden again. She disappears behind her bedroom curtain, and returns carrying a wax tablet, which she thrusts at Reynard.

Handwriting runs across it in several rows. Of course, Reynard cannot understand it, but he can tell every other row was written by a practiced hand. Every second row is scratched more messily, though the writing tightens by the end.

He recognizes the script of the odd-numbered rows. He has seen it on letters from the university, the ones he glances at before going in search of someone to read them to him.

"Lucia's been giving me lessons," Aveline says. "I'm learning to read and write. I won't spend my life tending war machines, father. I won't be a slave."

Reynard struggles to stand. He lays the tablet on the chair so he doesn't drop it. "You're turning your back on everything we are."

"You turned first. What about mother? What would she say about this war?"

This is enough. So Aveline wants to hurt him. Very well. He is a strong man. He can hurt back.

"You don't know what you're talking about," he hisses. "You weren't five years old when the chains broke. You know nothing of slavery. And less of your mother."

"Then tell me." Aveline stands her ground. "Tell me all about how beautiful she was. She must have had a lustrous mane, and silky wings. You've never cared for anything without wings."

When Reynard gathers himself after this, he is sitting in one of the hardwood chairs, warmed by a fire he doesn't recall starting. Aveline must be in her room, or out on the streets looking for one of her friends. He makes a pot of stew with fresh vegetables and broth, leaves a bowl out as a peace offering. It grows cold.

Long after the skylight darkens, he notices he sat on the wax tablet with the writing lesson. He hauls himself up, joints snapping, to put it someplace out of the way.

The foaling season passes. Aveline refuses to have anything to do with the adult gryphons, spends all her time exercising and grooming the yearlings. She cleans the stable, then cleans it again, and does everything she can to avoid her father. Once, she respected his willful determination to soldier forth on his own course no matter the consequences; now her old respect sickens her.

When the appointed day comes, the mares and geldings are led through the paddock gates into waiting trailers whose cloth coverings are emblazoned with the blue boar of Lascony. Each gryphon folds its wings and munches at the oats left for it, while the Lascon drivers lock the rear gate. Even Ouragan goes quietly, though Reynard has to lead him in by hand.

The trailers take them to the front lines, to the scraps of land Lascony and the Abelard League have been struggling over for longer than Reynard or L'Escalier have been alive. The gryphons fly over these provinces, bearing commanders who urge soldiers forward. The Lascons later use them as scouts. When things go bad, they become bombers.

They are struck with arrows, rocks from slings, ballista bolts. Many gryphons together can turn the tide of a battle, but the more who appear in the same sky, the more seem to die.

One day at the beginning of autumn, more than half the remaining gryphons cross a churning river to plant a bridge for the Lascon army to cross. A hidden Abelard ambush force surges out of the underbrush before the Lascons can hammer the planks into place. They throw nets at the gryphons and stab them and their riders with pitchforks until long after they die. Trapped on the other side of the river, the other Lascons are crushed by the main Abelard force. Less than half escape. Ouragan, the fierce, throws his untrained rider and takes to the sky, but a crossbow fusillade shreds his wing and sends him crashing to the ground. He dies on impact, a last act of rebellion against the men awaiting the satisfaction of butchering him with scimitars.

Two days after, the news reaches Locksgrove. Dominic L'Escalier walks out of a senate meeting, in the middle of a speech, and sends his steward to find Reynard aux Chatillon. Once again, Lucia arrives first, and finds Aveline, who, seeing the Professor hastily wiping mucus and tears from her face, knows instantly what has been lost.

Reynard descends into a café on the cliff face, on the fifth level of a boardwalk that rises another six stories above their heads. Tables form a constellation on the wooden walkway before the shop, which is recessed into the stone. L'Escalier has already claimed a table, and ordered two overlarge mugs of coffee. The other tables are empty.

L'Escalier gets up to pull out Reynard's chair. "I hope you don't mind the short notice," he says, "or the venue. This place used to be a big-time exporter's private roaster. His old house slave runs it now."

"What is it you want?" Reynard asks, rubbing his eyes. The coffee smells dark and strong.

"We can't just talk?" L'Escalier takes a long sip. "I'd have met you somewhere with stronger spirits, but it's hardly noon, and I need to keep a bit of respect with the people."

Reynard stifles a yawn. Aveline still does her share of the work in the pasture—more, if anything—but speaks to him two and three words at a time, and not at all when the work is done. Since their fight, he has not slept well.

L'Escalier sighs. "Very well. Yes. I do need your help."

Some giggling from below, maybe the crowd around a street performer. Someone wheels a cart along the next boardwalk up.

L'Escalier asks, "Have you heard the news from the war?"

Reynard feels a chill. He wishes he were back with the colts. "Nothing to do with me. Sir."

"Impressive that you should have missed it. I can't get people to talk about anything else." L'Escalier forces on a smile. Reynard gulps the bitter coffee. "The truth is it might have more to do with you than you realize. You helped Lascony once. They—or I—we're hoping you might do it again."

So that's what this is. Reynard's eyes drift out to sea. The sky is steel-grey, the breakers on the ocean like cold white fingers. Autumn is roaring past.

He hears himself say, "I can't. I only have colts and yearlings, not ready to ride. Find someone else."

L'Escalier shakes his head, lowers his voice. "There's no-one else. The others breed work animals or poncy show mares for rich traders. We are a new city, Reynard, without many options. You have the only war mounts I trust."

Dominic L'Escalier alienated Reynard's daughter, enslaved the things he cared most about, to die in a war about which they understood even less than he does. Now the Minister wants to do it again. To gryphons even less prepared, who will die even faster.

He could not have done any of these things had Reynard not consented. By the breaking of his chains, Reynard himself has been broken.

Reynard stands up and kicks the chair back, knocking it into another. "Tell Lascony you're done. I'm not selling the colts. They can't carry the payloads you want and they'll spook at crossbow fire."

"Sit down," L'Escalier says. "Drink your coffee until you can think rationally. Remember we have an agreement."

"We had a—" Reynard fumbles for words. "A business relationship. I don't work for you."

Now L'Escalier is standing as well, his mug forgotten. "You work for your city. Do you understand what's going on out there? The Abelards are marching on the Lascon capital. If they take it, and that is a matter of weeks," he pounds his knuckles on the table, rattling the mugs, "they will make Lascony a client state. And there is *nothing* between Lascony and Locksgrove save the few thousand militiamen the Senate can draft. We'll be overrun."

He steps around the table, looking up a bit to stare into Reynard's eyes. "Ask Lucia. She can read the signs, Reynard. Do you want to wear chains again? Do you want to go back to being a slave?"

Reynard lurches forward. L'Escalier narrows his eyes. "Go ahead. I didn't bring a bodyguard. Watch. *I order you to come out, guards!*"

Neither of his usual hulks materializes. The proprietor of the shop is stock-still with his hands in a vat of soapy water.

"Strike me," L'Escalier says. "But then say yes. Do you want them to take your daughter, Reynard? Do you know what they do to pretty girls like Aveline when they sack cities? Are your yearlings worth more to you than keeping her from that fate?"

Reynard's fist connects with L'Escalier's jaw. The Minister stumbles. He catches himself on the edge of another table and turns back to Reynard.

"Do it again, if you must."

Reynard digs his nails into his palm, and turns, caring only to put distance between himself and this man who burns everything he touches.

"Air support, Reynard," L'Escalier calls after him. "Scouting. Leadership. Flanking maneuvers. Evacuating the wounded. The Abelards dispatched entire cohorts against your gryphons. They determined the course of battles."

He stops. Without turning, he says, "I didn't raise them for that."

"Why did you raise them?"

A fisherman is rowing through the bay, headed for home. There is about to be rain. The eyes of the silent, waiting Minister drive Reynard into his own head, toward a fight with this question he has never before dared to meet.

"For the same reason you hold power and start wars," he tells L'Escalier. "Because we are good at nothing else."

"I didn't start this war." L'Escalier steps close again and whispers. "The Abelards despise us, Reynard. They wish we did not exist. Lascony alone keeps their wish from coming true, and there's about to be no more Lascony, unless you let go of your moon-damned yearlings."

Clear as day, Reynard sees each of the gryphons he has raised since he inherited the paddock. Unfolding its wings for the first time. Scratching at grass and bark and the walls of the paddock while its mother guided it around. Taking flight for the first time, its roars joyful, like a human child running for the sake of running. Its muscles flowing like water, with no motion wasted. Carrying a commander out to the battlefield. Falling from the sky, punctured with pikes, life leaking out.

Cursing Reynard aux Chatillon, with their last breaths, for delivering them life only to send them back into slavery to save his own skin from the same fate. Condemning him, in some strange gryphon language he would never speak, for his crime of delivering a human daughter into the praxis of suffering.

He cannot unburden himself of his debt. Cannot decide for a whole city. Nor for Aveline.

He says, "Yes."

Aveline and Lucia leave the University campus at dusk. It is hard to tell the time, since few people in the low tunnels are bothering to maintain the light cycles anymore. They stay huddled in their caverns with their families, or flee to sea, crowding the bay with boats. Collisions have occurred. Aveline doesn't know where they think they're going.

She herself is going to the empty pasture to take Lucia to shelter with Reynard—though she isn't certain Reynard knows why people are hiding. During their lesson, Aveline had to tell Lucia how her father sits in the shack most days, staring at the wall. They still are not talking, but she has begun to bring her father tea, which he sometimes even drinks.

Lucia can explain to him that the fall of Lascony took three days, and that Dominic L'Escalier has fled the city. None of it shocked Aveline, but to tell Reynard his one-time hero has abandoned Locksgrove will require Lucia's gentler touch. Her father still wants desperately to believe the Sovereign Minister is good.

A left, and a right. A few tunnels remain, and then they will be at the pasture. They're close enough to the surface to tell it's raining. *Will they drag us all away from here?* she thinks. *Will all these tunnels will start leaking, with nobody to maintain the seals? Will the gryphons that are left go feral? Will they prefer it that way? Will they remember us?*

In the shack, with wind howling and rain dripping through the roof, Aveline asks Reynard and Lucia about slavery.

Reynard is stuffing plaster into the cracks in the shed, blotting out a rain-washed view of the pasture with each one he closes. He wants to keep doing this for a while. There are some holes left. But then Aveline asks again in a small voice—"What is it going to be like?"—and Lucia can't answer.

His daughter needs him. It is the first time in a long time. Even before she turned against him, they were more like business partners than anything else.

Lucia is sitting on a sack of oats. She has unbuckled and unsheathed a long, gently-curved sword, and placed it on the table. Aveline is on the floor in the corner, her knees drawn up around her long pike. Reynard drops into one of the chairs.

"Not a death sentence," he says. "Some people made a good life. My father did, and his father. If you have a trade, you become more…more valuable."

"Reynard," Lucia says, but Aveline interrupts her. "I want the truth. All of it. Did slavery kill Mom?"

Lucia closes her eyes, rests her hand on the sword hilt. Reynard's throat clenches. He nods. "Your mother died because she was a slave."

The wind howls through the following silence. Amid the drumming of rain and the scent of wet wood, Reynard realizes they expect him to explain how she died. He will do it to fill the silence.

"The revolution didn't happen overnight. Much as it looked like it did." A gust of wind reaches into the lantern on the middle of the table, flickering the flame. "There were other fights. Earlier. In the streets, in the pastures, field slaves against the house. Itienne, your mother…she was out too late. Some people had died the night before."

"Slave or free?" Aveline asks.

"Don't remember." Reynard is talking now the way he breathed long ago with wild dead Ouragan. With the memory they enter the same rhythm, drawing strength from each other. With the story they survive a bit longer. "She walked into the middle of a skirmish. Not far from here. Carrying eggs. Our mistress wanted some."

He swallows. "Both sides said they don't know who hit her. And I never found out. I buried her the same night."

Now everyone falls quiet. Lucia grips the sword hilt. Reynard squeezes the wall putty in his hands, then, all of a sudden, drops it.

Aveline perks up. "Did you hear—"

"Voices." Lucia takes up the sword. "Both of you stay here."

Aveline jumps to her feet with the pike. "I'm coming with you."

Reynard finds the strength to stand. "You are not."

There's a pitchfork in a hay pile, ten paces away from the door. If he can reach it and return before any Abelard soldiers appear, he and Lucia might be able to bottleneck them in the shed door.

He doesn't know when he decided to fight, or to die. Perhaps it was the story, but more likely it was Aveline, who now gives him a look in response to his injunction. It is defiant, nakedly so, but not contemptuous. She does not mean to hurt him. She is like the wax tablet now, a simple statement of fact, telling him the way things are.

And it's all right. Just because she can protect herself, doesn't mean he can't protect her too.

Lucia puts her hand on the door. "If they have lights, we can sneak up on them. If not, nobody leaves this room."

"I need to run for the pitchfork," Reynard says. "They'll have armor. I can't fight bare-handed."

Lucia recalculates in her mind. The voice comes again, and Reynard strains to listen, but he can't pick any one out of the wind.

"All right. They may well still be too far away to see us in the dark. When I open the door, run to the hay pile. Then keep quiet and surprise them from behind."

Reynard nods. There isn't time for anything else. Lucia grips the edge of the door. Throws it open.

He runs. The ground vanishes under his feet. The paddock is dark, but the Abelards are carrying a light that shines a demonic red over the fences and pasture. Reynard grabs the pitchfork out of the hay pile, and whirls around.

Somebody shouts from within the paddock. "Lucia! Reynard!"

Reynard freezes. An Abelard might know Lucia's name. Maybe. But his?

"Lucia! Aveline! *Reynard!*"

He hears a sword strike point-first into soil, then, right after, a fist hitting bone. Rushing with the pitchfork, he arrives in the pool of light at the same time as Aveline, who lodges her pike in the tines of his weapon so he cannot move it.

Reynard turns from her to the man lying on the ground, who's managed to hold onto the torch despite Lucia having knocked him flat. Just one of Dominic L'Escalier's many talents.

"I deserved that," he admits. "But please don't do it again."

"Why not?" In the half-light, the sword glows like the blade of some ancient hero. Reynard and Aveline enter the paddock, where Dominic is getting to his feet under the watchful and enraged eyes of Lucia. "Tell me why."

Dominic holds out his hands. Other than the torch, he's unarmed. "You want to know what I did."

"I know what you did. Ran off in the night and struck a bargain with the Abelards. How many of us did you sell? Thirty percent? Fifty?"

"You're right." He dodges another blow, quickly adding, "Half-right. I did strike a deal, but I didn't sell humans. Don't you see?" He looks straight at Reynard. "I sold gryphons."

Reynard had thought this was done hurting him. But there is more still. "What do you mean?" he asks.

Dominic straightens up. "I already told you what a difference they make on the battlefield. Two dozen of them can be worth a whole light infantry, if a good general knows how to use them. They're living weapons."

Reynard is thinking of the foals in first flight, of the power of their wingbeats as he loses them in the sunrise. There is no creature in the world that knows so well where it's going.

"The Abelard League has wanted their own mounted force since they first fought the Lascon gryphons. And they were prepared to take Locksgrove to do it—their country is all mountains and mines, no pastureland. But they didn't want to. I mean, look at you three. Look at us. Everyone in this city is armed. Maybe the revolutionary militia can't stand up to a trained fighting force, but they would have had to fight tunnel by tunnel through the underground, with clubs and pikes hiding in every cavern." Dominic straightens up. "They'd have won. But with heavy losses. Nobody is ever going to take this city without watering the caves with blood. It's the way we're built."

"So you offered an alternative," Lucia says. "Trade money for the breeding stock, instead of lives."

"I told them we could only sell colts and yearlings, but they were happier with that than with losing them to the enemy."

"So war can go on in peace," Aveline mutters. "Having gained a third dimension."

Dominic turns toward Reynard. "I'm sorry I didn't tell you, but to be honest, I didn't think of the plan until yesterday. There wasn't time to explain."

"So it's over," Lucia says. "We're arms dealers to the continent now."

"You must admit it's a fine role to play," Dominic replies. "Everyone needs us alive and selling more than they need us destroyed."

"Yes," Lucia says, taking up the sword and sheathing it. Her eyes are dark, and when Dominic reaches out a hand to her, she neither takes it nor responds at all. "Yes. I must admit that."

Reynard drops the pitchfork with a thud. While Dominic is distracted, he takes the torch out of the Minister's hand, then turns.

Dominic jerks around. "Reynard—"

Behind him, though he doesn't see, Lucia throws her arm out. "Let him have the light. He'll need it."

"But where's he going?"

"I don't know. And don't ask. He's the one you made pay, Dominic. Not the Abelard League."

Another weapon hits the dirt. Someone hurtles toward the shed. Reynard keeps walking.

Once the tunnel city of Locksgrove is no longer underfoot, the pastureland turns to forest. The woods drip year-round with mist, the needles on the trees heavy with water, the soil slick with mud. There are just three roads. On one of these, Dominic met with the Abelard ambassadors. On the day the revolution began, fog made solid walls over all three.

Aveline follows her father's torch to the edge of the woods before she musters the will to call out to him. These trees have a threshold: the last farms clear-cut such a perfect line one can stand with a foot in and a foot out of the forest.

"Father."

He turns. It is light enough to see his face.

"Did you know I was following you?"

"I didn't," Reynard admits. "I knew I wanted to walk. Not much else."

"Why here?" She is drawing nearer. In addition to her pike—more of a walking stick now—and her coat, she has brought several yards of rope. "You're not a woodsman."

"No. But your great-grandfather was. Did I ever tell you?"

He must have looked like you, she thinks.

"He captured the ancestors of all the gryphons we sold," Reynard says. "Day by day, in the woods, never able to get farther than the line of soldiers stationed on the other side to capture fugitives. In two years, he brought back twenty-six. That's been a good number for our family."

"I brought this." Aveline drops the bundle of rope at her feet. "To make snares. Or a net."

He stares at her. His surprise, Aveline thinks, must mirror her own. Didn't she hate this man? Didn't she rail every day against his weak will, his blind equation of

L'Escalier to the whole city? Hadn't he made war on the Abelards?

No, she thinks. *No. He didn't.*

Reynard takes the coil of rope in his hand.

"Get new breeding stock," Aveline tells him. "And keep breeding. Father, you're the best at it. L'Escalier knows, everyone knows. So rebuild the pasture. No more staring at the wall." She points at the woods with her pike. "Get in there."

"Why?" her father asks. "Aveline...you were ready to abandon all of this."

She shakes her head, dries her eyes. "I didn't understand what Lucia was trying to teach me. Or to teach all of us. Nothing is good on its own. Sometimes, we just face down charging stallions, and...right at those moments the only thing that makes sense is to be kind."

Aveline lays her hands on her father's shoulders. "We can make them good, father. They're not weapons or even tools, they're hopes, yours and mine and their own. We can raise the gryphons free."

There is a long silence, broken by morning birdsong from within the trees. At last, Reynard says, "I think so too."

Aveline backs off, suddenly confused. "You do? And you came here without any equipment? What were you going to do, wrestle them?"

"I suppose..." These words are not calculated. She perceives he has just thought of them. "I suppose I was waiting for you to bring the rope."

In the next moment, a moment that lasts a long time, Aveline is grateful for the knowledge she has taken for herself. Not everyone knows the instant they have made a decision that will alter the rest of their life, but she does now. She will follow her father into the forest, into his understanding of beautiful doomed things. She will accept his skills, but she will also read and write, and in doing so, perhaps will save Locksgrove by saving the creatures it has made.

The best of it. The best of her father.

"Come on," Reynard says. "It's just early enough to catch one still asleep."

He slings the rope across his shoulders, and they step together into the shadows.

Samuel Chapman's story "The Foaling Season" was published in Metaphorosis on Friday, 1 June 2018.

About the story

I came up with the world of Locksgrove during a worldbuilding exercise with friends. It's based on revolutionary Haiti, with Dominic L'Escalier a stand-in for Toussaint L'Overture. Reynard aux Chatillon was a later addition, partially based on Jiro Horikoshi, the Japanese aircraft engineer whose dilemma is chronicled in Hayao Miyazaki's film *The Wind Rises*.

Reynard and Jiro share the same central dilemma, one also faced by Albert Einstein--if you're brilliant at something, should you do it, regardless of the consequences? In addition to this, I wanted to use the meeting of history and fantasy to discuss questions of slavery, freedom, and politics. Does a nation have a morality? If so, what responsibilities do the people in it hold?

After Haiti successfully established the only nation of revolutionary former slaves, Thomas Jefferson, among others, advocated for an international boycott of Haitian trade--in order to discourage other oppressed populations from following in Haiti's path. For all his high rhetoric about the Tree of Liberty, Jefferson's loyalty was to the economy in the end.

At the opening of "The Foaling Season," Locksgrove is in a similar predicament. At the heart of it is the question of what the gryphons mean: they could be symbols, pets, companions, or dumb products to be merchandised out. L'Escalier doesn't believe Reynard has the luxury to think of them as anything but the latter. Reynard's daughter Aveline feels differently.

In the end, though, I knew that I wanted the story to affirm the status of the gryphons as actors with their own agency.

A question for the author

Q: What is your favourite short story?

A: "Night Meeting" by Ray Bradbury from The Martian Chronicles. Nothing much happens in it--just a guy driving to a party and meeting a Martian on the way. During their conversation, however, Earthling and Martian realize they cannot tell the difference between future and past, and that therefore the only thing we can count on is the beauty of the present. Bradbury uses simple images to immensely moving effect. The whole book is great, but this is the one I can read over and over.

Honorable mentions: "Seasons of Glass and Iron" by Amal El-Mohtar, "Idle Days on the Yann" by Lord Dunsany, "Oh, Whistle, and I'll Come to You, My Lad" by M.R. James.

About the author

Samuel Chapman was born in Minnesota and raised in Wales. He lives in Walla Walla, WA, where he writes novels and short stories, fences at a classical salle, and works in water rights. In past jobs he's been a land steward, tour guide, writing tutor, bookstore clerk, and crew on a tall ship.

www.samuelpchapman.wordpress.com, @samuelchapman93

The Little G-d of Łódź

Evan Marcroft

On September 6, 1939, a Rabbi and Kabbalist named Yitzchok Falk sets fire to the Great Synagogue of Łódź. "The Germans will burn it anyway," he tells his apprentice they drag a body out of the trunk of his car. "Let it burn without victims, and for a good reason." The boy, Max, who holds the feet, only nods.

They carry the body in and lay it out in the prayer hall. It is a young man near Max's thirteen years and fifty seven kilos, dressed in his clothes. He died of a broken neck, not of their doing, and was obtained at great cost. From his coat the rabbi produces a rag-corked bottle and a heavy black key, the latter of which he presses into his apprentice's hand. "Everything is yours now," he tells the boy. "Do with it what you will, if you will good. But your life has become a precious resource. Keep it from those who want it and give it to those who need it." His voice breaks under the weight of emotion. "Do not loathe those who loathe you. Just live, Max. We are Jews; we know dark times will pass."

Max buries the key in his fist, but only nods.

He stays long enough to help his adopted father start the fire, touching flame to the parched books in the study hall, dousing the holy ark in petrol. He finds that a Torah scroll smolders with the same smell as any other paper. He escapes as the flames begin to creep towards the rafters, leaving his master to his last act of charity. The gunshot is a raindrop amidst a downpour.

Max flies through cobbled streets until it is safe to stop and catch his breath. Only then does he crumple up and discard his master's final words. There is no room left in his heart for them, for with apologies it is already so full of bile and venom and *hate*.

The key opens the hidden lock of a secret room in his master's house. There, where by lamplight Rabbi Falk taught him of the sefirot and the boustrophedontic Folded Name of G-d, are kept many tomes of ancient Tradition. The *Sodei Razayya*, the *Sefer Yetzirah*, and others more arcane still, illuminated ledgers of demons and angels, books of power, all disguised cleverly in the bindings of Christian bibles. Max takes them all.

The Germans will roll over this place in a matter of days and pave everything, stone and knowledge alike, into a road going east. Same as the synagogue, which would have burned tomorrow if not today. In boot tread and tank tread they will track all that is *jude* across Poland until there is only dust left of it.

But Max knows well there is power in dust.

Seven months later, in the spring of 1940, Max has a new family. The rabbi, ever prescient, made the arrangements for him well before he falsified Max's death. He has a new name; rest in peace, Max Steinberg, and welcome back from abroad cousin Oskar Kac. His aunt and uncle are Monica and Dieter, his little blonde cousin Else, and they live together in a modest house in the Sródmiescie district. They are ethnic German— happily registered *Volksdeutsche*—and they are Christians. Max could not ask for a better place to hide.

It is easy to be Oskar the Christian. In some ways it is an easier life than Max the *judenschwein*. The facets of the faith are not so different from his own. A crucifix is not the worst thing that can be tied around one's neck. His false family are Jewish sympathizers, educated people, and they are very kind to him. They have made sure he is comfortable in their cellar and allow him to eat supper with them. Little Else in particular is a blessing. She is a dim but charming girl who is happy to help Max fill the empty hours when it is too risky to be outside.

And yes, his features are Aryan enough that he can even walk about in broad daylight, so long as he carries his forged papers like he would clutch shut an open wound.

Max may walk free, but he has not escaped the ghetto. Is he supposed to not hear it when the Orpo executes men and women in the streets, or smell the bodies strung up until they rot free of the rope? That pigpen between Inflancka and Drewnoska Street is where his kind is deemed to belong, and at all times he feels its subtle gravity threatening to draw him in if he is not absolutely vigilant.

Yet he is there, watching from the crowd, as the wall is put up around the ghetto. The barrier is a flimsy thing, green wood garnished with barbed wire. The weight of all the bodies behind it would easily bowl it over. And why don't they? There must be thousands of them cramped into a tenth as many rooms turned cells. A universe of yellow stars. The few Germans who strut to and fro outside the fence would be drowned in them.

But those hot, fresh first days where anything could still have happened mature into weeks. More Jews are shipped in from outside the city and poured into the ghetto. What keeps it from rupturing like a full bladder, Max does not know—the Germans are geniuses in the science of cruelty. And still, he watches its occupants shuffle a little closer together, tromping in their own overflowing feces, making room.

They do not fear the *Nazis*, he has come to believe.

Not as much as they fear their sharp-edged *eye*. The eye that flutters from every storefront, that lolls from every shattered window. Bloodshot, lidless, its pupil a black windmill slashed into a cataracted iris, glowering over all. When the Orpo is gone, the eye observes. They call it the *Hakenkreuz*, though Max knows of many other names. The symbol came from somewhere in the Orient. India perhaps. It had meant only good things once, to many peoples, but the Germans can corrupt even the intangible, bend good to the work of evil.

In their hands it has become a lens for something to peer balefully through. Something that loathes the Jew and gluts on their suffering. Max knows not what name to call the entity. But whenever its indentured eye meets his, Max refuses to look away. Does the thing behind the *swastika* see the truth of him? Let it. Those trapped in the ghetto may be powerless before it, but he is not.

He has dirt, and a word.

In the cellar of the Kac house, Max is making a golem.

For the last several months he has scavenged and saved to purchase its components: Lengths of stiff wire, for structure; basic sculpting tools; eighty kilograms of clay in blocks. Concealing it all from the Kacs was a chore. Sculpting it by hand, by himself, in a night, is even harder.

Max misses the old rabbi sorely. This task is too much for just him. His hands know the way, but his father's had been there and back. Max is only fourteen. Too young to be alone.

Still, grueling hours transform the mound of wet clay into an approximation of the human form. Its eyes are featureless bulbs, its mouth a gash. No nose or ears. His creation is smaller than he anticipated it would be;

nearly two and a half meters tall but thin as a skeleton, its skull an oblong club. Max would have preferred to whittle it mighty and broad from the riverbank as Rabbi Loew did, but the curfew made that so dangerous as to be impossible. Its strength will have little to do with such trivia as mass and proportion.

Max stands over his work and sponges the sweat from his neck and brow. *My Adam*, he thinks, with pride. For was mankind not born through a similar art, cut out of the stuff of the earth?

For an hour Max circles his creation, whispering a string of names that scorch his tongue to pronounce, draping the golem in veils of meaning. Next he draws purified water from an urn and ladles it up and down the golem's chest. Wherever it trickles, the clay takes on the oily sheen of living skin. He strikes a match, holds it to the golem's feet until its soles are chapped and cracked as an old man's. Lastly, Max crouches over the golem and breathes into its dent of a mouth. His heart accelerates as its chest rises atop imaginary lungs.

Earth, water, fire, and air. There is only one thing left.

There is one thing Max did not prepare in advance, lest it slip into irreverent hands. On a slip of torn paper no larger than his thumb, he writes a shem—a Name of G-d.

He folds it in two, gigs it with a pin, and tacks it to the floor of the golem's mouth.

Eyes of solid clay snap open.

Max retreats into the corner as the golem climbs onto its feet. The hump of its scalp scrapes against the floorboards overhead. Overlarge hands swing limply at its sides. It is a mottled thing; red clay in places, ruddy flesh in others. Fingernails have sprouted on one hand, but the tip of its phallus has already broken off. It is imperfect, yes. And glorious as salvation always is.

Max would cry out, if it would not wake his family.

"Can you speak?" Max asks in Hebrew.

The golem shakes its head.

"Do you have knowledge?"

The golem nods.

"I have created you. Will you serve me?"

The golem nods again.

Max unfolds a photograph from his trouser pocket. "This man is *Hauptmann* Rudolf Pancke. He is an evil man: he has murdered many children of Israel for no crime. He profits from the theft of their possessions. Kill him, tonight, wherever he is."

The golem nods a third time. It does not look at the photograph.

"Men will try to stop you," Max adds. "If they are not Jews, kill them as well. When you are finished, do not return here—destroy yourself, or at least the shem in your mouth. Do you understand?"

The golem is already leaving.

The following morning Max swallows his exhaustion and requests to accompany the Kacs on their shopping. While Else is fitted for a new church dress and Mrs. Kac collects the week's groceries, Max cocks an ear to the gossip running wild up and down Piotrkowska Street.

Not four hours past, Rudolf Pancke was discovered murdered in his home, his throat crumpled as though by a vice, face black with trapped blood. His wife Gertrude was dead as well, her forehead flattened against their stovetop. Whoever attacked them tore their door of its hinges and took five bullets from Pancke's sidearm without leaving a drop of blood.

Max had been expecting to feel happy. Vindicated.

Instead, he feels hungry

A Jew must be the culprit of course. A rare brute of higher cunning than his breed, escaped from the ghetto with slaughter on the mind. Or perhaps one who had evaded being swept up with the rest of them, for despite assurances, there are surely many still skulking under floorboards like rats. Over the following days, Max watches the Orpo presence around the ghetto increase dramatically, In a show of force, they drag ten young men from their homes and execute them on the blackened steps of what had been the old Stara Synagogue. Those deaths are his fault as well. Max accepts that and moves on. They were dead long before he killed them.

With every new invader he sees on the street corner, he feels more powerful. They are war now, because of *him*. *Their* lives are in *his* hands.

But the same time, each reminds Max of just how many Germans there are in Łódź. Months of caution and preparation, a bucket of sweat, for only one head. Two, if he counts the wife.

He wants more. But how to begin? Where does one bite first to devour a mountain? This problem keeps him awake through humid nights. Max is starving with too much on his plate, from the patrolling officers who inflict a thousand little brutalities along their route, to that quisling Rumkowski who runs the ghetto in the German's stead. Who would be worth the time and risk, the blind retaliation? Of course he could simply knock down the walls of the ghetto, but that would hardly be productive. Animals escaped from the zoo are most often just shot.

Although he frets, he does not fear, for he knows his cause is just. In the darkened sky above the ghetto he has beheld the archangel Metatron, the right hand of G-d, with an aureole of flaming eyes about his brow and wings of gold forty thousand cubits in span. None but Max can see him—no, they merely duck under awnings and complain of the rain. Oh, if only the prisoners there could feel the hem of his alabaster robe pooled about their feet, they would know hope, for he who led the Israelites from Egypt has now come to Łódź. In one hand he holds a sword of smithied lightning, crackling and spitting; the other is pointed down in scorn at the ghetto administration headquarters.

The heavenly scribe speaks not a word, but its message is evident.

It is Else, of all people, who provides Max the breakthrough he needs. She has a little cloth doll named Odie, whom she carries with her everywhere. While playing one afternoon, a thread in Odie's leg catches on a jutting nail and tears beyond repair. She is distraught, until her mother sews the doll a new leg from an old paisley headscarf. Else sees happy enough with the result, not minding the incongruous limbs. The doll is still a doll. One material is as good as another.

How far might that principle travel before it broke down?

Golems have historically been exclusively from clay, for two reasons. The first is practicality: they have to be wrought from earth, and clay is easy to shape. The second is tradition; it has been done that way since the time of the rabbi Rava. But Max suspects now that this way of thinking has stunted the possibility of the golem. It is the twentieth century now; the world is wider and vastly deeper than it was.

Rabbi Falk taught him more than the Kabbalah in the years they'd had together. Max was better with letters and numbers than most his age, though his aptitudes were science and history. For instance, he knew that some thirty-five years ago a German Jew named Einstein proved the ancient theory that all creation is composed of invisibly small particles— particles that logically can then be rearranged to construct whatever one likes. It seemed to Max that if one were to examine any two items on a small enough scale, they would essentially be the same amalgamation of substances.

In that realm where atoms are the size of planets, everything is dirt.

Through the summer and autumn of 1940, Max sets out to make golems from everything.

Very quickly he proves his theory true. A man made of branches and twine takes little time and less artistic finesse than clay, and, as he discovers, animates nearly as well. When imbued with a name of G-d, a brace of twigs will crack and twist into a hand of five functional fingers. Knots will blink and suddenly be eyes, and hoary bark will sprout goosebumps in the cold. And most importantly, though at its thickest it may be no bigger around than his calf, it will possess the strength to crumble a brick in one fist.

With this first success to whet his appetite, Max attacks the subject with renewed fervor. He finds that it is easier to smuggle other materials into his room than clay, especially via the cellar's small window overlooking a strip of weeds beside the house.

From the moment the Kacs go to bed, Max toils at innovating the concept of the golem. Wood works well, as does sacking, and especially metal. Over the course of two sweltering nights in late August he patches together a child-sized thing of scrap pilfered from a garbage heap near the factory where the Germans have put the Jews to work. Although its gait is ungainly, its pipe neck inflexible, it handily eviscerates an Orpo captain with fingers of serrated steel, leaving him to be found in an alley the next morning.

That is good; two nights is not. Max can do better.

He finds efficiency in hybridism. Clay is ideal flesh, but sticks will function as limbs, and anything will serve for a head. With each golem the time and energy needed to acquire its pieces shrinks. What helps, Max finds, is to inscribe the shem directly on the skin of the golem, as not every one can have a mouth. It seems to provide them with a shade more humanity—broader swathes of flesh, more articulate digits—than his previous method.

Some turn out laughable, jiggumbob men with old kettles for heads, clopping about on wooden clogs. But function supersedes aesthetics. Broom-handle legs, knives for fingers, rags stuffed with rags for feet—all perfectly lethal. Night after night he sends them out with a name and a mission, infesting the shadows of Łódź with scuttling, clanking deaths wrought of its own matter. Max feels unfettered, a renegade genius in his field. What *else* had others not dared to attempt? He wonders how *small* a golem could be, how sneaking and insidious. Could a shem be written with a needle? A hair?

He wonders how *immense* as well.

He wonders that often.

Not every golem is successful. Some are destroyed by happenstance; an incidental scratch can obliterate a shem. And it was inevitable that one would be caught in the act or fail by some unforeseeable chance. On the night of October 12th, a Gestapo officer bursts into his headquarters with an arm lacerated in a thousand places, gabbling about shear-handed scarecrows. They public thinks him mad, but a month later, a boneless poppet made of a straw-stuffed Polish uniform is speared in the headlights of a truck full of German soldiers. A hail of gunfire blasts it to tatters, but whispers of it spread like fleas off a rat.

Golem. Max begins to hear the word from other lips.

Else asks what it means one evening as the family takes its supper. Max must feign disinterest. A golem, Mister Kac explains, in that tone fathers use to shrink adult concepts into child ones, is a big man made from clay and a magic word. It is a way for powerless people to become powerful. The legend goes that a Jewish holy man in a city called Prague created one to protect his people from their enemies. But although the golem was strong and fearless, it one day went mad and became a danger to everyone. So remember, Else, that sometimes the answer is worse than the problem.

Over the course of weeks, the Germans clamp tight about the city. They begin to move in larger groups. They publically scoff at the notion of a clay man murdering by night, but the streets start to empty themselves a little earlier come nightfall. Perhaps they, of all people, believe in some small way.

They think caution and numbers will make them safe. Max is overjoyed to prove them wrong, when at three in the afternoon on January the first, the devil Biebow himself is throttled dead in the warmth of his own office.

On the morning of February 3rd, Max lurks in the crowd outside the ghetto wall as the Germans begin to take the Jews away.

He had been hearing talk of Extreme Measures to be taken. There is no longer doubt that a Jew has been behind the murders, by means mundane or supernatural. Rather than root him out amongst many thousands, they're simply going to relocate the lot.

Day by day, trucks come and go carrying them away family by family. He hears word that they are to be moved by train to a place in the south called Auschwitz. How long the process will take remains uncertain, what with the logistics of it, and the war. Max feels a thin satisfaction. It isn't much, but it's something. He pushed, and the world stumbled. Only G-d knows what he can do if he only pushes a little harder.

Max returns home electrified with purpose, only to find a Nazi at the door.

He spots the man first and hangs back across the street. The officer is speaking with Mrs. Kac; he cannot hear what they are saying, but she doesn't seem afraid. After a time he nods goodbye and moves on to the next house in the row. He is going door to door looking for anything suspicious, not Max in particular.

But the demon that follows him is.

It rides naked upon a camel, a drooping animal harried by flies and striped with the shadows of its own ribs. Its head is a horse's lolling painfully upon its neck. In one hand it brandishes a golden scepter. Upon its brow is a flaming crown. Max goes absolutely still as its gaze sweeps down the street and over him without stopping. The officer keeps walking, and the demon canters after, unseen by all.

Max flees, but he sees now that the mazzikim have overrun the city. They skulk in the shadows of German officers, or ride upon their shoulders, tugging at the barbed reins of their fearful hatred. Toothless crones parade nude upon the backs of crocodiles; a mitered raven goose-steps before its host on ape-like hands; a fiery hakenkreuz of lion's paws rolls by, trailing a brimstone stink. More perch upon the rooftops and chimneys, terrors too real for Bosch's hell caterwauling in a tongue of lies and blasphemy.

These are the emissaries of the thing behind the swastika, for indeed those spirits that have the arms for it wear upon them a sash bearing its symbol. Far too late, Max understands the enormity of what he has antagonized.

The swastika is the eye of a god.

This is the most blasphemous thought he can have, but even so. Yes, a god, one unknown to the Patriarchs who articulated The Lord as the solitary power in the universe, for men know only what they can perceive, and though they knew great suffering, who among those ancient fathers could have even conceived of the unholy miracle that is the Reich? That ancient symbol of goodness, itself enslaved by Germans, has unwillingly become the aspect of an Anti-G-d, its beneficent meaning corrupted into domination and extermination. And just as G-d once tasked the Israelites with proclaiming his laws, so too did this evil counterpart uplift a nation of wolves and saddle its own chosen people with a covenant to become the world, devour the Jew.

Max returns home as calmly as he can, pretending he can't see what he sees. In the safety of his cellar he strips to the waist and pens upon his own body the names of G-d and other psalms of protection. The Evil G-d walks the streets of Łódź but does not recognize him as its prey. Forget the pretensions of dead mystics—only The Lord itself protects him now. *My Lord*, he prays, *hide me from the sight of my enemies. I only need a little more time.*

Max is a fugitive in a city he once strolled as a king.

He dreads now to leave his shelter, even with the nomenclature of G-d scrawled upon his chest. It is difficult to see the people anymore for the demons that caper among them. *They* are more real now than the men they orbit, and he must always pretend that he is blind to them. He no longer visits the ghetto, for that is where they congregate most thickly. And though he may creep about beneath their noses, he knows he is as pungent, as savory, a Jew as any other. *G-d's protection cannot falter*, Max assures himself with every spare thought.

But if it did...

He spends every moment preparing for the end, maximizing the reward for the risk that is living. From everything he can scrounge he breeds golems—dog-sized, hand-sized, lopsided, crippled by haste. These he stows in the crevices of the city, in trash bins and ditches disguised as rubbish, until the time comes when they will be summoned to their purpose.

The wreckage of the Great Synagogue yet lies where it fell. *The rabbi's grave*, Max supposes numbly, but he has not been coming for that reason. The Germans have not yet cleared the rubble away. What would they do with the plot? They did not come to Łódź to build. The pliable ground has begun to digest the old, charred stone. If Max stands in a certain spot, tilts his head just so, he can conjure patterns from the scree as one may invent faces in clouds. A heap of brick and mud becomes a protrudent knee; a grove of burnt rafters, a brace of ribs. What is the plot, he thinks, but the face of a block of clay from which anything can be cut?

Hidden in a slit in his mattress is a bundle of papers—sketches of an idea that has consumed his thoughts like a parasite. Diagrams in smudged charcoal arguing weight and pressure and balance, jottings on cost and time required. Discarded notions clutter the margins. Numbers smear into drawings—a Vitruvian man fully eight feet tall, yet no more than a reference point to the giant that stands beside him.

It can be done, Max has determined. He is only lacking in manpower, and he will not lack that for long. His mind is a furnace fueled by tradition.

Why could a golem not be tasked to build a golem? All he needs is a little more time.

He has little idea of how many will be needed so he works like a madman, shredding this throat with the names of G-d. He avoids the near certainty that anything will not be enough, that he will never be ready. Once he begins his work, the Anti-G-d will know and try to stop him. But no matter what Max will fight it, until either he is dead or is his fist is big enough to crush it like a grape.

On the morning of February 17th, 1941, Max awakens to a door banging open upstairs. It could be Mister Kac leaving for work, but it isn't. He is out of bed and running before he hears the first barked words of German. Barefoot and naked to the waist, he scrabbles up the wall and through the unlatched window. He does not see the pair of oily black boots waiting for him outside.

They take him by the wrists and drag him onto the grass. He is struck once in the mouth, and bits of his teeth spill everywhere. A heel stabs into his belly, and Max vomits blood and food across his face and chest. The swastika upon the officer's arm seems to wink at him, as that arm coils back, storing power. Through the haze of pain, he can see Mister and Missus Kac watching from the kitchen window, clutching each other.

The demons riding the Kacs laugh and point and yank on their bridles.

The world whirls on a broken axle around Max as one of the officers heaves him over his shoulder. As they carry him out into the street Max glimpses neighbors and passers-by watching in sick-faced silence. The Germans' idling truck lurches briefly into view through the crook of the officer's arm and Max understands that he is going into the ghetto like slop into a pig's trough, to fester and be devoured.

Through a mouth full of broken teeth, Max screams.

The truck's rear door swings open; the unwashed interior reeks of blood and bile. Max screams again—*anyone, please*—wringing his lungs out like sponges of terror, as they hurl him inside.

The two officers linger there, gloating over him. There is nothing left to lose now—it is struggle or die. Max kicks out, stomping his foot into the closest groin. The man bends double, cursing in German.

"*Verdammter jüdischer Bastard—*"

Max scrabbles onto his hands and feet to run for it, only to run up against the snout of the other officer's sidearm.

"Das ist es, was du bekommst, wenn du so nah stehst."

"Schieße schon die kleine Ratte ab."

"Ganz gut."

And as he turns to Max to fix his aim a blur of rag and metal drops from above and takes his hand off at the wrist.

"Was zum teufel ist—" the other blurts, scrambling for his pistol, but then the golem is upon him to, its knife-hands strobing with speed. The officer goes down shrieking, his skin coming away in peels. The survivor tries to run, but the golem is fleet as a fox upon its broomstick legs. In broad daylight, for the whole street to see, it slices the heels out from under him and efficiently disassembles him.

Max crawls from the truck to meet it. A dwarf of cotton-stuffed curtain with a pail for a head, it stares up at him through hole-punched eyes, gormlessly awaiting the next command. Max looks all around at the crowd retreating in fear from him—women clutching their children, men, clutching their wives—and at the cacophonic throng of demons baying for his blood from every rooftop and lamppost perch. They can certainly see him *now*, Max thinks. There will be no restoring that veil.

Max's heart begins to pound in his ears like a war drum. This is the moment, he realizes—the end whose approaching shadow chilled him awake through so many endless nights. He had worked so hard to hold it at bay but now it is here, and he is in it, and there is nothing to be done but embrace it.

Max had dreamed once of deific heights. Of crossing the land upon a colossus of his own creation, stepping between towns as one would stepping stones, and obliterating Germans with as little thought as he'd give ants. He had fantasized of trampling over Berlin and palming the *Reichskanzlei* into the dirt. Perhaps that had been too much to hope for—the whimsy of a little boy.

So be it. He shall become a man then.

What can be done with a giant can be done with a horde.

As Max marches through the snowy streets of Łódź, the golems he seeded the city with answer his summons. Tall, small, hodge-podge and whole cloth, they awake from their spider-holes and join his ever-growing procession. Some are mere spiders skittering along on sewing-needle legs, others monkey along on cork knuckles, on strong rebar bones. They are the matter of the city itself risen up to fight beside him, Max now understands. He never needed a colossus, no—the greatest champion he could possibly construct would be an insect beside the totality of Łódź.

People run screaming wherever he passes, their infernal jockeys hauling futilely on their bridles. Flocks of demons hurl abuse from the rooftops but they dare not stand against him. Delirious with pain, dripping blood with every step, Max feels stronger than ever before, a beast loosed from a too-small cage and free at last to stretch its claws.

No more cowering in a cellar. No more pretending to be what he is not. *No more fear.*

Those Orpo officers that blunder into his path find themselves torn apart by the horde. The golems carpet Max's cobbled path in glistening red. No, Max need never have hid. The Germans have nothing like this power. When Max looks to the murky heavens, he sees the Heavenly Scribe suspended there once more, the tip of his fulgurant sword blazing like a star above the ghetto. Yes, my Lord, Max thinks, his heart bursting with elation. He weeps, for his purpose has never been so blindingly bright. He is to be as Moses and take his people away from this forsaken land. He will teach them to make golems, and together they will raise the world itself into an army, G-d's final commitment writ across a billion clay brows. All land will be as the promised land, and milk and honey will flow forever more.

Yes, my lord, I understand and obey.
I will lead the last exodus.

When Max and his legion arrive at the edge of the ghetto he finds the Orpo waiting. A barricade of soldiers levels its weapons at his ranks of teeter-tottering scarecrow men. "Halt," the officer barks across the stretch of emptied street between them. *"Ergebe dich sofort!"*

Max sneers at the naked terror in the officer's voice. The Germans have placed their faith in the power to destroy human flesh, the most frail substance in creation. Max bids his army advance, and as one ramified limb the golems go bounding through the snow. A chorus of rifles retorts but it is like shooting at nothing; bullets pass harmlessly through dining cloth skin, ricochet off of candelabra claws. Some catch in interstitial physiology, where Łódź-matter has imperfectly become meat, but the golems are only sporadically filled with blood to shed. They crash into the German rampart and smash it instantly into panicked rubble. These soldiers have never expected to kill anything other than men; to shoot at a thing and for it to still live is a contradiction in their reality.

One by one, the soldiers fall and die. Soon there is only a wall garnished in barbed wire and a small, steaming aftermath. Many of his golems lay in pieces, overwhelmed at last by force of arms, but no matter— Max bids the remainder tear dear down the wall. Limping, bleeding, he steps into the ghetto for the first time.

Max expected celebration. His people flooding into the streets to welcome their liberating son returned. He expected anything.

But silence.

Each step he takes through the crunching snow echoes between looming tenements like a gunshot. The street for as far as he can see is marked by neither footprints or wheel tracks. Max cups his hands around his lips and hurls his voice as far as it will travel. A minute passes with no answer.

He is too late. His people, down to the children, have all been taken away. To Auschwitz, yes, but not to be resettled. He understands that now. Only ghosts still walk these streets—not the souls of the dead but those who will die when their train reaches its destination, for the tragedies of the future weigh like disappointment on the present. When Max closes his eyes he sees thousands of men and women, boys and girls, babies crawling, all gusting south, towards bullets still in their casings, graves yet to be dug.

He balls his fists, sobs tears and snot and blood. For all his power he cannot even save that many. How many millions more are steaming even now towards Auschwitz? How many more are already beyond him? Beyond salvation?

His ears prick at the growling of a distant engine. He turns, wiping his mouth—a German truck is fast approaching, barreling through the hole in the ghetto perimeter. Its wheels catch lagging golems and crush them to splinters; more are obliterated against its rusted steel scowl. A figure leans out the passenger's window and lets out a sound like cracking river ice. An invisible fist strikes Max in the belly and knocks him onto his haunches.

The urge to *survive* puppets him quickly onto his feet. Max screams a command, and those golems he has left throw themselves upon the truck. As they stave in its windows and climb inside, it swerves hard to the left, stopping dead against the wall of someone's house. Orpo officers spill out the back, taking the butts of their weapons to the fragile golems—swinging, smashing, stomping, hammering the holy names of G-d into the ground.

Max screams again—*Kill them!*—but what use? The golems that can already are, and the rest…

Max watches his army crumbles before his eyes.

All that he can do, is skirt the confusion and flee the way he came.

Max is going to die. The bullet shattered all his illusions on impact. He can feel it—the bullet G-d could have caught, but didn't—rolling in his guts. Growing, it seems, like a venomous pregnancy. He caps the wound with his hand, but still he leaves a trail of bright red breadcrumbs behind him as he flees the ghetto.

But still he runs, lurching through the crooked back alleys of Lodz, a hunted animal, a hunted animal pushing inevitability as far as it will stretch for it violently snaps back. Max squints blurring eyes at the overcast sky, begging the Heavenly Scribe for an answer, but Metatron is nowhere to be seen. *I'm sorry*, he silently pleads, but a soul's volume of contrition does not fill the heavens with angel feathers.

Max runs and stumbles and retches blood until somehow he arrives at the lot where the Great Synagogue once stood. Where the rabbi sacrificed himself to let Max live a little longer. The blackened stoop is the only whole piece left. As good a gravestone as the man will get.

Max stops to comb his fingers through its blanket of snow. *I am sorry to you as well, father. I could not live the way you wanted. I was too strong to live peacefully and too weak to succeed.*

What a fool—what a little boy I've been.

Max drags himself across the lot where he'd once dreamed idiotically of raising his champion. Flattened by snow, the distance seems infinite. How much further must he walk to escape the Germans? Much further than Łódź, he is certain. Paris fell before them long ago. He has heard that they have been bombing London every night for months, a dog worrying down a bone. Not even distant Africa is free of them, and that is almost the whole world. Max could walk for forty years and never find a place not branded flat and white by the swastika.

The dark times the rabbi spoke of will not pass. There have never been other times, only exodus, the flight from one boot-heel to another. One day, they will not even have that. In one year or ten the children of Israel will be extinct. The voice tasked with exulting G-d will be silenced forever. Max cannot see how it could be otherwise, for there is no Promised Land left to run to. Warding their homes with lamb's blood would only attract wolves.

When G-d's chosen people are gone, what good is his world?

Max goes rigid in the grip of revelation.

There is something more that he can do.

He still has his hands.

He still has dirt.

Yes.

An entire world of it.

Max falls to his knees and digs through the snow until he reaches the hard-packed dirt beneath. His fingers are blue by the time he is done shaping a lump of it into a doll-sized homunculus. For water he rubs snow between his hands until it trickles across the golem's chest. For fire he cups blood from his belly and bastes it with his body's dwindling heat. With a torn thumb-nail he gifts it a name of G-d.

The golem, half-flesh and half-earth, tears free of the ground and blinks at him with pinhole eyes, waiting for a command.

Why could a golem not be tasked to build a golem?
"Adam," Max whispers.

In that realm where atoms are the size of planets—

The golem nods.

—everything is dirt.

Max crouches over it, enunciating so that his words are not stolen by the wind. "You will create for yourself a companion as I have created you, as small as you can. You will inscribe upon them the name of G-d that I have inscribed upon you. You will command it as I command you, and then you will begin again. I command you and your progeny to be fruitful and multiply, to fill the earth and subdue it. I command you to wash away all that is touched by evil upon this world and to live virtuously thereafter. Do you understand?"

The golem is already at work

Max deflates into the snow to watch the golem sculpt a still more miniature version of itself and brings it to life. His eyes grow heavy as that golem immediately begin to reproduce itself in turn, eking fire from the friction of its earthen hands, while the original gathers soil together to start again. *Two times two is four,* Max thinks, slipping into a warm bed of snow. *Just as you taught me, father. Four times two is eight. Eight times two is sixteen. A billion times two is...*

Each golem is born in half the time of the one before, and is half the size. In less than an hour they are too small to be seen with the eye and as plentiful as the stars. With his last flicker of consciousness, Max watches grass and stone melt into the same dun-red as the earth, sees that voracious color rip through the snow like a dye through water. In that micro-plane where all is dirt, golems smaller than cell shave away the scar left by the Anti-G-d, rebuilding debased soil from the atoms up into fertile earth.

Into themselves.

The last thing that Max thinks before the golems reach him is, *it will be good.* The long suffering of man is at an end. Even awake he will feel nothing as they take him with absolute kindness, as they will all things, their trickle soon to be a flood enough to drown a planet. All souls, wicked and good, will go without pain into their common grave and be at peace. This fatally wounded creation will be *un*created, licked flat and clean by loving waves, restored at last to innocence. The anti-G-d will perish along with this world, and the next one will be better.

Its new people will be happy.

Max dies with a smile, and becomes them.

Evan Marcroft's story "The Little G-d of Łódź" was published in Metaphorosis on Friday, 2 November 2018.

About the story

This story came out of two weird bellies.

It was born initially out of a long-standing fascination with the difference between a good ending and a happy ending. A happy ending, in my definition, is one where conflicts are resolved in a way that is satisfying to the reader. The prince slays the dragon, the robot wins his freedom, etc. Everything is alright, and we feel good for having watched it happen. A good ending in my definition, however, is an ending that is satisfying to the protagonist, regardless of how that makes us feel. In my writing, I tend to care more about the protagonist than those reading about them. This story began in my mind at the end, which I saw as happy only in the unique mind of its hero and apocalyptic to everyone else. The hero dies. Every one else dies. The bad guys win. The world ends. Nonetheless, the protagonist's goal is fully accomplished, and I think we can all be glad for him. We're here for our heroes, after all, not the other way around. Our function as readers is to propel their adventure through our observation, and to presume that a character struggles for our entertainment is the height of arrogance, now isn't it?

This story was born secondly from my rejection of what I view as the 'customary' lessons of sci-fi and fantasy. I've read infinite stories where insurmountable obstacles are defeated by some combination of effort, bravery, love, trickery, imagination, and ballsiness. While it is nice to step briefly into a word where that happens, I've never found this to be reflective of reality, where oftentimes objectively small obstacles defeat towering heroes for all their trying. With this story I wanted to propose an alternate but equally valid message: that A.) sometimes no matter what you do you will fail, and B.) even complete failure can be overcome. The moral that built this story around itself is that defeat is not an outcome but a state of being escapable by operating outside of the context in which it occurs. When you lose at a game, flip the table. When the bad guys take over the world, blow the world up.

Also, the idea of a golem-based Gray Goo scenario is just plain cool. I think we can all agree on that at least.

A question for the author

Q: Have you ever wondered whether ideas are thought waves directed at you by an AI supercomputer located in the distant future?

A: I can't say I have, until now at least. Supposing that's true, I can't help but wonder if we're a form of story-telling to them. If our brain activity is directed by intellects beyond our observation, if what we say and how we respond to it is all decided by some other entity, if what we dream and what we do to pursue those dreams is decided by any amount of authorities at least one less than our eight billion, then are we not like characters in some vast story called Earth Circa 2018? I imagine those supercomputers tuning in to some time-piercing TV program to see how this million-year narrative is progressing, what plot twists are unwinding in this eleventy-billionth episode of Mankind. I picture a fair number of fans writing the producers complaining about plot holes and melodrama beloved characters dying unfairly. If that's the case then I guess I hope that I've got someone funny writing the character of me, because if I'm going to be just one mindless side character out of billions with no agency or free will of my own, then I at least want to have some good lines.

About the author

Evan Marcroft is a half-blind yeti-person with a sideways foot and an allergy to the sun. When he was a child he dreamed of writing important works of Earth-shaking beauty and settled for writing fantasy and science fiction instead. He currently lives in Sacramento California with a cat and a loving wife who foolishly believes he'll someday make real money doing this.

You can reach him on Twitter at @Evan_Marcroft and contact him for any reason at Evanmarcroft@hotmail.com.

Of Hair and Beanstalks

William Condon

25 December, being the Birth-day of Isaac Newton, Physicist:

Madam,
 Your stepdaughter has arrived and been installed in the tower chamber, per your instructions. This has already led to the predicted difficulties, as my dinosaurian bulk cannot fit within the narrow tower. When she refused to descend for supper this evening, I was reduced to flying outside her window and poking my face in.
 I found her combing her long hair, which raises my second concern: while I am ill-acquainted with human customs, your instructions to periodically observe her appear to overstep the bounds of propriety. However, as you are not only her stepmother but a human noblelady yourself, I shall bow to your procedural knowledge.
 Most dutifully,
 ANTRODEMOS, Dinosaur.

27 December, being the Birth-day of Johannes Kepler, Astronomer and loyal adviser to his king:

Madam,

While narrative is not my strength, as you have requested to hear the particulars of your stepdaughter's arrival, I shall attempt to recount them.

Her coach arrived shortly after the morning sun had burnt off the frost. It came as you described sending it: by the usual road, locked from the outside, and surrounded by six bodyguards. Upon the door's being unlatched in the courtyard of my castle, your stepdaughter disembarked with a sigh and addressed me in a despairing voice, "Mister Dragon, did Gothel send me here for you to eat me?"

I at once corrected her that (a) I am not a dragon but a dinosaur, for "dragon" is a word used in unreliable peasants' tales while "dinosaur" is a rigorous term used by modern scientists (and I know no more precise term of matching rigor that would correctly describe me); and (b) I do not eat humans.

She took these corrections with the dubious air I have observed from too many other persons, even in the nearby village. But, addressing me correctly as "dinosaur," she inquired of the conditions under which she was to live here. I replied with your specifications, to wit, that I was to "keep an eye on that Rapunzel every couple of hours, at least, to make sure she's not planning to escape or see any strange men – not that there're any wandering princes around your tower."

Although she appeared accepting in my presence, she was apparently unaware of my excellent dinosaurian hearing, for I later overheard her sobbing in her tower chamber.

Most dutifully,
ANTRODEMOS, Dinosaur.

1 January, being the Commemoration of Julius Caesar and Sosigenes Alexandris, Calendarists, who were sadly forced to give up Science for politics:

Madam,

Your stepdaughter intruded upon my workshop this morning while I was about a most delicate experiment. When I explained as much and ordered her to depart, she pertly replied that as I had been "peering at" her all week, she had rights to do the same to me. I replied that you had appointed me to supervise her. She refused response save to appropriate one of my human-sized chairs and say I "might as well continue."

Since forcibly removing her would be a greater disruption to the experiment than tolerating her presence, I did continue. However, I fear my measurement of the gases emitted is imprecise, since my attention was repeatedly distracted by your stepdaughter's fidgeting. I shall have to obtain further phosphates — and while that will not be hard, I fear what would result if she repeats this during next month's planned analysis of platinum, a rare and expensive metal from distant lands.

Fortunately, further interference was forestalled by the arrival of one of the local delivery-boys. I was (or, more precisely, my servants were) pleased to obtain further preserved vegetables and fresh milk; the boy also brought the soil samples I had requested from his farm. (A vascular stem plant of highly unusual height had grown there the previous autumn; I was unfortunately unable to study it before it was cut down and burnt.) It is fortunate there is no snow in this locale as there is farther north; that would greatly impede this sampling. Your stepdaughter, to my great satisfaction, remained in the courtyard for the rest of the morning.

Most dutifully,
ANTRODEMOS, Dinosaur.

2 January, being the Birth-day of Johann Titius, Astronomer and Taxonomist:

Madam,

As you have demanded an immediate response, I write in haste.

Your stepdaughter indeed remained in the company of Jack, the delivery-boy, for between one and two hours before (the gatekeeper reports) he expressed a need to return to his farm.

Being personally unaware of his reputation in our environs, I asked the castle cooks. They were at first unwilling to tell me, but finally reported that his name is Jack, his father died approximately two years ago, and he currently keeps farm with his mother (named Mildred). While his reputation has been besmirched with accusations of laziness and poor financial dealings, he has recently come into money and has hired hands to perform delayed maintenance on the farm. Further, he has always been acknowledged for his courage.

I regret that I cannot add to this testimony personally. Most of the neighboring farmers are frightened to speak with a dinosaur such as myself, no matter how often I reassure them I am not a dragon. Perhaps it would help if I introduced myself by a more precise taxonomic term than "dinosaur"? Sadly, I cannot tell which genus of dinosaur I would best be categorized under. None of the published descriptions of specific dinosaur genera fit me well, the Academy has not answered my letters asking for clarification, and I hesitate to create a new term by myself. In the meantime, the local farmers and villagers remain unacquainted with the delights of Science, and I am forced to interview my reluctant servants about Jack's reputation.

Regardless, I reassure you I have indeed been periodically inspecting your stepdaughter's room, as instructed. The customs of human nobility are difficult to understand, but as your castellan, I will comply and (I hope) eventually comprehend.

Most dutifully,
ANTRODEMOS, Dinosaur.

5 January, being the Birth-day of Xu Xiake, Geographer:

Madam,

I indeed agree that (even from my limited knowledge) Master Jack seems an ill match for your stepdaughter. However, might it not be an overreaction to forbid her from seeing any young men? Does not understanding come from experiment? Still, as I know some experiments bear overly high risks, I will comply.

Be that as it may, I roundly rejected her proposal of yesterday to hold "a dance, or a feast, or at least something" in honor of Twelfth Night as a frivolous gaiety which would distract from Science. "But you're a dragon," she replied. "Dragons might be that glum, but I'm not!" I again corrected her that I am a dinosaur, and invited her to join me in the mysteries of experimentation. Instead, she left for her tower, and I have not seen her since (save through the window, as per your instructions.)

Master Jack will next be coming on the ninth, as per his normal schedule.

Most dutifully,
ANTRODEMOS, Dinosaur.

10 January, being the Anniversary of Thomas Savery's inventing a smooth paddle-wheel:

Madam,

As your stepdaughter has continued protesting boredom, I decided to commemorate the date by a lecture on fluid dynamics. Sadly, despite my best attempts, both she and the castle servants appeared impatient. Finally, amid a discussion of the specific gravity of common air over different temperatures, she interrupted, "Can we use that paddle-wheel? Go boating?"

Taken aback, I protested the local stream was much too small — but I could demonstrate another invention of Captain Savery's: an engine powered by steam. She immediately agreed, and the visibly-curious servants helped us assemble the needed vessels and tubes. I lit the fire with my dinosaurian breath, and we watched the engine spurt water across the courtyard. It was a simple demonstration, but they seemed surprisingly engrossed.

Just after I had increased the fire (again at your stepdaughter's urging) and the engine started squirting water over the castle wall, Master Jack arrived bearing food. Your stepdaughter eagerly told him all about the engine, but after a few minutes (bearing in mind both your instructions, and her inaccuracies in attempting to explain the principles behind it) I drew him away into a longer discussion of gas dynamics. He attempted to follow, but was sadly ignorant of that science's mathematical foundations. I showed him out after approximately a half-hour.

Meanwhile, I overheard my servants wondering to each other whether I planned to set fire to the village to build more steam engines. I reminded them that I am no dragon but a dinosaur, and your castellan. They did not seem to be reassured, but I know not what else to say to them.

Most dutifully,
ANTRODEMOS, Dinosaur.

13 January, being the Anniversary of King Henry's Ban on Purported Transmutation of Metals:

Madam,

I must protest your interdict. I am not a dragon; just as I will not burn down villages, I will not hold maidens hostage for no rational reason or custom. I am a dinosaur, and a scientist. You have entrusted me with this castle, and you have charged me to keep watch on Rapunzel, so I will follow your instructions regarding her even though they be confusing and distasteful. Yet I will explain Science to whomever I wish: to Jack, if he wishes, or anyone else.

To my surprise, two days after my demonstration, Rapunzel asked me to teach her Science. I attempted to start her on gas dynamics, but as it did not hold her interest (nor had she the necessary math), we swiftly moved to mechanics. It appears that human fingers are much more versatile than dinosaurian claws; we have been able to measure the velocity of marbles after collisions with much greater precision than I could beforehand.

I hope this may distract Rapunzel from her ill-advised romance and convince the villagers that there is more to Science than lighting fires.

Most dutifully,
ANTRODEMOS, Dinosaur.

16 January, being the Anniversary of the Publication of an Organized Grammar by Elio Antonio de Nebrija, Linguist:

Madam,

Jack again arrived bearing foodstuffs, as normal. I met him at the gate, where (despite the suspicious glances I saw from some of the servants and passers-by), we passed a pleasant hour discussing physics before again being stymied by his sad lack of math. To my surprise, though, he suggested that next week I begin remedying that lack — a suggestion which I gladly accepted.

However, after I left, I am informed that Rapunzel passed some words with him inside the gatehouse (where she had been hiding) before the gatekeeper's arrival caused her to fall silent.

Before our normal physics lesson later that day, I asked Rapunzel what they had said. She refused to respond; I thought it futile to press her. Per your orders, I have cautioned the gatekeeper against a repeat.

Most dutifully,
ANTRODEMOS, Dinosaur.

22 January, being the Birth-day of Francis Bacon, staunch defender of personal observation:

Madam,

As instructed, Jack did not come to the castle today. Instead, I visited him at his farm. After reassuring his mother that I was not a dragon but a dinosaur (sadly, she did not appear to be reassured), we went out into the fields for a somewhat-satisfactory math lesson. He did not even mention Rapunzel, and the neighboring farmers who were eyeing us with unease looked relieved at my departure.

Meanwhile, Rapunzel herself continues to repeat physics experiments with me, but she refuses to analyze any results unless I work through them with her. I continue to fly outside her window as instructed, and to the best of my knowledge, she has not seen Jack since last week.

Most dutifully,
ANTRODEMOS, Dinosaur.

25 January, being the Birth-day of Robert Boyle, who clarified the nature of Chemistry by clearly delineating elements:

Madam,

I am not a dragon, but a dinosaur. Dinosaurs do not eat humans. Nor has Jack done anything deserving eating; he is a surprisingly apt student who has (despite your suspicions) engaged in no importune behavior.

Most clearly,
ANTRODEMOS, Dinosaur.

31 January, being the Death-day of Jost Burgi, Mathematician:

Madam,

I have indeed received your letters, and I am disturbed by how you continue to emphasize one subject and even descend to threats. While this castle does belong to you, I remain and shall remain an honorable dinosaur and scientist. I was under the impression we both understood this when I became your castellan?

I regret to report that, while doing my inspection last night, Rapunzel leaned out her window to lambast my "horrid suspicions" and "leering glare" which was "always watching" her. I apologized, saying that I was only following your orders; she replied that she would not study Science with me anymore and retreated glumly to her bed.

Thinking back, I am unaware what might have prompted such behavior, as nothing has changed from the last week.

I suppose you will be satisfied to hear that I did discover a rope ladder in her room; I burnt it despite loud objections.

Yours,
ANTRODEMOS, Dinosaur.

6 February, being the Birth-day of Scipio del Ferro, who solved puzzles in Mathematics:

Madam,

No, my silence does not mean I am conspiring with Rapunzel against you. Rather, there is nothing to report. Rapunzel has holed herself up in her room save for meals. She has apparently attempted gardening — I found the remains of strange vines under her window and have taken samples for future study.

Meanwhile, Master Jack has (despite your insinuations) not been in the castle, nor spoken with Rapunzel. I flew to meet him at his farm yesterday, where he continues to study Science diligently, belying his reputed laziness.

I might mention that I saw one of your Message-Men delivering Jack's mother a letter as I was approaching the farm. Since they were eyeing Jack and me with fear later on, I venture the opinion that your letter did not have its desired result?

Yours,
ANTRODEMOS, Dinosaur.

9 February, being the Death-day of Giulio Vanini, Natural Philosopher

Madam,

You will, no doubt, be reassured that Master Jack's mother has forbidden his return to this castle.

I was surprised when I saw Mistress Mildred bringing today's delivery instead of her son. She instantly fell to the ground when I approached her, eventually stammering (after much encouragement from me) that she "thought he really shouldn't dare" come here anymore. To my further inquiries, she added that I "should know really well why." As I did not wish to terrify her further, I let her go.

I fear someone is planning something, but I do not know what — and I do not know what experiments would show me the answer.

Yours,
ANTRODEMOS, Dinosaur

11 February, being the Death-day of René Descartes, who founded philosophy on doubt:

Madam,

To my shame, I confess my investigations were insufficient. This very evening, I discovered Jack in

Rapunzel's room, his having accessed it via another rope ladder. He and Rapunzel were talking, apparently about some ball or feast.

I interrupted their conversation by sticking my head in the window. They both immediately fell to the floor screaming and begging me not to burn them alive. I replied that I would neither burn my own castle nor kill humans needlessly, and demanded to know how long they had been seeing each other.

Rapunzel babbled that this was the first time, but Jack immediately said he had been coming every few days since late January. I thanked him for his honesty but ordered him to leave at once, which he did.

I see now that not only have my investigations been insufficient (for I missed Jack's presence), but so has my understanding of their characters. I have planted myself atop Rapunzel's tower for the present, where I shall meditate on this. I also await whatever advice you may have to give.

Yours,
ANTRODEMOS, Dinosaur.

13 February, being the Anniversary of Galileo Galilei's arrival to stand trial by those who protested how he presented Science

Madam,

I do not know how or whether this letter will reach you, unless I fly it on my own dinosaurian wings. Perhaps, should the besiegers triumph, one of them will send it with a letter asking for you to send a better and more human castellan. And, if they are correct in their claims, perhaps you will be glad to see their letter.

I find that hard to believe — did you not pledge your friendship to me? Did you not welcome me as the hoped-upon herald of future dinosaurs joining society and Science? Have I not been your good castellan these years? It is that which holds me back inside these walls: that a good castellan would not use his claws and fiery breath upon his people, nor a good scientist upon his neighbors. Thus, I wait in anxious hope that you will rescue me.

Yet the mob of farmers and villagers outside shout from outside every wall that you support them; that you have sent them letters asking them to rise against me as if I were a vicious dragon (I use the vulgar term by intent); that I am luring Jack to devour him; that my very silence proves my guilt and shame. I know Mistress Mildred did receive some letter from you, but surely she is misrepresenting it?

I have not sent out the few human guards, for they would be outnumbered; it seems every villager has come out in arms. I could fly out myself, but would that not prove their claims that I am no civilized scientist and unfit to join society? But if I continue to do nothing, would not the castle you have entrusted me be lost?

Your stepdaughter, I fear, does not share my doubts. She shrugs off the siege, saying that one captor will be no worse than another. And human politics are beyond me; might it be she is correct? But when I asked her to teach me of politics, she ordered me out, saying she needed to wash her hair.

As I reflect on the strange letters you have recently sent me, I wonder how much of the customs of human society I have failed to understand?

    Yours in confusion,
    ANTRODEMOS, Dinosaur

14 February, being the Birth-day of Georg Fuchsel, Geologist, who studied records written in rock many ages ago:

Madam,

I cannot but wonder how many letters will pile up unsent before this castle is overrun.

Meantimes, I underestimated Rapunzel's ingenuity and both her and Jack's dedication. While looking out toward her tower this rainy evening, a lightning flash illuminated it enough for me to see (with my dinosaurian eyes) a human shape climbing up from the siege lines!

I instantly flew over. It was Jack, climbing up a plant that had somehow grown in mere hours. I cut it with a thwack of my tail, meaning to catch Jack in his fall, but Rapunzel threw down her hair with a scream, and Jack grabbed onto it. He was too heavy for her to pull him up, however; I caught him in midair and growled "What is this?"

But he was unconscious.

I then flew up to Rapunzel, who was trying to haul in her waterlogged hair and massage her doubtlessly-aching neck. Her face white, she pleaded, "Don't send me back! Don't send me to my stepmother!"

I demanded why she did this. "Because I needed to!" she answered. I attempted to explain the difference between necessity and free will, but she interrupted, "I love him!"

Seeing the futility of further conversation, and not noticing any activity from the siege lines, I flew down to deposit Jack in the infirmary and write this letter. I am again at a loss as to what to do. Even my shipment of platinum for experiments is now unable to reach me. Perhaps it would have been better had you entrusted this castle to a human in the first place?

Yours in great confusion,
ANTRODEMOS, Dinosaur.

15 February, being the Birth-day of Galileo Galilei, Astronomer:

Madam,

As Jack has singlehandedly lifted the siege, I now give him my wholehearted recommendation as a fitting match for your stepdaughter.

Rapunzel met me before dawn this morning outside the infirmary, pleading for me to be kind to Jack. Still disturbed, I said I could not make any promises and reminded her that he had rebelled against his liege lady (you) and her castellan (myself). In response, she claimed you had indeed urged them to rebel, and made many other claims about you that I scarce would have credited two months ago. However, your recent letters' single-minded focus on keeping Rapunzel securely enclosed and watched makes her claims sadly plausible: that none of your instructions concerning her are ordinary, that you are accustomed to lose trust in anyone who is not cooperating with your watch of her, and that you would stir up any matter of rumors to keep young men away from Rapunzel.

I scarce would credit such claims normally — but have not these last months given as good evidence toward them as any experiment?

Shaken, I promised to keep an open mind about Jack, and we entered.

He was awake, and reading a mathematics book I had ordered left for him. Setting it down, he stared at me without words. When I reminded him of our collaborations in Science, he accused me of holding Rapunzel prisoner. I told him I was merely following your express instructions; he protested "Then don't! You shouldn't keep her cooped up here anyway! Does her stepmother want her held captive like a dragon's pet princess?"

I must confess I was shaken by this and asked him what to do.

Jack proposed an experiment: I would let him go, and if he ended the siege, then I would set Rapunzel free. That plan, Rapunzel added, would let me discharge my duty to you by keeping your castle intact.

Reluctantly, I saw that both other courses would have me acting like a dragon in one way or another. At a loss for what else to do, I expressed doubts that he could end the siege, but agreed.

"Don't worry," he said casually. Apparently, his stealth had been sufficient to slay a murderous giant earlier in the fall (whose castle he had accessed by climbing up a bean plant of unusual height.) "Just observe, like you said scientists should, right?"

I followed him and Rapunzel up to the battlements, where he waved his hands and announced to the now-silent crowds outside that I did not wish to act as a dragon, and that I would willingly let both him and Rapunzel go and promise never to hurt anyone without cause. The assailants replied, asking what proof I offered of this, and accusing me of planning to burn them all for my new steam engine.

At that, Jack laughed. "It was a human who invented that steam engine!" he exclaimed. "And this dinosaur's science can give you a lot of other good inventions, too! Right?"

Thereupon he turned to me, and I had nothing else to do but nod my head.

The crowd murmured in confusion, but they were evidently calmed, and some were throwing down their improvised weapons.

Jack then ordered the gates thrown open, and (with me observing) he and Rapunzel strode out to the crowd.

As I write this less than an hour later, I am still wondering if I did wrong. My trust in you is lessened — but did not experiment point in that direction? I did violate your instructions — but what else could I have done save act like a dragon and prove my enemies right? I did lose control of the situation — but is that not part of joining society?

Yours in even greater confusion,
ANTRODEMOS, Dinosaur

16 February, being the Birth-day of Georg Rheticus, who spread the truth of Astronomy

Madam,

I am pleased that we are finally once more in correspondence. Your letter clarified everything wonderfully. No, I shall not throw Rapunzel in the dungeons, nor shall I devour Jack, nor shall I do any of the other evil things you were insinuating I might do in the letters you wrote Mistress Mildred and the other townspeople (which letters they recently showed me.) Their earlier behavior was improper, but they do not deserve any grave punishment: Rapunzel, I now see, was reacting to her unjust imprisonment; and Jack is unaware of nobles' etiquette and unfortunately prejudiced against dinosaurs.

Therefore, I will not re-imprison Jack or Rapunzel. They are currently at Jack's house having luncheon with his mother, and they are already talking of betrothal. While I personally think this is far too hasty, I will no longer attempt to discourage them.

Further, Jack is showing no laziness in his scientific studies: he is already talking of double-checking the farm's boundaries using trigonometry and studying methods to improve the soil's health before the next planting. He has also given me new inspiration in my experiments — I have recently sent orders to sell the platinum and buy materials to study better farming. The recent siege showed I can no longer merely observe society; if I am to act, I shall act as a good scientist who uses Science for a purpose.

Perhaps farming is not the best career for Jack in the long run? If so, marrying a noblelady such as Rapunzel would not be unfitting.

Yours in Science and good sense,
ANTRODEMOS, Dinosaur.

William Condon's story "Of Hair and Beanstalks" was published in Metaphorosis on Friday, 7 December 2018.

About the story

"Of Hair and Beanstalks" merged three ideas I'd been pondering for a while. First, I'd been playing with the idea of a dragon who wanted to join society - how would people treat him? What kind of person would he be to do that? Then, I'd been wondering how the villains in fairy tales might try to justify themselves to their supporters. And, finally, I love the history of science and how it's dramatically changed the world over the last centuries. When I decided Antrodemos joined society because of that, almost everything fell into place for the story.

A question for the author

Q: When do you decide a story is finished?

A: When I first get through to "The End," I set the story aside and mull over how to fix the points I'm not satisfied with. Sometimes I can put my finger on the problems at once and how to fix them; other times I know something's wrong but need some time to puzzle out what. Then, I revise. I hardly ever agree a story's perfect, but there's a point where I know it's good and I don't know how to make it any better- and that's when I decide it's finished.

About the author

William Condon is a writer and programmer. He lives outside Seattle where he enjoys cycling and dreaming up new worlds.

Familiar in Her Angles

E.A. Brenner

The trees in this part of the Dragonwood are thin and lanky, like growing boys, like her own willowy limbs, but Lina has no interest in the trees, or young men, or the body that conveys her, stomping feet falling where they will. Her thoughts are for the great lizards, those remote majestic beasts sunning themselves on the high rocks jutting from the tree line. She looks up to patches of hot blue sky through the canopy of green leaves far above. Her feet are bare. It is the hottest part of the day, and everyone else is resting in the stone-coolness of the house. Around Lina the air is thick, dark, and green, sitting on her skin, sinking into her hair to run down her neck in rivulets. Every time a twig or stone digs into the sole of her foot, her heart leaps. *Soon,* she tells herself. *Soon. Please.*

She pauses her stomping to lift her hair against a light breeze. Heavy and thick as her arm, the braid falls to her feet and even a little beyond, dragging on the ground, pulling her head back until her scalp aches. Strands escape constantly, wispy things flying about her face. She wishes she could cut it off, pluck the hairs from her head, shave down to smooth unburdened scalp like her grandfather, like widows and oracles, bald beneath wimples. If her aching scalp were bald as a dragon's egg, she would throw the bones and divine her own path, be reborn from that egg and fly away with the dragons. But she cannot—Lina is not an oracle, a widow, an old man, or a great lizard. She is not free to do as she pleases. Lina was bought from a witch, on the promise that her hair remain unshorn. Lina was seen by the oracles as the wife for the Prince. She will marry him in a week's time, and become not only a wife and a princess but her family's greatest honor. The Prince's tower looms in the distance, beyond the Dragonwood. No matter which direction she walks, the tower grows closer.

Six months ago, the oracles came to their village, descended on the family estate, declared Lina the match for the Prince. They had seen it. "The desired outcome," they said as they sprinkled herbs in the fire and tied knots in thread pulled from Lina's clothes and bedding. They circled her beneath the full moon and smoked an owl pellet. The stink turned Lina's stomach and lingered in her hair for days. Over the shoulders of the oracles, she watched her mother and father clutch hands, eyes bright in the smoke haze. This was the sum of all their hopes and dreams.

Little Lina was already a miracle child when the oracles arrived, hoped for and prayed for, sacrificed for on the feast days and saints' days, and finally, when all else failed, paid for from a witch, a wandering oracle cast from the circle of the sisterhood. For Lina's mother, no more watching as her sisters-in-law dropped baby after baby, strong boys and girls, while her arms remained empty. Just a little hedge magic, a little twist of fate, a promise, and Lina came squalling into the clan of the wolf. That night, her mother likes to tell the story, the moon was in the constellation of the Tower, the sun in the Queen's throne. "The gods laid this path for you in the stars," her mother repeats over and over as they stitch her trousseau, tiny stars on the borders of towers and wolves' heads. "Your stars will make you a queen, my little Lina."

While no one is looking, Lina stitches her stars in the constellation of the dragon.

The royal household descends three days before the wedding like skeins of geese pausing their migration, raising a village of silk tents on the western lawns. Lina and Prince Ector are introduced. Ector's eyes are brown with flecks of gold and green, like dragon skin. They are warm and kind, but guarded.

They stare silently at each other, strangers shy of getting acquainted. Lina is more interested in speaking with Ector's cousin, the Duchess Honoria of Felchess, whose travelogue of her tour through the far eastern Dragonwood Lina has read four times. Honoria sits several tables away, waving a wineglass in the air to punctuate her storytelling. She is probably regaling the table with her account of the buffoonish tour guide who didn't know the difference between a male dragon and a nesting mother, whereas the Duchess, being well-read in the authorities on the subject, corrected the poor young man for the benefit of the tour group. Or perhaps she is not speaking of dragons at all, but only some court gossip to titillate her audience. Lina looks away, down at her own wineglass, in which she sees the distorted reflection of her hands, fingers curled into strange pale claws. She reaches toward the reflection and wraps familiar fingers around smooth glass.

Their families' murmurs grow edged with concern as Lina and Ector eat their first meal together in silence.

The evening is claimed by the women of the house, who brush her long hair, scrub calluses from her feet, hands, elbows, rub perfumed oil into her skin, share their secrets. She has been happily on the giving end of this exchange for many of the women in the room, but now that she receives these attentions, she finds the ritual an imposition. She doesn't want smooth skin and smooth hair. She wants scales and claws and fire. She wants to be a dragon. Some days she can almost feel the shape of it beneath her skin, an itch of dissatisfaction, subtle and patient.

A year ago, while brushing her cousin Caenis's hair in preparation for her wedding, Lina quietly voiced her discomfort with the idea that someday she would marry a man, not because she disliked men or marriage, but because she did not see herself as a wife, or some days even a woman.

"Are you two-spirited?" Caenis asked

"No," Lina replied, wishing then she hadn't said anything, wishing she could take it back, as the other women around them paused their conversation and listened. "I don't want to be a man, or live as one, or marry a woman."

"What do you want, then?" her mother asked. It was a gentle question, not a challenge, but Lina shrank away, suddenly uncertain of what to say. Wishing to be a dragon meant turning her back on these women, separating herself from them, from her whole family. She didn't want them to misunderstand, to believe she wanted to be something else because she thought so little of them and what they were. That wasn't it at all, but she had no words to express the itch inside her bones.

Now, as then, the room is pleasantly warm and full of family. Caenis brushes Lina's hair and whispers their favorite story in her ear: the tale of the unhappy princess who demands her suitors bring her the tail-tip spine of a dragon, but the would-be husbands must procure that needle-thin spike without killing the beast, an impossible task. Lina stretches out long and languid like a dragon on the midday rocks, lets Caenis's voice break against her like water as she turns her attention inward and questions her desire for the thousand-thousandth time. For weeks after her confession, Caenis and her mother questioned Lina about it, but she avoided answering. When the oracles arrived and declared Lina a match for Ector, everyone seemed to breathe a sigh of relief that said *well, there's Lina's answer. Now she won't be confused anymore, and we can all stop worrying about her.* But she is still confused. The oracles' pronouncement did not settle her mind; it only created more turmoil. Lina believes in the power of the oracles to guide people to the best path, but her desire to be a dragon has not been quelled. Nor has it settled into the kind of certitude that would allow her to say, "the oracles are wrong."

It is rare, but there are stories of people who defy the oracles. To do so requires a level of confidence in oneself that Lina does not possess. She has never been anything other than herself, and every other day, she wonders if her desires will change, worries that becoming something else will not settle her uncertainties at all, worries she will make the wrong choice if it is ever hers to make.

Her family celebrates her impending transformation into wife and princess long into the night, but the thought of becoming either stirs no emotion other than regret that the transformation she truly wants is fading into an impossibility. Her questions will never be answered.

The household sleeps the morning away and convenes at midday for another meal. Ector brings a book to the table and sets it down between them. Lina catches the

Queen's pinched look of dismay, but it is forgotten when she looks down and sees her copy of Jaffo's *A History of the Dragonwoods*. She knows it is her copy because the pages are marked with clumsily-embroidered ribbons from her childhood.

"I found this in the library," Ector taps the book with a long slender finger. "The marginalia look like your handwriting." He pauses, and when she doesn't respond, he adds, "Perhaps I should have waited until after the meal?"

"It's my book," Lina finds her voice on the other side of her surprise. "Have you read it before?"

Ector nods enthusiastically and ignores his food. "Three times! I searched the royal archives for a year looking for evidence to support Sir Rampion of Hunstead's claims about the offspring of the dragon and the wyrm, but no accounts of his Caravan of Marvels noted a single sighting. Does your family archive hold anything?"

Disappointing him feels like kicking a puppy, but Lina shakes her head and says, "No, neither our archive nor the neighboring estates have any accounts to verify Hunstead's claims. We do, however, have generations of observational studies of the dragons' mating seasons to show that his claims are specious. The dragons don't mate with the wyrms and wyverns, nor do they eat them."

To her surprise, Ector doesn't look disappointed by her revelations at all. "Fantastic!" He exclaims with his voice and his hands, and almost knocks over the water jug. "I didn't know the estates here kept records of the mating seasons. Do you think they'd send copies if I asked?"

"I think they'd send you anything you asked for." Lina puts a grape in her mouth before she states the obvious. He's the crown prince. He has only to ask and he receives everything, including the best-suited wife. Is *this* why the oracles saw her as the ideal match? They both love dragons? Her enjoyment of their conversation turns to dust in her mouth, and she swallows the urge to gag on the grape. She will spend her life talking about dragons with this man, and never be one.

Ector is too busy flipping to a page covered in her scribbled notes to notice her distress. She swallows some water and answers his questions with a smile. He asks for a tour of the woods in the afternoon, and she agrees.

There is a heated argument amongst Ector, his guards, and his parents when Lina arrives at his tent for their afternoon walk. The rest hour is over, and the heat of the day has gone down, but Lina has missed her opportunity to walk barefoot and alone. For this walk, she'll have to keep to the path with her shoes on her feet. If, that is, Ector is allowed to go into the woods at all.

"—dangers!" a guard bellows.

"The dragons don't attack people, and they certainly don't eat them," Ector rolls his eyes. "It's well documented—"

"Forgive me, your Highness," another guard interrupts, "but not everything you read in books is true."

"He'll be safe." Lina steps into the tent, into the circle of wary faces. "I go walking in the woods nearly every day. No one here has ever come to harm unprovoked."

Ector looks to his parents triumphantly. "My lady will make sure I am unharmed."

The Queen rolls her eyes, and Lina stifles a smile at the sight. Ector takes more after his mother than his father. "Oh, fine," the Queen huffs. "But take Honoria with you. And your guards."

Between Ector's questions and Honoria's questions and stories, two pleasant hours pass and Lina talks herself hoarse. No, dragons on this end of the wood are no wilder or tamer than the dragons on the other end of the wood. They mostly eat wild boar, mountain goats, and antelope, but occasionally snatch up sheep that wander from the herd. They bury their dead and mourn them, like the elephants in the lands to the south. There is an account in the library from a hiker who came upon the dragon's graveyard in a hidden valley in the central mountain passes. Lina promises to show the diary to Ector when they return.

They keep to path. They return safe from possible harm.

In the library, Lina leads Ector to the corner she claims for herself. All the books and folios about dragons line the shelves between the window and the fireplace, all within easy reach of a cozy armchair. While Ector's back is turned and he exclaims over her collection—"I stopped looking when I found Jaffo on the chair there this morning! If I'd seen all this I never would have made it to lunch!"—she plucks shed strands of her hair, so very long, from the chair's back and drops them to the floor.

Half a dozen times, she has sat in this chair and held a blade to her hair, sick of the burden, and half a dozen times her hand has been stayed by the intensity of her parents' fear. The hedge witch did not say what would happen if Lina's hair were cut, but her parents imagine fearsome consequences and have never allowed more than an inch to be trimmed from the day she was born. She loves her parents and dreads disappointing them more than she hates her hair, more than she distrusts a disgraced oracle's soothsaying; this is the only thing about herself she never questions.

Beside the fireplace is a mirror. Lina comes here to be alone and look at her own face, sometimes for hours, studying each angle, curve, line, and freckle for some sign of who she is, and whom she might become. Some days, her face seems that of a stranger looking back at her. Some days, she covers the mirror with a shroud, ill from her longings, wishing them away. Two years before, she tried giving up dragons, stayed away from the library for weeks, until she was so empty she lay in bed and wished for death. But the feeling was not strong enough to kill her, so she disdained it, got out of bed, and started walking the woods barefoot, seeking a different fate.

The diary she hands Ector contains not only an eerie description of a valley full of dragon bones, but also the clearest account she's ever read of a dragon spine and its properties: a slender needle-like growth fifteen to twenty centimeters in length jutting from the very tip of a dragon's tail, perhaps the vestigial remains of armored spikes spanning the backbone, now easily broken off or, the diarist theorizes, shed and regrown annually like a deer's antlers. Sharp enough at the tip to penetrate the flesh of a mammal. All accounts of the consequences of a dragon spine penetrating the flesh are unverified, old wives' tales of men made into monsters; no one in living memory can speak to the possibilities of a dragon spine. Unfanciful naturalists posit that the spines are not from dragons, but from some plant in the Dragonwood, and caution that they are likely poisonous, given the descriptions of their unnatural effects on the flesh.

In the middle of the night she returns to the forest, abandons the path, abandons her slippers in the undergrowth. She hopes for a dragon spine with every twig and pebble pressed to the soles of her feet, but her feet remain pristine. Even the dirt doesn't stick.

In the darkness, the Tower looms.

She can't say no. In two days she will marry the Prince. She will become a princess, the stuff of stories, but she yearns to be something from a different story. As soon as the oracles gave their pronouncement, her mother stopped asking what Lina desired. Before Lina grew accustomed to the strange question, her opportunity to answer it was gone. The words of witches and oracles determine her fate. The night grows warm, and she grows warmer from the fury rushing through her. When has she ever had a choice in who she is? Her hand falls to the knife at her waist, a ceremonial gift bestowed upon her at dinner. She must wear it through the next two days, to symbolically sever her ties to her family so she can be bound to another. Ironic, that fear of separating from her family has stilled her tongue for all this time, has stayed her hand from severing her hair, has wrapped her desires in doubt. Her fingers grip the hilt.

When has she ever felt brave enough to make a choice? When has she ever done more than leave it to chance?

Lina stands still in the forest, and the rage fades away, leaving an echoing chasm of doubt and regret and longing in her chest. If she refuses this marriage, her family will be ruined. Her forays in the forest are coming to an end, and so too her chance to go toward the thing she wants instead of away from what she doesn't. Every turn she takes, the Tower follows.

Her head aches from the heat and the weight of her braid, and she wonders for the thousandth time why the witch didn't say what would happen if she cut it off, only made her parents promise to let it grow and grow and grow. They have all been so afraid, so fettered by it, unable to see beyond it. Dragon or princess, neither gives one whit for the length of her hair. Perhaps she cannot choose the transformation, but she can choose to be unafraid of who she becomes. Lina draws the knife from her belt, steel so fine and sharp it hums in the sudden small breeze created by its movement. She lifts her braid, cuts it, and drops it to the forest floor, light-headed for the first time in her life.

Her mother flies into a terrified rage when she sees what Lina's knife strokes have wrought and must be calmed with fortified wine.

Ector compliments the close crop. "It brings out your lovely eyes," he says. "Doesn't she look fey, mother?" He smiles, and she sees his sense of humor hiding in the corner of his mouth. "Soon, all the ladies of the court will shear their tresses from envy."

Lina's mother looks so relieved she might pass out. The queen looks like she is trying very hard not to roll her eyes again. Ector insists Lina will become the muse for every court artist, the inspiration for every painting, the object of every swain's poem.

"It's more comfortable in the heat of the day," is all Lina says. Her mother glares at her, silent instruction to move along to a different topic of conversation, one that does not involve her deep streak of pragmatism in the face of romantic gestures. "I love to walk in the sun," Lina reveals, feeling petulant. Then she recalls that she intended to reveal nothing more of herself. She does not want to encourage Ector, even though she knows the conclusion is inevitable and she may as well make the best of it. But Lina is not the sort of person who makes the best of things. She came into the world with grasping hands, as her mother tells the tale, although Lina wonders where this desperate grasping person is hiding. She does not know her.

The prince smiles and agrees. "I love the heat here. It sinks into the bones. It can grow cold in the Tower." He holds her hands loosely, not limp, just loose. His grasp is easy and confident, his fingers warm and dry. His nails are neatly trimmed. Everything about him is neatly trimmed. He changes the subject and asks her if she believes that dragons shed their spines and grow new ones like deer and their antlers, as the diary-writer speculated, or if she thinks a dragon has only one spine for life. She can't see anything hiding in the corner of his smile now. Through the window over his shoulder, she sees a lone dragon fly above the forest, unusual in the heat of the day when they rest in the mountain caves and sun themselves on the rocky slopes, and her heart aches to join it.

They lock Lina in her room after the noonday meal, but she climbs out the window and down into the Dragonwood. She walks for hours in the heat of the afternoon, reveling in the breeze on her neck, the strange weightlessness. When she returns, her feet are clean, and her parents are sitting on her bed waiting for her.

They confiscate her rope, confiscate all the rope they can find throughout the household and even from their royal guests, and when they put her to bed that night, her father locks the windows from the outside. It doesn't matter. The wedding is the next day. Her fate is upon her. She lies sleepless and stares at the stars, sticky and listless in the oppressive air of the closed room, the warm night pressing against the glass.

She finally drifts into a strange state of quasi-sleep when a rock crashes through her window. The glass shatters, and the crash startles her to her feet. Picking her way over broken shards, she trips on a lumpy bundle, lost in the murk of the floor. Fumbling, she closes her fingers around it and draws the thing up close to her face to see it in the moonlight: a silky roughness wrapped around a chunk of stone.

The wrapping falls away in her hands, glides between her fingers. It is a rope. Pale, thick as her thumb, tightly braided. The silk running through it is familiar in her hands, a twining of colors in the strongest fiber, for she used it to decorate and bind her now discarded braid. The rope is crafted of her own hair.

Footsteps sound in the passageway outside her chamber; voices echo against the walls.

She doesn't stop to think. Instead, she unlocks the window and scales the outer wall, heart pounding every time her feet slip. The rope, hastily secured to the bed, holds. The house awakens beneath her, lights flaring, windows and doors heaving open. She reaches the ground and runs to the Dragonwood as her family calls after her in the darkness. It is middle night, when the dragons roam.

Without hesitation, she enters the wood.

The pain when her foot finds a spine in the darkness is so great she cannot stop herself from crying out. The trees absorb her screams, their dead leaves cradle her as she falls to the ground. The spine has pierced her foot, emerging through the top. She waits five agonizing minutes, counting the seconds with whimpers of pain, before drawing it out. She needs to be sure it will take. Blood runs thick over her fingers. The pain is a fire running up her leg. Her foot has gone numb. She wipes the spine clean and weaves it into the side seam of her nightdress, desperate with hope that it is the right kind of spine, that the tales are true, or, if they are not and she has failed, that it is poisonous and she is dead by morning because this pain is too much to bear for nothing.

Ector finds her sitting with her back to a tree, binding her foot with strips from the hem of her nightdress. He is gentle, pressing the torch into her bloody hands so he can carry her. "Did you find what you were looking for?" he asks. Flickering torchlight illuminates pieces of sympathy on his face. Nearby, loud voices and the bays of hunting hounds echo in the forest.

"I don't know," she replies, burying her face in his cool neck. She can feel her fever rising. "It's too late anyway."

They dunk her in cold water to bring down the fever, wrap the foot so tightly her toes remain numb, but nothing stops the fire in her blood. She sweats through three nightgowns until finally, at dawn, the shaking stops and she feels almost cool in the light of the rising sun. She sleeps for an hour, until they wake her to bathe and don her wedding gown. Her mother hides Lina's shorn head beneath a veil heavy with decorations and presents her to the Prince. He looks well rested, and she wonders if she dreamed him finding her in the forest.

The ceremony is traditional, except that the oracles officiate, a very rare boon. Lina and Ector are handfasted. They feed each other the bitter greens and the sweet, kneel and speak the ancient words. Over their heads the Oracles chant the binding spells. Most people forego the spells these days (none of Lina's cousins married under magic), but the royal house keeps the old ways.

Lina swallows panic in deep gulps at the thought that the binding magic might interfere with the work of the dragon's spine. Although she has no way of knowing if she's succeeded except waiting, she refuses to give up hope, even on her wedding altar, even as Ector looks at her, so pleased. He judders as she does, when the binding flows between them, a prickling suffusing the limbs, starting in her hand where it touches his, tracing up her arm, over her shoulder, and down into her chest to wrap around her heart. Pain flares in her foot, white hot. She gasps. Around them, the onlookers gasp with her, thinking they are witnessing one tremendous thing, when in fact it is another, all unknown to them. As she loses awareness of her body, feeling only the fire consuming her foot, she is glad she has this for herself.

The wedding party lasts all day and well into the night. The fire in Lina's foot is the only thing keeping her awake enough to grit her teeth and smile at the endless guests. She is surrounded by people, but loneliness rises within her. She is so weary, she feels removed from her body and her thoughts. Lina watches her mother and the Queen speak with the oracles. What did the queen sacrifice for the oracles' insights about her son? What did Lina's mother sacrifice to bear her? What is Lina sacrificing to change the course of her own life? One of the oracles catches her staring. They regard each other across the distance and the fading light, until the oracle smiles knowingly and winks. Confused, Lina turns away.

Ector—her husband—takes her hand. His fingers are long and cool. He waits for her to grip.

When she does, his smile is so brilliant it catches attention and a cheer goes up around them. She is caught between feeling secure and feeling lost. She wonders if the dragon spine is real, if it took, or if she is just nervous and fevered and married. He looks happy.

He leads her to a chair tucked in the corner of a garden hedge away from the crush of people. A flick of his wrist, a gesture, and three guards appear to stand perimeter around them, holding the guests at bay. A young boy brings a tray of food, a pitcher of water, and a carafe of good dark wine. While she eats for the first time in over a day, he confesses in a low voice, as though he had reached inside her and found her thoughts, "I believed I would feel different. They told me I would feel more settled after the binding, but I still feel restless. I want to see the Dragonwood again. I've never been there until yesterday." He doesn't comment on his participation in her midnight excursion. His voice is wistful as he continues, "I've wanted to visit so many times, since I was a small boy, but it was never permitted. And once we leave here, I doubt I will have the chance again. Is it silly that I hoped to meet a dragon, and charm it into giving me a spine?"

Lina reaches for more wine. It quenches her thirst, but not the heat in her belly. "'Why do you court me?' the Princess demanded." She quotes the story Ector has referenced, her favorite story, and waits for his response. Does he know it as well as she, as well as he seems to know everything else she loves?

Ector smiles. "To see you happy," he quotes the bard's response. The bard, who of all the princess's suitors brought her what she demanded: a true dragon's spine, from a live dragon. "For every time I have passed through your court, you have been borne down by a great sadness. I would see you free of it. I ask nothing in return but to write songs of your joy."

Lina finishes the tale: "The princess took the spine from his hands, and to the astonishment of her court, plunged it into her own heart. Instantly she was enveloped in flames, and when the flames died out, a great dragon curled around the princess's throne, for she *had been* borne down, by the curse of a wicked witch, transformed from a dragon queen into a human princess, trapped while her dragon clan suffered her absence. Freed by the bard, she returned to her clan, who rejoiced to be reunited with her. They granted the bard the boon of a hoard, but he did not retire to become a landed baron as people expected. He remained true to his declaration and traveled many countries singing songs of the dragon queen's joy."

Ector drinks his own wine. "Alas, I have no dragon's spine for you." He leans close. "I wanted to issue a decree that I would only marry a woman who could bring me the spine of a dragon. My mother went to great lengths to dissuade me, and in the end had to consult the oracles to make me see reason." He shows her humor, but there is a longing in his eyes, etched into the angles of his face.

Lina's attention is diverted as, one by one, the guards turn inward to face them. The fire in her foot flares. Beyond the guards, the crowd presses in. The garden corner shrinks. Faces peer at them over the shoulders of the guards. They are on display.

Ector's shoulders stiffen, and his face composes into a pleasant, somewhat vacant expression. She understands then, for the first time, that they share a cage. "The spines are just a story," she lies. His face falls, just a fraction, and she is surprised that she can read him so clearly when they are barely acquainted. Her heart breaks a little. She fingers the hem of her veil, where she has hidden the used spine, ready to confess her lie and give him this small gift in recompense for the trouble she might soon cause, but the Prince stands to meet his obligations and she is carried along with him, because they are her obligations now, too.

She didn't expect to love him. It makes this much harder.

The newlyweds are given a suite of rooms near the top of the Tower. Their daily complaints about climbing the many stairs become their first shared jest, because they would not trade their rooms for anything. The view of the forests is unmatched. In the morning and the evening, they watch the dragons spiral and swoop over the woods, hands clasped. They make love on the balcony, matching their cries to the screams of the dragons in the distance, and Lina has never felt so present and comfortable in her own body. It is a strange revelation, after so long contemplating what else it might be, but it does not settle her old discontent, and the tension makes her as restless as ever.

Ector was right about the cold at the top of the Tower, but the heat grows inside of her, stretching her, pushing its way out. She orders cold baths, sometimes three times a day. She feels hungry and faint and her thirst cannot be quenched by water or by wine. Her mother-in-law and the ladies of the court whisper of babies behind their hands and a hopeful anticipation fills the Tower.

Ector seems not to notice her heated skin, her agitation. He seems content, no longer the caged bird. Lina feels betrayed. She thought he understood, but he smiles and goes about the business of preparing to be king someday with purpose and drive. He speaks of all the things he is setting in order for the future but does not speak of the Dragonwood, even as they begin and end their days by watching the dragons.

Lina doubts everything. Perhaps there is no transformation coming. Perhaps her foot was pierced by an ordinary thorn. Perhaps she is simply overwrought with nerves and conflicting thoughts to the point of fever. Her husband makes her laugh, and doesn't tell her she is too much or too little, and would it be so bad, really, to live out her days with him? He is an ideal partner, and she is torn between a good man and a desire so entrenched she cannot open her hands to let it go. "Don't worry, dear," the queen pats her hand and mistakes her restlessness for other desires. "A child or two will draw you down to the ground." Her head feels heavy, as though her braid yet weighs her down.

On the day Lina singes her clothing simply by putting it on, her doubts fall away and she knows her time is coming. The heat and the pain are unbearable. She weeps, and even the cold of the mountain that blows past the Tower as the season turns brings her no relief. In spite of it all, her heart lifts in anticipation, then plummets with guilt when Ector looks her in the eye and smiles.

She tries to send him away, but he refuses to leave the room. He turns away visitors, barricades the door against his guard, and burns his hands to blisters holding her.

"I'm sorry," she cries. "I didn't mean for it to happen this way."

"Shhh," he kisses her hair, smooths the short length grown during their brief marriage. "You're perfect. This is perfect. I won't leave your side."

The transformation steals her breath. Bones melt in a fire and settle into new shapes. Hair and cloth burst into flames, filling the room with an acrid stench that does not smell to her the way it had to her old self. She is tangentially aware of pounding at the door, questions shouted, her own screams going on and on and on. Ector holds her gaze with his warm gold-flecked, dragon-skin eyes, doesn't flinch, not even once. In their short time together, she has only begun to plumb the depths of his endurance, the extent of his stoicism.

She thought she would grow larger, but she stays the same size, only rearranged. Perhaps, she thinks, she will grow as she ages. For a dragon, she's quite young.

She has wings now, and a long tail.

She breaths fire from her snout.

The room is very quiet.

Ector looks different to her new eyes. She can see the sadness in him, colored threads of blue and pearly gray. There are also patches of red and orange— excitement. "Marvelous," he breathes out, and then asks, "Can you understand me?" She tries to nod, a strange movement with such a long neck, and her body unbalances. Her new tail gets away from her, knocks over a table, topples a vase to the floor. The shards of pottery remind her of shards of glass, her window broken so mysteriously.

As though he knows her thoughts, he says, "I threw that stone at your window. I found your hair in the wood and made the rope, because suddenly there wasn't any to be had. I was hoping you'd find a spine." His face stretches into a vast, unabashed smile, and he lights up with a joy colored purple and yellow like pansies in sunshine.

Lina draws her tail around; it obeys her this time and goes where she directs. Her new limbs feel as natural as the old. There at the tip of her tail is the thing they both desired, a desire so strong it found its way into the stars and brought them together, from a hedge witch's baffling charge that Lina's hair remain uncut to the sly matchmaking of the oracles, everything intersecting to produce their desired outcome.

"May I?" he asks. She masters a nod and nudges him with her snout. Her love for him swells in her with an unexpected fierceness, and she wonders if all her feelings will be magnified into this heady, exciting wine of emotion sliding through her belly. There is no pain when he snaps the spine from her tail. He meets her gaze and, without hesitation, plunges the spine into his thigh. Like Lina in the forest, he cannot stop his scream of agony.

The door bursts open with a mighty crash, and the king and queen, half a dozen soldiers, and the court physician pour into the room. There are shrieks and cries at the sight of her, and Ector urges her toward the balcony. "Go!" he urges. He cannot stand on his leg—the spine remains very deep in the flesh. Soldiers raise swords and advance on her, but they halt as the Prince throws up one hand to ward them off. He pushes her with the other, balancing against her to hold himself up even as he tries to thrust her away. "Go!" he shouts over the din. "I'll find you!"

She pauses in the balcony doors. Evening has come. In the distance, the dragons begin their descent from the mountain peaks into the woods. They call out over the land, and a reply rises from her belly, tears from her throat. It echoes over the valley, and one by one, the great dragons turn to answer her. They circle in the sky, draw closer to the Tower, beckon her to join them.

She looks back to him one final time, and in the reflection of the glass balcony doors, she sees herself transformed, sleek and strange, yet familiar in her angles and her oldest imaginings. He says again, "I'll find you," and draws the spine from his leg, holding it aloft in triumph. When they meet again, he, too, will be altered yet familiar.

She launches herself from the Tower, rises on powerful wings, and takes flight.

E.A. Brenner's story "Familiar in Her Angles" was published in Metaphorosis on Friday, 21 September 2018.

About the story

In the summer of 2015, I read Angel Carter's *The Bloody Chamber and Other Stories* for the first time, and the first draft of "Familiar in Her Angles" popped out. I struggle to write short stories, so I was surprised how quickly that first draft came, amazed I managed to get from start to finish in only a few pages. I was reading a lot of fairy-tale retellings and fairy-tale theory that year, so when I realized I was playing with the motifs of the maiden in the tower fairy tale (Rapunzel, Petrosinella, Persinette), I leaned into it. Through several drafts I looked for ways to subvert the roles and tropes and also explore how we build and embrace our own identities. Also, I needed to write at least one dragon story in my life.

A question for the author

Q: What's an idea you're dying to write but haven't, and why?

A: An idea I've been dying to write is a Mission Impossible-style magical thriller. I adore over-the-top spy movies and magic-in-modern-times fantasy. I haven't even started such a story yet because I don't have a character or plot to hang the genre on. I'm waiting for the day my main character drives through my mind in an incredibly sexy muscle car and orders me to get in.

About the author

Elizabeth Brenner grew up in Toledo, Ohio and moved to Boston, Massachusetts to get an MFA from Emerson College. She loves hardware stores, making jam, stories about magic spilling everywhere, crochet, travel, and smart jokes. She makes a living as a managing editor for scholarly journals and is a member of the Boston Speculative Fiction writing group. She lives with her husband in Salem, MA.

Cheminagium

David Gallay

Pain, true pain, lives outside of time. It arrives in a shear of liminal precognition, the thudding sky before the storm. We formulate routes of escape, believing that the visitor darkening our door could be turned away with the right words. It doesn't matter what we do, what we say, whether the heart is flooded by prayers or screams.

Pain is patient.

The door always opens.

Col is only an arm's length away, huddled in his bed, a naked foot dangling over an empty boot, but I can't hear him. The ringing migraine swallows every word he says.

I press my thumbs to my ears and shake my head until my jaw clicks.

" … worse today?"

"I'm fine."

I make my way over to the window and rest my forehead on the cold glass. Outside, the first wisps of snow kick through the leaves. My eyes drift up from a patch of wildflowers sheltering in the lee of the woodpile, over the dawn-gilt crowns of linden, towards the towering heart of Spire Iberos. I squint into the glazed eyes of the keep. Usually they are dead as a fish, but this morning, there is movement. A candle floats from room to room like a stray thought.

"Our guest appears to have settled in," Col says. "He stopped by last night, while you were out. Nothing like the shaggy weed I remember. Barely recognized him. Twice, I mistook him for Mislav and had to bite my tongue. Remember that one, our bald cousin?"

Of course, I do. Mislav was once a frequent visitor to Iberos, related to us by some stray weave of marriage. His head gleamed like sea-glass. We used to wonder if he shaved it every morning or if that was simply his skull, painted and polished. He vanished out on the Ore-Fist curs a long time back.

In the keep, the candle flickers out.

"If you're looking for an excuse," Col says, "the mules he rode in on have been rooting up and down the hill, careless for next season's crop. Remind him where the stables are, make sure the bolts aren't rusted."

"Eir or Adal can take care of it."

A flash of annoyance crosses his face. He's always been ambivalent to our huldufólk, giving their ancient, withered bodies no more thought than one would a chair or broom.

"They have their own responsibilities," he sighs. "And you need a breath of light. Go see him."

There's nothing more he'd like than to shove me out the door, into the snow. But he can barely stand. Although we are brothers in decrepitude, his ruin exceeds my own. Instead, he rolls back to his patchwork map of Casses, our domain, our country, an island beset on all compass points by unpassable seas. The map is scored with pale chalk lines, one for each mystic curs seared into the landscape. These invisible rivers of velti old-magic radiate from the wellsprings of the Blessed: Spire Centonica at the tip of the southern archipelago, Spire Palus deep in the wild cliffs, and our home, Spire Iberos, an old iron nail struck into the toes of the northern mountains. Practiced travelers like Col can ride the curses from coast to coast without missing a meal. Used to be he'd be gone for weeks cataloguing those liminal pathways. Wearing his chalks down to the nub. Whenever I assumed the worst, that he'd finally lost himself to the blur of obsession, I'd inevitably find him curled up in bed, snoring that same musical wheeze from the days we shared a twin's crib, when his lungs were clean and his linens free of red.

The swallowing chain. A fish you cannot see. Yearning for the unlit taper. To crawl beneath your own spine. A long visit from a bad friend. Sleeping in the nailed bed. An argument with birth. The Blessed have a thousand words to describe suffering and just as many reasons given for it to exist. Pain is the cost of vigilance, for we Blessed stand watch on the bridge between Casses and darker countries beyond the sea, under the hills. Others believe that pain is a burden, a punishment, passed down from mark to mark, throat to throat. A reminder that the velti was never meant for us.

I learned most of this from my mother. As she tapped drops of poppy milk onto her lips, I asked how it was possible her Blessing brought her so much misery. After all, she could swim through the air as easily as an otter through the water. How could that be anything but joyful?

She gazed out the window. Her jaw already trembled from the bone-fever.

I yearn to touch the sun, she said. *I would give up everything. The desire consumes every spare thought. I dream of plunging my head into its fire, letting it consume me. I've flown so high that I could see over the mountains, to the sea. I would have gone further if my body let me, if my waking mind didn't froth into oblivion. Judoc, my darling, I would stab you in the heart right now if it offered even the slightest chance.*

Col was right about the mules. One has already breached the neighboring meadow, its flanks thick with burrs, while the other nearly snapped a leg by lodging its hoof down a rabbit burrow. With a calm but firm hand, I prod them uphill to the stalls. While drawing up a bucket from a well rimed with ice, I become aware of a figure crouched on the hill. He has a feral aspect, like a crow eying the seed in your palm.

"I had forgotten all about the mules," he says. "Seems I'm a bit fog-brained today."

"No worries. The curses can suck the wind from you."

Stig stands and approaches. He seems taller than I remember, or perhaps just thinner, stretched out. A worn cloak drapes off his lanky shoulders like moss from an alder. At the last moment he remembers to raise his chin up for a formal greeting. The mark on his throat is a scorch in the sand, mirrored glyphs of fortune. I desperately want to touch it. Instead, I mirror his posture so that he can acknowledge my own mark.

"My dearest, my Judoc. What brings that look of disbelief? Is it this?" he asks, rubbing his scalp. "Or this?" He taps his mark.

"That you're here at all."

"When I heard about Col –"

"Is that the nature of your Blessing? To hear the death clarion from the far side of Casses? Or perhaps you came to spark the kindling on his funeral pyre?"

The stinging words fly faster than I can swallow them back down. Stig accepts each blow.

"That would be something, wouldn't it? No, my gift deals with the flow of reason. Watch …"

He bends down and plucks a dead leaf off the ground. He makes a fist and crushes it inside, close to my face so that I can hear the dry crackling of its destruction. A pattern of greenish burn scars scores his knuckles and wrists, in some places carved down to the bone.

When he opens his hand, there are only flakes of copper.

"What do you see?" he asks.

"Nothing," I say, cautiously. "Dust."

"Then we agree, it was once one thing and now is another. What compelled that transformation?"

"You did. With your hands."

I sense a child's trick, such as when Col juggles acorns and they vanish in midair, only to reappear days later in my boots. Velti magic runs through the veins of the Blessed like a translucent thread. Col's acorns, the suck of breath when my mother's feet lifted from the ground, every curs weaving its way across the earth, the hum of rooted bones and witch-ravens weeping in the cliffs. I have my own meager gifts, and it appears Stig has found his as well, although I'm at a loss how. The mark is a birthright of the Blessed. It can neither be earned nor forged.

"Before the movement, before the thought, there was the intention. An intention birthed by your presence."

The migraine, absent until now, begins to make itself known again.

"You're saying I crushed the leaf."

"That's one way of putting it. I could also blame the mules, at which point I would have to blame myself, and then so on, and so forth. We can follow the water upstream and never reach the source."

"Then what does it matter?"

"Let's say I returned home a season ago?" He takes my hand, sweeps the remains of the leaf into my palm.

Before I can answer, he covers my hands with his own.

He closes his eyes. Fog drifts from his lips.

When it is over, I am holding neither dust nor the dead leaf reconstituted.

It is a honeybee, shivering in the wind. I protectively cup my fingers around it.

"The sun is peaking," he says and there's that half-smile I remember, those exquisite angles hiding under the softness of age. "Best get on with the day. I do promise to keep more watchful eye on the mules."

"Right. There's should be some chestnuts in the storehouse that haven't moldered yet. Keep them away from the western slope, there's a line of belladonna that'll turn them into frothing bags. If you want, I can send up a hulda to help. You remember Adal, don't you? He still has a touch with animals."

"No. Your huldufólk won't be necessary."

As I make my way down the hill, he calls after me.

"I searched for you last night, up in the keep, but the other chambers were all bolted or destitute. If my arrival has brought you any discomfort – "

A tingling pain flares in the crease of my palm. Stinger torn away, the bee curls up and dies. I scuff a hole in the dirt with my heel and gently place it inside.

"I forgot, you weren't here," I answer without turning around. "The bone fever consumed our parents, one after the other. That was a long time ago. Me and Col ... we sleep in the common halls now. The keep belongs to the spiders."

The last time Stig and I spoke, adolescence still dripped from our noses. We were deep in the trenches of another Iberos winter. Despite the freezing bite of the clearing sky, the walls of the kitchens were already sweating. Stig stood at the cutting board, thin as a reed, hunched over a platter of smoked eel. Focused on the sweep of the butcher's blade, he noted my approach with a sarcastic bob of deference.

I didn't expect to see you, divine one, he said between decapitations. *Rumor was you'd taken to your blankets again.*

Most unmarked wouldn't dare speak to a Blessed with such brazenness; it was only our friendship that granted him protection. As my own parents were often preoccupied and Col had grown bored with entertaining his smaller brother, most of my childhood lingered with Stig and his clan. His uncle especially treated us both like sons. We sat at his feet as he worked the potter's wheel and regaled us with stories of his people, gods and queens, pirates and demons. Me and Col spent a hundred afternoons staring at the treasures paraded across the shelves of his uncle's shop, ancient relics to be revered but never touched. Whenever our friendship bore injuries over the jagged shoals of boyhood, his uncle reminded us that good men are strengthened by their scars.

Col must have already been through here, I said. *No doubt spreading rumors of my condition while picking bones from his own teeth.*

Not my place to say, Stig laughed. *Fact is you look rotted. Let's take care of that.*

With three knocks on the wall, Maeija appeared out of the gloom. Like most huldufólk, she was a shrunken, pitiful creature, swathed in linens that barely disguised her oaken complexion and the weeping wounds of blue gaslight. While Spire Iberos may have had many tenants over its life, lore had Maeija a constant fixture, serving drinks and scrubbing floors back to the primordial mud. I would not be surprised if she was there to greet the first Blessed when they descended onto Casses in a storm of falling stars.

Of course, Maeija never bowed to me. A hulda has no need to acknowledge its rung on the ladder. With the buzz of cicadas under her breath, she addressed me in their strange backwards language, where tomorrow has already happened and yesterday is yet to come.

My Blessed, I recalled this threshing in your skull. If I served you better, would the pain have fled more swiftly?

Without another word, she slipped away and returned with an ivory cup. Her tea smelled foul, with bits of unidentifiable gray matter settling to the bottom, and drinking it felt like wires drawn across the tongue.

From one blink to the next, the ringing quieted. Maeija inspected my face. I often wonder what she saw there.

Better, mayfly?

Before I could answer, Stig nudged a bowl of eel bones towards her newly emptied hands.

Well, what are you waiting for, beastie? Ah, never mind, I'll do it myself.

Stig beckoned me to escort him outside. We walked against the wind, our fists clenched against the warmth of our stomachs. In the shelter of a shivering linden, Stig tossed the bones in the snow and withdrew a clay pipe. I once owned its twin, both sculpted by Stig's uncle. It's long gone now. We stood apart from each other, teeth chattering.

Sure you can't wiggle up a spark of velti fire? He nudged me on the shoulder. I flinched. *The tea usually lasts longer, yeah? Or perhaps it's your brother's wanderings biting at your ankles? Don't waste a worry. Col could walk with Death under the hills and find his way back blindfolded.*

That's not an exaggeration. I still remember the first time Col invited me along to walk the curses with him. He made it seem so easy, striding into the unknown, feet barely touching the ground. I only made it a few miles before keeling over to empty the contents of my stomach. He hooted, not out of cruelty but for the simple joy of having me along. I didn't see it that way.

After that, I avoided the curses, which meant avoiding Col. We became strangers to each other.

Which is to say, lingering outside the kitchens on that frozen morning, I wasn't thinking of my brother at all.

Despite all the tearstained promises made in the summer dark, the inequities between me and Stig had become unavoidable. Our boyish defiance snapped too easily under the heel of that imbalance. Although I reassured him it would be many, many years before I would receive my Blessing – ah, it hurts now to think how wrong I was! – he pled with me to refuse it.

I explained the Blessing was not simply a tradition, that without the mark to give release to the magic burning in my veins, it would eventually curdle both body and soul. Anyone who ignores the velti surrenders to the red hands of disease or despair.

And still, hearing all this, he continued to accuse me of selfish deformity!

We spoke in circles, grinding our arguments down to insults, to venom, to daggers. Did I suggest he should leave the Spire for various hells? And if I did, was it to hurt or liberate? I truly don't know. The forests of the past are unforgiving.

Well, plenty more fish to gut, Stig mumbled, the unlit pipe bobbing between his teeth. Then he clasped my hand and offered a startlingly genuine bow. The drumbeat of the velti pounded against my ribs. My last memory of him before he left Spire Iberos without word or warning was his gangly body slipping into the labyrinth of massive ovens with the ease of a fawn into the woods.

"I found it! Come on, stop dreaming. Wake up!"

Col stands over me, grinning madly, shards of pinking twilight caught in his hair. Before I can resist, he has me on my feet, a ratty cloak tossed over my shoulders. Insults curdle on my tongue before I remember his condition. Damn it. How is he standing? Where is he going? I push into my boots and chase him outside, past the fences and into the crackling frost. The trees thin out, their branches heavy with black leaves bowing inwards as we pass into the ephemeral corridor of the Grave-Green, one of the oldest curses.

Wheezing, he crouches in the snow. From above, I see lesions snaking down his neck, remnants of the latest huldufólk remedies.

"Let's go back," I say. "You can tell me about what you found, and I swear we can come back ... later in the season ... on a better day ..."

Col pulls himself back up. His eyes reflect the blood-dark spectrum of the sky.

He offers me his hand.

How can I refuse?

As we walk into the curs, the ground seems to speed from beneath us, as if every step doubles its distance. The trees whistle a strange tune. *Remember to breathe.* From Grave-Green, we pivot into other overlapping pathways – Serpents-Feast, Gallow-Seed, Ore-Fist, Tooth-Hook. The world fogs around us as we flicker, ghostlike, through wood and meadow, our feet barely touching the cobbled streets of distant Spires, our eyes blinking from flashing of rivers, lakes, sheets of ice crawling down the mountain. Occasionally, other travelers flit by us, women and men, Blessed and unmarked. I can still smell their skin long after their shades have passed. Perfume. Sweat. Wine. Disease. All of Casses flows through my lungs. *Remember to breathe.* At Col's insistence, we move faster and faster, until nothing remains other than buzzing smears of color. I cover my face with my hands, preferring the darkness.

"That wasn't so bad," Col says. He coughs into his hand and discretely wipes it under his arms.

The sun, returned a full hands-width up from the horizon, shines from a different direction. Instead of ice, the canopy drips with wet rubies of late autumn. It's difficult to determine exactly where we have alit; somewhere close to the southern rim I imagine. I begin to unpeel my cloak from the spreading tack of sweat, but Col stops me.

"Quiet. Listen."

The birds. Their song has changed from melody to keen. And there's this smell. Burning wood. The trees fall away as we step out onto a wide, rocky beach. The ocean surf inhales and exhales, pulling with it the smoke of a small campfire built at the edge of the tideline. Two figures kneel before the flames, warming themselves. Col strides towards them, palms facing out in in friendly surrender, those damn manic teeth wide and bright.

"You wouldn't mind if my brother and I join you?"

I shuffle in behind him, an afterthought. As we near the fire, my eyes pull apart more details about the strangers; their odd, hunchbacked posture and stunted proportions.

A moment of panic seizes my chest.

Wild huldufólk. Not the servile creatures of the Spire. No, these hulda are proudly undomesticated — no rags conceal their wizened bodies, no attempt to meet the delicate standards of human agreeability. It is a stark reminder that these are the aboriginal inhabitants of this place, long before the Blessed and the shipwrecked. Their kind were here when Casses was a nameless rock and likely will be when it is again.

The larger hulda, a female, lopes over to Col. She draws a claw across his chest and sniffs it. For his part, he doesn't flinch.

"My friends, last we met you claimed knowledge of a hidden road," he says. "A way across the waters?"

Before they can answer, I pull Col aside.

"You've been here before? When?"

"I go where the velti leads me, little brother." He punctuates the last two words with an acidity that leaves me mute. He spins back to the hulda patiently waiting out our human melodrama. "Well? The curs?"

"Whale-Breath," nods the smaller creature. I notice that the tone and texture of his skin has changed to match the rocks beneath us. "I recall you paid the cheminage this time."

I watch with increasing trepidation as Col makes a show of wagging his fingers, clucking his tongue. The velti charges with an odor of overripe fruit. The hulda seems not to notice. With a snap, two silver coins appear in the air, already spinning in the light. Col rolls the coins up and down his knuckles like a street performer.

"A trick my mother taught me. Here's your toll."

The hulda pass the coins between themselves. Appeased, they snuff the fire and lead further along the coast, into the marshlands. It occurs to me that the landscape's contours are not entirely natural. What initially appears to be a mound of earth transforms into the underbelly of an overturned ship. The further inland we push, the more displaced vessels we pass, like abandoned toys in a dredged pond. I can trace the outline of their unusual prows beneath the vines, intricate sculptures of wood and iron — the fangs of serpents, the talons of eagles, a wyrm caught in metamorphosis. We hike around the broken face of an angel, slugs and beetles cozying between her stoic lips.

The migraine returns, pressing the thumbs of my eyes into my brain. I grab a branch from the ground and nervously roll it between my thumb and forefinger. My Blessing, brought to boiling by the velti fires in my skull, whittles away the wood like an axe, sharpening it to a knitting needle, a porcupine quill, a surgeon's pin. I hone it down to nothing, and the ache whittles away with it.

We arrive at a pair of obsidian sarsens rising out of the earth like the fingers of a buried god. Weathered runes swirl across them, a language I don't recognize. The hulda fall to their knobby knees and offer petitions to the massive stones. The sun is now just an amber shard snagged on dimming felt.

"Now what?" Col asks.

"You stepped between them."

Grinning madly, his molars grinding, Col walks forward between the sarsens. I wait for the bitter tang of the curs to sweep him away.

Nothing happens.

Col looks around, confused.

Then the hulda do something I've never seen before. They laugh.

It's horrifying.

Infuriated, Col tears the scarf away to reveal his mark. "I demand you reveal the curs to me. We are the Blessed. The open wounds of heaven!"

This only makes them cackle harder. They remind me of imps scribbled in the margins of a holy text.

"What do you want?" Col snarls. "What is it? More silver?"

His hands clench tight, gripping the velti so hard I feel it shift in my marrow. A coin falls from the sky and hits the sand with soft thud. Then another. And another. A clamor of raining metal fills the air as Col's deluge crashes around us, bouncing off the sarsens, breaking through the trees, pelting the shoulders and backs of the hulda. Their merriment pitches into hysterics as the rain becomes a gale, then a hurricane of silver.

I should try to pull Col away. I should beg him to stop.

With a word, I could end this.

Wait. Listen to the velti delighting in the music of its own song.

How could I ever deny him this moment of rapture?

Instead, I find a half-buried wreck and cower in its berth. I close my eyes and pretend the drum of coins against the wooden beams is the thunder of a summer squall.

The heavy rain slows, stops. A lone crow coughs into the widening silence.

"Judoc," Col says after some interminable time.

As we make our way back to the homeward curs, I hazard a quick glance back. The sarsens stand against the night like silent judges, passively watching over the unmoving shapes of the hulda. Then I turn my gaze back to Col, carefully reading the tremors rippling outward from the marrow of his shoulders, the rasping of his chest, the blood freckling across his chin. Ironic that for a miraculous moment, my own head is clean from pain. I can see every leaf turning white in the moonlight. I hear the pads of our feet, the movement of tiny insects, the fading breath of the endless, unrelenting sea.

While my mother accepted the pains, named them like pets, my father refused to acknowledge them.

His mark granted the gift of prosperity. Anything he touched thrived. Fruit trees. Wheat. Horses. Exotic orchids that had no right surviving through the Casses winters. His own children, born dark-haired and opal-eyed. He inherited a crumbling outpost and nurtured it into a beacon of opulence. Both Blessed and unmarked came to tend their gardens within our walls.

How quickly fecundity can turn cancerous.

Within a few years, thorny vines strangled the orchards. Gluttonous rats ate through our granary. The horses tore their ropes and disappeared into the woods. The orchids, so frail and delicate, gave birth to evil smelling tumors.

We had to burn it all.

Stig watches with curiosity as I light the candles, set out the linens and washing basins, wave away the cobwebs. Eir scuttles in with a decanter of wine, pungent with acorns and cloves.

Eir fills my glass, but ignores the other.

I raise my hand to the reprimand the hulda, but Stig gently restrains me.

"Come now, poor Adal is nearly blind with age."

"That's Eir."

"Oh, well, I could never tell them apart." He toasts me with his empty glass. "Now, I thought you didn't come up into the keep anymore. Just me and the spiders?"

A second pouring loosens my voice enough to tell Stig everything; the cackling hulda, the forest of shipwrecks, the storm of coins. He listens carefully until it's all spilled.

"You see ... Col's gift is to surface the lost and forgotten ... could be anything ... but he always comes back to the curses."

"Yeah, even as a wild-runt, I remember him being waist-deep in those weird roads. Can only imagine how it was after a Blessing like that. Did he find what he was looking for?"

"Yes," I say. "All of them. A completed map of Casses sits in his brain like a pulsing rot. So ... I suggested that perhaps there were some secret curs leading ... elsewhere. The gamble worked ... for a while ... but ... my efforts may have only thickened the poison ..."

"Easy, easy. You stutter as if you plucked the strings of his fate."

He means it as an absolution but it only pricks my temper.

As if cued, Eir returns with a pewter serving dishes balanced on root-gnarled elbows. The hulda spoons out fragrant servings of cooked fruit, again only for me, before scuttling back downstairs. I slide my plate over to Stig.

He smiles, teeth jeweled by candlelight. "I have something to show you."

He pulls a figurine from his pocket, a primitive bird-like totem, its silver feathers smoothed away by the centuries. His uncle claimed it was an ancestral heirloom, passed down from the survivors of the apocryphal landfall that introduced their bloodline to Casses. When no one was looking, Stig would steal it from its high shelf for our garden games.

"I took it before I left," Stig says. "Do you recall the hours we spent play acting with clay dolls from uncle's scraps? I would pluck a cob-spider to play the álfar, wicked prince of the small folk, and this was its witch-raven. And you would be the great and powerful sorcerer from the wild cliffs ... what was his name?"

"Lord Ormstunga."

"Yes! Serpent-Tongue! And you hunted down the álfar, threw it in uncles' kiln. We watched it burn until we couldn't take the heat. Remember? So, tell me, what is your Blessing, divine one? Can you drag down the stars? Can you reduce men to their bloody bones?"

I explain my gift to sharpen a thing to its finest edge. Metal, yes, glass, wood, a knife, a sword, a needle. Also, sight, a dream, a song. Joy. Grief.

"Ah, what a waste!" he exclaims. "So many dull knives could have used your attention back when I worked the kitchens. I snuck down there today, you know. Thought I'd pinch a flask of gray tea for you. What a sight. Ovens dead, pantries furred with dust."

His mention of Maeija's tea rattles craving's cage. I ease the conversation back to the missing years.

"I meant to prove my own way in the world," he says, biting into a steaming pear. "I was an idiot. Barely a month on the road and I blistered through two pairs of boots and nearly starved. It was a miracle that your cousin stumbled over me."

Bells ring deep in my ears, metal on bone.

"Mislav found you?"

He laughs. "Even before taking pity on my empty stomach, the old man shaved my head to clean out the ticks. When he realized I wouldn't be whimpering back home, he let me wander the wilderness with him. In return I shouldered his library and offered up my meager culinary skills. But, Judoc, let's not be coy. You don't really care about all that. You want to know about my mark. Been staring at it all night."

No reason to deny it. "Yes."

"I don't know if you recall the huldufólk Mislav traveled with. Vile, scheming little beasts. No doubt relatives of your tricksters in the woods. One night, I caught them sitting on his chest, suckling the velti from his mark as he slept. I had just been working a rabbit, still carrying the butcher knife. And. Well." He glances down at his scarred hands. The smile remains, but his words struggle like a moth in the rain. "You've not felt pain until you've been kissed by that blue fire they bleed."

Stig refuses to divulge any details, other than that when it was all over, the impossible had happened; his throat burned with the mark. Since then he's been traveling between the Spires, unlocking the secrets of this strange and inexplicable Blessing.

I ask him if the Blessing hurts. How he deals with the pain.

He acts as if he can't hear me. A sour draft whistles through cracks in the wall.

"Look. Here I am, to rescue you from this dour pile of rocks. Don't you see? We're the same now, nothing left to stop — oy! Be careful! Your hand!"

"What?"

Did I spill the wine? Bright drops of red roll off my fingers. No, not wine. There's a flap of skin hanging off my thumb, sliced neatly by the lip of the glass, whose edge I've idly sharpened to a near invisibility. Strange, how it doesn't hurt. The cut is too clean. Stig leaps from his chair and quickly wraps the wound with linen. Roses soak through.

"Here, let me help," he says, grabbing my hand. He concentrates on the injury. The velti gathers around him, not naturally like iron to the lodestone, but with great resistance. I can taste its resentment. Its loathing.

Finally, Stig gives up and runs downstairs, calling my brother's name. I try to follow him, but somehow end up going the wrong way, stumbling down the steps leading out into the courtyard. The frigid night jabs through the bloodied linen. I thrust my hand into the frost to numb the wound. Framed in the windows of the keep, the hulda glare down at me. From here, their faces are unreadable, statues in the moonlight.

When the paradise of Iberos began to rot, my family followed close behind.

Our father withdrew into himself, hoping that his inattention might restore nature's balance. But even abstinence tills our flesh into fertile soil for all manner of affliction. As with my mother, bone-fever took root in his velti's abscesses. As winter crept in, they became haunts of themselves, Lord and Lady of a fallen Spire.

Col spent more and more time away from home, walking the curses.

Stig and I remained inseparable, even as our quarrels grew teeth. Weeks went by without me speaking a single word to my parents.

When our cousin Mislav offered to relieve us of a few hulda, the decision was easy. At a whim, my mother gave him Vigdis, a spry imp from the gardens, and Maeija. From what I heard, they did not complain as he led them into the woods.

I was not there, of course.

It was the evening of Stig's disappearance.

I had retreated to the darkness of the keep, heartache and hatred crashing through me like lightning and thunder.

With the caress of morning's cold incandescence, Spire Iberos shudders into snappish wakefulness like a dog yet to slip into its housebroken mask. The few remaining inhabitants amble outside, women and men, half-dressed, snorting clouds of vapor, to dump the contents of their night buckets into the weeds or knock the icicles from their roofs. Some face down the rising sun with clenched lips. With neither Blessed nor hulda in sight, the unmarked bask in a world where merely human is enough.

Stig joins me at the window. He follows the activity below us with the genial indifference you might have for an ant crawling across your arm.

"Col is waiting for us in the next chamber."

"Then you've seen him in the daylight. The shaking, the bruises? It's just how my mother was, at the end."

"And when he's gone, what will you do?"

A roar kindles in my head, bells within bells. I grab Stig by the shoulders and shove him towards the exit. It's shocking to feel the warmth of his skin through his shirt.

"You haven't asked about your uncle."

"No."

"Ulcer-blossoms of the stomach," I sneer, tongue sharpened for cruelty. "Died sobbing and alone."

He flinches but doesn't budge. "Join us at the hearth. Bring your blankets. Col could use some more."

When our mother died, my father stood with us at the edge of the cremation pit. As both flesh and disease burned away, he refused to watch as Col breathed in the smoke, sucking it deep into his lungs, blacking his teeth to ashen gravestones. His eyes were showing their whites when the smoldering mark finally appeared on his throat. First, the stave for hunter, overlapped by the sign of the underground. Finder of the hidden and lost. His Blessing.

My father whispered something into the ear of his eldest son. Then he walked down into the fire. He didn't scream and he didn't look back.

Col rested his hands on my shoulders.

It was my turn.

I wasn't ready. I tried to run away, to do what Stig had begged of me so many times, to forgo family, destiny, to remain a child.

Col braced me and held my head into the grim cloud that my father was becoming.

Breathe, he commanded.

I struggled to twist out of his grip.

No!

He jammed his fingers into my mouth, gagging me. In that moment, with ashes crusting in my nose, I hated Col, a hate that still scratches at the back of my throat.

Breathe.

I had no choice but to relent to the fire and the cinders and the heat of velti released with my father's final heartbeats. His ashes filled me, Blessed me, marked me, and when I was sure I couldn't take any more was when my brother urged me to breathe deeper.

"And here comes our little Lord Serpent-Tongue," Col says.

Stig offers me a half-empty bottle of wine like the taper of a supplicant. When I don't move to take it, Col smirks and draws the blankets tighter around him. A bruise spreads across his face, dark as ink in the dim firelight. Several more of his teeth have fallen out.

Spots of dread whirl at the edge of my vision. How long have they been conspiring? A tight knot cannot be unraveled in the dark, but if enough hands tug the strings it may be undone by accident.

"Brother, let me help you back downstairs —"

Col glares at me. "No. You need to listen."

"To him?" I try to hide the urgency in my voice, even as the edges brighten, the pressure builds. "He's a kitchen boy who stumbled his way into his mark."

Stig runs a scarred finger around the bottles lip, making it sing. The spots pulse faster, dark feathers against my temple. "Transiency is the natural state of all things," he says. "Even the hardest, oldest stone is remade by a single drop of rain. It's a difficult lesson to learn." He passes his hand over the bottle, and the velti reduces it to a pile of quartz-glinted sand. "Or that might all be poetic nonsense. What do I know? Maybe you're right and all I'm good at is scaling a fish before it stops gulping for air."

Despair slips into the room like a ghost. It stares into the fire. Finally. I've been waiting for you. I don't care if the velti starves for attention, if it eternally pries its fingernails into the seams of my skull.

Nothing would make me happier.

Then another coughing fit rakes out from Col's lungs. Before his voice falls apart, he manages a hoarse whisper into my ear. "Don't you dare give up on me. Not yet."

After finally convincing Col to return to his bed, I peel back the wrappings around my thumb. The cut shines in its rawness. Some scabbing at the edges, the rest gapes like a drowning fish. Without asking, Stig inspects the wound for any slickness of infection. Why does such a simple act nearly bring me to tears?

I take my hand back and ask Stig why he believes he can save Col rather than be the final tap of false hope that nudges him over the edge.

As an answer, he produces a slight book, clasped in bronze, bound in pebble-gray reptilian leather. If my face betrays any reaction, he doesn't notice.

"It's an ancient war-tongue," he explains, tracing its spidery script. "Mislav claimed no knowledge of this book, that he had never set eyes on it before. Must have been a lie. Right? Yes. That's how I knew it was important."

"And he taught you how to read it?"

"No, he never had the chance. I taught myself – or, rather, I used my Blessing to transform into someone who always could read it. A small adjustment, really."

A small adjustment. That's how it always starts. Maybe just a taste, enough to prove it to yourself. A taste leads to a morsel to a meal to a bottomless feast, eat, eat or ache, eat or wither, until you realize, too late, that perhaps it's *you* that the velti has been devouring all along.

"There's a ritual described inside," Stig continues. "To carve out a new curs. It requires certain forms of velti, which we have between the three of us. And I know the perfect place to try it." He picked at the scars on his hands. "I'm sorry, should have told you right away. Not sure why I didn't."

"It's fine."

"Judoc, don't you think, now that we are both Blessed, there shouldn't be any more secrets between us? There doesn't need to be. Right? There's something I should tell you, about your cousin. Mislav, he didn't find me. I was waiting for him. I swear, I only wanted his guidance –"

Before he can speak another word, I take his damaged hands in mine. "It's fine."

With enough practice, any lie can be sharpened into the truth.

In all those years, away, did I think of you?
　Stig, why don't you ask?
　Then I could tell you.
　Yes. Constantly.
　I obsessed over you the way Col does his maps.
　What you might look like, what you might be doing, where you might be. I saw you sleeping in a night-blue forest of pines. I heard you walking the marble streets of Spire Palus. I tasted the salt of the western sea on your teeth.
　Visions of you sparked against a constantly spinning whetstone of resentment. I would wake up in the middle of the night, velti currents knotted in my hands.
　I would tell you how strange it was, as Iberos collapsed, as my parents burned and my brother sank into desolation, that I remained healthy, even as I rarely exercised my Blessing.
　How, in all that time, I never felt a drop of pain.
　Not until the day you returned.

The tall grass snaps underfoot as we march through the fields. Our boots glitter with ice. We suck cold air through our teeth, where it warms along the roof of our mouths before rolling down into our lungs. Stig pauses occasionally to tug his cap back over his reddening scalp.
　"Almost there," he says, multiple times, first as a joke, then more serious as familiar woodlands thin out to a horizon of cobalt stone. There is nothing alive out here, not a single sparrow, hare or beetle.

Col seems oblivious to the cold. Hope rouges his cheeks. I bet he's already imagining names for this new curs.

Approaching the mountains, the trail shakes off its snowpack to reveal crests of shale, uneven steps as likely to cast an unlucky traveler off as carry them forward. Up here, the hissing wind becomes more insistent. It seeks out any patch of exposed skin, groping at us, promising cool, dry kisses, if we only take off our cloaks, our scarves, our boots.

Stig pauses to gauge the way ahead.

"See those twin ridges of rock jutting out? My uncle called them the Sleeping Dogs. First time he brought me out here, I was certain that wolves or mudsnakes would devour us in the night. Nothing happened though. I suppose even devils find it too cold up here to bother."

Evening drops quickly. Other than a hazel shaft of sunlight pricking over the mountains, nightfall drains the world of color.

A coin flashes in Col's palm, then disappears again.

We reach a flattened palm of untouched snow sheltered between a copse of ice-heavy alder on one side and the elbow of a Sleeping Dog on the other. There's a stillness here, the quietude of an ancient chapel, present and sacred, nature holding its breath.

We are exactly where we need to be.

"We best start," Stig says. "Before we lose the light entirely."

Col tastes the air. Nods. The lines of his body grow rigid, even the creases on his face, his grimace sharp as a scythe.

Stig sidles up to me and pulls my face close to his.

"Are you ready, divine one?"

He's giving me one more chance. To stop everything, to turn around and trudge back down the mountain and let events unfold as they should, a story already written where the Blessed of Spire Iberos fade away, our inheritance reclaimed by the ivy, the moss, the worms, our lineage forgotten to everyone except the huldufólk who had yet to meet us. Before our extinction, there might even be a time of warmth, rising from the decay in a rush of wine and tea, blood to blood, the sighs of aging friends.

And if I can see that possibility, so can Stig.

Above us, dark clouds churn through each other, trapped between the dusk and the mountains. As if driven by instinct, we concentrate our Blessings. The velti responds. Even as the pain flickers away, I start to say something, I can't even tell what, a dozen shapeless words rising from my ribs, when the sun goes rust and velti wildfire leaps from Col's throat, to Stig's, to mine. Magic pops and spurts between us, burning away our emotions, its alchemy shifting the elements to air, to water, to glass.

I was a babe when Maeija came to me.

She looked then exactly as she does now, as she probably did when the earth itself slipped the fiery cowl of its birth. She crept into my chambers in the middle of a moonless night with what would be the first of many cups of gray tea. As my headache dulled, she climbed up onto my bed. I will never forget the jab of her knees through the blankets. The smell of her breath, like the heavy air from a cavern deep underground. The rough brush of her bark-scaled lips against my ear.

There, as I laid in the darkness, paralyzed by terror, she related the entirety of my life, backwards.

You rose from a broken corpse, she said, *up, up, into the keep, through that very window on the other side of this room. The sickness shook you like a doll, softer and softer, through a winter and a summer. Then you barely felt the fever at all, other than a twinge in your jaw. Yes, just like you see in your mother's jaw now. Then, your brother walked out of the ocean, relief turned to anger, to despondency. He can barely remember being dead, all those guts eaten by crabs. He rejoined you here in the Spire for many years, some happy, others less so. The bone-fever burned brightly in him, before fading, before your mother and father pulled themselves out of the ashes ...*

Please, enough, I wept. *I don't want to know this.*

Don't be frightened, mayfly. It is a story already told, a stone resting at the bottom of the sea.

It's horrible.

She drew her claws through my hair, gentle as a kitten.

Perhaps, together, we tipped the stone as it settled? Speak truthfully. What else could you have done for your own blood? Was it all worth it to take away their pain?

All I had was family. They were my whole world. Even Stig, despite all his charms, could never grasp the beautiful and terrible magic that stitched the Blessed together in threads of white and black.

Anything, I said. *I would do anything to save them.*

In that way, we were the same. She pressed a thin book into my hands. It felt oddly alive. I swear there was a fading pulse under its skin. *This came back to me in the cage of a corpse. It wrote itself. You slipped it in with others of its kind. You chose a darling of unlike blood carry it. You kept it hidden for a hundred turns of the moon.*

As she climbed off my bed, I asked her how this could possibly save my family.

Left alone, a quiet love retained its simple form. Hit with an axe, it shattered to dust. But, carefully fletched, whittled over time, you turned a green sapling to a needle, its life sharpened to pierce the world's skin.

Me? I will cure them? That is to be my Blessing?

It was too dark to see, yet I knew she was grinning.

Mayfly, that was my weapon.

Stig screams into the unnatural gale swirling around us.

"Col, now!"

My brother, weak, skeletal, raises his hands into the velti. It appears first as a smudge, then a shadow, then a shape. Massive. Dark. It crashes to the ground and I recognize it as one of the obsidian sarsens from the forest of shipwrecks. It totters precipitously over us like a finger about to crush a beetle, before settling into the snow. The second sarsen arrives with a thunderclap, taking its place by its twin.

Col collapses in exhaustion, tongue lolling.

I look over to Stig. He's concentrating on the empty space between the sarsens. Under his guidance, the air dulls like a cataract, softening the sharp angles of the mountains beyond. With a final grunt of effort, he becomes midwife to a shivering curs that limps and lurches out from the gap.

The velti seethes around us. Col grimaces, lips wet with bile.

"Behold," he cries triumphantly, "I name thee the Broken-World curs."

It is not complete. To enter now would be like walking into oblivion.

A tempting thought.

According to the book, three Blessings are required to create a new curs. Col's gift of finding brought the sarsens to this location. Stig changed history, making it as if this end of the curs were always tethered to the stones.

As for reaching the other side ...

Stig hands me the bird-like totem, our witch-raven, the relic of a distant continent. Sparks roll down its silver wings.

I take the totem and roll it between my velti-slicked palms until it softens like wax, keep spinning until it forms a rod, then a spear. With shaking hands, I aim the tip towards the curs. The velti wind draws it forward as if pulled by a string.

The curs ripples at the impact. But it does not open.

I knew it wouldn't.

"Oh," Stig says.

"Your uncle probably thought it was real."

Col has curled up in a soft pile of snow rusted with vomit. He's barely breathing.

"It's over," I say. "Help me carry him home. Better to die in his own bed than out here."

Stig looks to Col, then to me.

Many strains of acquaintance may sprout in the thin soil of our footsteps; comradery, love, lust. Friendships blossom like wildflowers. However, a perfect bond, a heart that returns to your side through seasons of pain and selfishness? One that, when presented with the opportunity, would choose to sacrifice itself for your own happiness? Infinitesimally rare. Like my father's impossible gardens, it must be meticulously cultivated. Take a scythe to the weeds, to the stragglers, to the less desirable offshoots. Creation is an act of cutting away all other possibilities.

"Something else we can try ..."

There's a thousand things I should say now. I have been practicing them all my life.

Stig, perhaps, once, you truly were a friend to a monk who found you in the woods. Perhaps, once, he died peacefully in his sleep, and you stood too close to his funeral pyre. A smudge of the velti singed your throat. Enough to taste. To want more. To abandon what you were and eventually, through slaughter and desperation, to dream yourself to my equal.

Stig, you always were my equal.

Stig, don't make me choose.

Stig, the truth is, I chose this a long time ago.

My lips refuse to speak, even as Stig embraces me and his mouth covers mine, as his breath fills my lungs, as he draws the velti from me, Ormstunga, Serpent-Tongue. He already understands. Perhaps he knew from the moment I agreed to come to this barren place. What portion of our lives is constructed from such feints to ignorance, burying our wet natures to play the roles required? We tell ourselves we can step off the stage at any time. But controlling our story takes an act of creative violence, one whose expanding design refuses easy perception, even as it alters everything it touches.

While it's undeniable that all humans are alien to Casses, via some unnatural symbiosis the Blessed anchored themselves to this rock. Stig's people never had that chance. We bound their identity to exclusion. Their blood. Shipwrecked. Unmarked.

He is the shape hidden in the wood.

I am the blade with which to carve it out.

"Wait," is all I manage to say before the velti reads our intent and explodes with a prehistoric wail, rooting out from the marks in our throats, encircling us, forcing us closer, pressing my hands to his chest, then sinking into his chest, one knuckle, two. He buckles as his knees fuse together. His ribs explode outward, the bones jutting from the skin in a spray of red. A sheen of moss crawls upwards from where his feet used to be, bursting from the muscles beneath. That's when he finally screams.

Ever since Maeija's prophecy, I have only prayed for one thing; that this moment would be painless.

I should have known better.

Stig, my darling. This is our Blessing.

His face is last to transform. His eye sockets pinch shut. Teeth crack. Muscles harden. He has become a milestone of bone and flesh. As the velti lifts him up and carries him into the white maw of the curs, I can still see a hint of his smile in the scratching runes.

The Broken-World curs erupts into brilliance. A corridor of light pours out like a crimson thread from the needles eye. It effortlessly flows across the rough, between the ears of the Sleeping Dogs, presumably crossing the mountains and the ice freckled waters beyond.

Through the warped glass of the curs, plagues of flies rumble over a wasteland of sand and vermillion scrub. No, not flies, distant warships, floating in the air. Entire armadas of those carved totems skate across the surface of a burning horizon, just as my mother did, that effortless glide. Will they become the wrecks in the marshlands? Am I seeing the past or the future?

It doesn't matter.

Pain exists outside of time.

The curs warbles. Something emerges from the other side. It is difficult to look at. My eyes slide off its shifting collection of limbs, arms and legs, intertwined with serpentine roots of gaslight. It takes no heed of me or Col as it picks through the snow, constantly changing shape, shrinking, hardening, a liquid mandala becoming stone.

I know what this is.

Prince of the small folk. Mythic creature of pure velti.

Álfar.

It pauses at the bloody pile of rags that were Stig's clothes. A sinuous claw plucks the leather book out from the carnage and gently attaches it to a weeping sore of matching shape on its flank.

Then it sees me.

Orbs of blue flame flicker in its sockets.

"Judoc of Iberos. Your life made a nice splash dropping into the pond of time, mayfly."

My mouth goes numb with the taste of gray tea.

"Maeija?"

"A good name. Perhaps I will take it one day."

A thousand questions sting my tongue to silence. All I can manage is stutter.

The álfar whispers into my ear.

"The knife in its velvet sheath needed not know why it was made, or in whose forge it was birthed. It only needed to know how to cut."

A second phantom steps through the curs, then a dozen more, a hundred, an upended waterfall of thrashing shadows pouring from the curs and spilling across the mountains. Horror clamps my ribs. Is this an invasion? A plague?

A reclamation?

An invisible wind takes them up, light as spiderlings, and carries them into the night. As fast as they arrived, they are gone. Gone into our dead past, their future.

Stars prick through the thin clouds.

I crawl over to Col and press my ear to his chest. Still breathing. I leverage him over my shoulder and make my way towards the curs. My arms brush against the milestone. It is warm, slightly yielding. It reminds me of when Stig and I sat on our hands and watched his uncle work the sculptor's wheel. It always fascinated me to see a simple lump of clay transformed by nothing other than his naked hands. He didn't need the velti to infuse the inanimate with grace and beauty. Once, he sculpted us miniature replicas of ourselves, perfectly detailed down to the fingernails. I remember Stig cradling his brittle boy in his hands. I remember crushing mine under my heel, not for the sin of accepting gifts from the unmarked, but for the unfairness of it being unfeeling clay all the way through.

I drag my brother's limp body past the milestones, into the curs, toward the ragged dawn of a distant shore.

David Gallay's story "Cheminagium" was published in Metaphorosis on Friday, 9 February 2018.

About the story

This story began with the image of a two men standing before a gate in the mountains. At their feet was a body, crumpled in the snow. I knew the two men were brothers. The body remained a mystery until I heard someone define "cheminage" on the radio, as an old word for a toll to pass through the forest. That's exactly what the body was. Everything else flowed from the tension of that triangle and the strange red sky on the other side of that gate.

A question for the author

Q: What kind of pieces are the most fun to write (action, lyrical, etc.)?

A: The human mind has an underrated capacity for acceptance. The pieces I find the most fun to write are those that arise from characters placed in unexpected, uncomfortable or even horrific situations and then watching them navigate their way through it. No matter how dark or bizarre the circumstances, the act of living always finds its own lyric beauty.

About the author

David Gallay is a writer of speculative fiction and horror. After receiving a B.A in Creative Writing from Binghamton University, and currently resides in Wisconsin where he leads a double life as an IT SysAdmin.

@svengali

The Stars Don't Lie

R.W.W. Greene

The Dean of Admissions took off his spectacles and polished them on his dappled lower shoulder. "You will be the first man to attend Chiron Classical University, you know."

"I'm a woman," Lesa said. "A female of my species. I know the situation is unusual, but—."

"I used 'man' in the inclusive meaning of the word." The Dean's rear hooves shifted on the thick grass. "Unusual. Yes, it is unusual. You should not expect special allowances to come with your ..." His mouth twisted. "Rarity."

Lesa shifted her weight to spare her aching right ankle at the expense of her somewhat less tender left. Neither the Dean nor his office had offered anything resembling a chair, and she had not expected the three-mile hike——a near jog, really——from his office to the sculpture garden in the center of campus. They had toured several venerable buildings en route, all round, with gently curving hallways and long, low ramps instead of stairs.

The Dean had finally brought them to a halt near a statue of a noble-looking centaur being speared to death by five Greek soldiers. It appeared to be a common theme in the garden.

"I don't expect any special treatment," Lesa said.

The Dean whisked his tail. "I remain surprised a woman man would want to study here. Your kind usually frowns on the sciences."

"Only the old sciences," Lesa said. "It seems like we're always finding new ones."

"I have read about your space vessels and computers." The centaur academic accented the third syllable of the word like it tasted bad. "Imagine trusting so much to soulless things." He pulled a folder out of the haversack slung across his withers. "You'll find a map of the campus in here. A meals schedule and the like." He licked his lips.

Lesa took the folder. "Where should I go from here?"

"Your dormitory, perhaps. A lovely centauride—a female centaur—from a good family has been assigned as your roommate. You will meet with your program advisor Monday morning, so you are free until then."

Lesa reached up to shake the graying centaur's hand. "Thank you for this opportunity."

"I did nothing." The Dean ignored her hand and rested his own on his bare paunch. "I was simply outvoted."

Believed a myth for much of the past two millennia, centaurs were rediscovered in 1996. In Ancient Greece, where they originated, centaurs once numbered in the tens of thousands. Today, there are less than 12,000 individuals, living in small communities in isolated parts of the world. Infant mortality among the centaur is extremely high, so, although they are long-lived, the population is in decline.

—Actor David Duchovny, narrating for National Geographic's "Myths Among Us" (1999)

Lesa pulled the map out of the folder. The offer letter from Chiron Classical had come out of nowhere six months before. Lesa had never heard of the school and knew nothing about centaurs beyond what she could find online. Still, she reminded herself, the chance to study divination at one of the oldest universities in the world was too good to pass up.

The campus map was hand-drawn and beautifully lettered on thin parchment. Her dormitory was ... She put her finger on the building's icon as a placeholder and lined up the compass rose with the waning sun. Due west. She shaded her eyes with her hand. A low, stone building nestled in the crook of two hills about a mile and a half away. An easy trot on four legs, likely a half-hour slog on two. She stuffed the folder into her satchel and slung the bag over her shoulder. Another hike would be a great start on those ten pounds she wanted to lose.

The distance proved deceiving, and an hour later she reached the sliding door at the front of the building. The door handle was at least a foot over Lesa's head, and she had to use both hands to operate it. Lesa's satchel slipped off her shoulder and dangled in the crook of her arm as she slid the heavy door open. She put the pack on the worn tile inside the dormitory before using equal and opposite strength to get the portal shut again. The number δ was written in flowing calligraphy on the top-right corner of the folder. Lesa found the number's mate within the dormitory and knocked.

"It is open," said a voice within.

Lesa set her belongings down for the second time and stood on tiptoe to reach the handle. The door slid open with a screech.

"I put a repair request in for that," the centauride inside said. "I will probably graduate before it gets fixed."

"Maybe it just needs some oil." Lesa wiped sweat from her forehead with her sleeve. "I'm Lesa."

Her roommate was a chestnut with white socks, her human skin several shades lighter than Lesa's own. From the waist up, she put Lesa in mind of a naked, Olympic-caliber, beach-volleyball player.

"I know who you are." The centauride's hooves pushed straw around the worn wooden floor. "Before you speak, I want you to know that this was not my idea. I do not like men, and I did not want one for a roommate."

"Noted," Lesa said. "Good thing I'm a woman."

The centauride blew a fall of rust-colored hair off her forehead. "Whatever you call yourself. I do not like woman men, either."

"It's just 'woman,' or 'women' if you are disliking more than one of us." Lesa hung her satchel on a peg beside the door. "It's okay if I use this?"

The centaur swished her tail. "I am Rhiannon." She pointed to the far end of the room. "That is your side."

The floor was carpeted in fresh straw. On Rhiannon's side, a canvas-covered wedge was mounted low on the wall. The centauride could lie down next to the wedge and lean her upper body on it to sleep. Her walls were covered in tapestries and warmly lit with alchemical lanterns. A sword, shield, and archery kit leaned in the corner next to a tall loom.

Lesa's side of the room was empty. "There's no bed," she said.

"Try the campus stores. That is where I got mine. Otherwise ..." Rhiannon shrugged.

Lesa nodded. Cost wouldn't be a problem. Two years before, using numerology, a new algorithm, and coffee grounds from her neighborhood 7-11, Lesa had won $43 million in a nationwide lottery. After taxes and paying off all her friends' student loans, most of the winnings had gone to charity, but she could still be comfortably and independently middle class for a few lifetimes. "I don't see an outlet in here," she said.

"Perhaps there is one near the toualeta. Outside the back door."

"Are the showers there?"

Rhiannon's face was blank.

"For bathing."

"Baths are every other morning. Line up along the fence and wait for the helpers." The clock on the wall chimed. "It is time for pémpto."

Fifth meal. One of eight that centaurs consumed daily, according to the information in the folder. "You might want a jacket," Lesa said.

"Or I might not." The centauride slid open the door and clopped into the hallway. Lesa snagged her satchel off the peg and followed.

The shadows of the hills behind the dormitory had crept into the yard in front of it. "The dining hall is that way." Rhiannon pointed roughly northeast and galloped away, leaving Lesa to close the heavy door and walk alone. She consulted her map. A two-mile trek in the growing darkness. *No special allowances.* Lesa shouldered her satchel and followed Rhiannon's receding figure.

Former bush pilot [Charlie] Landsdowne gestured wildly as he recalled finding the centaur village.

"They were just, you know, standing there. I figured I'd gone crazy from the cold or something. I think they were just as surprised to see me!" Landsdowne said.

Landsdowne said he stayed in the centaur village for four weeks while he recovered from injuries he sustained in the crash and wondered what his hosts planned to do with him.

"They didn't talk much to me," he said. "But I could tell they spoke English. They knew what I was saying well enough."

The centaurs eventually carried Landsdowne to Waterton Lakes National Park, on the US/Canadian border, and left him at a ranger station there.

"But not before I got pictures!" Landsdowne crowed. "You'd think they'd never seen a camera before."

— New York Times, February 15, 1996

The dining hall was a high-ceilinged timber-framed roundhouse above the sculpture garden. Long before she arrived at the door, Lesa could see the light from the building's large windows. Inside, a central fire pit warded off the cold, and dozens of centaurs stood at high trestle tables to eat. Chestnut and bare skin was a common color scheme, and Rhiannon was well camouflaged.

A centauride with gray braids yanked the pull rope of an iron bell and chased the din with a hoarse shout. "Kitchen closes in five minutes!" She held up her hand to show all her fingers. "Fill up and get out."

Lesa lined up with six or seven centaurs while they ignored her and jostled for space. It turned out to be far safer at the end of the queue than in its middle, so Lesa was the last one at the serving window, which was at least a foot above her head. She jumped and waved her hands to get the attention of the serving staff.

"What do you want?" one of the serving centaurides said.

"Dinner," Lesa said. "I'm a student."

"The kitchen is closed." The centauride ran her hand through her short hair, making it stand on end, and glared down at Lesa. "There is nothing left."

"I don't need much."

"You are a man." She squinted. "I had heard one of you was coming. We have bet on how long you will last."

"I'm a woman." Lesa pulled her smartphone and a deck of tarot cards out of her jacket pocket. The phone wasn't getting a signal, but she didn't need it to run her custom tarot app. "If I tell you something true about you, can I at least get a sandwich or something?"

"You are in the Divination College?" The centauride laughed. "If you tell me I am going on an unexpected journey and that I am going to die surrounded by friends, I am closing this window right now."

"Hold on." Lesa dealt a row of cards and took a picture of it with her phone. She opened the photo with her app and studied the results. She noted the pattern of age spots on the centauride's face and added it to the data. "Your husband is cheating on you. She's a blonde, bleached blonde, and she ... likes the White Sox?"

The server snorted. "She has a white sock on her right back leg. She works in grounds keeping. Her name is Layla, and she can have him."

Lesa put her phone and cards away. "I only said it would be true, not unknown."

The server pushed a plate to the edge of the window. "All I have. Take it or leave it."

Lesa balanced the plate on the end of her fingers until it was low enough to grasp firmly. "Thank you," she said, but the serving window had closed.

There were no human-scaled tables and few openings in the barrier of horse posteriors surrounding the centaur tables. Lesa took her plate to a corner and crouched with her back against the wall to inspect her meal: four raw carrots, half a grilled onion, a wad of alfalfa, and a chunk of near-bleeding meat the size of her fist. *And me with no way to reach Instagram.* She took a picture anyway and put three carrots into her satchel for later. She ate the meat and onion first, then the alfalfa, with a carrot for dessert. *Happy first day to me.*

Back at the dorm, Lesa could not suss out how to light the alchemical lamps. So, she worked in the dark, kicking up a platform of straw on her side of the dorm room and piling clothes on top of it until she could no longer feel the scratchy poke of dry stalks. She used her satchel for a pillow and pulled her jacket over the top of her for warmth.

Things will get better, her great-grandmother would have said. *The stars don't lie.*

Lesa woke at midnight with a full bladder and no idea where the door was. She powered on her phone, which she had switched off after dinner to save the battery, and picked her way past her sleeping roommate to the door. She opened it slowly, which only prolonged the screech, and glanced back to see if Rhiannon had been disturbed. The centauride smacked her lips and resumed snoring.

The hallway beyond the door was dark, too, and Lesa held the cellphone high in search of the back door. It opened onto an empty paddock. Right outside the door, Rhiannon had said. Lesa took two steps into the small and space and placed her bare left foot squarely in a pile of

"Shit!" No toilets, either. No toilets, no toilet paper, no beds, no food, no ... "Shit! Shit! Shit!"

Lesa's phone dimmed and buzzed to remind her it was running low on juice. The only thing worse than pissing outdoors was pissing outside in the dark, so she made short work of the task and went back inside. Rhiannon's breathing was slow and steady, and the room was warm with beer breath and horse farts. Lesa returned to her pallet and pulled her jacket up to her chin.

The stars don't lie. The stars don't lie. The stars don't lie.

Lesa feigned sleep until she heard Rhiannon lurch up from bed and leave for próto, first meal. She had not rested well on the straw pallet, and her back hurt. Worse, she had to pee again. She pulled on her boots

and went out to the paddock. She squatted behind a bush and tried not to notice the chill nor think about what she would have to do when her bowels caught up with the time-zone shift.

There was no power outlet in sight, but Lesa found a cold-water sink. She moved a log from a nearby woodpile and stood on it to reach the tap. The cake of soap on the sink side was rough-cut and smelled like pine tar.

Back in the dormitory, she ate a carrot and went through her folder. Próto was ending soon, but there would be another meal in about two hours. Lesa pulled on her jacket and hiked to the university's library and stores, a multi-story stone building with white pillars in the front. A low, curving ramp brought her to the front door, which was locked. She leaned against the wall and ate the other carrot.

Before she saw the bookish centauride, Lesa heard her hooves clattering up the ramp. The centauride was carrying a parcel, and she clutched it to her chest when she saw Lesa.

"A man!" the centauride said. "How did you—?"

"I'm a student," Lesa said. "Supposedly, a memo went out."

The centauride's throat bobbed. "I have never seen one of your kind before."

"Well, I've talked to exactly four of you," Lesa said. "I need to get into the stores."

The centauride nodded. "I am here to open them." She pulled a large brass key from a belt pouch she wore around her human waist and used it to unlock the door. She slid it open and waved Lesa in. The centauride activated the overhead lamps while Lesa found her way around the dusty room: pens, ink, parchments, tapestries, lamps ...

"How do I turn those on?" Lesa pointed at the lamps.

"They respond to body heat," the centauride said. She held up her hand. "Just touch them."

Lesa put both hands on one of the lamps on the shelf. It failed to light. She added another hand. "It's not working."

"Nonsense." The centauride clopped next to Lisa and put her hand on the lamp. It lit almost instantly. "See?"

Lesa tried a different lamp. It didn't light, either.

"The stories are true!" The centauride drew back. "Cold blood! Men are descended from snakes!"

"Wait a minute." Lesa rubbed her hands together, warming them with friction. This time, when she touched the lamp, it lit. "Centaurs must have higher body temperatures than people. Where are the beds?" Lesa said.

The centauride pointed to the back of the store, where Lesa found a half dozen wedges like the one on Rhiannon's side of the room.

Lesa picked up two of the lamps. "How do I pay for these?"

"You use them until you graduate, then return them. You are allotted two more, plus a bed and academic supplies."

"I don't think I can carry more," Lesa said. "I'll have to come back."

"We can deliver." The centauride pushed a piece of parchment across the countertop. "Write down what you want and where you want to receive it."

Lesa put the lamps back and scratched out a list with the centauride's quill and ink.

"I can scarcely read this," the centauride said.

"Scarcely will have to do." Lesa wrung her cramped, ink-stained fingers. "When will all this be delivered?"

"This afternoon," the centauride said.

Lesa looked at her smartwatch and swore. It had reached the limits of its battery life. "Can you tell me what time it is?"

The centauride considered. "It should nearly be time for déftero." She looked longingly at her parcel. "I brought mine, but you should hurry along and get yours."

Lesa steeled herself for another hike. "The dining hall is north of here?"

Imagine being half hoarse! [Host pretends to clear his throat.] Sorry, half horse! Four legs, two arms, one head, a tail ... one little mouth! [Camera zooms rapidly in and out on the host's mouth.] How do you feed a horse-sized body with a person-sized mouth? Lots, and I mean lots of food! Horses need up to 15,000 calories a day. That's like eating seven cheese pizzas every day! Centaurs are hungry all the time!
— Bill Nye, Bill Nye the Science Guy, Season 4, Episode 21 (1997)

Getting to the dining hall was only a thirty-minute walk, so Lesa took her meal back to the library. The Divination section was in the basement, and she curled up in a quiet spot with her parcel of meat and vegetables and an original copy of the *Prophecies of Socrates*. The philosopher's so-called guiding spirit had answered questions by sneezing — right for "yes," left for "no," so its answers were frustratingly one-dimensional. Compared to Nostradamus though, who pulled everything he wrote right out of his social-climbing butt, the old Greek was a paragon of accuracy.

Lesa made her food last until dark and reluctantly reshelved the sheath of scrolls. She answered nature's call in the lee of the library building and set out for her dormitory.

Clouds had settled in and the night was even darker than the one before it. Lesa walked hard, trusting to the stars to bring her back to warmth and light. She shivered and pulled up the collar of her jacket.

She was passing the pond on the edge of campus when she heard it: an undulating moan for attention like a baby's cry. It sounded as if it were coming from the water. She stepped off the path. The cry grew louder, then doubled. A second cry was coming from further along the bank of the pond. Then a third. A chorus of cries echoed off the water like a daycare of the damned.

Lesa backed away. Self-divination was seldom accurate, but it didn't take a soothsayer to know the pond was bad news. She checked the stars again and got back on the path to her dorm. The cries dimmed as her route took her away from the water.

Without working electronics, Lesa had no idea how long she had been walking, and the sight of her dormitory's front door was welcome. Lesa's order from school stores was piled outside the dorm room's screechy door. She set up the lamps and experimented with the wedge. It looked like a sex pillow a former lover had talked her into using once, but it was more comfortable than the pile of straw.

Lesa went over her reading notes until her drooping eyelids hinted at sleep. She reached for the closest lamp and swore. The centauride at the stores hadn't told her how to turn the things off. Lesa draped them in clothing until the glow softened and lay down on her wedge.

"Lemme see that cup, baby girl."

Lesa took the last swallow of mint tea and offered the cup to her great-grandmother.

"Wait." The old woman held up one wrinkled hand, a gold band shining dimly on one finger. "Swirl it 'round first. Like this. Three time." She demonstrated. "Then shut yo eyes and think 'bout what's comin'."

Lesa closed her eyes while her great-grandmother upended the cup over a saucer and let the remaining liquid drain away. She opened one eye to peek. "What's it say, grandma?"

"Hol' on a minute I'll see." The old woman picked up the cup and looked inside it. She tapped the rim. "Sez here you need to mind yo' mama better. Stop givin' her the fits."

Lesa rolled her eyes. "I already know that! What's it say about my future?"

Lesa's great-grandmother, Lesa's namesake, looked deeper into the cup. "Sez you goin' to be important one day. Not famous, not powerful, but important to somethin."

"To what?"

The old woman shook her head. "That's all ah see. The stars don' lie." She put the cup down. "Let's go out t' yard and get some peaches for dessert."

Lesa lined up near the fence for the Sunday morning baths but fled when she saw the army of helpers armed with scrub brushes and hoses. The centaurs chatted and laughed as the helpers, collared wendigos, hosed them down and scrubbed their hard-to-reach areas. Lesa went back to her room and applied another layer of deodorant.

Several groups of centaur cantered past Lesa as she hiked to the dining hall for second meal. Most ignored her, but one dark-haired centauride called her a pórni as she rushed by, and a scrawny male threw a potato at her. Lesa picked up the potato and put it in her satchel for later.

The dining hall was quiet and sparsely populated. Lesa got to the serving window before the last call.

"Where is everyone?" she said.

"Drunk. Or getting over drunk," said the server with the adulterous husband. "Like this every Lord's Day." She handed down a plate of food. "Settling in?"

Lesa shrugged. "I'll know better tomorrow. I have a meeting with my advisor."

The centauride tapped the side of her nose. "Do not leave us too soon, man. I have money riding on you. If you hold out the week, I collect."

Lesa turned from the window and found herself airborne as a centaur's hindquarters struck her. She landed on the floor amongst her vegetables with the wind knocked out of her.

The offending centaur squinted and twisted his human torso to look around. "Feels as if I hit something. Did anyone see what it was?" His friends laughed. The centaur walked in a circle, pretending to look for something on the ground. "Something small, maybe."

Lesa could not catch her breath. She spotted Rhiannon, who was hiding a smile and trying hard not to look at her.

"Smells like pórni in here!" The centaur who had knocked Lesa over grinned. "Does anyone else smell it?" He brought one of his front hooves to the floor in a hard stomp.

Lesa staggered to her feet. "Real mature, ass——." Her words came out as a wheeze, but the centaur wasn't listening anyway.

He pointed at her. "How did this get in here? I thought they set traps for vermin."

"That's enough, Polkan!" shouted a gangly centaur from the edge of the crowd.

Lesa stepped back to the serving window. "Can I get another plate to go?"

Lesa took her food and went back to the library. *The stars may not lie, but sometimes they forget to mention things.*

The Centaurs are best known for their fight with the Lapiths, which was caused by their attempt to carry off Hippodamia and the rest of the Lapith women on the day of Hippodamia's marriage to Pirithous, king of the Lapithae, himself the son of Ixion. The strife among these cousins is a metaphor for the conflict between the lower appetites and civilized behavior in humankind. Theseus, a hero and founder of cities, who happened to be present, threw the balance in favour of the right order of things, and assisted Pirithous. The Centaurs were driven off or destroyed.

— Wikipedia, Centaur entry

Lesa had carrots for breakfast the next day and pulled the best-possible outfit from the pile of wrinkled clothing she had slept on. The Divination building was nearly five miles away, so she set out early, hiking as the sun settled into its track. She climbed the long ramp to the door of the round building and wrestled it open. Her advisor's office was down the hallway on the right.

At her knock, the advisor, a centaur with a long white beard, bade her enter. The office smelled of old parchment and ink. "You must be Ms. Carter," the centaur said. "I am Mentor Rhaecus."

"I'd kill for a chair," Lesa said. "I just walked five miles on two carrots."

Mentor Rhaecus tapped his chin. "I'm sure we have something ..." He rang a small bell. There was a rattle of claws in the hallway outside and a pit bull-sized creature made of black fetish rubber dashed in and slid to a stop in front of the professor's desk. "We need ... a chair," the centaur glanced at Lesa as if awaiting correction, "for Ms. Carter."

The dog thing licked its slavering jowls. Its fur was stiff and spikey like a toilet brush, and it had a long, muscular tail, which ended in a human-like hand.

"Go, now!" the centaur said.

The dog thing ducked its head to the centaur and dashed back out of the room.

"Was that ...?" Lesa said.

"An ahuizotl. South American. Very hand-y fellows to have around." His smile was self-amused. "They do most of our fetching and carrying."

"They eat people!" Lesa said. She had received a mythological-animals coloring book for her eleventh birthday and filled in every page. Ahuizotls hid in caves near lakes and cried like human babies until a good Samaritan came around. At that point, the ahuizotl would drown the Samaritan and eat his or her eyes, teeth, and fingernails.

"Only the wild ones do," the centaur said.

Lesa forced her eyes away from the door the man-eater had left through. "I suppose you want to talk about the caribou," Lesa said.

Mentor Rhaecus smiled politely. "As you wish."

Lesa scowled. She had assumed her work predicting caribou migration in northern Alaska had put her on Chiron's radar. The algorithm she programmed compared data sets derived from astrological computations and austromancy (divination using wind patterns), and the result prediction proved accurate within five meters.

"I ended a near famine," Lesa said.

"Lovely." The Mentor smiled again.

"Do you even know my work?"

"Work?" The Mentor's breath made the quills on his pen rack flutter. Goose feathers mostly, although one or two might have been from a swan. Special-occasion quills, for writing letters to must-have students. There wasn't a computer in sight. There was no way news of Lesa's success with the caribou had reached him.

The ahuizotl re-entered the room with a drooling friend, each carrying one end of a low footstool with its hand tail. Tail hand. There were hands on the end of their legs, too, each rubbery finger tipped with a sharp claw. The ahuizotl sniffed eagerly at Lesa's legs and mewled like a crying baby until the professor shooed them out.

"They're quite safe. They prefer water to land," he said and closed the door behind them. "But you should perhaps carry a weapon of some sort. One or two of the ahuizotl may have escaped to the grounds and returned to savagery. Not a problem for a healthy centaur, of course, but ..."

Lesa thanked whatever intuition had kept her from venturing near the pond and sank onto the stool, which left her head at least three feet lower than the professor's desk. "This isn't going to work."

"Nonsense," Mentor Rhaecus said. "I saw it clearly. You absolutely must be here."

"How did you find out about me?" Lesa said.

"A Norns cast. Runes are a specialty of mine."

"You invited me here based on pulling three rocks out of a bag."

The mentor shuffled his hooves. "I cross-checked, or course. With osteomancy. My teaching assistant narrowed the prophecy down to you. You'll meet him —."

"What do the rocks and bones say about what I'm supposed to do?"

The mentor's tail swished. "Something of great import, no doubt. The runes were very clear: You must be here."

"I want a bed," Lesa said. "A real human bed. And a toilet. And a golf cart or something to get around in."

"I am sure you were told that you would receive no spec—."

"A bed that I can sleep in is not special treatment. Neither is a way to get to get to class on time."

"There might be something in the muse—."

Lesa rose from the footstool. "I want a weapon, too, something to keep away the ahuizotl."

"And the wolves."

"Wolves?!" The campus was in the Canadian Rockies. It stood to reason there would be wolves. "Yes, the wolves. And I want electrical power in my room."

The centaur wrung his hands. "Your requests will take ti—."

"I want them soon," Lesa said. "If I 'must' be here," she frowned, "I want them very, very soon."

After the meeting with the mentor, Lisa followed his instructions downstairs to the Divination Lab. The large space reeked of tea and incense. A gangly centaur with curly hair and glasses pranced up to Lesa as soon as she entered. "You're here!" he said. "I found you, but I never thought you'd ..." He extended his hand. "I'm Pholus. That's how humans do it, right? With hands?"

Lesa shook his hand carefully. "Lesa. Nice to meet you. You're the mentor's TA, right?"

The centaur was nearly dancing with excitement. "Your work is inspired. So precise!" He put his hand out again. "Read my palm. Will I get tenure?"

"It doesn't work like that," Lesa said. "For something so specific, I'd need—."

"We can do it later," Pholus said. "Let me show you around the lab."

In short order, Lesa got the tour and met the other graduate students: five nerdy centaurides and a dark-and-broody centaur named Elatus. "I studied your algorithms." Elatus shrugged. "I was not impressed. I could do the math with quill and parchment."

"It would take you twenty-five years to do the calculations," Lesa said.

The centaur flipped long, black hair out of his eyes. "I could still do them."

One of the centaurides, her name was Hippe, laughed. "By the time you finished, it wouldn't be worth anything. Time doesn't stand still!"

"Did you bring it?" Pholus said. "Your computer?"

Lesa reached into her satchel and pulled out the battered MacBook. "Do you have an outlet I could hook up to?"

They did not. Lesa set the MacBook on one of the lab tables, and the grad students crowded around to see it.

Elatus yawned. "I am going back to work. Some of us plan to graduate." He trotted off, flipping his long hair insolently.

"Do not listen to him," Hippe said. "He is still angry he couldn't get his thesis proposal approved."

"What was the proposal?" Lesa said.

"Anthropomancy. Reading the entrails of a fresh human sacrifice. He wanted us to adopt two human children for the purpose." Pholus adjusted his glasses. "The vote was not even close."

"I would hope not." Not being alone with Elatus was suddenly high on her to-do list. "I thought there would be more students.

"Divination is not the most popular of disciplines," Hippe said. A lot of the families do not believe in it."

Before they broke for lunch, Pholus galloped down to the basement armory. "Most of us have our own. These are the best I could do." He handed Lesa a sword, hilt first. "It's a gladius. Third century."

Lesa took the weapon. Her psychometry was not well developed, but she got flashes of a large battle under a torrent of rain. She shook off the sudden feeling that she was up to her sandal straps in bloody mud.

Pholus presented her with a second object. "You will not be historically accurate, but I thought you would prefer this to a scutum."

The round targe, about the size of a large cheese pizza, was unexpectedly light. "I've no idea how to use any of this," Lesa said. "I'm an academic."

"We start weapons training as foals." Pholus showed Lesa how to put the leather-covered shield on her left arm. "It's Celtic. Sixteenth century." He stroked his thin beard. "I have no idea how a human should stand. You want to present the shield first. Keep the gladius back to strike."

Lesa experimented with her stance and adopted a left-foot-forward stance, her right foot angled in back.

"Hold on." Pholus trotted away and came back with his own sword and shield. "This is completely unfair, I have experience and reach on you, but let us try it. Slowly. Block with the shield." He swung the sword at Lesa's head, giving her plenty of time to lift the targe. "Now, attack ... thrust, not cut ... with the sword. Slow. Step forward on your right hoo—foot—as you do."

Lesa thrust with the sword, stepping forward for power and reach.

Pholus pushed the gladius aside with his own sword. "Now recover backward."

Lesa's feet crossed in the attempt, and she nearly fell. "I'm never going to be good at this."

"You do not have to be all that good to hold off an animal. Use the shield to push it away. Strike it when and if you can."

"Easy to say when you're an expert."

Pholus laughed. "I am terrible at this. Ask anyone."

"Well, I am more terrible." Lesa dropped her arms to her side. "What do I do with this stuff when I'm not fending off wolves and ahuizotl?"

"The shield goes on your back. The sword goes in this." He handed her a belt and scabbard.

"I'm just supposed to wear these all the time."

Pholus slung his shield over his withers and returned his sword to the scabbard on his back. "When you are traveling between buildings. At least when you are alone. But you should not be alone. It's not just wolves," he said. "There are bears, too. Have you ever used a bow?"

"Never."

"That is harder to learn. I will get you one and find you a tutor."

Lesa tried a slashing cut with the sword. "This is ridiculous. It's 2018."

"Is it?" Pholus said.

"What's a pórni?"

Pholus lowered his sword. "Literally it means "slut," but it is also a derogatory term for any human female." He cleared his throat. "I am sorry about what happened in the dining hall."

"It was you who shouted at him." Lesa nodded. "What's his problem with me?"

"Mostly he was showing off for his friends, I think. But centaurs and men do not have the best history." He sheathed his sword. "Polkan's older brother was a fetishist. A human lover. He had tapestries of women all over his walls. Killed himself when it was discovered. Polkan does whatever he can to distance himself from that." The massive astrology clock in the corner bonged. "Middle meal! Do you want me to walk you to the dining hall?"

Lunch was friendly but awkward. Pholus introduced Lesa to some of his circle, but the conversation was made difficult by the fact she couldn't see over the table. Pholus and his friend, Endeis, a second-year Alchemy candidate, accompanied Lesa back to her dorm.

"What is that?" Endeis pointed to something parked to the side of the sliding door.

"It's a lot better than a golf cart," Lesa said. She caressed the handlebars of the black and chrome motorcycle. "A 1952 Vincent Black Lightning. I've never seen one in this condition. Where did it come from?"

"Probably the museum. All kinds of strange things in there. Experiments." Pholus said. "Can you ride it?"

"Will it have gas?" Her father had been a Harley Davidson fan and had given her a rebuilt 1963 Sportster for her sixteenth birthday. She began the finicky process of starting the antique. Build compression and ... it fired up and started to rumble.

"It's really loud!" Pholus pointed to a brass cylinder incorporated into the gas tank. "Looks like it was converted to run on alchemy. Probably need to refill that once a year or so."

Lesa adjusted the choke to smooth out the idle. There was a helmet attached to the saddle. She put it on and slung her leg over the bike. "Race you guys back to the Divination Lab?"

She won easily and waved them on before returning to her dorm. Only a very unusual wolf or bear would brave the noise the Vincent produced. She parked near the front door of the dorm and shut the bike down.

Rhiannon was in the room, working her loom. "You found your machine." She nodded toward Lesa's side of the room. "They delivered that monstrosity at the same time."

The bed was humongous, gold-leafed wood with a canopy, the thick mattress filled with down. A set of portable steps was required to mount the thing. Lesa climbed the steps and sank so deeply into the mattress that she lost sight of the rest of the room. "What are you making?" she said.

The loom sounds paused. "I am a history major, so I am making a historical tapestry."

Lesa clambered out of the bed with some difficulty and moved the stairs so she could see the tapestry her roommate was weaving. "It's beautiful!"

Rhiannon grunted noncommittally. "King Pirithous' wedding. The bride seduced a centaur guest and accused him of trying to rape her when her fiancé found out. Your ancestors cut off his ears and nose and drove him into the woods."

"Pirithous was king of the Lapiths, right? That's in Greece. My ancestors came from a lot further south and a whole different continent." Lesa studied the tapestry-in-progress. "Did you spin and dye the wool, too?"

Rhiannon stomped her front hoof. "I told you I was not interested in being friends with a man."

"Woman," Lesa said.

"Regardless." She pointed toward Lesa's side of the room. "That is your space. I expect you to stay out of mine."

Lesa stepped off the small flight of stairs. "Your call. I just figured, since we're living together, that it would be easier if —."

"It would not." The centauride wheeled and headed for the door. "And do not touch my things!"

Lesa pulled the stairs back into place near the bed. The business end of a heavy-duty extension cord was poking through a crude hole in the wall. Lesa followed the cord outside to where it petered into a clay alchemical jar. She shrugged, added a power strip to the chain, and plugged in her phone, watch, and computer to charge. On the wall next to the bed was a rack for sword and shield, and Lesa hung her weapons. Beneath it was an ornate box with a round lid—a chamber pot.

"Just what the doctoral candidate ordered."

She used it and tugged experimentally at a jeweled chain at its side. With a hiss, a thin film of blue liquid poured into the bowl, dissolving everything inside it before vanishing. The bowl sparkled. An alchemical chamber pot, even better. There were a sink and small shower unit, with hot and cold running water, in the corner.

She returned to the Divination Lab the next morning, clean and well-rested, for the daily department meeting. She commandeered a small bookcase and climbed on top of it to put herself at eye level with the centaurs. Mentor Rhaecus led the meeting, asking each student for an update on their projects. There were thirteen diviners in the program. Elatus was focusing on entrails. Hippe was heavy into fractomancy. Pholus was doing a dual degree in geloscopy (divination through laughter) and nggám (divination through spider behavior). Another centauride in the group was studying ambocomancy, or divination through dust, which Lesa had never heard of, and the I Ching.

"Et tu?" the mentor said when Lesa's turn came around.

"Still finding my feet," she said. "But I can already see where I could help everyone else out. It's like you're stuck in the Dark Ages. Elatus, your project alone —."

The gloomy centaur glowered. "Stay away from my work, human."

"Speak for yourself," Hippe said. "I'd love to some help with my project."

Mentor Rhaecus brought his hands together sharply. "Hippe, I doubt your thesis committee would think well of such methods. Perhaps the man should keep to her own studies." He held up his hand to forestall debate. "That's enough for the day. Meeting adjourned."

Lesa waited until the mentor was out of sight. "That's ridiculous. Just cataloging your fractals in a searchable database would save you hours a day, but I bet we could —."

Hippe shook her head. "Rhaecus is my thesis advisor."

"Pholus?" Lesa leaned in so she could see the centaur's face. "What about your project? I could—"

"You could bring us all to ruin," Elatus said. "The way your kind always has."

Pholus smoothed his beard. "Give it a little time, Lesa. Maybe start working on something for yourself and in a couple of months see what happens."

"Did you actually just say that?" Lesa said. "We're diviners! If anyone can see what happ—."

"Have you had breakfast, yet?" Hippe interrupted her. "Let us get something to eat and talk about this later. Pholus?"

The gangly centaur shook his head.

"Just we mares, then." She helped Lesa off the bookcase. "Food will help."

Lesa kept the Vincent down to about 15 mph, allowing Hippe to cover the distance at an easy canter, but a twist of the throttle could have left the centauride and everything she represented in the dust.

"Let us take them outside," Hippe said when they'd gotten their trays of food. They walked a little ways from the building. Lesa sat on the remnants of a rock wall while Hippe folded her legs and lay down.

Lesa frowned at the meat and vegetables on her plate. "What am I even here for?" she said.

"I could not say this in front of the others," the centauride said, "but I want your help. Pholus does, too. We have talked about it."

"What about Mentor Rhaecus?"

"As you said, we are stuck in the Dark Ages. He is one of the reasons why."

Lesa gnawed on what she hoped was a hunk of mutton, but it might have been ahuizotl. "What about Elatus? Who shoved that stick up his—?"

"He is a descendant of Eurytion. He and his cousin, Rhiannon." She whisked her tail. "It will take much to get them to think kindly of a man."

"That was thousands of years ago!"

"The families have long memories." Hippe finished her meal and heaved herself to her feet. "I will not go back to the lab with you. I believe my estrus is beginning."

"Your estrus?" Lesa put her hand to her mouth. "Oh."

The centauride smiled. "I do not have to exile myself but doing so can prevent bad choices." Hippe's hooves moved restlessly. "We will talk more about my fractals and your algorithms in a few days."

Lesa finished her breakfast alone and headed back to the lab. With her electronics fully charged, she began experiments with shufflemancy, telling the future by what song came up on a random playlist. If she could write an algorithm that correlated it with ambulomancy (divination by walking), she might be able to create an app that would keep exercisers safe. She worked the problem until lunch, then returned to it until it was time to head back to the dorms.

Pholus shook his work lamp, disrupting the alchemical process that kept it alight. "Are you coming to the party?"

"What party?" Lesa had been wandering around the lab listening to a randomly-generated punk-rock playlist to gather data. If there had been a party announcement, she'd missed it.

"One of the frats at the War College."

"When does it start?" Lesa said.

"Nine. But if you go, don't go until ten, ten thirty. No one gets there early."

"Maybe." The music had put Lesa in a dancing mood, but she doubted it would last through the evening, and she wasn't sure she'd survive a dance floor full of centaur. She rode back to her dorm in the dark. The air was chilly, and she made a mental note to research snowmobiles when she went back to New York for the school's Sagittarius holiday in November. If she picked up a few more MacBooks and some routers, she could set up a local network for the Divination College and ...

Lesa parked the Vincent and went through the now-familiar process of sliding open the door. Inside the room, she hung a few posters and unpacked a quilt her great-grandmother had made her. The down mattress had far too much acreage for the quilt to cover, so Lesa folded the blanket and put it on the foot of the bed.

Rhiannon came in around 9:30 and failed to greet her roommate.

"Are you going to the party?" Lesa said.

Rhiannon propped her sword and shield against the wall. "Are you?"

"Doubt it." Her experiments combining shufflemancy and ambulomancy were showing promise. Few divination methods performed accurately on the diviner, but Lesa had made it around the room four times, blindfolded, using the beta version of her new app.

"Wise choice." Rhiannon clopped to her mirror. "You might get stepped on." She put a tea kettle in the room's brazier and let the water heat as she washed her face, ran a brush over her short hair, and rouged her nipples. When the tea kettle whistled, she spooned loose-leaf tea into a pot and poured water over it.

"Is that some special centaur-party tea?" Lesa said.

"It is Earl Grey." Rhiannon retrieved her sword and wiped the blade with a rag. She took a jar of oil from a shelf and applied a light coating to the blade.

"Are you expecting a fight?" Lesa changed a value in a line of code and the user-interface of her app turned green.

"Best part of a centaur party." Rhiannon poured tea into a travel mug and slung her shield over her withers. "Do not wait up."

The temperature in the dorm room was chilly by human standards, and Rhiannon's Earl Grey had smelled good. Lesa waited until her roommate had slid the door closed before getting up to see if she had left any tea in the pot. She lifted the lid and inspected the leafy dregs inside. There wasn't enough to make a decent cup, but —

Lesa nearly fumbled the pot while setting it down and ran to Rhiannon's mirror. She pulled two hairs out of Rhiannon's brush and dug into her pocket for her Zippo. Lesa lit the hair on fire and used her smartphone to film the smoke as it curled to the ceiling. She sent the video to her laptop, added the information from the tea leaves, and crunched the data.

"Shit!"

Lesa grabbed her sword and shield and ran for the Vincent without closing the door behind her.

Howard Stern: You know, I saw in the news the other day that centaurs, part-person, part-horse, are real. Swear to God. [Leans into the microphone] Do we have that clip? Play that clip.

[The clip plays. In it a centauride runs toward the camera in slow motion, breasts bouncing]

H.S. That is something. Can we see that again?

[The clip plays again, with a bow-chicka-wow-wow soundtrack]

Robin Quivers: Guess they've never heard of sports bras.

H.S..: Why cover that up? If my wife had breasts like that, I would never let her cover them up.

R.Q. Never.

H.S.: Apparently centaur women are only interested in sex four days a month.

R.Q.: Do they go into heat? Like a horse?

H.S.: They do. For those four days, they are the hornier than college girls on spring break. For the rest of the month. Nothing.

R.Q.: I wonder how the male centaurs feel. Can they even reach their, you know, to take the pressure off?

H.S.: Maybe they get each other off. Would you [bleep] a centaur, Robin? [Ten seconds of the clip plays.]

      — The Howard Stern Radio Show, CBS. (1996).

The party looked like a blending of a livestock auction and a free-love festival. Centaur dancing consisted of rearing and wheeling while clutching ceramic jars of strong beer. Lesa climbed on top of a table and spun until she spotted her roommate, who was filling her jar from a freshly tapped barrel.

"Rhiannon!" She cupped her hands around her mouth. "Don't drink it!"

Rhiannon did not hear or opted to ignore. She lifted the jar to her lips.

Lesa jumped from the tabletop to the back of the nearest centaur. Another leap, another centaur, and Lesa was atop the drinks table and in range to dash the jar out of Rhiannon's hand. For good measure, Lesa pushed the just-tapped barrel of beer onto the floor, where it burst.

"What are you doing?!" Rhiannon said.

Lesa dropped to the floor. Her roommate towered over her, nearly a thousand pounds of angry, human-hating muscle and bone with heavy hooves and a newly oiled sword.

Four legs and a gangly body came between them. "What's going on?" Pholus said.

"The beer is laced with something!" Lesa said. "It's going to —!"

"Get the jar," Pholus said. "Give it to Endeis."

Lesa picked the jar off the floor and gave to the gray alchemy student. He sniffed the jar and ran his finger around the rim. "Smells like ...." He licked the tip of his finger. "Definitely." He turned to Rhiannon. "Did you drink any of this? It's a hormone simulator. It will bring you into season almost immediately."

"Shit!" Rhiannon flushed. "I feel it. Which one of you basta—?"

A centaur on the other side of the table whooped. It was Polkan. He flared his nostrils. "Smells like a paaaarty!" The males around him began to react, too, excited by his pheromones as well as the ones Rhiannon was beginning to emit. They jostled each other and pawed the floor with their front hooves. Someone started a war chant.

Lesa slipped her arm into her shield and drew her sword. She put herself between her roommate and the approaching centaurs. "Any fucker who touches her gets gelded!"

"We will get her out of here," Pholus said.

Lesa looked at him suspiciously.

"She does not affect me the same way," the gangly centaur said. "Endeis and I, we are lovers."

Lesa and Endeis provided cover while Pholus led Rhiannon out of the dining hall and into the cold air outside.

"How are you feeling?" Pholus asked the drugged centauride.

"Better." Rhiannon rubbed her forehead. "I think I am okay to get home."

Four centaurides came out of the dining hall. They were disheveled, and their swords were drawn. "We will go with her and make sure she gets to her room safely," one said. "The party is over. Polkan will not sleep comfortably tonight."

Pholus watched them leave and ran his hands through his hair, making it stand on end. "That could have been a real mess. How did you know?"

"Her tea."

"Just that?"

"Smoke patterns. I burned some of her hair."

They studied the stars for a while.

"Do you think this is why the Mentor said you had to come here?" Pholus said.

Lesa rested her head on his lower shoulder. "Maybe."

"Want to go the Alchemy Lab with us and get drunk?"

The Alchemy Lab had a hookah bar, and Endeis insisted Lesa try his favorite smoking blend while she and Pholus talked about his thesis. The night ended at dawn with a draught Endeis gave her that took away her hangover and made her feel like she'd had a full night's sleep. Lesa got the Vincent started and powered back to the dorm for a shower and a change of clothes.

Lesa parked in front of the dorm and stopped short. Someone had put a stepladder out, which made it much easier to reach the latch and open the door. There was another ladder in front of the door of her room, with a note. Lesa pulled the scrap of parchment off the ladder and puzzled out the scrawling calligraphy. *I still do not like men,* it said. *But women might be acceptable.*

Lesa put the note in her pocket. She didn't need to see the future to know it was a good sign. *There you go, Great-Grandma. Not famous, not powerful, but I might be important to something here.* Lesa climbed the ladder to open the door.

The stars don't lie.

About the story

"The Stars Don't Lie" started out because I wanted to write about someone overcoming a disability. I teach high school, and most school days I visit a little coffee shop run by kids in the special-education program. It's one of the best parts of my day. The idea of a human attending a centaur school came from that. Lesa, the main character in "Stars," is not disabled in her own world, but in a world made for creatures who are taller than her, have more legs, are faster and stronger, etc. she faces challenges.

The rest evolved in the writing. I was in a bit of a slump after hitting a dead-end on a rewrite, so I started pecking away at the story. I do a lot of my first drafts on manual typewriters. It's easier for me to get into the zone and stay there when I write on something that can't connect to the Internet. I usually write in small blocks that fit here and there into my schedule, so getting into the zone quickly is important.

I researched while I wrote and came up with the idea for the Divination College, and, since I often warn my college-bound my students about the dangers of college parties and drinking too much, a story was born.

The first draft topped out at 8,000 words, the second draft climbed to 10,000, draft three dropped to about 9,000, and that's where it stayed.

A question for the author

Q: Do you have a garden? Have you ever grown your own food?

A: I grew up in rural Maine, and my family always had a garden and chickens. Summers I hayed, picked potatoes, and blueberry raked. Nowadays, I live in a smallish city, but we still do a garden every year, and there is nothing more satisfying than going outside and picking a salad. We also have a couple of apple trees that do well, a peach tree, a couple of quince trees, and blackberry bushes. My wife likes to can, so we get a lot out of the fruit. The asparagus does pretty well, too. About five years ago we got into beekeeping, not as much for the honey as to have the little guys around. They are good neighbors.

About the author

R.W.W. Greene is a New Hampshire writer with an MFA he exorcises in dive bars and coffee shops. Greene collects manual typewriters, keeps bees, and, by day, teaches writing at a variety of institutions.

rwwgreene.com, @rwwgreene

The Dream Diary of Monk Anchin

Felicity Drake

I went to the museum's special exhibition on Seitokuji Temple alone, as was my habit. In the corner, there was a glass case full of portraits of the temple's famous poets.

The last portrait made me stop to take a second look. Unlike the other monks, this one was gazing directly out at the viewer. His face was painted in the standard Yamato-e style, just lines for the eyes and a hook for the nose, but there was something strangely expressive about the minimalist painting: a slight tension in the angle of his eyes, one hand holding a brush in midair, as if hesitating.

The bald little monk stared up at me out of his portrait, as if he were trying to speak to me. The plaque beneath the painting read:

Monk Anchin (1244-1316)
Collection of Seitokuji, 14th century, artist unknown

There was no background or architectural detail in the plain portrait, but there was a lit candle-stand beside him, a common pictorial convention for depicting nighttime. Why would the artist take pains to portray Anchin, unlike the other poets, writing by candlelight?

Taking my notebook from my purse, I added Anchin's name to my notes on the exhibit. He couldn't have been a particularly notable poet. In high school, I had made a habit of memorizing poetry—which endeared me to my classical Japanese teacher and precisely nobody else—and even I had never heard of Anchin.

Before I left, I even spent 3,000 yen on the glossy exhibition catalogue, so I could take home a copy of the painting. My own research specialty is medieval Japanese women's diaries, and at this stage in my career, there isn't time to waste exploring intriguing tidbits outside my field. But seeing Anchin's little face, I couldn't resist the urge to find out what he had to say, what seemed to be on the tip of his tongue in his portrait.

It took some doing, but I tracked down a journal article about Anchin. The issue came out of the university's offsite storage facility crumbling and dusty. It was an obscure journal from the 1930s, with an article written by a professor I'd never heard of: "Annotated Selections from the Dream Diary of Monk Anchin."

I'll include an excerpt from the introduction here:

Monk Anchin's remarkable diaries are a treasure of the Kamakura period that have been overlooked for too long. Previous scholars have neglected his diaries, perhaps because of their length and the difficulties of his written style. Notably, in 1834 the scholar Ishizawa Takeru dismissed Anchin's diary as "an idiosyncratic work with minor poetic value and little historical interest."

It is regrettable that because of this early scholarly misinterpretation, no one has attempted a full transcription of the diary. Ishizawa reached his conclusion by reading the brief excerpt traditionally contained in 19th century anthologies, and I suspect that Anchin's dream diary has not been read from beginning to end in all the intervening centuries.

It is true that Anchin's diary is a singularly ahistorical text. He offers no information about daily life or special events at the temple; the diary reveals to us very little about the life of a monk at Seitokuji in the Kamakura period. Similarly, although his classical Chinese poetry was well-received by his contemporaries, subsequent generations considered his verses undistinguished.

But his diary is, nonetheless, a monumental and unique work: with fifty volumes representing the fifty years of his life after he took Buddhist vows, it is perhaps the world's longest continuous dream diary, full of insights into the unconscious mind of a highly literate, devout, and, yes, idiosyncratic man.

We can speculate about Anchin's life from court and temple records. Born the fifth son of a minor aristocrat, Anchin achieved some early success as a poet, but never received an official appointment at court. He never married, and took the tonsure in 1266, at the age of twenty-two. Although he spent the rest of his long life at Seitokuji, he was by no means disconnected from society; he contributed poems to social gatherings at the capital and frequently traveled on long pilgrimages.

I have selected the following excerpts from Monk Anchin's diary on the basis of their poetic or psychological significance. It is my hope that their publication will contribute to a reexamination of his life and work.

Since nothing had been written about Anchin in all the intervening decades, the professor's hopes had apparently gone unfulfilled.

Dreams were an unconventional choice of subject for a medieval diarist. But if he was best known for his dream diary, it explained why the anonymous artist had painted Anchin, brush in hand, beside a lit candle. As if he had just awoken from a dream and was hurrying to write it down. I've always been a vivid dreamer myself; when I was a teenager, I'd even kept a dream diary for a few years. I shredded it before I went to college, which I now regretted.

I settled down on my couch with a glass of wine and the diary excerpts. That was how I spent most of my nights alone at home, anyway, with Bach, Bordeaux, and books. And there was a certain transgressive pleasure in spending an evening away from my research or my students' papers, in the unfamiliar company of Monk Anchin.

First entry, undated but presumed to be from 1266:
Last night I saw a dream so strange I was compelled to take up my brush, to write it before it fled from memory. In my dream, a woman came to my bedchamber and sat beside my pillow.

"It's a shame when a good-looking man takes vows so young," she scolded me. "You've robbed the women of Kyoto. I'm terribly put out. At least we can meet in dreams, can't we?"

Her smile as she teased me was incomparably lovely. She outstretched her arms to me, and I saw that she wore her robe turned inside out—which once was thought to bring good dreams, as in Ono no Komachi's poems of longing.

When I reached for her, my hands passed through her body as if through mist, and she disappeared.

1267, the new year:
The first dream of the new year tells what is to come. A dream of a hawk is said to be auspicious, but what should I make of the dream I saw? Two hawks flew

together through a clear sky. A cloud came and went, and there was only one hawk remaining.

1273, tenth month:
In last night's dream, I had retreated from the temple into solitude in a brushwood hut. There I would live in absolute simplicity, apart from the vulgar world.

A female pilgrim knocked at my door and asked for shelter from the rain. Although I should have turned her away (as the lady of Eguchi turned away the wandering monk Saigyō, so as not to tempt him), I allowed her inside and made her tea to warm her. We composed poems about the rain.

There is no escape from worldly desire, is there? Not in a temple, not in seclusion, and not even in one's own heart.

Anchin's dream reminded me of a dream I'd had as a teenager.

In my dream, I was waiting on a train platform. Rain fell down in a curtain from the overhang. I was in my school uniform, and my shoes and socks were soaking wet; a puddle grew on the concrete at my feet. The platform was deserted. Trains passed by without stopping, as if I were the only person left in the city.

A man joined me on the platform—an ordinary-looking salaryman in a gray suit, carrying a briefcase. He bought two cans of hot tea from the vending machine, and although all the benches on the platform were empty, he sat right next to me. But I wasn't afraid. We drank our canned tea together, as if we were the best of friends.

I was so young when I had the dream, I could hardly remember any more than that. It must have been written down in my old dream diary, but that was long gone. But I still remembered the thrill of it: to have the attention of a man, to be alone with a man, had seemed naughty and wonderful. It had felt so real. I remember waking up and hurrying to the mirror to see if my cheeks were red.

That had been just the silliness of a girl, of course. In my waking life, men had never paused to look at me, and I had never dared to speak to them. Since I'd started working at a women's college, it had become even easier to avoid men. I had been on a few dates, arranged for me by my worried parents or friends, but the silence had always stretched too long, and I'd never had a second date. There weren't many Monk Anchins left in the world, not many men interested in listening to a plain middle-aged woman talk about the fourteenth century, or in sharing a pot of tea and reading poetry together. 'Born in the wrong century,' my colleagues sometimes said about me, which I know they didn't intend to be cruel.

I brushed a few fragments of the journal's yellowing paper off my lap and set it aside for the night.

That Saturday afternoon, I sat at my usual table in the back corner of the department store's top-floor café, carefully arranging my papers and pens around the delicate china saucer and plate.

It was 900 yen for a thin slice of dark chocolate gateau and a cup of milk tea. Just a little luxury, something to sweeten the routine of grading papers. I hadn't made it to that coveted position of full-time professor at a proper university, where perhaps even grading papers would be a joy; at forty-one, I was still an adjunct lecturer at a two-year women's college, correcting grammatical errors and encouraging my pupils to look up information in books rather than on Wikipedia.

After an hour's work, I set aside the half-finished stack of papers and pulled out the rest of Monk Anchin's diary instead, savoring the bitter chocolate gateau as I read the last diary entry, written shortly before his death at the age of seventy-two.

1316, seventh month:
Now that I have been celibate for fifty years, all that was left of desire should have long since burned away, and yet...

I've seen the same woman in my dreams for years and years. I believe that I saw her once with my waking eyes. Not when I was a young man in the capital, and she a beautiful maiden, but when we were both withered and old.

It was at the height of cherry blossom season, when the temple was crowded with travelers. Through the crack of a door, I saw a little girl pretty and fresh as blooming dianthus, playing beside her grandmother. Unaware she was being observed, the woman didn't conceal her face; whatever beauty she'd had in her youth had long since faded, but her eyes were sharp, and her voice as low and sweet as a koto string as she read aloud to her granddaughter. And I knew it was her —not the greatest beauty, not the most charming or the most learned—but the same woman I'd seen in my dreams. I saw her in the waking world only this once, perhaps fifty years too late.

In my dream that night, she came to me, and she said, "When you were twenty, and I only seventeen, we both attended the Kamo festival. You stood beside my carriage then. I saw you, so dashing in your cap. I lifted my blinds in hope that you might catch a glimpse and slip a poem to me, but you turned your head left instead of right, and then you were gone. If you had turned your head right, do you think we would have known each other by daylight, not only in dreams?"

Last night, I saw her again. There were five-colored threads tied to her hands, which she offered to me to hold, like a bodhisattva welcoming me to the Pure Land.

"We'll part soon, even in dreams. I'll see you again," she said.

"Will we share a single lotus in the world to come?" I asked her.

"Do you think it's so easy to become a buddha? In seven hundred years, I'll make sure to come here once again. Promise me that you'll find me at Seitokuji. Promise me that you won't forget."

How appropriate that I saw her on Tanabata, a celebration of reunited lovers. Seven hundred years—whether Seitokuji still stands, or whether it is ashes, I'll be here once more.

In my career, I've read dozens of medieval diaries. I haven't found a publisher for my monograph yet, but still, I believe I'm something of an expert. Most medieval diaries, at least the ones that survive today, were intended for broader literary consumption, and therefore were thick with classical and poetic allusions, but Anchin's prose was unornamented and personal—almost uncomfortably so. It was unlike any medieval text I'd studied. I briefly wondered whether I should prepare a paper on the dream diary of Monk Anchin for a future meeting of the Medieval Diary Literature Research Group, but I couldn't imagine speaking about him in public. I wanted—strange as it was—to keep him for myself.

Monk Anchin died in 1316; thanks to his diary entry, I knew that he must have died shortly after Tanabata, the seventh day of the seventh month. It was a rather stunning coincidence that this summer happened to mark seven hundred years after his death, the year that he promised to return to Seitokuji to find his dream-bride.

I tried and failed to put it all out of my head. Over the next weeks, I read and reread Anchin's diary. I returned to the museum exhibit to sneak forbidden photographs of his portrait. And in my dreams, I saw: a pair of dark eyes, a crescent moon, a curl of smoke, half a line of poetry, dark woods stretching out beyond the cypress pillars of a temple's veranda.

One night, after the stimulation of Glenn Gould's magnificent Goldberg Variations and perhaps a too-generous pour of wine, I visited Seitokuji's official website. The temple still existed, and like some other temples struggling to pay the bills in an irreligious age, it offered overnight lodging for tourists. In addition to a gallery of inviting photographs showing off their austere guest quarters, contemplative gardens, and delicate vegetarian meals, there was an online reservation form.

According to the Gregorian calendar, Tanabata fell on July 7th, which was right before final exams and not a convenient time for me to disappear. But Anchin would have been using the old lunisolar calendar system, and the seventh day of the seventh month in the old calendar actually fell on Tuesday, August 9th (according, at least, to the online calculators I used). That was the summer holiday, and no one would notice if I left the city to go on a little pilgrimage.

With just a few cabernet-emboldened clicks, I had my temple reservations and train tickets booked. Perhaps it was silly of me, but I couldn't help but think that someone ought to be there to commemorate his life. Was I the only person alive who cared about Monk Anchin? No one had ever bothered to fully transcribe his diary. No academic had written an article about him since the 1930s. How sad to think that he had lived, died, and been utterly forgotten. What if he returned, after the promised seven centuries, and no one were there at Seitokuji to see it? I didn't want to let the date pass unwitnessed. That was all.

Monday evening, the night before Tanabata on the old calendar, I arrived at Seitokuji. I'd visited plenty of temples for research trips or sightseeing, to the point where all the intricately carved transoms and mossy rocks started to blur together, but this felt different. With every worn step I climbed, every statue I admired, I imagined that Anchin had stood in the same spot seven hundred years before. I'd never had a personal connection to a temple before. I had to remind myself that I still didn't have one: I was engaging in shallow literary tourism and self-indulgent fantasy, nothing more.

There were other guests staying at the temple as well. In the public bath, I sat across from a pair of little old ladies from Osaka chatting about the next stop on their vacation. In the corridor, I saw one of the temple's monks struggling to communicate in English and hand gestures with a family of Chinese tourists, and I wondered how they'd ended up at out-of-the-way Seitokuji. Seitokuji had a long enough history, but I'd assumed international tourists would be likelier to visit Kiyomizudera for its waterfall, or Ryōanji for its rock garden.

My room was spare and elegant, just bare mats, a futon, and a buckwheat-husk pillow. No television or wifi, which I appreciated; other than the slight buzz of the electric lights, I could imagine that I was back in the thirteenth century. A monk brought my dinner in on a tray: tiny bowls of tofu, vegetables, and rice, delicately flavored and artfully arranged. I wondered if Anchin had eaten so well here in his day, or if temple fare had been humbler then.

After dinner, I brought out my reading. Thanks to some archival wrangling, I'd gotten my hands on a copy of a facsimile edition of Anchin's diary. The copy quality was only so-so, and it was frequently indecipherable, but still it felt like a miracle to see Anchin's own handwriting. From the boldness or faintness of his brushstrokes, I could imagine the passages he had rushed to write, or the places he had hesitated, brush in hand.

After dark, I went out to the temple's veranda alone. Here, far from the city, I could hear cicadas singing and see the stars.

Anchin must have seen this same night sky, I thought, seven hundred years ago.

I sat on the edge of the veranda and stared up at the distant, unchanging stars. In my head, phrases from Anchin's poetry shattered and recombined. I felt so close to him here.

The faint scent of incense tickled my nose. No—cigarette smoke. My nose wrinkled and I had to pinch it to keep from sneezing. I glanced back over my shoulder and discovered the culprit: the teenage boy from the family of Chinese tourists I'd seen earlier that evening. He was leaning against one of the temple's cypress pillars, smoking a cigarette and staring off into space.

Well, the presence of an intruder, and one so rude as to smoke a cigarette in a nine-hundred-year-old temple, damaged my reverie. But I was hardly about to leave my perfect spot for stargazing. I'd been here first!

I tried to refocus. The smell of cigarettes was distracting.

I looked over again, and saw the boy stubbing out his cigarette and neatly disposing of the butt in a portable ashtray. Polite. I thought he might go back inside then, but no such luck—instead, he sat down cross-legged on the veranda, no more than a few meters away from me. He pulled out a little notebook from the pocket of his oversized jacket and hunched over it, pen in hand.

I took the time to look him over while he was staring down at the notebook. He couldn't have been much older than nineteen or twenty, and his gangly frame still had that elbows-and-knees pointiness of adolescence. His hair was long and shaggy, hiding some of his acne-scarred face.

Trying to retain some sense of solitude, I turned away and closed my eyes. I had come here to be with Anchin, to see if he had returned after the promised seven hundred years. Silly, yes, but...

My mind drifted, and among the cicadas' song, I heard another sound: the scratching of pen on paper. I glanced to the side, and there was the boy—biting his lower lip and writing away in his notebook. He looked utterly absorbed. My irritation at him ebbed slightly; in him, I saw a shadow of the bookish girl I had been when I was his age.

He looked up at me, and we were caught awkwardly staring at each other. I nodded politely at him—he stared at me, then hunched his shoulders and offered a tiny smile.

"No Japanese," he apologized, in heavily accented English.

"No Chinese," I answered, and I couldn't help but smile in return. I wondered why he and his family had come here.

I thought it might end there, but he stood, crossed the gap between us in just a few steps, and sat down again, right beside me.

"Can you read this?" he asked, again in English, and handed me his notebook.

He had been writing poetry—poetry in classical Chinese, at that! What a rare bird. Did they teach poetic composition in Chinese schools these days? My own students were about his age, and it was a struggle to get them to read even the most accessible poems, much less compose their own.

I took a moment to look over the poem. Clumsy in places, almost brilliant in others. A sudden pain ran through my chest. His handwriting was charming, neat and somehow masculine in the boldness of his penstrokes. And the poem wasn't bad at all.

"I can." For a few minutes I didn't return the notebook to him.

He handed the pen over to me, and I realized that he was hoping I would write a response. Ridiculous! As a medievalist, I'd read my share of poetry in classical Chinese, but I'd never written a single line of my own. Instead, I wrote out a quatrain that I remembered from Monk Anchin's diary. Anchin's poetry was in classical Chinese, so the boy could read it, and his style seemed to suit the atmosphere of the night.

I handed the notebook back to the boy, and he bent over it for a moment—then his head snapped up, and he stared at me open-mouthed. His brow tightened, and he said slowly, deliberately, "That is... very... good," as if it caused him physical pain to be unable to say more, to express what he was thinking. His English was almost as bad as mine.

"It is not mine," I admitted, because I could hardly take credit for Anchin's genius.

"Show me more?"

We wrote back and forth to each other. Some of his poems were his, some were famous verses that even I recognized. I replied to him with Anchin's poems, some half-remembered Li Bai, and a few poorly turned couplets of my own.

"My name." He wrote it out and pronounced it for me in Chinese; I had to repeat it several times before he nodded. I wrote my name and did the same for him. He looked so serious while he practiced saying my name.

The crescent moon had risen high above us while we wrote. I pointed to it, and he stared up at it with such earnestness, as if he'd never seen the night sky before. My throat hurt, my chest hurt. The stars reflected in his wide, dark eyes.

Suddenly, I was struck by the overpowering urge to tell him about Anchin. I hadn't mentioned Anchin or my unseemly obsession with a long-dead monk, not to anyone.

"Seven hundred years ago," I began. If only he had understood Japanese! It was a struggle to find the words in English. "There was a man. Here." I had forgotten how to say *monk* in English.

"At this temple?"

"Yes. He wrote this." I gestured to the poems I had written. "He saw dreams... every night, many dreams of a woman. He said he would return here—after seven hundred years—today—to meet her."

His forehead wrinkled in confusion, evidently unable to find the right word in English. He wrote a phrase in Chinese in the notebook, punctuated with a question mark. At first, I didn't recognize the simplified characters, but then I understood: *reincarnation?*

"Yes, that," I answered, pointing to the word in the notebook.

"Do you believe?" he asked.

"I don't know."

"I don't know also." His shoulders hunched forward and he stared down at the aged wood of the veranda: "I had a dream last year. I saw this temple, the moon, the... statue of Guanyin? Like tonight."

It was impossible, of course, but there were times one wanted to believe in the impossible. I had to acknowledge it: if Anchin had come back, it was in this boy's body. His great, dark eyes; his bold handwriting; his clumsy, potent poetry; his ungainly hands trembling in his lap as he tried to tell me about his dreams.

Why did he have to be a boy? Why did he have to be born in the wrong country? After seven hundred years waiting, couldn't we have been spared this?

"It's late. I should sleep," I said, because I didn't know the right words to say to him in English or in any language.

"Don't go."

A boy half my age, with acne-pitted cheeks and eyes as big and trusting as a golden retriever's... It would have been wrong to kiss him. I was old enough to be his mother. So I didn't—I didn't even touch his hand.

We sat together on the veranda without speaking, without touching, until the sun rose and the temple bells rang to wake the monks for the morning services.

It would have been rude to skip services after staying at the temple, so I dutifully attended, kneeling in the back of the hall. I hadn't slept a wink. The scent of incense, the dull gold gleam of the image of Kannon in the altar, and the monotonous chanting of the monks made my head spin.

I had met Anchin—had looked into his eyes and recognized him—and still the world continued to exist. The vulgar world, into which one or both of us had been reborn in the wrong time and place.

After services, the family of Chinese tourists said goodbye to the monks and hauled their bags down off the veranda.

I watched as if in a dream. The father swung open the trunk of the car and began loading up suitcases. The mother opened the passenger side door.

The boy tapped his mother on the shoulder, then ran back to the temple. He vaulted up the stairs to the veranda and stopped short, just a few feet shy of me. And then he stared, as if he were waiting for me to say something.

I tried to memorize his face. This was my last chance.

"Seven hundred years," I told him. "You will come again in seven hundred years. I will wait."

Would Seitokuji Temple still stand in the year 2716? Seven hundred years—I couldn't conceive of it. Even the few decades of solitude remaining in this lifetime were too much to bear.

He stared and stared, and then he shook his head. "I will study Japanese. When I graduate college... I will come here again. Two years. You will wait—you promise?"

I wanted to tell him that that was insane, that he was a young man with promise and a life and country and language of his own. That I was too old for him, old and strange and unbeautiful, not at all worth uprooting a life for. That I was willing to wait until the next lifetime, when perhaps we would be born in the same decade, the same country. That my delusions about Anchin were born of middle-aged loneliness and regret, that he was being swept up in teenage melodrama, that we both knew perfectly well *there is no such thing as reincarnation...*

But how could I say all that to him in English?

Instead, I said: "Two years, or seven hundred years. Either is okay. I will wait."

He reached out and touched the back of my hand with his fingertips. And then his mother called for him in Chinese, and he was gone, running off like a deer back to the car.

I watched him climb into the backseat of the car. The door closed. The car drove out of the parking lot and onto the winding road descending the mountain. It disappeared among the trees.

Felicity Drake's story "The Dream Diary of Monk Anchin" was published in Metaphorosis *on Friday, 20 July 2018.*

About the story

A few years ago, I went to see a special exhibition at the Idemitsu Museum in Tokyo, and I was particularly charmed by a portrait much like the one in the story.

Researching or translating premodern texts can feel like having a conversation with someone from the past, sometimes in a surprisingly intimate way. I wanted to write a story where that feeling of intimacy goes one step further, and to explore different ways people can connect (through reading, writing, dreams, language barriers, or reincarnation).

A question for the author

Q: Aliens. Are they out there?

A: In a vast universe, surely they are—although maybe in unfamiliar forms, or so far away that we can't meet them (yet!).

It's exciting to think that something so consequential is still totally unknown. It's good to have a little sense of mystery in life.

About the author

Felicity Drake is a writer based in New York. She writes fiction and interactive fiction.

www.felicitydrake.com, @DrakeFelicity

Not All Those Who Wander Are Lost

Douglas Anstruther

-1-

Carla sat on the edge of the metal railing that lined the motel's third-floor landing, gripping its paint-chipped bars with long, slender legs. Black lace stockings disappeared into a tattered bathrobe and a lipstick-stained cigarette rested between her fingers.

She liked the feel of the breeze on her legs, the thrill of the twenty-foot drop below. She wasn't a danger junkie, far from it, although she could have probably found a safer way to make some cash while Ash was at school — a florist, maybe, or a cashier. She had job offers, but the hours weren't flexible enough, and cashiers got robbed all the time anyway.

"So." The man standing behind her cleared his throat. "Are you married?"

"Me? Nah. Never tried it." She looked back at him. "How about you?" She thought he'd said his name was Stig, but she wasn't about to use it. Guys didn't like it when you got their name wrong, even if it was fake.

He stared past her into the mid-day heat rising from the oil-stained and cracked parking lot. He was kinda cute, like a movie star from the nineteen fifties: chiseled jaw, dimpled chin and blond curly hair. His stained and wrinkled dress pants contrasted with the smooth skin of his chest. A patch covered his left eye.

"Yeah," he answered in a faraway voice. "I think so."

"You think so?" A column of ash fell from her cigarette to splash across the cars parked below. "You mean you don't know?"

"I lost her. I lost them all. Two sons and a wife. I'm trying to find them, though."

She looked at him, her face a squint as she took a drag of her cigarette. "Whadya mean?" Her words came out with a cloud of smoke. "You *misplaced* them?"

"The places I go." He paused, shaking his head. "It gets complicated."

A new sadness in his eye caused her attitude to soften. She liked the guy. He seemed nice, and there was something mysterious about him. He came across somewhere between a world-weary sailor and a lost child: just a first impression, but she was usually right. "Look, I'm sorry. I, uh, I hope you find them." She stubbed out the cigarette and shrugged the bathrobe down a few inches, revealing breasts swept by the ends of her long black hair. "So, you ready to go again?"

After, she fell off him, scooped her bathrobe up from the floor, and headed to the TV in search of the remote, threading her hands into oversized armholes on the way. She always brought her own bathrobe. It was portable luxury: armor against the squalor of the cheap motels that even the sticky remote couldn't pierce.

She returned to the bed, settled back against the headboard and started pushing buttons. The TV remained black, and after a few seconds she sighed and tossed the worthless device onto the bedstand with a clatter.

At the sound, the man sat upright like a sprung trap. He frowned at the remote, then sank down and stared at the ceiling. As he moved, Carla briefly saw the black silhouette of a raven tattooed at the base of his neck. The image recharged his air of mystery and piqued her curiosity. She remembered their discussion on the landing; maybe exploring some of his secrets would be even more interesting than her missed shows.

"So, where did you see them last?" she asked.

"Hmm?"

"Your family. Where was the last place you saw them?"

"It's not really like that. It's that I can't find the path back to them."

"What do you mean, 'the path back to them'? Were you camping or something?"

He looked at her, measuring her up in a way she'd seen before. She recognized the instant he decided that she wasn't important enough to lie to. She didn't like the look. It took something from her, and the secrets the johns told her, usually how they hated their kids or planned to leave their wives, weren't worth the cost.

"I travel through time," he said. "That's where I lost them: among the possible timelines."

"What?" Her sardonic expression went unnoticed, unable to penetrate his study of the ceiling.

"I move forward in time, look around, go back, change something and then when I move forward again things are different. The possibilities form an immense branching tree, and I lost them somewhere in its branches."

"Seriously? You've been to the future?" She leaned in and conjured a seductive voice harvested from a lifetime of movies. "Do you know what happens to me?"

"A little."

"Prove it." She flounced against him on the bed, now playing little girl. "Tell me something about my future."

"You're going to steal my wallet when I take a shower in five minutes."

"Pfft, that's some reverse psychology bullshit. I'm not gonna touch your wallet."

He just stared ahead and shrugged.

"C'mon," she said, disappointed he wasn't playing. "Tell me something better. You know, like a fortune teller."

"Your son, Ash. He's going to die in three weeks."

All her voices and personas fell away like chips from a poker table thrown over before a bar fight. She peeled herself from him while wide-eyed shock slid into an angry glare. "That's not funny," she said with a dire tone. He kept staring at the ceiling, oblivious or unconcerned. "Hey. I said that's not funny!" She shoved him, but he gave no response. His calm indifference was a stiff breeze against her kindled anger but she didn't know what to do. Finally, after crouching in a frustrated rage for several seconds, she threw herself off the bed, snatched her cigarettes from the bedstand and stormed outside, slamming the door behind her.

A few minutes later, she returned to find the bed empty and the sound of running water coming from the bathroom door. She changed quickly into her clothes, stuffed the bathrobe into her massive purse and headed out. Before the door closed she paused, went back inside and wrestled the wallet from the man's jeans, where they lay in a heap by the side of the bed. She slammed the door again as she left.

It wasn't until that night that she realized he had used her son's name.

-2-

The roar of machinery forced their tiny guide to conduct the entire tour by shouting. The young woman, transformed into a bright orange blob by layers of safety gear, led her three charges through a maze of complex and expensive-looking equipment.

The company's Chief Technical Officer, a tall woman in her mid-thirties, had joined Stig and Osmond to answer questions that never materialized. Osmond couldn't remember the CTO's name. He figured her real role was to tackle him or Stig if either started taking pictures of their proprietary do-hickeys. She had somehow managed to retain a feminine shape despite the safety gear, and Osmond considered testing his theory, but he knew that Stig would make a scene soon enough and he didn't want to interfere.

Dr. Stig Gangleri, his best friend since college, and co-owner of Aesir Consulting, managed to look good in the gear too. It contributed to a mystic shaman vibe, with his bright blue eyes shining through the protective glasses like twin beacons of magical enlightenment. Osmond's own gear had consigned him to Club Blob, along with their guide.

They followed the guide through a vast underground warehouse filled from floor to ceiling with twisting, brightly colored pipes and tanks. Osmond only heard half of what the guide said and understood even less, but it didn't matter. Stig was the show pony. Osmond only made it happen, then made sure Stig didn't get lost on the way home.

"Temperature and pressure are all monitored remotely, as you can see here." The tour guide looked back at the group and paused. "Dr. Gangleri?" She looked around, causing Osmond and the CTO to do the same. Stig had disappeared.

They scattered to look for their missing companion and eventually found him in an aisle they had passed earlier, with his arms crossed and head tilted back, staring blankly at the bend of a pipe.

"He hasn't listened to a word I've said," the guide said, exasperated.

"What's he looking at?" the CTO asked.

"Oh, probably nothing," Osmond offered. "He gets like that sometimes. His mind takes him somewhere else entirely, but trust me, this is your man."

No one seemed particularly interested in going to get him, expecting instead that their collective stare would bring him back in line. Osmond knew different, but was in no hurry. He didn't want to ruin the magic.

"What are his credentials again?" the guide asked, incredulous.

"The professor has PhDs in both theoretical physics and statistical analysis."

"Hmph," the guide said, still unhappy that her shouting had been in vain.

"But it's not the credentials that matter. My associate has a photographic memory and an amazing gift for extrapolation and leaps of intuition. He's a genius the likes of whom you've never seen."

"He doesn't look like he could put his shoes on in the morning," the guide muttered.

"Hey now, show some respect!" All eyes turned to Osmond, who found himself glowering over the petite guide like a great ape defending his territory.

"Sorry. Sorry. It's just that—" He shook his head and tore away from their stares to look back at Stig. "He's a great man. You'll see."

They shuffled in place awkwardly for several minutes before Stig broke free and wandered back to the group, unaware or unconcerned that they had been waiting.

The tour guide resumed with a sigh. "Dr. Gangleri, thank you so much for joining us." Her eyes flashed to Osmond, whose affable smile deflected her sarcasm. "What I had been *trying* to explain is that data from the remote sensors is actually processed at the—"

"At the point of collection, the same way the retina and many other biological sensors process data." Stig finished her sentence to hijack the conversation, then promptly changed the subject. "You will have a seam failure in three days. It will begin there." He pointed at a structure in an aisle they hadn't reached yet. "It will cause one death and nine million dollars in damages."

"With all due respect, Dr. Gangleri," the guide said in a tone suggesting any debt of respect had been fully settled, "if you had paid attention, you would know that a failure of that nature is impossible because—"

"Because all seams are robotically resistance-welded within a tolerance of point zero one percent. That doesn't matter. Material strain from micro-temperature fluctuations will lead to the failure." With arms still folded across his chest he walked briskly down another aisle toward a section they hadn't visited. After a few seconds, the rest of the group caught up. The guide's face glowed red beneath the plastic shield and the CTO had a look of intrigued skepticism. Osmond tried and failed to suppress a grin. He always enjoyed seeing Stig do his thing.

Suddenly, Stig stopped and pointed at what seemed a random direction. "That pile has a heat leak which is throwing off your calibration. It won't be caught for three months and will result in the loss of a major grant."

Then he swung around and pointed to a drain grate on the floor. "Rats. A sink overflow upstairs at the end of the year will lead to an infestation. It'll never be discovered, but the ammonia from their urine will slowly degrade the sensors and prevent you from ever achieving the project goal."

The guide and the CTO both stood stunned, mouths agape. Osmond smiled broadly. "And there you have it," he said. "You will, of course, find Dr. Gangleri's predictions to be one hundred percent accurate. Payment has already been confirmed and no refunds are available. However, I assure you, none will be needed."

The CTO straightened herself and turned to Osmond, "I look forward to Dr. Gangleri's report, especially the technical analysis that supports his conclusions."

"Oh, my dear." Osmond wrapped his orange arm around her shoulders. "There will be no report. Our work here is done. You've been pointed in the right direction; the rest is up to you. One word of advice, though: if you can't figure out how he's right, assume he is anyway, okay? Best avoid that death and all that wasted money." He dropped his grin and looked at her steely-eyed. His voice took on a serious edge. "He's *never* wrong."

He released the stunned CTO and moved over to Stig, placing his gloved hand on his friend's back to direct him toward the exit. "Thank you, we really must be going now."

"But, Dr. Gangleri," the CTO called out as the two men moved away. "How do you know all this?"

Stig stopped and turned. "I saw it happen."

-3-

Stig walked down the short hall that divided living room from kitchen. It was always the same house with the same familiar smell of old wood and the same creaking floors, even if *he* wasn't always the same. The thought sent his hand rising up unconsciously toward his healthy left eye.

He had grown up here and inherited the place from his grandmother on his twenty-first birthday. He had been happy in this house: in the past, as a child doted on by his grandmother who had raised him as her own, and again, in a future he couldn't find. The rest of the time, its emptiness felt like a cold that the heaters couldn't warm.

Sometimes, when he turned the corner into the living room he didn't know if he would find his grandmother sunk into her old overstuffed chair reading spy novels or his sons sprawled across the floor playing while his wife watched sleepily from the couch.

This time, the room was empty except for hundreds of sheets of paper that covered the floor. His heart sank. He had no reason to expect otherwise, but hope grew from a different place than reason.

He walked into the room, stepping carefully on the edges of the pages, which puckered between foot and carpet as he went. Each page contained a portion of an immense branching map of the possibilities he had explored. He remembered them all perfectly, every detail of every moment. Yet nowhere in this map could he find his family. His memories of them were as vivid as any of the branches beneath his feet, but somehow they had become detached from the tree of possibilities. He couldn't find his way back to them. He had lost them.

He knelt down among the pages and traced each branch, looking for a lead, a promising direction to explore. He had recited this mantra a thousand times before. It had become an invocation, a prayer to be happy again.

A loud knock at the door interrupted his reverie. There he found Osmond Higgins, always best friend and sometimes business partner, fidgeting on the step. Osmond was a big man with a ruddy, pock-marked face and gaps between his teeth. He gave Stig a wide smile and a bone shaking pat on the back.

"Hey, Stig. I need some papers signed and wanted to drop off this check." He marched past Stig toward the kitchen. "That last gig was great. They already confirmed two of your predictions, and I gotta say they are loving you now. Word of mouth, my friend, word of mouth. That's what will send us into the heavenly realm of outrageous consulting fees." He opened the refrigerator and closed it with a grunt of disappointment. "Do you even eat?" He turned to Stig and smiled, "How are you doing, buddy?"

"Good," Stig answered, wandering back to the living room.

"How's your, uh, project going? What did you call this again?" Osmond asked, following his friend into the paper-strewn room.

"It's Yggdrasil. The tree of life."

"Right. All the possible futures you've explored, looking for your, uh, family. It's a lot bigger than the last time I was here. You've been busy."

Osmond stood back and squinted at the mighty opus. Through sheer artistic accident, the heavily annotated branching connections did look like a massive gnarled tree, spread across several hundred pieces of paper. Cramped, looping symbols inscribed along its length lent it a texture of mossy bark and hundreds of tiny oval notes dangled from the branches like leaves. The entire left side was stunted and dark, as if the great tree had been hit by lighting. There, the symbols crashed into each other with a sense of urgency, giving the branches a scarred, sinister appearance.

"What are the leaves, again?"

"Decision points. Variables that are likely to significantly alter subsequent events."

"Um, in English?"

Stig sighed. "Possible directions of future exploration."

"I see. And where are we now? What branch or twig or whatever shows us having this conversation?"

Stig pointed to a spot near the upper right edge of the tree. "We're here."

Osmond nodded and leaned forward. "May I?"

Stig motioned for him to proceed. "Carefully."

"Of course."

Osmond tip-toed between the pages, careful not to disturb any. The page Stig pointed to looked like all the others. Thick dark lines connected it to the surrounding pages. Strange symbols and occasional words, places and names crowded around the lines. Stig had once tried to explain his personal system of time-travel notation, but Osmond had retained nothing.

Osmond looked up. "Well, I don't understand it, but it looks pretty impressive."

"It's a rough map. A way for me to see how the pieces fit together as I explore the timelines, following leads, looking for them."

He looked down at the great tree on the floor, superimposing it over the one in his mind. He could move through it much the same as in the trees he had climbed as a child. With almost no effort, he could release his grasp of the present and slide down to another time, catch himself on the crook of a past fork, then pull himself onto a different branch using memories as footholds, until he reached its terminus, where time would resume its measured growth. He had clambered over every inch of the tree but couldn't find his family. His recollections of them, although intense, were as unsubstantial as sunlit mists, and wouldn't support his weight.

"What are all those branches that start behind us? Like those over there." Osmond pointed to the left side of the tree.

"Those branches are what happens when I drop out of college."

Osmond shivered like a teenager at a campfire ghost story. "You mean 'if you had' dropped out of college. I was at your graduation, all of them. So, those other branches never happened. You know that, right?"

Stig shrugged. "I still go there. Those branches are as real as any other."

"My friend," Osmond said, "don't you see? You aren't time traveling. You're daydreaming. I once read that Henry Ford could design a machine and then run it in his mind. You're like that, except the machine you're running is the world. You imagine alternate pasts and possible futures with such detail that you feel like you're

311

there, living them, but the entire time you're really here, in the present, with the rest of us, running simulations.'

"Maybe," he said, with a patience that bordered on boredom.

Osmond shook his head and scanned the left half of the tree. "Honestly, I'm not sure it's healthy for you to keep going back there. It's like you're building entire fantasy worlds and then living in them."

Osmond had expressed these concerns in every timeline. To him, only the timeline he was on was real and all others were the products of Stig's overactive imagination. Stig understood that — his friend couldn't travel from one to another, he couldn't see that no present had more claim on reality than any other. The surety of experience inoculated Stig from doubt, but each time Osmond raised the question, he received another dose of the contagion and there were times when he wondered if maybe Osmond were right. Perhaps he had lost more than his family. Perhaps he had lost the present.

"Hey, I see the name Carla a lot over here. Is that the woman you've been looking for? Your wife?"

"No. Just an acquaintance."

"Well, you'll have to introduce me to her someday. You know, if she's real."

-4-

"Excuse me. Sir? Mr. Gangleri!" The voice came from his blind spot but didn't startle him. Stig finished threading the key into the front door of his house then turned toward the road. A woman hurried toward him from the other side of the street. She looked like a stressed-out soccer mom, with frazzled, pulled-back hair, and jeans tucked into boots that made for awkward running. He traced her path back to an old Honda Civic where cigarette butts on the ground attested to a long wait.

"I'm not sure if you remember me." she said, breathless from her short jog. "I'm—"

"Carla Munn. From the motel." He turned back to the door lock. "I remember."

"You, uh, left this. At the motel." She produced a bulging flap of leather and held it out to him straight-armed. "It's all still there."

Stig took the wallet, tucked it into his back pocket and walked inside, leaving the door open behind him. Carla glanced back at her car for a moment before following him into the dark house and closing the door behind her. She found Stig in the kitchen, filling a glass of water.

He leaned against the counter, glass in hand, and watched her. He could see her unease, her keen awareness that she was in the middle of someone else's house, no longer on neutral ground. For all of her daring and bravado, she wouldn't be here without a good reason.

"Look, I don't," she stopped and shook her head. "This sounds crazy, but I need your help. It's my boy, Ash." Her eyes started to fill and her voice cracked. "He's dying." She burst into tears and sat heavily at the kitchen table, sobbing. Stig leaned against the sink taking occasional sips from his glass. He wanted to console her, but it would be awkward, strange. He didn't need to visit the future to see that.

"You knew it was going to happen," she said, her voice an octave higher than usual. "Somehow you knew."

Slowly her sobbing subsided and with a determined face, streaked with mascara and snot, she collected herself and continued. "Two weeks ago, Ash spent the afternoon playing with his cousin." She paused for a moment to search her purse for a tissue which she unfolded and used to wipe her face. "Three days later Ash got a real bad headache, a high fever and a weird rash. Later we found out his cousin had been sick too but got better on his own. Ash just kept getting worse. I've never seen anyone so sick. At the hospital they put him on a breathing machine. They said he had meningitis." She started to tear up again. "Now they say my little boy is brain dead and they want to pull the plug. Mister Gangleri, you've got to help him."

Stig set the empty glass on the counter and frowned. Her formality always caught him off guard, but what did he expect? She didn't know all the times they'd been together, all the permutations. Carla was a recurring feature of these timelines, the forbidden fruit of the dark side of the tree. To her, he would be little more than a stranger, a one-time customer, but he knew her well and thought of her, in a strange way, as a friend.

She stood up and grabbed his sleeve. "Did you hear me? You've gotta do something. You said you time travel or something. You could prevent this. Please."

Stig spoke dryly. "If I were to go back and prevent his death, it would create a new timeline. This branch would still exist. He'll still die here."

"Take me with you, then."

He shook his head. "I'm sorry, Carla. But it doesn't work that way."

"I don't care!" she shouted. "At least in some other universe or whatever, my baby will live. I don't care. Please, save him. I'll do anything, *anything*." She moved her hand up and ran her fingers jerkily through his hair. "Please."

"You won't know. You'll never know." He seemed to be talking to himself. "Whether or not it's real for me, it can never be real for you."

-5-

The students, slumped in various degrees of boredom, occupied the lecture hall's available seats unevenly. Stig had arranged to have an old chalkboard moved from storage, and he wheeled it in front of the modern equipment before each class. He enjoyed the feel of the chalk on his fingers, the staccato tapping as he wrote. A breeze from the windows, propped open by an antiquated crank system, carried the smell of the old building to him and threatened to send him to another time. He resisted and kept talking.

"As you move through time, each particle is continuous. So you see, from the perspective of spacetime, it's not a particle but a thread: unbreakable and woven with all the other threads of matter and energy like a tangled mass of spaghetti. From this perspective, motion is an illusion. It's merely a bend in the thread. Not only are the threads unbreakable, but Einstein showed us that they can only bend so far: the speed of light." As he spoke he drew frantically on the chalkboard to illustrate his point.

"Our brains consist of an immense tangle of these threads. The present is merely the point along them where a particular set of perceptions and thoughts converge. Time does not pass. It is an illusion, an artifact of consciousness."

Stig looked up to see blank expressions on the few students that were still awake, with the exception of one young lady at the back of the class whose hand rose silently.

He squinted his eyes to see the owner of the hand. "Yes. Ms. Verdandi?"

"So, if each thread of matter is unbreakable, does that mean that everything is predetermined?"

"No. Because of uncertainty."

"Quantum uncertainty?"

"Bah. Everyone is obsessed with quantum this and quantum that. Flip a coin. There's enough uncertainty in that mundane act to change the course of history." He reached into his pocket, pulled out a coin and prepared to flip it. "There are two possible outcomes. Heads you pass, tails you fail. Do we have a deal?"

"Uh, no. I need an 'A'," she said.

"Couldn't the result of the coin flip be predicted?" another student interjected. "Like, if you knew the location and momentum of every atom in the room?"

"That information is not only unavailable, but unobtainable." Stig flipped the coin, trapping it on the back of his hand. "Even though all the matter and energy in the room consists of unbreakable threads, we now have two possible futures: one where Ms. Verdandi passes and another where she fails. With this simple act I've caused them to branch."

He raised his hand to reveal the coin resting on his palm.

"Dr. Gangleri, I didn't agree to this."

-6-

Dishes clattered as Stig's grandmother gathered them from the table and brought them to the sink. The sound sent shivers of Pavlovian dread down his spine, hollowed him out and filled him with bile. He sat, frozen, at the dinner table, scarcely able to pick at his plate. He had visited this terrible scene too often, in pursuit of the myriad possibilities that sprang from it.

The dinner had been like any other. His grandmother hadn't spoken much during, but at the sink she found the courage to say what had been on her mind the whole time. In a faux casual tone, she spoke over the running water and jangling silverware. "Your mother called today. She says she'll be in town for a day after the holidays. Just a short stopover between movies. She's moving from one set to another clear across the country. Isn't that interesting?" She flashed a quick look at him over her shoulder.

It was one of the rare occasions where his decision didn't matter. Seeing his mother that day stirred a deep pond of sadness and disappointment but had no lasting effect on the timelines. Either way he ended up on the same branch.

"No, I think I'll pass." That wasn't why he had come.

She nodded silently and kept washing. "So, Stiggy, are you all ready for finals?"

"Yes, 'ma."

"You going to get all A's again this year?"

"I always do, 'ma."

"I can't believe you're going to be a junior in college. You grew up so fast."

Stig stared at his plate, pushing peas around with his fork. In some branches he kept eating, slowly finishing his meal while his grandmother cleaned the dishes, but to access certain hidden branches of his possible futures, Yggdrasil demanded a toll, a sacrifice of a not-quite-metaphorical pound of flesh, a price as arbitrary and cruel as most things in life.

With ice in his veins, he stood and carried his plate to the sink. There, he turned on the water, activated the garbage disposal and pushed the remaining food into its roaring maw. The rumble of the disposal changed abruptly to a loud hum and all motion ceased. He looked at the fork, still dangling from his hand. The first time had been an accident, but every time since had been calculated. He stuck it into the drain. The infernal mechanism sprang back to life, jerking the fork from his hand. A blur of motion was followed by an odd coldness in his left eye. Three drops of blood splattered into the sink, one after another, before he felt any pain. The disposal had torn the fork apart and launched a tine into his eye. Reflexively, his hand rose. No matter how many times he went through this, he could not prevent that hand from rising up and making its grisly discovery.

Stig studied the cracked and peeling plaster of the motel room ceiling. He had spent less than an hour here, but he had done it many times. Did he know the pattern of blemishes any better from his numerous visits? He could have drawn a detailed map of the ceiling after the first time, but it felt familiar now. If Osmond were right, he had imagined each visit here, including this one. But by that logic, the present could be anywhere, even here, and his two-eyed memories as a professor and successful consultant could be the fantasies. This felt real. All the branches did.

"So, where did you see them last?" Carla asked, sitting in her bathrobe beside him on the bed.

"Hmm?"

"Your family. Where was the last place you saw them?"

"It was winter." Stig let the ceiling blur and fade away. "There was a fire in the fireplace. It was actually too warm, but it felt nice. Cozy. My wife lay on the couch. The boys sat on my feet and held onto my legs while I walked around the living room and tousled their hair. I can hear them squealing with laughter and see my wife smiling up at me. So beautiful."

"Huh," she said, uncertain what to make of his story. "That sounds nice."

"Have you ever wondered if the things that are happening to you are real or if you're just imagining them?" he asked.

"Well, I've had some pretty vivid dreams," she said. "You know, where you wake up and it takes a while to figure out it was all a dream. Is that what you mean?"

"I don't think so. I don't know. I never dream."

"Never?"

"Never," he said. "Dreaming is all about forgetting. I don't forget."

"Don't people go crazy if they're not allowed to dream? Maybe that's why things seem unreal to you.

You have to be able to forget things that didn't happen to know what did."

"I'm not crazy."

"No, of course not. No. I didn't mean that you were. I just.... Hey, listen, I think I'm going to go take a shower." She stood and looked at him. "We, uh...."

"Yes?"

"We better settle up now. Chances are you'll be gone when I come out."

"Ah. Okay." He rolled over to the side of the bed where his pants lay in a heap, fished around for his wallet, and sat back up. He pulled some bills out and handed them to her.

"So, if I don't see you again, uh, good luck with your family and all that."

"Thanks."

She headed to the bathroom, scooping up her pile of clothes and purse on the way. Just before the bathroom door closed Stig called out.

"Carla."

She stopped and looked back, surprised he knew her name. "Yeah?"

"Don't let Ash play with his cousin next week. His cousin has meningitis. Ash will — he'll get very sick."

Her look of perplexion deepened. "What? How do you know all that?"

"I just do. I, uh, know someone. A doctor told me. It doesn't matter. It's important, though. Okay?"

Visibly shaken by his warning, she gave a slow, "Okay," and closed the bathroom door on her puzzled look.

-8-

"You still with me?" Osmond asked.

Stig sat at the small coffee shop table looking through the window at the busy street outside. He looked up slowly and seemed to rediscover Osmond sitting next to him. "Yeah," he said.

"Well, anyway, I'm sorry," Osmond said.

"Don't be. I understand."

"It's almost as if no one wants to hire a one-eyed guy with no credentials to look over their most precious tech secrets these days, am I right?" Osmond asked with a gentle punch to his friend's shoulder.

"Yeah."

"Seriously, though, have you ever thought about going back to school? Finishing college?"

"Not really."

"Why not?"

"I already did that."

Osmond was puzzled for a second, then understood. "Oh. In other timelines. Right."

"The degrees don't matter," Stig said, staring at the table. "I know everything that the college professor version of me knows. I'm the same person. I've lived both lives. Many lives."

Osmond tapped a finger on the table, trying to think of a polite reply. "The problem is," he said, "other people don't know all that. They don't know what you can do. I mean, I can't even remember all the times you've helped me. Hell, you've saved my life at least twice."

"I'll always help you, Oz. You're my best friend. The year I spent in and out of the hospital after the accident, you never left my side. In all the branches, you're the one constant. I can always count on you."

Osmond put his meaty hand on Stig's back and squeezed his neck. "That was a rough time. Tell you the truth, I didn't think you were going to make it — between the surgeries and the infections." Osmond trailed off shaking his head. "You're lucky to be alive. Anyway, I'm sure our business will take off. We just need a lucky break." He let his arm drop and swirled the dregs of his coffee, lost in thought. When he looked up Stig, was staring out the window again.

"Hey Stig," he said. "Do you think that maybe you could work that mojo of yours to impress some bigwigs? You know, like hold back some CEO just before a piano falls on them, or something like that."

Stig answered without taking his eyes from the street outside. "Maybe."

During their years together, Osmond had grown used to their one-sided conversations. He kind of liked them. He joined Stig in looking out the window, and a longer silence followed, each of them lost in their own thoughts. It was Osmond who once again broke the quiet.

"You know how you always say you're time traveling and I always say you're only daydreaming?"

"Yeah?"

"Well, I was thinking. Have you ever followed one of these branches of yours all the way to the end?"

Stig looked up. "The end?"

"Yeah. I mean, it seems like if you follow any branch of your tree out far enough, you'd eventually die, right?"

"I suppose."

"Well, if you followed a branch all the way to the end and lived to tell about it, wouldn't that prove you're daydreaming and not actually time traveling?"

"I imagine I could leave that branch before I die. Go to another branch."

"Hmm." Osmond scrunched up his face. "I guess. But then that would make you pretty much immortal since you always have another branch you can escape to if you're about to die." Osmond held his arms out dramatically. "I sit in the presence of an immortal, time traveling God."

Osmond saw the serious, thoughtful look on Stig's face and broke out laughing. "I'm teasing you, man."

Stig stared at him blankly.

"You're not," Osmond said.

"Not what?"

"You're not a God. You're just a smart man. So smart that sometimes you're really quite dumb."

Stig just nodded.

"What do you think would happen," Osmond asked, "if you didn't leave a branch before you died?"

"Are you asking me what's after death?"

"Yeah, I guess."

"I don't know."

-9-

"Mr. Gangleri, I can't explain why the antibiotics aren't working, but they aren't. The infection is out of control. The last scan showed a fluid collection eroding through the optic canal. We need to take you to the operating room today to have it drained."

The doctor stood by the door, ready to make a quick getaway. Stig's grandmother sat attentively next to his bed, completely overwhelmed, her spirit broken. Each time he sacrificed his eye to see the branches beyond, he also sacrificed his grandmother's happiness. The sicker he became, the higher the toll she paid. He had seen her in worse shape dozens of times and had buried her as many, but he hated being the cause. Maybe this would be the last time.

"Today?" she asked.

"Yes, we have to try to control the infection. Do you understand, Stig?"

"I do." He understood more than the doctor knew. The antibiotics weren't working because he hadn't been taking them.

The doctor spoke a little longer to his grandmother, had her sign some forms and vanished.

Lying under the glaring surgical lights, Stig waited for the anesthetic to take effect. The morphine barely touched his pain and he shook violently with chills. Each visit to this early bough of Yggdrasil came with multiple surgeries, but he had never been this sick before. He should have been frightened, but instead he just felt exhausted: tired of being separated from the ones he loved and tired of being lost in the tangle of Yggdrasil.

"His blood pressure is dropping," a voice said. He understood the tone, not the words.

The pain faded, and the light grew brighter. The murmuring voices and electromechanical sounds of the room withered like shadows before the advancing light until only silence remained. Silence and light.

He felt himself walking before he saw anything. Walls emerged from the blinding nothingness to form the familiar hallway of his home. He reached the end of the hall and turned the corner hopeful, as always, of what he would find. There, rocking a baby over a bassinet while another slept peacefully nearby, stood his wife. When she saw Stig, a warm smile spread across her face and she lowered the sleeping baby into the bassinet. She hurried across the room and gave him a long hug, burying her head on his shoulder. When they separated she held his face gently and looked into his eyes.

"My love," she said. "You must leave this branch. It ends and your work isn't complete."

"But I finally found you." He took her hands from his face and held them tightly. "I want to stay here, with you."

"Much of Yggdrasil remains undiscovered. Your destiny is unfulfilled," she said. "You must continue."

"I can't leave you. You were too hard to find. What if I never find my way back?"

She laughed gently. "We are easy to find. All branches lead here."

"I don't understand. I've searched Yggdrasil for lifetimes without finding a way here. I shouldn't be here now. This branch — I'm only nineteen and my grandmother still lives in this house. I couldn't have met you yet."

"Silly. You've been looking for us within the tree, but we live beyond the tree of possibilities, in the space between the branches. You've found us here, in this house, because this is familiar to you, but we are not tied to any one time or place. We are always with you, like air against a tree, rippling its leaves and rustling its branches."

"But I've been with you before. How?"

"You caught glimpses of the impossible when your mind was freed."

"From anesthesia? During surgery?"

"Yes. But you must go now, or Yggdrasil will never be complete."

"I don't know where to go. I think I've lost the present. Without it—" He paused and shook his head. "Without it, I can't tell what's real."

"The present is where the future turns into the past. It follows your mind like a mirage. You know this better than anyone."

She released his hands. "Now go, and return to us after you have accomplished great things and grown tired of wandering."

The ebb and flow of chaotic motion outside the coffee shop window mirrored his thoughts, and mesmerized Stig in a way he found hard to resist. Osmond's voice pulled him from his reverie.

"You know how you always say you're time traveling and I always say you're just daydreaming?"

"Yeah?"

"Well, I was thinking. Have you ever followed a branch out to the end?"

"No. Not to the end. But close enough to see what's beyond."

"Oh?" Osmond looked surprised. "What's there? What did you see?"

Stig looked up from the window and smiled. "The impossible."

Douglas Anstruther's story "Not All Those Who Wander Are Lost" was published in Metaphorosis on Friday, 31 August 2018.

About the story

I wanted to explore the idea that perfect prediction of the future could be confused with, and possibly be indistinguishable from, actually experiencing the future. As I wrote, I discovered that for someone with the ability to do this, the concept of the present became less relevant, and along with it, the notion of mortality.

In addition to the intentionally unanswered questions of whether or not Stig is really immortal and whether or not a real, objective present exists that he has lost, the story raised other questions along the way. I wasn't able to address these in the short story format and they were better left to the reader's imagination anyway. For example: If Stig's mental facilities are impaired (from drugs or sleep) does he lose his ability to jump away from danger? Is there some sort of meta-time that allows the linear progression of Stig's own experiences? If he doesn't go back to a thread, does time pass on it? If there were two people with the same ability, could either one extend the same thread? I do hope that the list goes on and that many more questions are raised among readers.

A question for the author

Q: If someone wanted to make an animated series out of your work, based on the title or recurring themes, what would it look like?

A: There are a few times in the story when the present isn't holding Stig's attention very well and we find him spacing out. Is he considering a leap to another branch? Maybe he's moved on to another timeline and is letting the one we see coast on autopilot.

An animated series could show these other timelines in the background, constantly impinging on his attention, threatening to carry him away, competing with each other to be his next destination and coloring his decisions and mood with knowledge of alternate histories and futures that the people around him haven't experienced. It'd look pretty trippy.

Also, dark. I like my animated series dark.

About the author

Douglas Anstruther was raised among the long cold winters of Minnesota. At age seven he discovered that there were other worlds beyond our own and was astonished, and frankly disappointed, that no one had thought this important enough to mention earlier - a sentiment he still holds today. At some point he married his lovely wife, Dana, went to medical school, had three very nearly perfect children and moved to Wilmington, North Carolina. When not tending to people's kidneys, Douglas likes to read, write and talk about history, linguistics, space, AIs, the singularity, and everything in between. He particularly enjoys writing stories that will rattle around in the readers' head for a while after the last page has been turned.

www.facebook.com/douglasanstruther, @DouglsAnstruthr

Velaya, the Dreaming City

Six parts after Dunsany

Beston Barnett

Part 1

I set out for Velaya as a young man, having only just pledged to wed. I was to marry Belqis, flower of our village and light of my eyes, in whose father's orchards I had played since my childhood. Our marriage should have been enough for a lifetime of happiness. But I believed then—as so many young fools do—that dreams were the currency of happiness, and I carried with me dreams as yet unredeemed. And though I tried to conceal it, Belqis, my betrothed, sensed my dissatisfaction and, knowing its source, spoke to me, saying:

"Always you have shared with me your dreams of Velaya. You have whispered to me of silver domes and white carved stone, of miraculous waters which run in aqueducts through strolling parks, of red and gold kites which fly from the cliffs and gild the sky, and of so many other wonders that for me the Dreaming City lives in the sound of your voice. Always it has been your dream to visit far-off Velaya and know its mysteries.

"And yet, once we are married, it is possible that duties to our fields and orchards and to family and to our as yet unborn children—think of our beautiful children, my love!—may keep you from ever travelling to such dreamed-of distant lands. I am selfish and do not wish to bear that disappointment. Therefore, though each day apart will be a trial, I say: go now to Velaya and return to me with eyes brim full of silver and green and red and gold, eyes that have beheld the Dreaming City. For though I love you now and with all I know of my heart, it may be that I will love the man who returns to me from Velaya even more."

Thus—as ever—did Belqis amaze me with her generosity.

Of course, I protested.

I said, "The duties you speak of are to me nothing but joys."

And also, "Our full and happy lives could admit of no regrets."

And also, "My dreams of Velaya are a child's dreams, but my dreams of the coming together of our lives are the dreams of the man I wish to become."

But Belqis knew my heart, and she overcame my protestations. And truthfully—young and foolish though I was—I knew myself blessed even then to be understood so well and trusted so completely.

And so Velaya rose up triumphant in my mind's eye.

I set out by cart and was soon come to lands beyond any I had known. I traveled by overgrown tracks through fields cultivated with grain and by wide highways that the legionnaires had of old hewn through the impassable forests between cities. Coming over rocky wastes and through orchards of olives, I had my first sight of the sea and felt myself remade in its grandeur and its sadness.

And though I was clumsy with the language of the dock-hands in that first port, I was able by signs and nodding to book passage over the sea and to come finally to the yellow shores of that great desert land of which Velaya is the very jewel and heart and center. From there, caravans of camels in long trains came and went daily. Here were found traders, journeymen, diplomats, shepherds, but also pilgrims, and these were my true kin—the pilgrims—those that had been granted visions of Velaya in dreams.

When I had replenished my stores and purchased a blanket and hired a camel-puller, I too joined a caravan and left at dawn for the last four days of my pilgrimage.

That first night in the desert was cold; a cold of open spaces like none I had known. As the drivers settled their camels into corrals, I huddled with three pilgrims around the remnants of our cooking fire, and we drank the clear local liquor called *raktash* and each of us was fired by the *raktash* with bright longing for Velaya.

And out of this bright longing, the woman who had traveled from distant lands far to the West spoke, saying:

Part 2

"It is said of the gods of Velaya that they are fierce but also generous, that their dreams dwell often along the white and shining cliffs, and that in their dreams, miracles are worked. For it is within the power of their miraculous dreams to grant the gift of *flight*.

"Aspirants travel great distances to petition this gift of the gods. Settling in the squatter's quarter known as the Aerie, aspirants build themselves the nests of sticks and mud which will be their homes for at least the next season and often much longer. During the days they lie in their uncovered nests, absorbing the rays of the sun, taking the lightness of the sun into them, willing themselves to lighten. Then in the cool spring evenings, they descend in their white robes to the taverns and meeting places of the city, and there recite the light-filled 'cloud poems' for which Velaya is justly renowned.

"As the sun fills their bodies with lightness, so aspirants fill with a floating feeling, and in the summer they are often seen wearing lead weights around arms and ankles as ballast. Much of their poetry in this season eulogizes the peculiar sensation of untying the weights from their limbs in the evening, of experiencing that weightlessness which presages the hoped-for gift. In this season too they begin work on the red and gold paper constructions which they will fly from the lower cliffs with such drama during the kite festival.

"It is in the autumn that aspirants often decide to petition the gods. It is not a decision shared or discussed, but must be reached alone, known by the lightness in the heart, by the tense spreading of invisible wings. Many, through doubt or humility, never decide. But on a clear morning in the first cool days after summer, a small white-robed figure may be seen climbing alone the Dawn Stair and mounting to the heights of Veliara, tallest of the white cliffs, though it does not face Velaya as the others do, but is hidden and turned away behind a great knee of limestone rubble.

"And what happens then numbers among the great mysteries of Velaya. For it is not known if there is some right phrasing or secret password or if perhaps the heart of the aspirant is weighed against that of a feather or if it is purity or yearning or some inborn talent or simply the dream of gods whose dreams must of necessity be ineffable. The aspirant makes his petition and steps from the cliff. The gods dream and judge. And some aspirants—most, it is said—end there at the base of Veliara, and their bleached bones remain uncounted, for the base of the cliff of Veliara is sacred ground and to visit there is forbidden.

"But there are some—a few? one a year? a decade? a generation?—who are caught in the cupped hands of the gods' dreaming and who fly."

The woman from the distant West paused then and drank. We all drank, each in turn—the *raktash* like hot sand that singes the throat and afterwards consoles it—before she continued.

"And there are those who say that long since passed are the days in which the gods of Velaya heard petitions. The city fills with white-robed aspirants, yet fewer and fewer climb the Dawn Stair each year. *Where are these chosen flyers,* they say, *aloft on god-dreams?* And in the dark corners of taverns there are others who whisper that the gods' interest is only with the pile of aspirant bones at the base of Veliara and not with those that would fly above it.

"But as for me, I am unwavering. From my youngest days have I dreamed of flying and known those dreams to be the best part of myself and true.

"And one day I will take my place among the flyers above Velaya."

We stared into what embers of the fire remained then, each of us inhabiting the image of the city that our minds conjured glowing there in the coals, and I sensed the others drift one by one into sleep.

But I lay awake, I know not how long after, with my mind in the jaws of frightful premonitions. A veil seemed pulled aside, and all was revealed and inverted and churning. *The city is a trap,* I thought, and my thoughts were like jaws that closed and closed again. I saw a procession of young men and women with broken wings, sun-blind, their limbs contorted. *The city is a trap. It calls to the gullible, to the pilgrims, to the dreamers like myself, and it eats their dreams.*

I saw the pile of bones at the base of Veliara, felt myself pressed beneath them.

I slept.

In the morning was a great hubbub of packers and camel-pullers and coffee wallahs calling across the expanse of cold, spent fires. I stood, wrapped in my blanket. In the noise and the smell of the coffee and the gray light of the new day, my last night's imaginings paled. I thought of Velaya and Belqis, the dreamed-of city and my beautiful wife. Both awaited me, and by this I knew myself a pilgrim twice blessed, who followed two stars. Gathering my few belongings, I thought, *And what if the allure of Velaya eclipses that of Belqis? What if its red and gold kites, its white walls, its taverns full of poetry, what if these seduce me and make me forget my heart?* Yet—after one month, after two—I would return to my Belqis and tell her what I had felt and seen, for the tale of such beauty must have an audience, and always Belqis had been that audience for me. I believed that I knew myself; that I would return to her. For though Velaya filled my mind with imagined colors, Belqis still filled my heart.

Velaya might be a trap for some, but not for me.

All that sweltering day I sat and swayed on the princely hump of my camel as the great caravan spread out around me and advanced. And at end of day, we came again to a camp in the desert where the day's caravan heading northward from Velaya met our southward-heading caravan, and again there was the chaos of stocks and tents and animals and cooking fires scattered like a wide mirror of the stars which are themselves scattered in a band across the night sky. And again that evening my three companions and I reclined together around our small fire and ate and passed the local liquor *raktash* that so opens the hearts of travellers, one to another.

Then into that tranquility that descends upon the desert at day's end, the young man from the distant North spoke, saying:

Part 3

"I have heard it said of the gods of Velaya that they are loving but shy. That they love their people is certain, evidenced by the many miracles they have wrought in their city, chiefest among these the Miracle of the Waters, which rise up in the desert city in green pools and playful fountains to delight and succor its people. Yet the gods of Velaya are also shy, timid of applicants, unwilling to reveal themselves except to the most pure and the most devout. But in their love, they have left stones hidden in and below the city which the pure and devout may find and with which they may commune with the gods. For it is thus that the gods find the miracles they bestow upon Velaya: by mining in the hearts of men.

"There was a man stranded at the base of a cliff deep in the desert, lost, dying of thirst; this was the first applicant. How he came to be there, how he came by such purity of heart and devotion of spirit, these things are not known. But there in his distress he found a stone, and this was the first of the Dreaming Stones. It was a sand-smoothed oblong of jade, and through it, clasping it to him, the man communed with a god; this was the first of the gods of Velaya, who is called simply Vel, and who mined in the heart of the man through the Dreaming Stone and found there Velaya's first miracle: the Miracle of the Waters.

"He was the first applicant; since then, there have been many. Successive generations of applicants have come and striven and searched and some—the pure, the devout—have found the stone they sought, and the miracles they carried in their hearts have transformed Velaya into the jewel of the desert. The massive statues of the First Dreamers, the tiered Night Gardens, the filigreed temple of Vel-Abir—all these were miracles wrought by stone-finders of old. The Dawn Stair itself was among the earliest miracles: the heart-wish of a father whose daughter loved above all else the flying of kites; his plain river stone appeared to him one evening at the bottom of a humble pot of soup.

"Many applicants are miners or prospectors or vendors in the gemstone markets for which Velaya is renowned, where they daily handle seraphinite, jade, epidote, chrysoprase, beryl. Others work in infrastructure, shoring up stone work, re-routing water systems, sculpting architectural ornament, or simply cleaning the floors of palaces and homes. Always and at every hour, applicants search for their Dreaming Stone, listening for its distinct call, opening their hearts in purity and devotion. An applicant serves the city and his dearest wish is to have the next great miracle—the cliff statues, the gardens, the stairs—called forth from his heart through the stone of his dreams, and thus to live on forever as a part of the city itself.

"And, yes, there are those who say that many years have come and gone since Velaya was re-fashioned by miracle-stones. They say that the city is too big now, too impure with commerce, or that the last Dreaming Stone has long since been found. Or in darker moods, some mutter that perhaps the gods find their nourishment no longer with the pure and their stones, but with the suffering of the applicant who goes blind cutting gemstones or who is crushed in the mines beneath the city or who is worked to death cleaning, every day, year upon year, the palaces, the walls, the sewers."

The young man paused, and drank as if to rid his mouth of a disagreeable taste.

"But as for me, I am undeterred. Since earliest memory have I dreamed of holding a green stone to my breast, holding it and calling forth wonders. And I believe that one day, when I have hallowed the city in my eye and in my heart—with purity, with devotion, with humility—then shall I find my place among the miracle-workers of Velaya.

"For this was I made."

We lay then silent around the dying fire, each of us awed and entranced by the Northern man's story. The Dreaming City shone before my mind's eye—as I knew it must before the others'—wonderful, exotic, like a child's glass marble given by a parent returning from long travels, alight with possibility.

And yet, as the others drifted into sleep, the image of the city tilted in my mind. I saw it as from below, up from the blackness of the mines that coil through its foundations, and there I saw old men and women, frail and blind, who struggled through those tunnels ceaselessly and in vain. And I saw that those tunnels were the entrails of the city, its very intestines, and all those zealous seekers no more than digesting meat trapped in a horrible peristalsis. *The city is a trap*, I repeated to myself.

The words echoed, the coils tightened. *The city is a trap.*

Somehow I slept.

The next morning broke with the same confusion of activity as before, and yet I felt it overlain with a new sense of urgency and reverence. The Dreaming City waited only two days ride to the South. We pilgrims rode lost in thought as brides to a distant wedding who in their thoughts take leave of their former lives and prepare as best they can to be transformed. And all that sun-bleached day I meditated on what it might mean to be disappointed by Velaya. What if I found its streets dirty, its vistas uninspiring, its palaces gaudy, its gardens wasted, its denizens petty, its meeting places unwelcoming, its waters untended and unclean, and all my many dreams, mirages? What if I found more truth in the eyes of its beggars, than in the hauteur of its gods? These thoughts were terrible. I would be broken. And would I then return to Belqis and ask her to fulfil her vows to a broken man?

And thinking thus I remembered Belqis, my other pilgrim's star. I remembered her not as simply an audience or a symbol of home, but as she truly was—generous and understanding and kind. I knew that she would accept and remake me, that I might be dispirited for a time but that I would be remade in our lives together and in the lives of our children, and that one day we might all smile together at the dreams of my earnest youth. A weight lifted from me, like a fever breaking. I believed I knew myself. I believed I knew Belqis. And as we arrived at the final camp and the porters flew about their accustomed tasks, I thought, *I shall see what there is to be seen of Velaya, whatever that may be, and I shall return to my beloved and tell of it.*

The city might be a trap for some, but not for the man for whom Belqis waits.

And as the preparations for the night's camp began, there were pilgrims who said they could see already the white cliffs of Velaya off to the South, but I could make out only what seemed a sand storm, a shimmering white smudge on the horizon.

Just as in earlier nights, my companions and I built a small fire, spread blankets, and shared out dried apricots and patties of lentils. We passed the local liquor *raktash* in a small gourd between us, hand-to-hand and solemnly: a libation. It would be our last night as a company, and our hearts were so full with the awesome nearness of the Dreaming City that I expected no one to break the thoughtful trance which had come upon us with the cold and the dark. Thus were we all surprised when the silent woman—a woman from far to the East by her clothes, whom I, for one, had assumed spoke none of our common tongues—began to tell of her dreams in a clear and quiet voice, saying:

Part 4

"Among my people we have an idiom: *wary as the gods of Velaya*. We say this of the baker who will not share his recipe with his apprentice, or of the midwife who will teach no one the secrets of her trade. That the gods of Velaya keep secrets is known. Of the secrets of flight and of communion we have had eulogies already; but they keep also secrets for changing lead to gold, and making broken things whole, and living eternally young. And why are these secrets kept so dear? Are the gods given to spite or jealousy? Or might they perhaps be wise to allow only the few and the dedicated to learn the working of such miracles as might undo less worthy supplicants?

"The madrasas of the Dreaming City are built on this simple faith: that both wary *and* wise are the gods of Velaya.

"Students flock to the madrasas from all the lands that we know, and from the moment they step through the East Gate, their lives are bounded by ceremony and study. During their first years, most complement their research by taking apprenticeship with the glassblowers or the metalsmiths or in the guild of the nurses. After graduation, many may take up the mantle of professorship or medical practice, but the final stage in the lives of the scholars of Velaya is always solitary and secret study, for it is in mimicking the gods themselves —*wary and wise*—that they hope to discern that which their dreams have intimated: the recipes, formulas, incantations, codes, and mechanisms of the miraculous.

"Of the great madrasas, two dominate: the alchemists' university and the hospital. At the lower levels, these institutions operate as schools, as wards, as laboratories and libraries; they buzz with students, patients, and journeymen, all moving about their labors. But as scholars attain the higher levels, treading spiral stairs into the towers that sprout from these centers of learning like shoots in spring seeking upward for a purer air, so their silence deepens. In the highest rooms— within the very domes which so distinguish the city—the most learnéd study in deep solitude where the only sound is the turning of pages and the scritching of pen against parchment. And even above that, it is said, there are floating rooms hidden by art of magic in the upper air where adepts neither read, nor write, nor discourse at all, but simply stare into the secret mysteries of the universe.

"Of course, such institutions must have their detractors: students embittered by failed examinations or families dissatisfied with the care given a loved one. The scholars of Velaya, they say, neglect the world around them for the sky above and lose their way in mazes of their own making. In seeking the miraculous, the scholars wish to be gods themselves and so must fail.

"And perhaps, whisper the spiteful to one another, the whole towering hierarchy of study and sacrifice is as a honeypot laid by the gods—oh so wise and wary, the gods—who would lay a honeypot to feed off the best and brightest, their would-be usurpers.

"But as for me, I am undaunted."

Here, the Eastern woman paused and raised the gourd of *raktash* to each of us in turn, looking steadily into each pair of eyes from beneath the folds of her hood before continuing.

"In my dreams, I stand below the silver domes with a balm in my hand, a miraculous balm to heal the sick and make whole the maimed. And in that dream, the sick and the maimed come to me, and I heal them and, by my hand, I make them whole.

"Be it prophecy or be it illusion, I shall follow whither such a dream leads, because it is a good dream, and because it is mine."

Silence settled on us then, and we lay staring into the last lit embers of our fire. The Eastern woman's tale had been so eloquent, her dream so noble, we each of us felt that a grace had been laid upon our little camp and a blessing upon our dreams. I felt certain that the premonitions which had haunted me on previous nights would not recur.

But as the others closed their eyes and the dim fire gave way entirely to the dimmer light of cold desert stars, I began to think of Velaya in the abstract. Of what does it dream?—Velaya—for it is called the Dreaming City, and not the City of Dreams. Are the dreams of the city and of its gods one? And what if the city's dreams are of men that never leave, but circle endlessly its siren streets, seeking but never finding dreams of their own?

Then, of a sudden, the image of Velaya—that image which had been in my mind since my earliest memories and which had grown in these final days of my pilgrimage to fill every corner of my inner sky—that image tilted again. Now I saw it not from belowground, where its mines twisted and turned, but from above, where countless layered labyrinths made of naught but wind and vapor ornamented the air between the domes and radiated outward and upward in towers and coronae. And through these labyrinths, hidden in the air, crawled old men and women, scholars, always alone, always seeking but never finding, their robes too threadbare to keep out the cold. And I saw that if the mines were the digestive tracts of Velaya, then these insubstantial mazes above the city were its brain matter, and the scholars lost there were as its very neurons. And I saw that this beast of a city nourished itself on a steady stream of pilgrims but shat out only bones. And I saw that the great breathing of this parasitic beast, squatting there one day's ride through the desert, was the nightly going out and gathering in of its dreams, dreams like lures, like siren song, like golden netting, and these dream-lures were made in the crucible of its inhabitants' desperation and longing, made under great pressure and flung out in invisible waves from its trembling need.

The city is a trap, I thought, *but not for me. I am neither flyer nor miner nor scholar, and I have Belqis.* I would pass through unharmed, like a white egret that flies over the swamp and returns, unsullied.

My mind calmed. I shifted beneath my blanket and turned on my side and thought that now I would finally rest. A pleasant silence of sleepers and cold stars spread out around me. Tomorrow, all the colors of Velaya awaited.

And with that I came fully awake. Another scenario visited me—a possibility I had not before considered—and it set me shivering, for it had the halo of truth about it. What if Velaya seemed at first a disappointment and, after a week of seeing its uninspired sights, I was ready to depart and prepare what disappointing words I would say to Belqis, but then I spied there something colorful and vibrant, something truly *of* the city of my many dreams? Of course, I would have to stay and explore it—a café where poets gathered or a crumbling temple in the gardens, a place where something unfolded which was worthy of being described to my Belqis. And after I had learned enough of the vain poets or the maudlin temple and was preparing to leave once again, what if I should stumble across some other image or experience which seemed to speak more to the heart of the mystery of the Velaya for which I had first set out? A little girl building a kite with her grandfather perhaps, or a green-robed monk planting a yellow flower, or the great cliffs glowing from a certain perspective in a certain light. Would I not then stay and explore a while longer, if only so that my tales for Belqis would be that much more captivating?

And with each new delay, my absence from Belqis would grow. The longer I was away, the more amazing my stories would have to be on my return. Otherwise, how could I explain to her why I had stayed away so long? I imagined myself desperate—after six months, after a year, after five years—struggling to find something, always just around the corner in Velaya, worthy of telling my Belqis. Something amazing enough to heal the wound of our long separation. After five years, what could possibly be amazing enough? A miraculous balm? A god-stone? A pair of god-gifted wings?

Now was I frozen in fear, feverish, trapped in the coils of my own premonitions. I saw the pile of bones, the mines like intestines, the mazes pulsing in the air, and I saw myself following a trail of glittering clues through the streets, pacing out mandalas, the true Velaya always just ahead, and I, desperate and in despair. And what then would become of my Belqis?

No. Sometime well before dawn, I made a decision. I would not say goodbye. I would not face the disbelief and disappointment of my companions.

I arose and padded through the camp and found my indignant camel-puller and informed him of my change of plans.

I would not venture on to Velaya.

Part 5

And that is the story of my life. The central story, the story on which the rest teeters. A coward's less-than-heroic story about a long journey and an abandoned dream. That is how I viewed it for many years: an abandoned dream.

I returned to my village and married Belqis. At first I lied to everyone: I told fanciful but brief tales of the wonders I had seen. To those who asked why I hadn't stayed longer, I said that the time away from my beloved had been too painful, that I had been eager to start our lives together. This was half true, and Belqis, caught up in the excitement of the wedding, allowed me these half-truths for a time.

But my wife is an observant woman. After we had been living together for some months, she began very delicately to probe my stories, and I broke down almost at once. In real torment of soul, I told how three nights of terrible premonitions in the desert had defeated a lifetime of dreams. I recall how we sat at our little table long after the village slept, drinking the tart early cider our orchards produce in that season and speaking in low tones by the light of a single candle. And how she did not reproach me but looked at me all through our conversation with tender compassion. Yet still I felt myself a failure.

"I failed the first and simplest test of Velaya, a test of the resilience of my dreams. I am revealed a coward."

"My beloved, you were made to choose between the city and me. It is not cowardly to choose love. I honor you."

"And I honor you and love you ... yet I cannot help but feel unworthy now of that love."

And Belqis held my hand and, from that night, she seemed to love me as much as ever she had or even more.

And in the years that followed, our fields were fruitful and our flock thrived and our village prospered. We were blessed with three children, two girls and a boy, all beautiful and full of life. In motherhood, Belqis grew in beauty and wisdom. We were blessed. And yet at times—in truth, *often*—I seemed to see our blessings as through a veil, a veil that separated me from my feelings and from other people. A veil that filtered color from the world. At these times, I felt myself a hollow husband, a hollow father.

Rarely in those years did we mention my journey, and never once did Belqis reproach me for my failures. Never, at least, until the naming of our tavern.

For some time, she had talked of opening a tavern such as our village lacked, a proper place for travelers to eat and pass the evening, and for village meetings and dances in the colder months. I supported her, and when the structure was complete and the first fire was lit in the barroom hearth, Belqis showed me the signboard that would hang above the front door. The board was carved and colored wood, white cliffs against a blue sky, with the words, *The Dreaming City,* engraved across them in painted silver.

It had been so long since those once magical words had passed my lips; I felt stung, mocked. I hesitated, then spoke carefully.

"I did not know you had decided on a name."

Belqis did not look at me, but smiled at the floor. "It is a beautiful name for a tavern," she said. "Travelers will recognize it, and the village will find it exotic and exciting... Do you like it?"

I sensed that she was tense, that maybe the whole project for this tavern had been leading to this moment, to this sign and this name—that now was the time to show my gratitude for her years of forbearance—but I didn't trust myself to speak. Coward that I am, I made an ambivalent "mmm" sound and nodded.

The tavern was a success. Belqis took some pride in preparing the days' meals and the nights' rooms, in welcoming travelers and introducing them to our local cider. She seemed in her element there, a fish in good water. I spent more time in the fields or teaching the children to tend the flock and the garden and the orchards. Of course, I visited the barroom some nights, though I was uncomfortable with the travelers and their talk.

But one cool autumn evening with the fire's warm glow burnishing the few faces in the room, a young man traveling alone began to talk of Velaya, and it was as if his voice spoke to me across space and time, from another fire in the desert far away and years ago, but immediate, present. He said he loved birds and had dreamed as a child that he could speak to them. Later, he had heard that the secret to the language of birds could be found in a distant city far to the South. Many had scoffed, insisting that the birds had no language or that the stories of men who spoke with birds were only legends, but he remained true to his dreams.

I was transfixed.

When he had finished, Belqis looked at me and away—subtly and quick—and then she offered a glass of cider to the young man who loved birds.

To the room, she said, "A glass of cider and a bowl of stew on the house for any traveler who tells a story of the Dreaming City!"

There were no more storytellers that night, but word spread, and eventually our tavern became known throughout the countryside and beyond as a trading post for the lore of Velaya. Pilgrims would travel many miles off their routes to spend an evening or two at *The Dreaming City* and to share a story. We heard from warriors who dreamed of invincible swords, and lovers who dreamed of fairy brides, and would-be wizards who dreamed of taming fiery dragons. And sometimes—as the months became years—if the night was slow or the weather was bad, I might volunteer a story of my own journey. Never of the city itself, but of the dock-hands I had encountered and the sailing ship, or of the sounds and smells of the great caravans.

And am I now content? Am I healed? I am still ashamed of my brush with the city. And yet also I am haunted by a kind of wary nostalgia for the road and its mysteries. I am not entirely content, but neither am I the hollow man I was for a time. There is color again.

And tonight after a late evening of stories in the tavern, as I helped Belqis into bed and lay down beside her—wise Belqis, clever Belqis, flower of our village and light of my eyes—she turned to me and spoke to me softly.

She said, "Our flocks and our orchards do well. The tavern prospers."

"Yes, my love," I said and touched her gray hair.

She said, "Our children are grown and married and have children of their own. You have taught them to tend the farm and I have taught them to tend the tavern, and our children and our grandchildren do these things well and with love."

"Yes, my love," I said and touched her shoulder.

She said, "All these things we have done with love and now we have time."

"Yes, my love," I said and took her hand, though I did not yet know what she meant.

And she said, "We can go to Velaya together."

Part 6

I am Belqis and the dream of Belqis and I am old.

I was old already when we set out. Old and dying, if truth be known, though it had been my constant concern in those last few months to hide my growing infirmity from my husband and my children.

They were not so very difficult to deceive. My children worried about their own children, not about me, and this relieved and comforted me, for it is as things should be between the generations. As for my husband, I believe he saw me still as a young maid—the dream of Belqis he had returned to all those years ago—and I loved him for this harmless delusion and indulged him.

But I could not deceive myself. What had at first seemed the common ache and stiffness of age revealed itself over the course of some months to be a creeping paralysis. I could no longer turn my hips or unbend my back to reach the shelves in the pantry, my ankles would not flex, and my right hand was perfectly wooden, like the false claw of an amputee, so that I poured cider now only with my left. I was become an old fire-ravaged tree. I succumbed branch by branch, the sap hardened, the xylem and cambium no longer coursed with living water: I knew that soon I would be only pith, only dead wood.

And so I determined that we should travel as aged pilgrims to Velaya, to the Dreaming City, where my husband could at last complete the great interrupted arc of his life, and I, like a canny cat that when its time has come slinks away from family and friends, I could go there to die.

We left with fanfare and the blessings of the whole village, and I, swaddled in quilts, waved from our hired carriage and smiled and wept and knew that I was dying and never to see my children again. And that was hard—very hard—but I have always endeavored to live gracefully, and I chose to die gracefully as well.

After only two days, we had traveled farther than I had ever traveled before. After two weeks, nothing at all was recognizable to me: not the language men spoke, not the trees, not the very color of the earth. In the mornings, birds I did not know sang songs I had never before heard. My body continued to stiffen, but through the apertures of my ears and eyes, a new lightness entered me, made of awe and surprise and a comforting sense of our smallness when considered against the expanse of the wide world.

And still I did not speak to my husband of dying. Not until at last I beheld the sea—the true, storied sea, wide, steel gray, implacable, against which all human conceit is but loose sand—only then did my unwillingness to speak of dying fall away from me at last. We booked passage, and there on deck, amid the strange back-and-forth calls of the sailors as they clambered through the rigging and the sharp smell of sea wrack, I pressed my husband's hand.

"Now that we have left the road for the sea and can no more turn back, we must speak of difficult things."

"My love?"

"You know that my body is failing, that I walk only with great difficulty, that my hands have stiffened to such a degree that I can no longer feed myself. You take my arm and you guide me, you put the spoon in my mouth, and you do these things lovingly. I am made to feel young and loved and I am grateful. But we must speak the truth of these things." I held his eyes. "My husband, I am dying."

"Of course you are not... Or we are dying together, yes, and will do so for many happy years. My love, let us not talk of such things, but enjoy the sea breeze and the sun. Here, I will adjust your chair to better catch the light."

I said, "I have a disease. A paralysis is moving through my body, slowly, stilling my hands, my legs, my back. It will reach my lungs or my heart soon. Sooner than you have imagined... I am sorry."

He looked at me, amazed, but I would not look away, though tears started from my eyes. "Then we will turn back," he said. "If it is as you say, I will speak to the captain immediately and we will turn back. I must bear the blame for encouraging this pilgrimage. We will go home where you can rest and you can mend."

And my husband made as if to stand and go, but I spoke softly, so that he bent to hear me.

"I will not mend and there is not time. I am sorry. It has been a good life with you and our families and our children and the orchards and the tavern—a life full of love—but it is ending. And now I wish to see Velaya."

Then he sank before me and held my knees and wept.

We said much more to one another, that day and in the days that followed, but we did not turn around, and gradually my husband came to support my resolve. And though my condition worsened, so that I was more like a bent plank of wood than a woman when finally we made port, he bathed me and cared for me and passed the evenings of our sea voyage with descriptions of the great caravans he had known of old.

But the port town, when we alighted, seemed diminished from the bustling center he had described, and the wide caravanserai with its many stables and markets was pitifully empty. I saw disappointment on my husband's face and also confusion, and I, in my debility, could do little to help. Eventually we found someone in the dusty market who would take us the four days to Velaya on camelback, though our guide's fare was exorbitant and his camel seemed skinny and old, even to one who had never seen a camel before.

We set out the next day, and the going was hard for me. We rode together on the one camel, my husband and I, because I was so light and because I was too stiff to sit without falling, so that my husband had to tie me to him atop that strange fleshy hump. The heat of the day was punishing and the cold of night, bitter. I spoke almost not at all, for my breathing had become shallow and short. I feared that the paralysis had come to my lungs at last, that I might not make it to the city.

On the third morning, we woke alone in the desert with no water—camel and guide gone—and all but one coin stolen from us.

I could not walk. I could barely breathe. But far on the horizon, my husband said he could see white cliffs, and so he hoisted me into the air, as a bridegroom crossing the threshold with his bride, and began to walk. All that day he walked through the broken desert carrying his wife before him like a cord of wood and the sun beating down. And all that night with the cold stars staring. And more than once he stumbled, but never did he let me fall, and I could do nothing to help but to coax my laboring lungs on, and each breath a trial.

At dawn we came to Velaya.

And having never seen the Dreaming City myself, I could not know with certainty that it had fallen, that it was a husk of its former glory. I had heard only stories of Velaya, and who can say what is fantasy and what is real in a story, no matter how earnest the teller.

But the city was certainly a husk. The Northern Gate was pockmarked; its arches had fallen where their keystones no longer held. The domes of the madrasas which had not collapsed had been stripped of their silver. The streets were dusty and steep and uneven and empty of inhabitants except for a few market-folk in colorless rags selling trinkets and dried nuts from the shadow of low doors.

But my husband entered with his head held high in the dawn light and his eyes stern and his dying bride in his arms.

"We are come to Velaya, my love," he whispered.

And on the blanket of a sun-wizened old rag-picker, from among dirty sandstone idols and chipped crockery, my husband chose a small earthenware jar the size of a hen's egg and traded for it our last coin. And squatting there in the street with myself in his lap—never putting me down—he opened the jar, and with his two fingers scooped from it a gray ointment, and opening my thin black robes, he rubbed the ointment onto my chest.

"A balm of Velaya, my love," he whispered.

And at first I felt only a tingle, but then air rushed into my lungs and I breathed as deeply as a child breathes who wakes from a long and untroubled sleep.

And I would have lain there in his lap breathing and praying and giving thanks—for I had surely been touched by a miracle—but my husband stood with me in his arms, and continued walking up the broken street and in his eyes was a burning intensity. The rag-picker called after us, and some children, ragged also and all skinny, came from the doorways out of curiosity or wonder and followed us on up the street, and more joined, until we were leading some dozens of street urchins in a motley parade. And we wound through the abandoned city until we came, all of us, to a wide plaza with a shallow pool at its center, the pool dry and half-filled with wind-blown sand and its tiles all cracked. Then my husband reached down and grasped a pebble that two of the boys had been kicking and raised it to the light for me to see—a piece of broken cobble with green flecks in its clay—and then he held it to my chest and held me close to *his* chest.

"A stone of Velaya, my love," he whispered.

And as he held me to him, water burst forth in a great arcing spray from the center of the pool and the children all screamed and the mist from the spray of water soaked into our robes and into the rags of the children as they ran and jumped and splashed into the pool. But my husband held me and rubbed more of the ointment into my hands, and as he rubbed the sore useless tendons and the stiff little bones, my fingers returned to life and ached and flexed and clutched his fingers in desperate gratitude. We drank from the pool together, cupping our hands, the clear cold water running down our chins and necks, and rainbows danced in the arcing mist.

There were more shouts as the city-folk came running into the plaza, clapping and ululating and wading in. But my husband lifted me again in his arms, though he did not need to do so for the miracle of the ointment was spreading through my body and I felt my knees tingle and my shoulders and my neck, and a great relaxation came over me, like a fist that has been too long clenched finally unclenching. He walked with me up into the city, through abandoned alleys, past temples, past the eroded faces of old stone gods and the disjoint columns of palaces, and as we walked higher and higher, the wind blew across our wet clothes and the sun warmed us and our skins felt magical. And we climbed up into the cliffs above the city by a long white stair cut from the living rock.

"The Dawn Stair of Veliara, my love," he whispered.

Far below us, from the shoulders of the great cliff, we could see the water from the pool as it shimmered in the sun, and the water overflowed into ancient canals and along aqueducts that had run of old throughout the maze-like city, and the spreading of the new water through the city was as the veins of a leaf held to the sky, except that the veins of Velaya were silver and shining. Then my husband set me carefully down, and though my feet had not felt the ground for some days, I was suffused with a curious lightness, as if I floated like a cork on water. We continued on up the stair, hand-in-hand, always higher, and we were not tired, and we climbed until at last we came to the very summit of Veliara and stood at the cliff-edge looking down into the shining maze of the Dreaming City.

And there was no terror and there was no trial. My husband bent and placed upon that high ground the stone and the small jar of balm and then he took up my hand again. We were not judged. We felt no fear and no uncertainty. We felt no need to leap into the unknown, for we rose from that place on wings we had always known we had.

Beston Barnett's story "Velaya, the Dreaming City" was published in Metaphorosis on Friday, 16 March 2018.

About the story

"Velaya" was very much inspired by Lord Dunsany, who was a writer of quirky little fantasies in the pre-Tolkien era. I had been fooling around with different voices and styles in my writing, and thought Dunsany's high, Biblical language would be interesting to mimic. Of course, what you set out to do is never quite what you do do, which is true for the protagonist of my story as well.

A question for the author

Q: Are titles easy or hard for you? Do you start with the title or the story?

A: Titles are the best! Really, coming up with titles is like coming up with band names: it's pure id. I usually do it after the fact, with an eye to seeing the title in a list of other titles. Something to stand out, but without, I hope, being too obnoxious.

Chapter titles are even better. When I was revising my (unpublished) novel, *A Catalog of Devils,* I suddenly realized that I could give the 40 or so chapters titles. I went through each chapter, looking for my favorite phrase or word and used that. It was like bringing all the best, trickiest bits of my writing to the forefront. It sounds absurd, but out of the year and a half I spent on the novel, that two hours of titling chapters was the emotional highpoint.

About the author

During the day, Beston Barnett designs and builds furniture in San Diego. At night, he plays Romani jazz. The rest of the time he is reading a book, or eating with chopsticks, or—in the best of all possible worlds—doing both at once.

Copyright

Copyright 2019, Metaphorosis Publishing

Cover art © 2018 by Saleha Chowdhury
salehachowdhury.com, @AroUnleashed

"The Bagel Shop Owner's Nephew" © 2018, J. Tynan Burke
"Hishi" © 2018, David A. Gray
"Just a Fire" © 2018, A. Martine
"Koehl's Quality Impressions" © 2018, Tim McDaniel
"The Foaling Season" © 2018, Samuel Chapman
"The Little G-d of Łódź" © 2018, Evan Marcroft
"Of Hair and Beanstalks" © 2018, William Condon
"Familiar in Her Angles" © 2018, E.A. Brenner
"Cheminagium" © 2018, David Gallay
"The Stars Don't Lie" © 2018, R.W.W. Greene
"The Dream Diary of Monk Anchin" © 2018, Felicity Drake
"Not All Those Who Wander Are Lost" © 2018, Douglas Anstruther
"Velaya, the Dreaming City" © 2018, Beston Barnett
   Authors also retain copyrights to all other material in the anthology.

Our patrons

Our Patreon supporters mean a great deal to us. Not only do they provide financial support, but they're great morale boosters. Our supporters in 2018 included a host of great people:

- Karen Anderson
- Yaroslav Barsukov
- Lauren Sullivan
- Harrison Perry
- Helen Stubbs
- Ian Millington
- Peri L. Fletcher
- Tamara L. DeGray
- Sarah Das
- Jason Ray Carney
- Albert McFarland
- Richard Johnson
- David Rae
- Sunyi Dean
- Dimitra Nikolaidou
- Karen Chaffee
- L'Erin Ogle
- Christopher Pearce
- Pauline Yates

More information about supporting us at Patreon is available at: www.patreon.com/Metaphorosis

Metaphorosis Publishing

Metaphorosis offers beautifully written science fiction and fantasy. Our projects include:

Metaphorosis Magazine

Metaphorosis, a weekly magazine of SFF short stories, including stories from all the authors in this anthology. Find out more at magazine.metaphorosis.com, and sign up to be notified of new stories.

Metaphorosis Books

Recent books from Metaphorosis can be found at books.metaphorosis.com, and include:

Metaphorosis 2017

All the stories from *Metaphorosis* magazine's second year.

Metaphorosis 2016

Almost all the stories from *Metaphorosis* magazine's first year.

Metaphorosis: Best of 2017

The best science fiction and fantasy stories from *Metaphorosis'* 2nd year.

Metaphorosis: Best of 2016

The best science fiction and fantasy stories from *Metaphorosis'* 1st year.

Reading 5X5   **Reading 5X5**

Five stories, five times   *Writers' Edition*

Twenty-five SFF authors, five base stories, five versions of each – see how different writers take on the same material.

All the stories from the regular, readers' edition, plus two extra stories, the story seed, and authors' notes.

Best Vegan SFF of 2017   **Best Vegan SFF of 2016**

The best vegan science fiction and fantasy stories of 2017!

The best vegan science fiction and fantasy stories of 2016!

Susurrus

A darkly romantic story of magic, love, and suffering.

Made in the USA
Middletown, DE
22 February 2019